PECKHAM
DIAMONDS

Also by Georgina Hunter-Jones:

Fiction

Atlantic Warriors

Non-fiction

Helicopter Landing Sites in Great Britain and Ireland

Children's Books

Ronald the Postage Stamp
Wizard Wheeze
Nola the Rhinoceros

Student's Books

The Twerple who had too many Brains
A Student's File, or the Yawning Gap

PECKHAM DIAMONDS

GEORGINA HUNTER-JONES

FLYFIZZI
Publishing
MMV

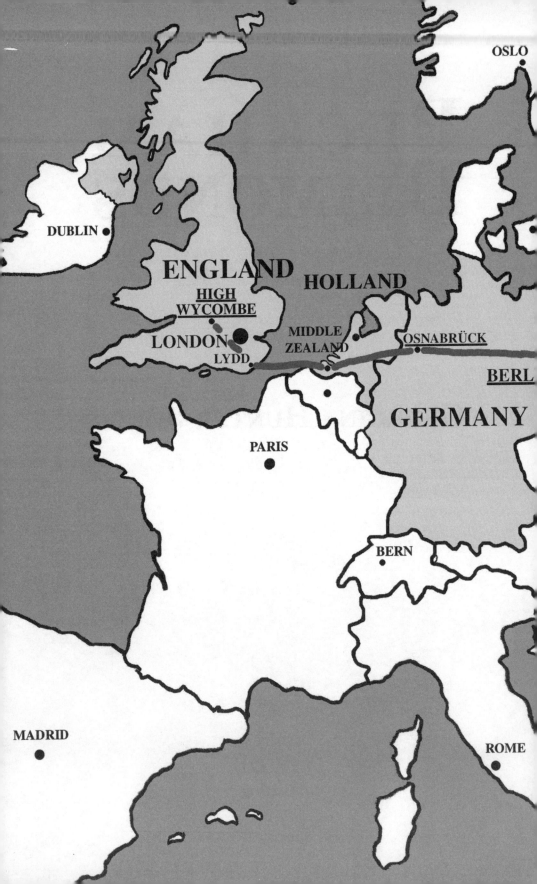

This book is dedicated to my father and mother,
without whom I would never have learnt to fly.

Peckham Diamonds was first published in 2005
FlyFizzi Publishing
59 Great Ormond Street
London WC1N-3HZ
England

This book is fiction and all the characters and incidents in it are
completely imaginary. Any resemblance to anybody living or dead is entirely accidental.
Some of the institutions and airfields mentioned in the book do exist but all the
characters within and around them are entirely imaginary.

Hardback: ISBN 1-900721-35-X
Paperback: ISBN 1-900721-30-9

A catalogue record for this book is available from the British Library.

Designed by Hilaire Dubourcq
Typeset in Georgia
Printed and bound by Alden Press, Oxford

Table of Contents

"Every action.... is in an historical sense not free at all, but in bondage to the whole course of previous history, and predestined from all eternity."

Leo Nikolaevich Tolstoy

Transfer Values: 1878

Sergei Denunciovitch, like his father, his father's father and his father's father's father, was a loyal servant to the His Highness the Tsar and Emperor of all the Russias, to his mistress and to his country. He repeated that to himself every time the aged Russian boat rolled with the rough waves, and his stomach heaved in response.

Now, fagged by months of travel, he searched once more for a smooth spot on the straw pillow. Then grew still, digesting a change in the creaking moans of the old wooden boat. Through the solidity of the snores around him he registered a change from the endless wrenching of twisting wet boards to another, a shore-bound sound, a repetitive man-made clanging of metal on metal. Remotely he smelt the distant sweat of horses supersede the gluey tang of fish, and heard the shorter chords of shallower water under the keel.

Suddenly he was awake, staring at the crudely nailed wooden walls. Around him others were mumbling in their sleep, their hot breath congregating in gobs of condensation which dropped down from the cold pipes like internal rain. Sergei, used to the density of the fetid air, now noticed a leafy green smell enter the cabin. They had arrived.

He stretched, his fat stomach bouncing like a ball on a bench, then jumped up as excited as a child at Christmas. Grabbing his straw and sacking bundle, and without another glance around his stinking quarters, he hurried out the door and leapt up the ladder onto the deck.

In front of him on the deck, quivering with apprehension, were clusters of people with dirty faces huddled in family groups, clinging to their bundles and their children like survival equipment. Most were Jewish, refugees from the pogroms. Sergei had no interest in them but looked around for his companion. He was nowhere in sight.

Sailors in ragged uniforms barked ill-understood orders. Thin faces flinched nervously then peaked up, staring forward with nervous appreciation. Ahead of the boat shadows and shapes appeared piecemeal out of the dull grey fog. An anchor chain, then the prow of a moored ship, then the long dull expanse of a ship's flank which somehow merged into the flat greyness of wet stone heralding the harbour entrance. There was a rawness to the air; a painful, astringent edge to the mist but the exhausted travellers did not care. For them shore-side abuse and profanities were like music, ground-born stinks like medicine, after months and months of lonely bird cries and the painful wrenching sighs of a boat at sea.

Sergei felt the lightness of relief. They had arrived in Harwich in Essex, in England, even the names sounded romantic to Sergei. He might never see his homeland again, but he was at his destination. He had completed his job and would be well rewarded. Money to buy silks and satins. Money to buy a horse, and a watch. Money... his imagination stalled but he already felt the coins in his hands and jingling in his pocket. Coins. No, gold. Gold and silver.

As the large ship bellied into port the offshore smells grew stronger. His own village, north of Katya, smelt too, of urine, horse manure, wood fire, tea in the samovar, smells all laden with mud-encrusted beauty. This tincture of horse manure and tea, oak and coke, was sodden with new English scents of lavender, metal and rust. Behind him honest poverty, his only possessions his sharp sabre and his loyalty to his master, ahead was his future. He had travelled far. Only one man had been his friend and confidant on the voyage, a man from his own village, although with a different master, but, although Sergie looked around for him, the man had disappeared in the furore and excitement that surrounded the docking of a heavily laden cargo ship.

He pressed his little bundle tighter to his chest, musing that if anyone knew what was amongst the straw they would cry out from shock. Though not as shocked as he himself would have been to learn what was going to happen to it in the next hundred and fifty years.

He muttered a name and address to himself. It was short, but it was enough. Then, as he walked down the notched wooden board that led onto the quay, he heard one of the crew point him out as 'The Russian' and knew he had arrived. His money and his new future were waiting just around the corner.

No Dancing in the Aisles: 1994

The winter sun was still hovering in the car park when Ali walked into the supermarket, ready to do battle with the crowd. Crevasse-like aisles were packed with elegance-challenged humanity. Blocking the first was a robust woman with Martian-faced children and an overflowing grocery-carrier. Ali grabbed a trolley, angled it to joust the woman from her position between the bananas and the grapefruit with a well-timed blow, but stopped, seeing her opponent crush a grape between strong fingers, dropping its emptied skin on the floor like a used sweet-paper. The children pushed past in a fanfare of triumphant whines, and Ali, blenching, picked up a basket and fled sheepishly for the area of nightly peace: the wine department. "I measure out my life in supermarket trolleys," she thought, using her favourite method of self-defence: silent critical pastiche.

Reflected in the polished bottles she saw a young, tall, well-built red-head, who stooped not to conquer but to disguise her height; something she had done since school days, determined to fit her stout buoyancy into the traditional mould. Then a hand slapped down on her shoulder, her neighbour Dindas, and she turned away from her reflections. "Hey there Ali, had a good day?"

Recovering herself she replied: "Not bad. I've been in court."

Dindas raised his eyebrows and leant back against a shelf of bottled water. With any other neighbour it would clearly be a violation or non-payment order, but Ali was a nice white girl and as far as he knew had a job, although he was never certain what she did that kept her out such odd hours. Never asked. Dindas only saw the beneficial and knew how to keep his mouth shut: he was an excellent neighbour.

Ali saw his look and laughed, picking up a bottle of Merlot and putting it in her basket. "Not like that. I was a witness for one of my students, to prove he was with me at the time 'they' said he was caught by council cameras violating the bus lane. That's all."

"Right, right, right." Dindas still looked a little skeptical but, swinging a plastic-wrapped pack of Cumbrian water bottles into his trolley, asked curiously, "'Eh, man. See anything nice?"

Ali had seen nothing except her student and his lawyer. "No, and it took two hours before they threw out the charge. Ridiculous!"

She slipped a second bottle of Merlot into her basket, defiantly, remembering her student's angry suggestion the camera inspector was too drunk to read the correct time that he entered the bus lane.

"Yeah, man," said Dindas shaking his head, "them police are mad, with the things they do. You keep a quiet life, no drink, no nothing and then they get you for all that nonsense. A man two doors down is up on a charge for letting his dog dirty the streets, you know, and everyone knows he only has a cat. 'Eh man."

Dindas's laugh spurted out in exultant fashion like a shower of tiny translucent stones, making Ali laugh too. They slapped palms, said it was good to see each other and danced away, one past the bulging cake shelves towards the bread, the other steering through still boxed juice cartons to the olives.

After a dispute in the Exotic Foods aisle with the cascading trolley of an obese man, who swore at her, Ali hustled her way to the checkout. No dancing in the aisles here, she thought, as she waited for three abundant trolley-loads to pass through before her small basket reached the front.

"You'll have to take it out," snapped the girl in the orange polyester top. "It's not my job to take it out of the basket. That's your job." She turned and gossiped with the orange back in the parallel line.

Despising herself for being so feeble Ali did as she was told, thinking: "Oh girls, girls, silly little, valuable things. Young vulnerable girls."

Outside the supermarket, amongst red and blue parking areas, Ali saw Dindas, his head moving about sharply like a hunter looking for game, coming out from behind a taxi tattooed with advertising. She pushed a lost trolley towards the collection area hitting his, both rearing up like competing stallions. "Sorry!"

"No problem," he said, adding he was waiting for his brother and that they were off to their sister's place for a cousin's brother's funeral. They hi-fived again and Ali watched the brothers drive away in the mud brown car with its slipped bumpers. The elastic tie-rope around the boot joggled up and down as they drove over the sleeping policemen.

Before she had moved to Peckham Ali used to wonder why people allowed their cars to get into such a state, now, after three break-ins, her own car had a yawning gap where the suicide-seat door leant backwards. She covered the hole with recycled plastic like half the other cars in south-east London. Peckham streets were great places for home-garaging.

[11]

Ali drove home. As she parked she watched a woman dumping unwanted suitcases; lifting them out of the boot she dropped them on the pavement and, without a backward look, got into her car and drove away. Ali stared at the accumulating rubbish beside the railway line: blue plastic bags nestling against food cartons; moulding shoes glittering with broken glass (Ali called it Peckham diamonds); mattresses dumped across the pavement, even an old desk, and wondered how anyone brought up amongst this deluge of human debris could ever hope to admire nature or appreciate beauty. She re-seated the plastic over the suicide-seat door-jam gap and, with a burst of optimism, locked the car door.

Someone had peed against the gate, the smell mixing with Indian spices from her neighbour's cooking. Going inside she checked involuntarily that she hadn't been burgled. Her house so far remained unviolated, something she put down to Dindas's status in the community and the fact he was one of the local church leaders; covering both fields as it were. Ali herself was agnostic, typical of her upbringing and age, but she felt Dindas and his gods kept an eye on her house and was glad he was there.

Inside her small Victorian house, with its 'little patch of concrete some estate agents call a garden', she collapsed into a chair. She knew she ought to read the paper; ought to know what was going on in the world, but stared at the black and white type without absorbing a word. Reality was so dull, she much preferred fantasy. Her head fell back against the green flowery sofa, a present from an aunt, and she fell asleep.

The Nightingale Sang

Over the other side of London, in a high ceilinged office in Mayfair, a dapper man in a Saville Row suit was questioning his secretary.

"Do you know anything about diamonds?" Mr Charleston asked, his back turned, his voice bouncing off the closed French windows and echoing around the commodious converted coach house.

Margaret very much wanted to reply in the affirmative because she knew a trip to Russia depended on it, but sadly she saw she was going to be the stay-at-home. "Not a thing, I'm afraid."

Charleston wasn't surprised but he went on talking, more to clear his thoughts than to question her. "Could you recognise one? Tell a good one from a poor? Or even tell the difference between a diamond and broken glass?"

Margaret said nothing. She had worked for Mr Charleston for seventeen years, knew his ways. She waited patiently, allowing her mind to dwell on thoughts she had had many times before. She looked past him onto the patio, thinking it was suitable for a glass of champagne to celebrate a successful deal, but little else, that the property developer had known his market: he was not selling to those who wanted large gardens any more than to those who would put up with leaks, poorly fitting doors and horrendous plumbing just because the price was right.

Instead he had created a wall of subtly introduced panelling, well-spaced pictures of Ancient Greece, and on a small plinth, a rearing bronze horse whose wildness was tamed by a small, plucky, saddle-less rider. Absolutely suitable, Margaret thought. Absolutely.

After the right amount of time she broke into his thoughts with a quiet, "No."

"Umm," Charleston replied, awoken from staring at the pools of water on the decking. "Know anyone who does?"

This time she was able to surprise him. "Actually, yes."

He turned to face her. A sizeable woman, she had the ample kindness of those who have spent most of their lives at home looking after children, and he would have been pleased to help her. However, like many long-term wives, she had such complete faith in her younger, smaller husband that she was inclined to offer him for any and every situation, usually without justification.

"Your husband?"

Her voice regretful, with just a slight feeling that perhaps she should have offered him first, she said, "No, a friend. At least he was trying to explain the difference between carbonado and proper diamonds the other night. It was funny we were having spaghetti carbonara and he, because he's foreign he doesn't always understand accents like mine, well he thought..." she tailed off, realising her boss was not listening.

"Ah," said Charleston, wondering if her amplification of her husband's abilities extended to her friends. "Can you arrange for him to come and see me? This evening at Brooks's. Book a table for us, will you. Eight o'clock. Make sure your friend has a tie, or lend him one. Call Marcel, tell him I'll need picking up at the club tomorrow at nine. Have the engineers fixed the artificial horizon in the 109? Good, then we'll take the helicopter. Ring my wife, tell her I'll be home tomorrow. What is your friend's name?"

Margaret went away to make the phone calls, wondering, not for the first time, what it would be like to assume that everyone else would immediately fall in with your plans. Probably the only person who ever defied Mr Charleston was his stepdaughter Alice. Margaret grinned, her salebrous face pouching up like a rabbit. She rather liked Alice, who was headstrong and difficult, clever and wild. They said she was German, but Margaret didn't believe it. Call it woman's instinct if you like, but every year she and Tom went to Mallorca with the children and those Germans weren't a bit like Alice.

After Margaret had gone Mr Charleston turned again to the rain, his wiry hands unconsciously clenching and unclenching behind his back. It was not just the diamonds that worried him, although that was all he could tell his kindly but indiscreet secretary, but a letter he had received which threatened his stepdaughter. Although the tone had been ingratiating and he knew whence the threat came, it was not something he could deal with himself. He knew he needed a professional; one who was clever, knowledgeable and discreet, and knew about diamonds. Someone, Mr Charleston's 65 years of life had taught him, rare.

Peckham Princess

Ali was woken by the obtrusive double ring of the cordless phone, compensating for its unattached status by making twice the noise: like some of her girl friends. Groggily she picked it up and pressed the little green button. The dialling panel shone in the dark room, mirroring a repetitive slashing light from a street lamp that flickered on the edge of extinction.

"Alison, it's Gavin," said the voice on the other end, unnecessarily, she thought, since she didn't know anyone except her boss with that way of ending a sentence on a rising whine like a lobster entering the boiling-pot.

"Hello."

"You didn't do your test today!"

It sounded like an accusation.

Her mind drifted back to the low cloud base and poor visibility of the morning, followed by the rain and high winds of the afternoon. "No, the weather was terrible. I'll have another go tomorrow."

"Just as you like," he said, and as the 'ike' swung upwards she wondered if it was indeed the lobster's last gasp or just air escaping from the shell. "But don't do it on our behalf."

"What?" Ali asked, shocked out of sleep. Of course she did it on their behalf, she couldn't teach without it, that was the game the Civil Aviation Authority played. You did tests, paid highly for them and then had the privilege of working for a living. Oh what fun, but what did he mean, he knew the score.

"Look Ali, I don't want you thinking we are going to be still employing you in the summer. Rather than bother with the test you may as well stop now. We won't be needing you."

Ali was shocked. Good teacher though she was, she had not spotted this problem hovering in the wings. Didn't even know that 'the sack' came from the French word for travel documents.

"You don't want me anymore?" she asked incredulously. Incredulous not because she and Gavin had a good working relationship, but because she had recently won the CRAABI (Civil Regulation Aviation Authority Best Instructor) award and was indeed a popular teacher.

It was true she and Gavin had disputes over many aspects of instructing practice, but that was all part of the game too, wasn't it? Good teachers discussed different ways and came to a conclusion that was best for the student. Didn't they? Not that Gavin was a good teacher. Indeed he had a phrase, 'discussion is criticism' which he used often.

"Hey, wait a minute..." she began, but Gavin had no time for her problems.

"No," said Gavin. "Discussion is criticism! You can use our helicopters, if you like, to do the test but we'll have to charge you the full rate. Well, goodbye."

"But..." Ali tried, but she was talking to herself. Gavin had gone off to ring the students to inform them they'd have to fly with him from now on. Luckily for him most students took advantage of the discount on advance payment.

Ali felt that odd, bashed sensation of the newly sacked. Partly delighted she no longer had to work for a man she considered a boring fraud, partly terrified that she (who was so interesting and pure) could not pay her bills. She realised she was shaking.

She went to the fridge to get herself a glass of white wine, stopped, thinking she mustn't drink too much because she had a test tomorrow, then remembered she hadn't after all and filled her glass to the brim. 'Let's get drunk,' she thought, but knew she wouldn't. Whoever cried, 'drink and be whole again' hadn't allowed for Ali's natural abstinence: Ali lived her life as though waiting for an emergency call.

'There is never a thunderstorm or blare of trumpets to announce a new beginning,' she thought, bolstering her spirits. A new job? No problem. The economy was jittery, shares falling and helicopter jobs rose and fell with the loose change in people's pockets, but she had contacts. And her prize. This was just a delightful new challenge. Another challenge. And she had thought those only came in her private life.

On the street a man thrown out by his wife started to yell obscenities for entry. Ali grimaced, she been there too. Next door Dindas began hoovering to drown out the noise and on the other side Mrs Singh turned up the sound on her satellite channel. 'Welcome to Peckham, have a nice day.'

Smolensk Kristall

In the next few days Ali rang schools from Brighton to Leeds. All said they would love to employ her full time - sometime soon, and until then would keep her name on file. In the meantime freelance work.

Freelance work. She could hear the tinkle of small change. Freelance flying meant hours by the phone like a hopeful debutante; driving to airfields where they were profuse with apologies: meant to cancel but had forgotten; the weather had just changed to rain, the cloud just lowered, the student just cancelled: so sorry; so foolish: so incontrovertible. And, of course, occasional flights.

After a month she had grossed £500. Her mortgage took half, council tax another £100; the rest she lived on. She felt like a cross-threaded screw constantly rubbing away its support system.

One flight, however, was different from the rest. Ali had been asked to fly as a safety pilot for an eighty-year-old former Air Transport Auxiliary pilot, who wanted to go to an air-show east of London. They started from White Waltham and, after a distinctly exciting journey across the Heathrow Zone with a woman who remembered London before there were commercial airliners, radio requirements and airspace restrictions, they arrived alive, only to be told they could not land as an aerobatic display by Yaks was in progress.

"Nonsense," said the old girl, "they may be Russian but they're on our side now!" And landed, narrowly missing the departing aircraft.

Ali, still suffering from shock, was pottering around in the diluted sunshine examining the now on-ground Russian Yaks that littered the airfield, when a thin man with a pipe-stained beard and long legs and arms, which stuck out at angles like a cricket, approached her.

"Ali! How the Hell are you?"

Ali smiled. Pete: aviation's John Cleese. His mannerisms used to unnerve her, until she met his beautiful but even weirder son, then she realised it was simple family affectation. "Hi Pete. Fine. How are you?"

"I'm good. Good indeed." He filled his pipe holding it between his teeth, his voice, which came out in tobacco sucks, showing he was thinking of something else. "What are you doing these days, Ali? Still teaching?"

"Sort of. I'm a bit between jobs... if you know what I mean."

Pete leant on the nearest Yak's wing his peaked face looking suddenly attentive, as though she'd turned unexpectedly into a supermodel. "And you might want something?"

She nodded. "Umm."

"Well you know what, I might have something. It would be temporary and it won't pay very well, but... is your instructor's licence still valid?"

"Yes." Ali had debated with herself whether to renew it when she saw the dearth of jobs, but had financed herself through the test because she thought without it she'd end up becoming a plane washer or a re-fueller. What else could she do? Although there was a desirable vacancy for a bus-lane-camera-inspector in the local Peckham paper. "Yes, it is."

"Good." He banged his pipe against the Yak and refilled it. "Have I got your number? Still the same as it was?"

Ali gave him her card. She'd made them herself on the computer and although they were a little limp, she was proud of them.

He glanced at it without seeing anything, mechanically waving it up and down, as though testing its tensile strength. "Can you travel easily? I mean go away for a month or two without problem? No chap hidden in the wings?"

Ali thought about it. It's not easy to leave your house for a month or two once you get established: there are bills to pay, cars to protect, letters stack up, the telephone goes unanswered. But there was always Dindas next door. And no chap hidden in the wings. Not even Jake. A Squirrel from Lippets Hill Police Station circled overhead, and Ali looking up noticed that the 'eye in the sky' at the front made it look as though it had a beaky nose. An eagle for the flying beagle?

"Yes."

"Good girl," he said, in the voice you'd use to a dog. "Good girl. I'll ring you." And he walked away, waggling a few long tobacco-yellowed fingers.

'Between the idea and the reality...falls the shadow,' Ali thought, wondering if he would really call.

Ali waited by the phone with even more trepidation now, but the phone calls remained sparse. She did a few days at various London airfields and once drove all the way up to Leeds for a day's flying. Even as she worked she wondered about

Pete and if he would call her, if he really had something that would involve being away a couple of months. What could it be? A job in New Zealand? Or, rather more likely, France? Perhaps it was another job in Leeds. Pete used to have a school in Scotland but had given it to his son, who had then run it into the ground. Pete now lived by doing exams and the son was said to be working for a detective, but she didn't really believe that. After all what sort of detective needs a helicopter pilot; or could afford one? Flying was full of gossip.

Weeks passed. The winter moved on to spring, daffodils and crocuses bloomed and birds began to sing in the trees, even in Peckham which had more than its fair share of cats and foxes. Then, half way through May, Pete phoned.

"Ali," he began without any opening Cleese-isms, "are you still open for a job?"

"Yes, probably," she said, although she was really getting desperate.

He ignored the probably, indeed probably didn't hear it as he was instructing someone in the background to go out and get the helicopter ready.

"Good, it starts in August, and will last a couple of months, maybe longer. I can't pay much, but I'll cover all your expenses. £1,000 a month, payable here, I'll have it put in your account if you give me the details. Don't argue with me about the money, it's yes please or not at all!"

Ali didn't argue, she was still averaging £500 a month and £1,000 seemed like unheard of luxury, especially with expenses covered. "I'll do it, but what is the job?"

"Oh," said Pete, rather too negligently. "It's to escort a group of pilots to Russia, to Moscow. I'll be there too, and Daniel, you'll be sharing a Robinson R22 helicopter with a girl who hasn't got her licence yet, but is learning. You'll be teaching her on the way. I'll fax you a few details, but basically be prepared to leave Lydd on August 1st in the morning. You'd better stay there the night before. I'll get you a hotel. You can leave your car at the airport."

He rang off.

"But why?" Ali asked the flashing handset. "Why? And with whom? Who wants to fly to Russia in a tiny, two seater helicopter? And why?"

Between the idea and the reality...falls the shadow.

Dindas was delighted to look after her house for a month, two months, as long as it took. He'd been in Ali's house before and he knew why she hadn't been burgled: even the TV wouldn't have fetched a fiver and there was nothing else. She had a lot of books, but who'd want them, and pictures, ditto, and some rugged old-fashioned furniture which some aunt had parted with before departing herself: to Capri.

≈≈≈≈≈≈

Alice Springs

If information giving had been left up to Pete then it would have been as sparse as vegetables in the desert and Ali would have turned up at Lydd on the 31st of July ready to fly to Russia, probably without a visa, but luckily there was Alice.

Alice was the student Ali was to accompany to Moscow and it was Alice who finally told Ali the purpose of the flight.

"Oh, didn't you know?" she asked, amazement filling the telephone and reverberating on around Ali's archaic room like a child climbing across the furniture. "We are taking part in the World Helicopter Games, you and I are the British Ladies team and we're going to do our best to win."

We are? thought Ali, aware they hadn't even met, let alone flown together and she had no idea of the rules of the competition or even how to enter. She murmured weakly. "Shouldn't we perhaps practice first?"

"But we are going to," spat Alice, even more exasperated, clearly thinking little of her future co-pilot. "Pete must have told you about the trip to Shropshire? The weekend after next?"

When Ali rang Pete he was urbane, delighted that she should practice and offered to send his JetRanger to pick her up, unless she wanted to fly there with Alice.

"Yes," said Ali smartly, "I think it makes sense doesn't it, that we fly together at least a little before we enter a World Class competition."

"Absolutely right, my dear, absolutely right. We've borrowed an R22 for the duration and you can fly that over to Shropshire. If you go down on Friday you can pick it up from Exeter and fetch Alice from her home in Herefordshire, on the way up to Shropshire. I'll fax you the details."

This time he did. Plus that these expenses (such as they were, bar bill, food off base) she could cover herself. Ali couldn't help wondering why, why any of it? Why didn't he teach Alice himself, why did they need her? Why enter a competition of this sort? To be fair if they were entering a Ladies Competition then he did need her, but having decided to involve her why tell her as little as possible? It made no sense.

Between the idea, and the reality, between the motion and the act, falls the Shadow.

But, Ali told her questioning mind, forget it, think of it as a paid holiday and relax. Wonder instead what is Russia like. The only thing Ali knew about Russia was from Dr Zhivago and that it snowed a lot in winter.

On Friday the weather was beautiful. One of those late spring, early summer days with blue skies, light winds and an elegant slanting scent in the air. Ali planned to take the early train down to Exeter and a taxi over to the airport, where she'd been told the Robinson helicopter was awaiting her out on the apron, fully fuelled and oiled.

In Peckham Rye, on the way to the station, she passed a car, its windows broken recently as clusters of reflective 'Peckham diamonds' on the pavement showed. Inside was a build-up of cardboard boxes. Once Ali would have marvelled at the oddity; but now, as a long-time resident, she knew that on her return she would see a burnt-out shell; that the boxes were the firelighters and the diamond cutters were merely waiting until the next darkness. Perhaps the police should also live in the area, but why would the police come out for mere Peckham diamonds.

Ironically, in spite of the precious gems that lined the streets, Peckham, the town on the hill, had some very beautiful buildings. Carty's, Makers of Vats and Wooden Tanks, reminded residents that there had been a village here in the seventeenth century. Tall terraces of jostling Georgian houses, with flat fronts and wrought iron balconies, gave way to stubby Victorian cottages with hopeful bay-windows. Yards that once resonated with blacksmiths' tools and parks, where pudgy milkmaids had once dallied with local lads, now had garage music and estates of graffiti-boys. If Peckham had once been a country child it had now developed into an urban teenager.

The train was expectedly crowded, Peckham being the home of the early morning cleaner and those who didn't choose their hours of travel.

A crowd flowed over London Bridge, so many, I had not thought death had undone so many.

There was the perennial smell of pee and hospital medicine which infected the trains on the South East London loop. Ali glanced suspiciously at the dampness of the partially disconnected cushions, hanging by a sinew like a child's first tooth. The trains were modern with automatic doors but not a single window had avoided the graffiti-boys' scratch, while dried chewing gum spread dark blotches in the plush.

Ali had read about the sense of comradeship one finds on trains; on the Peckham to Victoria route this was absent, replaced only occasionally by actual abuse, as when Ali asked a small child who was using her knees to practise kick boxing to desist. The mother screamed that Ali was a posh totty who held her nose up at ordinary folk with babbys. Ali stood for the rest of the journey; an angrily empty circle around her as the inhabitants of the carriage regarded the politically incorrect pariah. Mostly, though, the crowded occupants just rubbed each other sore, silently watching the passing elegance of the white tower boxes with their defensive windows like gun-slits in a fort.

At Victoria she swapped her modern graffiti bus for an old one with slam doors but miraculously a few unscratched windows. Here Ali had a bench set of four all to herself. She picked up a copy of The Guardian someone had left behind. A headline proclaimed 'The Mystery of the Tsar's Missing Diamonds Solved'.

"When the 'Devoshka' sailed into Portsmouth in the summer of 1878," the Guardian story revealed, "somebody was waiting to greet Sergei Denunciovitch, lowly palace courier of the Tsars. A Somebody who knew in his bundle of almost unnoticed straw was a string of diamonds so perfect and brilliant that women in Russia had killed to wear them."

The writer went on to contradict a Pravda writer's story about the theft of these diamonds from Tsar Alexander 11 of Russia. By paragraph 3 the Guardian writer had exposed these were not, in fact, stolen diamonds since Alexander had given them to his mistress, Katharina Dologorukova, only pretending they were stolen to pacify his suspicious wife. Katharina, terrified of the ensuing furore, had sent the diamonds to Britain. However, when she tried to reclaim her diamonds, after the death of Alexander's wife in 1880 and her own marriage to Alexander, both Denunciovitch and the diamonds had disappeared. Now, it seemed, there had indeed been a theft, but from Katharina not Alexander.

When asked for their opinion by the journalist, the Government of Russia declared any diamonds found belonged to them and the British must not try to appropriate them like the Elgin Marbles.

Do they mine for diamonds in Russia? Ali mused. Unable to answer herself she turned on to the sports section. She wondered why, although the helicopter championships were clearly a sport, there seemed to be an unwritten rule they never got mentioned in the newspapers.

Ali alighted at Exeter. Growing along the station were tall wrought iron Victorian lights with curving heads that never would have been left to grace a Peckham platform. Even here two light shades had been dented by a flying bottle and looked like ladies in Ascot hats bowing to one another.

Ali felt curiously happy. She took a taxi to the airport, wondering if this was at her expense or Pete's.

On the concrete apron sat a bronze-coloured Robinson helicopter, a sleek aerial toffee apple. She noted from the manual that it was a new machine, bought only six months ago and with less than one hundred hours on the engine and airframe. She laughed with relief when she saw it had a GPS attached to the side of the console for navigatory ease. The idea of trip to Russia with only a compass and map seeming suddenly like unnecessarily hard work.

Ali puttered around the pad, checking the helicopter for cracks and leaks, her well-trained senses alert for tell-tale signs. Although it was now 10 o'clock the wind was only just dispersing the fog and the sun sent rays of tingling dust through the lifting and separating clouds, promising a beautiful day.

Behind her in the hangar the clang of dropped tools and the voices raised in discussion ("that is wh-ay, that is wh-ay." "I'll tell YOU what...") supported by the surging monotony of the radio, proclaimed that the engineers had come off their tea-break and were back at work. Somewhere across the apron there was the repetitive ping of a reversing lorry and a steady banging, which sounded like someone compelling metal into a new, possibly helicopter-friendly, shape. Accompanied by the whine of an electric screwdriver, capable of drowning out a hive of bees, these were sounds of the airfield. The romantics who complained that aircraft destroyed rural peace had no idea: helicopter noise was merely a trumpet in the orchestra.

Satisfied that the helicopter was flyable she went into the office to check the weather to the north and ring the tower to book out. Around the slightly dilapidated office were Certificates of Approval, a rotor blade with winning names painted on it in white, and pieces of engine for student study. Two of the walls were decorated with maps and a broken white board leant on a cupboard full of books. A couple of mugs dropped into the bin reminded her of an engineering director who destroyed coffee mugs wherever he found them. She felt the pain of nostalgia and hurried through into the Chief's office to find the phone.

Before flying away she lifted the helicopter up into the hover and absorbed the feel of the machine. The way it held steady at low manifold pressure, without vibration and with the confidence of an excess of power in hand, gave her a perception of how well the helicopter could do in the championships; if only it had the experienced pilots to match. She wondered who owned it, and if they knew it was about to fly off to Russia for some only partially determined project.

Ali called Exeter tower, taxied up to her departure point and took off for Alice's parents' house in Herefordshire. As it was more than a two-hour flight she had planned to land somewhere on the way, to fuel up for the further flight onto Shawbury, but Pete had told her not to bother: Alice's parents had their own bowser. Why, naturally, was not explained.

As Ali climbed up to 1,000 feet, buoyed by the high pressure, she left behind the shadows of the airfield. Below her she could see the amorphous effect of the sunshine on the buildings distorting their outline, but up here in the liberated sky only the clouds could put her and her helicopter into shade. Clouds which, suspended like escaped powder puffs under the morning sun, gave the ground a motley dappled feel. Her heart shuddered, echoing the vibration of the machine. To Ali such an effect meant emancipation from man-created restrictions, here above human invention only nature could curtail her freedom. Man and his petty restrictions were relegated to the world below. She flew steadily along, watching Apollo cruising lazily in and out behind the small tufts of cumulus, giving the impression the clouds were bustling across the ground, although in reality the wind was almost still.

The air was so clear she could already see the Bristol Channel in the distance and, to her left, the glimmering blue of Barnstable Bay. Behind her the English Channel. She was conscious of the affirmation that Britain was an island and that she was a moving piece of air over land between seas. It gave her an oddly disconnected feeling, like a bee flying over soil without flowers.

In the bright metropolis of their flowers, the banker bees are busy with their gold!

The M5 was busy with traffic. As she passed the visual reporting point at Cullompton she saw the cars were down to a crawl and wondered how many drivers looked up and envied her flight; how many dreamt of converting their cars to Little Nellie like James Bond and joining her up here above the maelstrom. She flew on down the valley between Exmoor and Taunton and then, to avoid the danger area of Bridgewater Bay, turned east over the uxorious

Quantock Hills. She changed frequency and talked to Cardiff on the radio but stayed out of their zone. The girl at Cardiff ATC warned her the area around Weston Super Mere was busy with traffic, and she saw a Stearman, the sun glinting on its wing-walking rig pass beneath her, out of Bristol and on its way to a show somewhere into the unknown west.

A flick of sunshine upon a strange shore.

The pilot saw the helicopter and waved a white gloved hand. His mumbled radio call confirmed him as an airline pilot in another guise.

The Bristol Channel was so full of boats it looked as though a flotilla of tiny ships were on their way to war. Toy-like white sails gleamed flutteringly below her, others had collapsed and their crews struggled like disputing soldier ants to raise them, and some were just unattended thin poles reaching out of white ovals, like miniature traffic beacons.

Many pilots didn't like flying over great expanses of water and would even avoid the Bristol Channel, but Ali had no such squeamishness. Unusually for someone trained as an engineer she believed in her machine and trusted that it was no more likely to fail over water than over land.

North of Cardiff she flew over the M4 which, like its southern brother, was a bumpy line choked by stationary holidaymakers escaping London congestion. Climbing up to 3,000 feet to remain clear of the Black Mountains, she skirted around Ebbw Vale, its derelict mining equipment still scarring the rocks like black bones picked bare by vultures. Here the shadows from the clouds etiolated the ground, running across the slopes and reminding Ali that Jake's intellectually clever friends debated whether the view from the sky looked like an unfinished canvas or a finished one. Although there was not much wind Ali remained aware of possible fluctuations from the mountain drafts, but the little Robinson ploughed on with hardly a flutter.

Every now and then she saw a little cloud at her height. Then she would turn and chase it, and catching it smash it into a thousand little white puffs, as though hundreds of tiny smokers had all breathed out at once.

Looking at her map trying to identify the high peaks she was passing Ali saw Brecon famous for its beacons, and Hay-on-Wye known for its books. Then, before she was ready for it, Hereford came in sight on her right and she knew it was time to deflect towards Leominster.

Alice's house was between Leominster and Tenbury Wells, built in a defensive position between the hills and the river. On the site of an Elizabethan Priory, it had been burnt down by Cromwell's men at the height of the civil war. Though some of the period outhouses remained, the present building was mostly eighteenth-century with nineteenth-century additions, plus those pre-Cromwellian outhouses and cellars. Ali had bought a guide book for the area and Alice's house was one of the notable buildings mentioned therein. An addendum explained that although the house had been open to the public in the early part of the century it had now reverted to private ownership. Adding: not without some local opposition. Ali wondered what this meant. Perhaps locals had enjoyed picnicking in the grounds, or missed the opportunity to spread graffiti on a mansion of the wealthy. Or perhaps, as Hilaire Belloc would have pointed-out, "It is the duty of the wealthy man to give employment to the artisan."

The house came in sight before she was ready for it. Ali gasped. It was a palace!

The guidebook had said: 'An illustrious building designed in the era when your house confirmed your personal magnificence. The imposing curtain wall and gatehouse were built shortly around 1370, when King Richard 11 granted Bishop Field a licence to crenellate. Positioned on the edge of a knoll the impression is that the builder had been aiming to combine strength with elegance and had come down more heavily on the side of defence. However, in the nineteenth century the windows were illuminated with mythological animals, and a turret gives a story-book aspect to the house.'

Certainly if perennial weather could be guessed from architecture the prevailing winds were strong enough to uproot trees and the rain invaded any potential crevices. However, the hard edges of the buildings had been softened by Gothic spirals and whorls, one chimney in each stack of four supported a stick of candy sugar, whirling and twirling around the pipe.

Ali was alternately intrigued and appalled. There was something *jolie laide* about the whole edifice. You wanted to dismiss it as a piece of hill-tribe architecture and yet your eye kept being drawn back to it, like an ugly old man in the middle of a gaggle of beauties. What sort of people lived in a house like this?

Ali checked the GPS; this was indeed the right house. Alice-the-exasperated, as Ali had come to think of her, lived here in this amalgam of winter fortress and Alladin's cave. What sort of person could she be? Perhaps a 'Fat white woman whom nobody loves.' Or 'a green girl unsifted in... perilous circumstance'. Either way they had a long flight together into unknown lands to come.

She circled to check the best approach path and, seeing a clear line through the trees onto the park, decided to let down there and taxi on up to the front lawn, hopping over a small fence.

Even as she flew the fence and taxied up the lawn, preparatory to touching down, Ali could see a girl opening the French windows; unwisely judging by the contortions of the curtains. As she landed and began shutting down the helicopter she wondered if this was Alice, or perhaps a maid; there was something about the way the girl looked that made Ali doubt she had access to helicopter-flying millions and a house this size must have staff. But the girl seemed too tall, too athletic to be a maid, and the way she stood holding an Alsatian, which Ali now spotted in the shadow of the curtain by her side, made you think police.

The rotors stopped, Ali opened the door and the girl and dog walked towards the helicopter. The dog was clearly more than a pet and the girl wore a pistol on her hip. Ali's first thought was to joke 'do you have a licence for that' while simultaneously realising she must have. Ali had never lived in any kind of jet-set world and she avoided the news and real life wherever possible but even so she had read about rich people taking their personal protection to parties. This woman and her dog must be bodyguards. What sort of people need bodyguards?

"Hello," Ali said, "I'm Alison Gee."

The girl nodded. An unusual response for Ali, who had lived the last few years of life embarrassed by the comic. You couldn't blame her parents, Shaun Baron Cohen had been using his own name when she was born and they had named her Alison, which she hated so much she insisted on being Ali. Then Ali Gee became a household name and Ali was constantly causing disappointment amongst strangers. There were two immediate responses, one was profound laughter, the other was denial. Older people knew only Auden's Miss Gee.

"I heard you were coming," said the bodyguard in a pulverizing voice. Ali's eyes were propelled to the gun. "Mr and Mrs Charleston are awaiting you in the drawing room."

Great! An inquisition. Ali was tempted to say the weather and the time were pressing and they had better get going, but felt the kindness of the soft air on her cheek and meekly followed the Alsatian across the smooth, green lawn and in through the newly painted French windows.

The room behind the dancing curtains was the library: dusty teak shelves reached from floor to ceiling, large coffee table books balanced on rows of leather first editions, paperbacks leant against fat cloth-bound dictionaries. School books interspersed between sets of green leather Who's Who and red leather Debrett's. Guinness' Records jostled for space with Alastair Cooke, novels, histories and maps. The room had a mellow and smoky scent like a Gentleman's club on the morning after a full gathering. On a discreet deep red Turkish carpet lounged a sprinkling of hard, black lacquer chairs and those armchairs you find in the clubs, covered in hard green leather with studded pockets punctured by round buttons giving way into layered wrinkles like a fat man in tight clothes. Ali followed the girl and dog through into the huge hall beyond.

The hall was panelled and dominated by a table about the same length as Ali's house in Peckham. In the middle of the table was a china bowl of pot-pourri strangely covered with cling film. All available space was covered with things: a stuffed fox in a case, a leather vaulting horse, pictures higgledy-piggledy on the walls, racks for coats, hats, umbrellas, even one of those wooden calling-card butlers, fire dogs, whips, riding hats, letters, and, oddly, plastic picnic knives and forks, all lying around haphazardly as though a flurry of busy people had rushed through the hall dumping things as they went. But their steps echoed across the room with emptiness.

A large oak staircase ran off to the right and Ali was vaguely aware of a gallery above and many doors leading off the hall, but the bodyguard, negotiating the table, opened one straight ahead of them. To Ali's surprise, there was another door immediately beyond. Standing in the dark, claustrophobically between two closed doors, Ali felt as though she was in a wooden lift and would soon find herself on another floor. Had she known it, that was a game Alice used to play as a lonely child: standing between the doors, pressing her fingers into the panelled wood, pretending she was climbing up many floors to the roof and thence to fly away to find another family.

The bodyguard waited until Ali had joined her in the small compartment between the doors, shut the outer door and knocked on the inner. They went through into a room that yelled yellow, although deeper inspection revealed lime green chairs amongst the daffodils, perhaps an eccentric purchase by a colour-blind aunt.

The extremely large room had been reduced to sections by clever use of colour and mirrors. Beside the marble fireplace were three yellow brocade sofas with supporting wood, pale as milky lemons, distributed around a predominately yellow Persian rug. Inside the protected world of the upholstery, on a Georgian table, was a bowl of sweets, again covered in cling film.

Outside the sofas, towards the middle of the room, was a round rosewood table, covered with magazines and everyday items; ashtrays, cigarette lighters and lamps, and to one side an eighteenth century mahogany musical box and some gentle Edwardian chairs and a table. At the far end of the room was the modern world: an enormous wide-screen television between two deep red sofas and a bean bag on the polished wooden floor. Ali suddenly noticed the dog had stayed behind. When had he slipped away? Was he not allowed in this room? Did she have mud on her shoes?

Belatedly she noticed there were a couple of people in the room. Mid-sixties, a grey-haired couple, both of middle height and slender they fitted the room so well they blended into the furniture. Presumably these were Alice's parents. The woman, who was dressed in a light tweed suit from another era, stepped forward and put out a frail hand, so soft and fragile that Ali could feel two wedding rings on the thin fingers. Mrs Charleston looked like a British aristocrat from a long line of dedicated breeding.

"Good afternoon," she said and her voice was so quiet Ali had to lean forward to hear her. "Miss Gee. How kind of you to take Alice flying. I hope it's no trouble."

Ali shook her hand and murmured something hopeless, then shook the man's hand too. Charleston, who wore cords and a cashmere sweater like any weekend professional, seemed crisper, his smile efficiently effective behind the exterior aura of relaxed suavity. He looked at the bodyguard and asked where Alice was. His voice was firm, and there was a touch of some foreign accent in it.

"I'll fetch her," she replied respectfully and left the three of them alone.

"Please," said the woman, her delicate hand fluttering over several chairs, "sit down. Would you care for a drink? No, you're flying of course. Perhaps a coffee? Tea? Something cold?"

Ali shook her head and sat lightly down on the edge of the yellow brocade, wondering if it clashed with her hair. "Red heads," her mother had told her, "should not wear purple or yellow, but unfortunately they so often do."

"Yes," said Charleston smiling, "of course you will," and looked significantly at the now returning bodyguard, who disappeared again.

"Nice house," said Ali politely, "very magnificent."

"Thank you," murmured Mrs Charleston, "it's been in the family a long time."

Yes, thought Ali, so it seemed.

There was a noise from the lush gardens outside, Ali looked up and felt a spasm of shock. Ali had been looking forward to meeting this mysterious woman who wanted to fly a tiny helicopter to Russia. A woman who, on the telephone, sounded so certain of herself, so much in control, so mature, but the girl who came in through the French windows at the modern end of the room, away from the world-excluding sofas, looked as though she had hardly left her teens. Ali had been expecting a woman around thirty, and yet Alice had that fullness of face, that fuzzy bloom and awkward elegance of a young animal. She was so thin she looked like one of those fish whose stomachs you can see expanding as you feed them.

The girl was almost as tall as Ali, and like her had red hair, but while Ali's hair verged on the side of blond Alice's was the colour of clay. She wore jeans and ankle boots with a heel, which made her strut, and a string of wide flat plastic beads around her neck. She was not a good-looking girl. Unlike the refined features of her parents, her face was hard with a large nose and a prominent forehead. Her chin receded into her neck and gave her mouth the appearance of pushing forward ahead of the other features.

Her mother, who had sat on the sofa opposing Ali, turned around, her elbow flopping back over the milky lemon wood. "There you are darling, this is Miss Alison Gee. Come and say hello."

Ali felt a strange emotion pass through her. The woman spoke as though to a child, and yet Alice was probably actually nineteen or twenty, an adult. Now that she was closer Ali could see that although she still had the fluid grace of a young thing she was more poised, more aware than a child. These elegant grey birds must have been elderly parents when she was born. This was something Ali knew a lot about, her mother having had another child at the age of forty-six, giving Ali, then sixteen, a baby half-brother. Ali could still remember the amazement she felt when her mother told her she was pregnant, although perhaps she should have expected it since her mother had just married for the third time.

"Hi," said Alice fingering her hair nervously, "good flight? I saw you land. I was on the other side of the haa-haa. I've just been riding." She threw what looked like a defiant glance at her mother and smiled rather coquettishly at her father, patting down her hair.

She smoothes her hair with automatic hand, and puts a record on the gramophone.

The tea tray arrived and Alice sat down next to Ali on the yellow sofa. Mrs Charleston moved up to pour tea from a silver pot, into cups that were as slender and fragile as her hands. Ali watched the liquid trickling into the thin ceramic wondering if the hot and cold would suddenly explode, leaving a quivering, shaking hand exposed above the void.

Time yet for a hundred indecisions, and for a hundred visions and revisions, before the taking of toast and tea.

"Have you been flying long?" asked Mrs Charleston as she poured.

"Yes, oh yes," replied Ali, jerked back to a friendly reality, "I started at university, in the air squadron. More than ten years ago. I flew Chipmunks, and the Tiger Moth for a while, then I went on to Bulldogs and from there to the Twin Comanche..."

"Splendid," murmured Mrs Charleston politely.

Ali could see she was relieved that this was not some 100-hour girl Pete had produced from nowhere and was about to cite some more types to add to her reassurance when her host broke in.

"Now," said Charleston briskly, "how long do you estimate your flight to Russia will be?"

"Around twenty-five hours each way," Ali replied. "We're doing the flight out over five days."

"So quick," breathed Mrs Charleston, while her husband continued his inquisition.

"Now, have you planned refuelling points?"

"Yes, we..."

"Good. And where to stay? If you have any problems I have a manager stationed in..."

"I'm ready if you are," said Alice brusquely, "shall we go?"

Her father gave the shocked look of a priest heckled by a goldfish, while his wife, spontaneously diplomatic, began to murmur about light and weather. Alice stood up, her face closed. "Ok, let's go."

Ali, taking in the strength, the weakness and the tension, the ghosts and the aura of sadness in the room, nodded automatically and went to shake hands with Alice's parents. She felt she ought to reassure them, to say that their baby would be OK. She couldn't help wondering if she was supposed to be acting in lieu of the bodyguard. Just consider this a holiday and relax, she told herself, but felt a surge of incompletely understood pain and wasn't sure how it related to the family.

By the time they returned to the helicopter it had been refuelled and the front perspex had been washed and polished by invisible hands. When she mentioned this to Alice the girl shrugged, comment unnecessary. They climbed in and Alice took the pilot's seat on the right hand side, Ali the instructor's.

"Are you learning on the Robinson?" Ali asked, uncertain how much to prompt the girl.

"Sometimes. I've done some hours on a Sikorsky S76, some on an EC120 and our Agusta 109 but most in the R22. I know how to start it and so forth, if that's what you mean."

"OK, good. Is Pete teaching you?"

Alice made a scornful noise. "He was, but he's such a show-off... you know him... all that rubbish about the density of air displaced by a space ship and twelve being God's number. The latest one is that all ATCs are called Caroline. Silly. Too silly. No, I had a girl, but she left. I'm looking for someone else."

She turned the key, the engine purred and the blades whirled eagerly. There was little vibration and Ali, thinking again what a clean machine this was, made no comment.

The hop over to Shawbury was such a short one that Ali suggested to Alice that they fly a little into the mountains on the way, to get used to the helicopter and to each other.

"Wicked," said Alice, her fuzzy face defining with excitement. "Let's go and buzz the wind farms. My parents loathe them, they say they can hear the clatter they make in their sleep. Frankly, I'd rather hear the thud of a heavy rotor blade any day."

Ali laughed and told her that Frank Robinson had said that he disliked the tinkling of the ice cream van.

They headed west past Shobdon, dodging shoals of graceful gliders, then dropping low into the hills along the river Teme in the narrowing valley where it competes with the railway lines. They scooted along the train tracks at fifty feet, watching their shadow bumble over the sleepers like a child dragging her school bag. The shadow reduced to miniature as they shot rapidly up to 1500 feet, when the line went into a tunnel, and then widened out again as they floated down the other side into the flat expanse of the Ithan river plateau. Here Alice flew so low the longer blades of grass shuddered in the wind and above them walkers on the peaks looked down in part amusement part disapprobation. Ali and Alice giggled and waved: *girls just want to have fun.*

At Newbridge they left the railway and turned instead to follow a disused line. Only the high hedges remained to remind them railway noise was once a cause of complaint. Past Rhayder, Alice singing raucously "raiders of the windfarm", they climbed up to the edge of the escarpment and there before them, banging sloppily in the light wind and reflecting the afternoon sun, was a field of moving white crosses, a noisy graveyards for giants.

"Phhrr," said Alice disdainfully, "just look at them. Let's go and hover over them and see if we can make them turn faster. It looks like a junkyard on a hill."

But Ali looked at her watch and decided they must turn for Shawbury, where Pete and the others would now be expecting them.

"Come on," she said, "bet you it takes twenty-five minutes to get there."

Alice looked at the clock on the console. "Twenty! And that'll be on the deck."

"You're on. Winner gets to pay the fuel."

"Ha, it's free. Present of her majesty."

Alice climbed to 3,000 feet and saw, spread below them in the clear air, the craggy rocks and hills of the mountainous range. These gave way to neater fields and well tended countryside which led to the enclave of Shrewsbury, its brown and grey buildings swaggering with all the pretension and pomposity of a small market town but kept in check by the severe outline of the motorway by-pass. Beyond that was the airfield of Shawbury, runways tethered in a long grey line like a team of exhausted donkeys.

Ali called Shawbury on the radio as they got closer and was given directions to approach directly across the runways, up to the control tower and land. As they flew low across the wide grey expanse of military airfield, approaching the elegant brown and white tower, Ali saw well manicured grass, polished tarmac and washed concrete. An airfield that was constantly being renewed and refurbished. She knew she was flying in a wealthy country, which still felt the pressing might of its past.

Empire after Empire at their height of sway, have felt this boding sense come on. Have felt that huge frames not constructed right, and droop'd and slowly died upon their throne.

They parked the R22 on the apron, in a little white circle with an H. Its nearest companion helicopter was a sleek Gazelle in military camouflage: a lizard reclining in the sun. The larger helicopters were parked on the other side of the apron where they would not agitate the frailer craft.

Alice landed rather neatly, the little R22 prupping gently onto the tarmac with a relieved sigh. Ali was even more impressed by the landing, either the girl had been taught well or she had natural ability.

They shut down and got their bags from under the seats, Alice's having been placed there by the invisible hands. Alice had fine leather tooled brag-wear from Gucci, which made Ali's worn duffel bag look cheap and uninviting. Clearly the boys on the apron thought so too as they jostled to take Alice's things and the loser took Ali's. They escorted the girls into the barracks.

Alice and Ali's shared room had a pine wood emphasis, with an IKEA desk, table and wardrobe, and two single beds whose cheerful striped covers cried out there was more here than mere utility.

Left alone with instructions that drinks would be served in the officers's mess at six, Ali suggested to Alice that she had the first shower.

"No," said Alice, "you go ahead. I'm going to ring home, say we've arrived safely."

Ali said nothing but it struck her Alice was a bit too old to have to check-in with her parents. Still, families were always a source of bafflement to her; even her own.

≈ ≈ ≈ ≈ ≈ ≈

Outside the Garden Ring

In the dull listless early morning air an equally dull and listless girl walked, her baby strapped to her back with as old shirt, her hair tied in a shabby parched shawl. The girl was young but her face was matured by life and the scowls that painted it as thoughts crossed her mind. The brick path that she walked down was littered with dog mess and parts of the paving stones were cracked and broken, but the girl didn't notice. She had lived here so long the litter and the pointless iron fence, which didn't prevent dogs getting onto the mythical flower-beds to soil them, were part of her daily routine.

She walked up a short flight of steps into the lobby of a tall block of flats, greeting the *dezhurnaya*, who sat there swathed in baggy sweaters, with a muffled murmur. Acknowledge by a nod of the headscarf, she walked past her, up three cracked linoleum steps to the lifts, where she waited amongst bits of blistered and peeling floor for the creaking sixties metal box to shudder to a halt. A crowd of people swept out of the lift, but she noticed neither their number nor the smell of camphor and spice which clung to their woollen coats. This was a daily occurrence for her and no more notable than a fly crawling up the window.

She entered the lift and pushed a button mounted on the formica. With a grudging grunt the box heaved its way up four floors, stopped while some other people got in, then out again cursing her, realising she was going up. A few voices shouted that the many should have priority over the few, but she joggled the button harshly, the doors shuddered shut and they moved up a second time.

This time she got a clear run up to the twelfth floor. Here she got out, walked past a broken window to a formica covered door. She rang the bell. Inside was the noise of children, and even the girl smiled briefly as she undid the arms of her shirt-strapping and swung her baby forward into her arms in one strong movement.

A large woman, muffled in layers of clothing with a red apron dancing on top like a cherry on a cake, opened the door. "*Dobraye utra*," said the girl politely. "Good morning."

The woman nodded her greeting and took the boy from his mother automatically feeling the nappy. She reminded the girl she hadn't yet paid for his keep this week, and the only reason she was able to keep her prices so low was that everybody paid in advance. No exceptions! She had been lenient with her, because she understood her situation, but we all have to live, we all have problems. Life, the old woman sighed lustily, is hard for all of us these days. All of us!

"Tonight," replied the girl, her face drooping. "I'll pay you when I return."

The woman nodded, but though her face was nearly sympathetic she shut the door firmly.

Galina turned and made her way back down the lift, now joined by more people at various floors and, once again in the lobby, walked out into the brightening early morning. She skipped towards the Metro station, joining a growing crowd, who were like her heading to the centre of Moscow to their jobs.

Galina travelled from the last stop on the Metro, way beyond the Garden

Circle, so she could always get a seat on the train. As the train moved down the line more and more people swamped the carriage, until the air became fetid and it was hard to breathe. She stared at the rivets, at the seats and at the newly arrived advertising which had taken the place of party slogans, trying to believe she was somewhere more beautiful: somewhere cool and empty. Britain, perhaps? Great Britain. Named for the wealth of its people? She swivelled her pupils, making sure to avoid any eye-contact.

As the train moved more centrally the architecture became more beautiful, the stations more heroic. Once this would have meant something to Galina, once she felt a sense of joy in the elegiac nature of the cathedral-like surroundings, but now it merely alerted her to her arrival in the centre of the city. She stood up and began to fight through the tightly packed masses to reach the door.

Once in the illustrious architecture of Teatralnaya she pushed past the begging babushkas without a thought. When she first began to work she had given to beggars, now, though, she realised that it was a tough life. She was young, she needed to live; if necessary the old must die to give her life. It was sad. It was bad. It was Russia. It was the way of the world.

After a short walk she arrived at the office of her employer, a small German firm who employed her to translate Russian into English and fortunately had not yet discovered her English was not really very good. Getting this job had been a break for Galina, and she was determined that the German would never discover how much she used the dictionary. Luckily the office was only staffed by her and another Russian secretary and the German employer only came to Moscow occasionally. As long as everything was ready for his presentations he made no comment, and so she assumed he was content.

Today the German had sent a message to expect him next week, and to arrange for his flight to be met. He would need, the message continued, a driver while he was in Moscow. Galina smiled. This was good news. She knew she could get a friend to drive him. She would charge her employer many times the Russian rate and pay the friend the normal rate. One of the perks of her job. To celebrate she made herself and the other secretary a cup of coffee.

≈ ≈ ≈ ≈ ≈ ≈

Mohs' Scale

Ali walked past identical pine wood doors all standing to attention except one, which had fallen open revealing a room the mirror image of their own. At the end of the corridor was a communal room with a bank of cubicles. She stripped off and stepped into a powerful, hot shower, with a head that allowed her 'massage' or 'diffuse' water settings. This was something she'd almost forgotten existed, used as she was to her dripping-rain shower and the vibrating horn music of the air locks back in Peckham.

Thoroughly massaged, Ali returned to the bedroom where Alice was sitting on her bed reading a women's magazine.

"Do you realise they don't even have a television in here," Alice snapped as she walked back in, "fucking barbaric!"

"It's a barracks," Ali replied surprised. "I expect they're either out training or studying or something. Do you think we should pay for them to watch TV?"

"Oh, Christ! You're not going to say wasting tax-payers' money are you?"

Since that was exactly what Ali had meant she was silent. The good rapport they had developed in the helicopter clearly was not going to continue. With a disgusted flourish Alice picked up an elegant Tiffany's bath-bag and went to shower.

By the time they were ready to leave Alice was friendly again. She complimented Ali on her dress, and wished she could wear black too, "But I just look like a Holstein cow. Mind you if I wear white I look like an Aberdeen Angus. You're lucky your hair is lighter than mine, mine is a real trial."

Ali laughed, assuming she was meant to. Even as she marvelled at Alice's charm her mind wandered away to disappointing dates when her partner had disappeared with a short brunette. Unaware she was missing an opportunity to connect with Alice, Ali remained silent and mused on the subject of tall redheads and their ability to be striking; even when they would rather remain in the background.

"Come," said Alice, her voice just a tone different, "let's go and wow them."

Let us go then, you and I through certain half-deserted streets, the muttering retreats of restless nights in one-night cheap hotels.

As they walked through the barracks to the mess Alice sparkled beside Ali, telling her about her love of horses and helicopters, making jokes, and being entertaining in the manner of a sophisticated child.

"When I was twelve," she told Ali, "I won my first horse show. I wanted to go into the juniors but they wouldn't have me because I rode a horse not a pony, so my mother lied about my age and I went into the seniors; and won! When they found out they were furious, but couldn't take away my cup because they didn't have a minimum age. Another time I'd won the cup, but we didn't realise it and had already gone home, one of mother's friends brought the cup round but she arrived at the same time as the sewage lorry; we didn't have main drains out there when I was a child and we misunderstood..."

They arrived at the bar laughing. On the surface Ali liked her, but on a deeper level she already found herself growing wary of the girl's effervescence. What would it be like flying all the way to Moscow with such volatility?

She's young, Ali told her deeper self. Forget it. Enjoy your paid holiday.

Pete was already at the bar, chatting to a stocky man with short brown hair and glasses. The man, whom Pete introduced as Tim, was buying drinks and the girls arrived just in time to be included in the round. Pete came forward to greet them, and he too, like Alice, was shining with the light of entertainment.

"Girls you both look absolutely stunning. Ali I should never have recognised you, you look so elegant..."

Ali raised her eyebrows, but the gaffe was unintentional and Pete was already away into further compliments, this time on the subject of Alice, who pirouetted coquettishly when her skirt was admired.

They moved over to sit in a corner, by a window still tickled by the evening sun and giving a view down the long lawns to the shingle drive. While Alice and Pete entertained the company with vying wit, Ali looked out the long windows and watched a group of men walking up from the stables. Probably ex-stables, as she hadn't seen or smelt any horses, perhaps this was once the home of a Cavalry regiment she thought lightly. She had never taken a great interest in the military and even had to stop herself confusing the Fleet Air Arm with the Air Force. The young men reached the front door and all but one entered the building. That one, an elegant and attractive blond boy, broke away and walked towards the long windows of their room lighting a cigarette. Behind Pete but in front of Ali one window was half-open, at least enough for a grown man to enter that way if he bent low and swung his leg across. That was exactly what the young man did. Sitting astride the high frame, swinging and bending all in one fluid movement and arriving standing inside the room his cigarette still glowing.

"Cool!" said Alice, who was sitting next to Ali and could see the show.

Pete turned around, then turned back to the group, his face beaming. "Well! Isn't that typical of Daniel! He can't just enter the room like other men." He tried to force his proud father's face into disapproval, as Daniel sauntered towards them.

"Everyone all right for drinks?" asked Daniel, off-hand as though he hadn't just put on a show for them. "You must be Alice. I'm Daniel."

Alice gave him her hand. In spite of the wide chairs that separated her from him, Daniel took it, bowed low over it and kissed it flamboyantly. "Enchanté! Ali, Tim, Governor. Good to see you all."

"I see he's cut off the moustache then," said Ali, as Daniel walked towards the bar to get another round. Her voice sounded more curt than she intended and Pete's face drooped in disappointment. "Yes, I think he decided he was through the Chevalier stage," he said. "Or maybe I told him too often how ridiculous he looked."

Ali felt mean. As though she'd mocked a man's baby, which of course she had, and he'd tried to be nice about it. She wanted to say something to make up, but so great was her disdain for this show-off that she couldn't think of anything nice to say. Alice, on the other hand, was watching Daniel with ostrich eyes.

A couple of men approached their table and Pete jumped up hospitably.

"Graham, Robert so glad you could make it. I thought you weren't going to be able to get here until tomorrow."

"No," said the taller man, his bearded face moving under his glasses reminding Ali of a chipmunk. "Robert thought he was going to have to stay and baby-sit his daughter, but then his brother had a free day, or something, and his wife was able to get home slightly earlier than she thought. All very complicated but it made it possible for us to leave this afternoon and we shunted up here as fast as the Squirrel could go." He looked around the table, took in the girls. "Hello, hello. I'm Graham, this is Robert. You girls coming to Moscow too?"

"I'm Alice Charleston, this is Ali Gee, we're coming and we're going to win. Watch out boys!"

Ali wondered if she meant it. She was sparkling so much Ali would have thought she'd been snorting something back in the room, if she'd shown any tell-tale signs, but Ali had lived with an addict and knew that although they were magnificently devious there were always the signs for the initiated.

Robert went to the bar, while Graham sat down by Alice, showing white socks between his Timberlands and chinos, and asked if she'd seen the rules yet. To Ali's surprise she said she had. Fiddling with her beads, she looked back at Ali and, smiling slightly, said she'd photocopied a set for her too. Ali was impressed, especially as the girl went on to discuss methods of holding the bucket in the slalom, which showed she'd not only read it but had thought about what she'd seen. Ali listened to their conversation but it was like a foreign language she understood but didn't know well and she could neither initiate a new topic nor keep the original one going.

It occurred to Ali, sitting there listening to Alice sparkle and the men laugh, that Alice used rather formal English, like a foreigner who had learnt it in school rather than imbibed it from her parents. It was true she said things like 'wicked' and 'cool', but her English was actually correct even to the point of being old-fashioned. Ali noted there were no 'hopefullies', and 'almost uniques' dotted around, nor did she confuse 'less' with 'few' or 'I' with 'me'. Perhaps it was due to the influence of older parents, who had taught her strictly and monitored her language. Mind you, thought Ali, my brother gets away with all the sloppiness of a *ditch born drab*, but then he is not an only child, however much he may wish it.

After dinner the young ones went what Pete called 'ashore' into Shrewsbury, while he and the wrinklies stayed behind at the bar. Ali wasn't sure it was better to have a smooth face.

She, Alice and Daniel joined Rob and Paul, two Naval Gazelle pilots based at Yeovilton, and a group from Shawbury which included Toby Jones, a rotund baby-faced boy, and Adam Brookes (who was known as Doc) his sandy haired navigator, splitting between Toby's Audi and Adam's Volvo Estate.

Ali sat in the boot of the Volvo, watching the traffic behind her as they sped into Shrewsbury as though pursued by a rival team. An old Sainsbury's bag floated along behind them, never quite catching up nor falling away. Ali watched it with amusement. It seemed like a smaller dog, following bigger companions. Then suddenly it lifted in a gust of air, and falling connected with the front of a black car, staying there attached to the fender like cappuccino fluff on some drinker's lip. Ali was sorry when the black car turned away and wondered how long the bag stuck firm.

She was the last to leave the secure warmth of the car. When she edged out into the cold square, with its high rectangles of houses from an earlier era, the first thing she saw was Daniel standing hips pushed forward, shoulders coolly relaxed, blowing smoke rings like any Peckham pimp. Alice had her back to him and was chatting animatedly to Rob, a sandy-haired man with spiky fox features. She was asking about local discos.

"They're crap," he said, his long nose quivering as though scenting a chicken, "all yokels and no presence. There's a great little pub over on the far side of the square though, some of the best beer in Shrewsbury."

"That good 'eh?" said Paul, who was taller and darker than Rob and laughed easily and a lot. "Better hurry then."

Alice looked at them, laughing capriciously as though their jokes were new to her. Perhaps they were, thought Ali, remembering the girl's youth.

In the pub Phil and Toby hailed a couple of mates, Nudger Smith, and Knobby Clarke and, after some brief conversation with the girls, faded away to play darts. In a smoky back parlour they could hear the dull thud of darts connecting and the scratching slap-plop of failure.

Rob began discussing cars with Daniel. Daniel had been a racing driver and loved driving fast in and out of the traffic, hopping from one lane to another like a pigeon avoiding shotgun shrapnel. Daniel outlined the details of his brief career in between smoke rings. "I drove a single seat racing car, miniature F1. Lying in the car cockpit everything close to hand. The clutch is fucking sharp, the gears are conventional shift pattern but fucking difficult to do. Sure footed yeah! With the aerodynamics contributing to both cornering and braking it is designed for fucking performance! I found the best engine was the time when we experimented with a turbine..."

Paul listened to Daniel for a while, then turned to Ali. "So, I hear you girls are keen to win. Rumour is it you've been practising like maniacs."

Just shows, thought Ali, how poor rumours are. "Hardly," she laughed, "we only met today."

Paul stared at her, unbelieving. "Come on! You can't put that one over. I know you've been using the fields behind the Charleston place, we sometimes fly over and watch you."

Alice picked up a copy of the Sun some previous drinker had left behind and waved it at Ali and Paul, giggling. "Look here! They're so keen on breasts, why don't they have some penises?"

Slightly shocked Ali laughed. "To enlarge the audience you mean."

Rob broke away from Daniel's monologue. "That's disgusting!" he said.

"Ha," Ali riposted brilliantly. While Alice asked he if he'd thought of modelling.

"You're a pair, aren't you," said Paul, "you'll have poor Rob blushing, he's not a palm pilot."

"Nor a crop duster?" asked Alice innocently, while the boys stared at her and Daniel tried to reclaim their interest.

Beautiful Balas

The next morning was the start of one of those hot days-in-waiting, now holding a fresh, cool smell but soon to become so still it seems almost silent. A heavy silence, as though the molecules of the air had become too dense for sound to pass through, but perhaps the heat simply kept all the noisy people asleep in bed.

At exactly zero nine hundred hours they met in the classroom for a briefing from the station commander.

"Good Morning Gentlemen, and Ladies."

The man on the podium had the slim fit look of one who would slip straight from Major to General, by-passing the fatter stages of Colonel and Brigadier. "And welcome to Shawbury. May I say how glad we are to have the British teams here, both gentlemen and ladies. And well done to those of you who have already done some substantial amounts of practice." His smile gave a sufficient caress without becoming obsequious. "Now, a brief word about flying here at Shawbury and then I will pass you over to Lieutenant Coriolis for the weather."

He went through a few basic regulations and then Lt Coriolis took the floor; the weather was CAVOK, winds so negligible they were laughing and no probability of change.

The commander then turned to the map behind him and outlined the 'practice area' and the best approach. Ali felt vaguely amused, imagining that he was more used to giving serious briefings about the position of the enemy, range of fire and aircraft vulnerability, than training areas and what to do in case of broken poles. Alice, however, was totally absorbed and took notes.

After the briefing, including a heated discussion on the team uniform, they went out to the apron. The sun radiated down from a clear blue sky and the rising temperature caused little eddies of heat to shudder off the tarmac. Ali looked into the distant hills and thought that on a normal Saturday she would be teaching people to fly somewhere in the south of England. How different, how unusual to be here in the heartbeat of the nation, close to the west coast, looking at a Russian future. The whole idea gave her a frisson of pleasure and she danced jauntily out to check out their helicopter and start up for the flight to Ternhill. To her surprise and Alice's anguish, Pete informed them that he and Daniel would fly out to Ternhill and they could go in the back of Rob and Paul's Gazelle. In an attempt to make Alice feel better he added. "But you can fly home."

"Great," spat Alice, stomping across the glowing tarmac to the Gazelle.

As they approached the helicopter they saw cat-like radio whiskers decorated the front for UHF conversation. Ali was about to speculate on their use when Alice said: "You can see they don't give a donkey's about us winning. Well, we're going to show them, and everybody else. The fuckers!"

Ali said nothing, looking forward to a ride in the Gazelle. The uniformed boys were already checking the machine.

"Hi girls, flown in a Guzzle before? No! You're in for something special!" said Rob. "This is the Jaguar of the fleet and I'm the F1 pilot."

"Yeah," said Paul, "and we all know what F stands for! Specially with UP after it!"

They flew north east to Ternhill, the helicopter playing field, adopting a rather roundabout arrival route which, Ali speculated, might have had something to do with normal military defensive behaviour but had little to do with commercial practice. She looked out of the window and Alice glanced again at the rules, while the boys chatted together.

"Lt. Coriolis 'eh? What a joker, can't wait until he becomes a Colonel, Colonel Col can I feel your force?"

"Colonel, I feel the pressure over your ridge!"

As they flew over the practice field Ali saw below her red-topped poles set out in pairs forming 'gates' for the slalom course, an ugly stake-mounted metal square with a missing piece, which Alice explained constituted the high obstacle, and a group of four flat-topped mushrooms; the low obstacle. Beyond that was a dog kennel, with a large square hole in the roof for the skittle drop. In the distance, behind a second slalom course, were some crosses marked on the ground with white paint, the target for the flour bombs. Ali thought 'James Bond', and wondered if the SAS trained here. She could almost see Lotte Lenya snooping behind the mushrooms.

Rob and Paul landed beyond the doghouse and let their guests out, before moving off to practise their slalom run, saying: "At least we won't have to practise navigation, plenty of that on the way to Russia."

"What do we do now, do you think?" asked Alice, watching Pete take the R22's doors off and lie them on the ground. "That's our helicopter Pete and Daniel are mucking around in. We're paying for it, we ought to be flying it."

Ali said nothing, but it answered one question anyway. She wondered what percentage of Alice's transaction she was getting and how much Pete had kept.

For an hour or more Ali and Alice sat on the ground watching Daniel and Pete have yet another attempt at the slalom, knock the bucket into yet another set of gates and miss the final table. It was not a good spectator sport, that was indisputable. Ali yawned and reminded herself to have a good time. The sun was warm, she was being paid, the ghosts of her past were fading in this new, fresh company, what more could she want.

"What do you think of those guys Paul and Rob?" asked Alice. "Aren't they a couple of jokers."

"A poor degenerate from the ape, whose hands are four whose tail is limp," said Ali. "But Daniel now..."

"I think he's an oblomovist" said Alice.

"A what?"

Alice grinned naughtily, "Since you're so keen on quoting I thought you'd know it! It's from a well-known Russian novel "Oblomov" by Goncharov. Oblomov is the name of a landlord. The exact word is "oblomovshina," it means a lazy sausage who loves the good-life. You'd better get to know it. Russians use it all the time!"

"How do you know?"

Alice jumped up. "Come on," she said, "it's our turn now. We've spent hours doing nothing and I damned if we're going to let them have another practice. We won't win this way."

And she sped off towards the slalom starting line waving her arms.

By the time Ali caught up the Robinson had landed and Pete had changed places with Alice. Daniel was sitting in Ali's seat, his leg astride the collective, chatting to Alice. He climbed out as she arrived.

"Ah, the conquering hero. I must give up my seat. I hear you and Alice are out to beat us." He winked and drew back, Ali said nothing and climbed into the machine in his place thinking: *A man of action forced into a state of thought is unhappy until he can get out of it.*

Ali took off and flew back to the start, where Alice collected the bucket of water, and then rose under starter's orders to begin flying through the 'gates'. However, only half of her mind was concentrating on the flying. The rest was impressed again by Alice's determination to try and win in spite of the enormous obstacles facing them. She had been like that herself pre-Jake. Jake, love of her life and problem of her love.

All hope abandon, ye who enter here!

Perhaps she was letting Alice down. She glanced at the girl leaning out of the Robinson door, holding the rope, trying so hard not to swing the bucket and silently promised to be more positive.

"How we doing?" Ali asked through the radio mike, "am I too high? You'll have to tell me. I can't see the poles."

"Yes, go down and right a little. Ok. Hold it there. Good we are through. Next gate. First one on the left, entered from the other side. We need to be below the red lines and above the ground. And I have to be careful letting my hand get too low or we'll be disqualified."

Alice had really read the rules.

While they practised on the left-hand course, the military Gazelles were moving around on the lower field. The girls could occasionally hear them over the radio, when they yelled at the judges, made facetious remarks or let off a stream of expletives at another pilot, all other times the radio waves strummed lightly, blissfully free of noise.

Then suddenly there was an explosion. A noise like someone dragging an umbrella across a metal fence rattled across the radio. Followed by complete silence. Then a new voice called 'Mayday' rather blandly, as you might curse in slight annoyance, and outside the Robinson Alice and Ali saw their judges halt, turn to look at the lower field and suddenly, as a bunch, begin running in that direction still clasping their clipboards.

"What do you think has happened?" Ali asked.

Alice craned out the door, trying to see what was happening, stretching her seat-belt to its limit and twisting towards the back of the helicopter like a horse trying to bite its tail.

"I don't know, but it's something on the lower course, everyone is running that way…"

Ali allowed the helicopter to yaw 180 degrees right, so they could see behind them. It looked as though one of the Gazelles had landed on top of the low obstacle. Under the sleek lizard they could see yellow and red shafts with rough, broken wooden edges. The Gazelle was still upright but tottered a little, slanted to one side. The pilots were out and they and others were running about with all the direction of termites whose mound has been invaded by the heavy feet of hikers.

Ali taxied the helicopter slowly over to the lower field and landed. Daniel came up immediately, his gait excited. He lit a cigarette.

"Paul's had an engine failure, he put it down safely but unfortunately it squashed the low obstacle, we'll have to fix it when they move the helicopter. He's mad as a half-burnt peasant. His gophers going to get it all right. Just look at him!"

Paul was by this time out of the helicopter and was shouting at one of the clipboard holders. The man was trying to answer back but the angry pilot was not letting a word edge past his furious tirade. They watched him for a moment, then Alice said in a slightly bored voice, "come on. Let's get back and practise. He's OK isn't he. Nothing more's going to happen."

Ali lifted up the collective and they turned back towards the upper course, to once again try to get the bucket through the gates without spillage.

When they met Paul later that evening he was only half angry and appeared more puzzled. The helicopter had run out of fuel. However, the gauges showed half full. But then there was one of those mix-ups typical of military cost cutting. The fuellers were now civilians, and the one in question was an agency man, brought in because the regular guy was sick. The agency could find no record of having sent a man, and the man himself had disappeared, however he had signed the book as having given the helicopter full fuel. And yet, contrary to those sticking gauges, the tanks were completely empty.

"Shit!" Paul said with a laugh, "I know those fucking Ruskies will do anything to win but I thought that Shawbury was a little too far for their empty pockets to reach. And I don't want to have to blame the damn gremlins. Besides who'd want to kill Rob and me? Ex-girlfriend? Or maybe," he said smiling at the thought, "the miscreants were after you girls!" He laughed heartily.

Ali joined in the laughter, but Alice's face froze like angry granite.

So that was it for practice, the rest Alice and Ali would have to somehow fudge. Pete told Ali to take the helicopter back to High Wycombe where he'd found space in a storage hangar for it and to keep herself available for the odd job or two. She gave Alice a lift back to her parents' house but this time didn't even shut down, just let the girl out and headed off to High Wycombe. None-the-less the girl had impressed her, such grit was rare in the nineteen-year olds Ali knew; the Peckham estate girls who followed men and had their babies, and the working girls who wanted to.

When she got home she discovered there had been a leak in Peckham's Victorian plumbing and consequently the water had been turned off all weekend, resulting in another outbreak of frustrated 'diamonds' decorating the street.

Komdragmet Circles

Galina worked all through lunch. She seldom ate much, never out and usually sandwiches that she made for herself. The boy would have eaten with the old woman, so he could just have sandwiches himself later. He was a good boy and, as long as she let him watch the television, he wouldn't complain. She would take some of the translations home tonight and work on them with the dictionary, so the Russian secretary wouldn't notice. Probably the girl would say nothing, but you didn't want to trust anyone, you could never be sure.

While the secretary was out for lunch with friends, Galina rang a car-owning acquaintance to ask if he would drive her German boss when he was in Moscow. Ten years ago her friend had been a government driver, making money *na levo*, to supplement his salary, by selling off state fuel on the side to private drivers. Sadly, the government had now reduced their drivers in one of their wild cost cutting exercises and such perks were no longer available to him in his regular job as a taxi driver. He was always glad to get extra work like this from Galina.

She had already told her boss how much it would cost and he accepted the price without comment, her friend did too. Moreover, he asked if he could pick up her this evening and drive her over to pick up the boy and then take them both home. She hesitated before agreeing. She had told the old woman it was difficult for her to pay because of her terrible, low-paying job, if she now turned up in a car, with a man, the woman would raise the price and not give her the previous leniency. After some deep thinking Galina's desire for a ride prevailed and she agreed, but told her friend he would have to wait around the corner from the old woman's flat, so there was no chance of the nosy cow seeing her getting out of a car. She told him it was because the boy's father watched her closely, which he accepted. She also decided to pay the woman half of what she owed, that would stem some of the whines. Putting the phone down she had another celebratory cup of coffee.

≈≈≈≈≈

Octahedral Rocks

Ali was showering three days later (water having finally returned to Peckham after a five day absence) when Pete rang. He had a client for her. A guy called Tom Moore wanted to be transported to Welshpool and back, the next day. Pete sounded relieved that she was free and reminded her to take her hangar key to the airfield.

Before I go, Tom Moore, thought Ali, looking at the map and making Alice's house a GPS way-point so they could fly overhead and amuse the observant Alice if she glanced up while riding, *here's a double health to thee.*

When Ali arrived at High Wycombe she realised she hadn't focused on the word storage, as in storage hangar, strongly enough. On the Sunday evening, after the practice, Pete had told her to leave the Robinson out on the tarmac as there wasn't space for it in the hangar until the following day. Even this, though, had not alerted Ali's instincts to the possibility of finding the helicopter fifty feet back in a hangar full of tools, builders pallets, bricks, trolleys and (more under-standably) another plane and an American van.

She stood by the unlocked door and stared at the chaos within. The helicopter was set rather neatly in the midst of twenty or so of the pallets, all piled high with a variety of heavy looking objects. A beautiful swan and her guarding maids; but unfortunately the Robinson could not dance itself free. Ali could push the pallets to one side of the hangar, the tools and the bricks she could lift, the plane could be left where it was as the helicopter blades had enough clearance to sweep over-head, but only if the van was moved. The van had no keys.

She stared at it. Kicked it. And suddenly, her fury mounting, shook the damn thing. And the keys felt out of the sun-flap.

"Wow!" She hadn't even thought about it. Of course if you leave a car in the hangar and in the way, you leave the keys in it; somewhere. Although it took her a while to get the column-mounted-gear-stick to work, eventually she drove it out of the hangar, moved all the concomitant obstacles and hoisted the Robinson up onto its wheels. She had just managed to squeeze the helicopter past the plane and drag it up onto the tarmac, giving thanks for two blade machines, when a short middle-aged man with an expanding stomach and retreating hairline flounced towards her.

"You're late," he said (sounding more Tom Cat than Thomas Moore). "I espe-cially said I wanted to leave at 8am and it's nearly that now. Are you ready?"

Ali started to explain but he waved away her words. "I don't want excuses," he said. "No details. Just get ready; fast."

Ali, understanding why Pete had been so keen to give away the job, muttered to herself: "For it's Tommy this, an' Tommy that, an' 'Chuck 'im out, the brute!' But it's 'Saviour of 'is country' when the guns begin to shoot."

"What's 'at?" asked Tom Moore, pausing and eyeing her quite as suspiciously as his forebear might have done the King.

Feeling better she smiled, checked the helicopter over, and pushed it up the slope to the pad, while he walked beside her; keeping his distance as though the machine might bite. "You're tall, aren't you," Tom said, "strong too. Must be difficult getting boyfriends. You'd always be looking down on them. Men don't like to be dominated."

Ali said nothing, wondering if she gave him a quick jab on the nose would she end up in prison or as a hospital visitor.

"Done a flight plan have you? Many pilots I've flown with are so damn casual they simply rely on the GPS and freewheel it when it all goes wrong. Pretty slack to my way of thinking..."

Ali looked at the natural visibility indicators around the field; the clouds, the distant hills, the Union Jack lapping lightly in the breeze and, satisfied, went in to get the paper weather. He followed her, remarking he'd better keep an eye on her in case she slipped off for a quick snifter. "I've heard about your type of pilot," he said mysteriously.

While Ali helped him to strap into the helicopter he complained about the size, said his legs were cramped, pointed out he usually travelled in Squirrels or JetRangers, and said it was only because Pete had offered him such competitive rates (for after all money doesn't grow on trees, even though he'd been working all his life to earn his keep not like some lay-abouts who thought the government should provide).

"When I do business in America," said Tom, "they pick me up from Wilmington Airport in a Sikorsky, an S76 no less, and fly me right to their factory. None of this pay-your-own-way there. This country has a lot to learn about business, I can tell you."

Ali said nothing.

They took off, with Tom rather surprisingly suddenly crying: "Chocks away!" and headed out towards the Golden Ball. The mist was lifting and clearing in the valley and the day had that first-time-ever feeling of early morning that lifted Ali's enervated spirits. Somewhat cheered, she followed the M40 up to Oxford, counting the sets of road-work-induced queues. This time, though, with her critical companion, she did none of the low zooming indulged in with Alice but maintained a stately 2,500 feet, while watching out for planes that also liked to cruise along at that height.

After talking briefly to Oxford ATC, while passing Blenheim Palace, Ali turned onto Brize Norton's frequency. They warned her to keep a look out for a low flying Hercules and parachute dropping at Weston on the Green.

Flying over Moreton-in-the-Marsh they passed the mock village used for fire practice on the disused runway, and over the Cotswold Hills to Evesham.

"I used to own a shop in Pershore," said her companion, "but you can't get people to work nowadays. They want more time off, more sick leave and more holidays than it's cost-effective to give them. So I sold it to a competitor. Let him worry about staff shortage and horrendous wages. I concentrate on what I do best. And it does me good."

She said nothing, concentrating on flying over the M5, which this time was flowing freely, and south of Worcester. Then suddenly they were passing the little nodule of hills which sheltered Alice's mansion. And there it was, on the nose, sitting in a little bed of mist, looking like some fairy tale Schloss on which an evil witch has put a spell.

Turning onto a new track over Alice's house Ali looked out the window, wondering if she would see the girl looking up at her, perhaps across the ha-ha with her horses. There was no one in sight. Looking sideways she realised her companion had stopped talking and was watching her.

"Big house, isn't it?" he said. "Complete waste of money. Empty for years and years. There were plans to make a compulsory purchase, to turn it into a school, or a set of apartments, or use it for some kind of corporate games place, or simply pull it down. That's what I would have done, effing monstrosity, but you know how out of fashion that is these days."

"But it's not empty now," said Ali, indicating the smoke whispering out of one of the chimney stacks.

"An illusion," he said, "must be morning mist. You would be surprised how much in life is not what it seems: the still wet Rembrandt; the newspaper-idolised wealthy man who doesn't have the price of a bus ticket in his pocket; the investor-created gold mine. I bet half the royal families in the world are wearing fake (good quality fakes, mind you) jewellery, having pawned the real thing. No! Big houses are an anachronism, a thing of the past..."

And I have known them all already, known them all, Have known the mornings, evenings, afternoons, I have measured out my life with coffee spoons.

Ali said nothing, she looked again to see if there was any sign of Alice.

Flying towards the Welsh border Ali climbed to 3,000 feet. There would be no searching for windfarms now. As the country became mountainous it also became less populated, and the occasional village popped out of the hills, marking a river, road junction and forming a good landmark. Here churches still dominated the centre of small towns and you could still believe in their mediaeval inheritance.

She called Welshpool near Craven Arms but no one replied until she neared Bishop's Castle and called again.

"Sounds like loads of pubs," said Tom. "Those hill-tribes were all so fucking drunk they thought even the villages were beer holes." He laughed too loudly for the small cockpit and Ali stifled a shudder.

Finally the ATC replied, telling her simply there was no traffic and to make her approach to the 22 threshold and taxi to the grass parking area.

As she entered the long valley Ali put the QFE on the altimeter, watching as her height theoretically unwound on the instrument. She was still at 1,800 feet so she descended to the 1,000 feet needed for circuit height. Above her the town of Montgomery looked down on the small, passing helicopter with the stateliness of a town that has seen civil wars, passing governments and fashions and yet remained ostensibly unchanged.

Welshpool poises on a branch of the River Severn, at the base of three sets of hills making it impossible to see until you are almost on the airfield. Beside her Ali could feel Tom fidgeting in case she had got the wrong valley. Then, when the long dark strip of runway came into view, she felt him relax like some ancient mariner who has finally spotted the lighthouse from the stormy sea.

"Here we are at last! I know you pilots never really know where you are until you see the hangar door."

She landed and he jumped out of the helicopter without waiting for it to shut down. "What time will you be back?" Ali yelled as he scampered away.

He shrugged. "You'll see me when you see me. You've got a night rating haven't you?"

"Yes. But single engine commercial flights aren't allowed at night."

But he had gone. Business first. No excuses. No details. If he came back late they would have to stay here for the night or make it an instructional flight. Ali hoped he wouldn't.

After shutting down Ali pushed the little Robinson over to the fuel pumps. She thought of Rob and Paul and the Gazelle as the swish of the electric pump forced the low-leaded mixture into her tanks. Satisfied the Robinson was completely full she walked down the mown grass parallel to the runway, entering the buildings where the airfield ended in a severe edge. She asked a thin-faced man behind a high desk if they had a cafe. He waved a silent arm at a small hatch.

The hatch was empty, and when she walked into the cafe so was that, apart from small formica tables dotted haphazardly around. Eventually a woman came out from the back, started on seeing her saying accusingly, "I didn't know anyone was here!"

"Could I have a coffee?"

"Yeah, why not. Milk and sugar?"

Ali sat down, opened her book and began to read. The tea-lady, however, being alone and bored, had other ideas. Having brought Ali her coffee she hovered around the table, dabbing disjointedly at the neighbouring formica with a filthy cloth. Then she tried a more direct attack.

"You a pilot, dear?"

Ali looked up, smiled politely and said "yes," before ducking back to her book.

"That's nice dear. I always thought I'd have made a good pilot if I was younger."

Ali smiled at her book.

"But when I was younger, see," said the tea-lady, clearly feeling Ali couldn't have fully understood, "I wasn't free. Not like you young girls nowadays. You know sometimes I envy you, being able to have money and fly as you like. I'd have made a good pilot. I like to watch those boys going round and round and round, you'd think they'd get dizzy, but at least they can't get lost. I suppose you fly planes do you?"

Ali gave up and said, "no, helicopters."

"Oh! Was that you with Mr Moore? In that little one. He usually comes in a much bigger helicopter, you know," she said, looking rather resentfully at Ali who clearly had prevented Mr Moore from travelling in his usual style; probably by using some dreadful female wiles. "He's quite a man round here, Mr Moore. Important like."

Ali smiled.

"He's got something to do with jewellery, you know. He travels everywhere. Not just shops but bigger things with diamonds."

Ali wondered what bigger things with diamonds might be: huge clocks? Factories? Dealings with African potentates? Smuggling perhaps? But the tea-lady was distracted by the thin-faced man, who had left his perch outside to come in for his dinner, and Ali was left alone to read her book.

Tom returned after a few hours, long before dark. He appeared quite drunk and fell asleep not long after she took off, slumping against the door so heavily that Ali hoped desperately it wouldn't come open if they went through turbulence, leaving him hanging by his straps like some Fellini paparazzo.

The return trip was quicker as the breeze had got up and the tailwind chased them all the way to High Wycombe. Again as they passed the house Ali saw no sign of Alice, but she noticed the Alsatian in the garden and was rather relieved that Tom's remark had obviously been nonsense, in spite of his importance to the tea-lady.

Tom's final words as he left the aircraft were: "You're pretty quiet for a pilot aren't you? Personally I like a bit of chat with my driver, a bit of a laugh. I've always had a good sense of humour but there you go! We're all different aren't we. Goodbye."

"The bookful blockhead ignorantly read, with loads of learned lumber in his head," Ali quoted crossly, hoping he heard her.

Driving back home she listened to the plastic rain-guard over her door-jam beating in the relative airflow like a cold skeleton pleading for entry. The events of the day reverberated with the plastic. If the house had really been empty for years where had Alice's family been living? Mrs Charleston had said it had been in the family a long time and it didn't seem like a recently occupied property, apart from the newly painted Yellow Saloon, even there the smattering of lime chairs seemed to indicate the clutter of longevity. The dust of history certainly looked to have accrued on the books, as on the family themselves.

Whom to believe? Tom the diamond cutter, who normally flew in bigger helicopters. Or the family? So many people talked nonsense. Why? The wind jolting the plastic became noisier around 30 mph and quieter again over 40 mph, by 60 it was either streamlined or made her so deaf she didn't notice the clatter.

That evening Ali, as usual unable to face watching the television, played computer games. (Jake had told Ali that television was the ultimate fiction, giving us the cloak of invisibility we crave to wander through unknown alleys and war zones, adventuring but totally safe: but she did not believe him). Then Pete rang.

She wondered if he was going to offer her another trip with Tom the Prelate, but instead he needed her to bring her passport and a photocopy to the Russian Embassy the next day. He clearly assumed, rightly, that she had no work to do.

"We need visas," he explained, "luckily they'll let us do a group one. I'll meet you at the embassy at ten o'clock."

Valyuta Pear

Galina had arranged for her German boss to stay at the Sovietsky Hotel, to the mutual satisfaction of herself and the hotel. As usual her boss had not questioned the cost. Galina imagined he probably charged the amount to a client, or perhaps took a write-off against tax. All the way everybody gained. She definitely liked this field of business.

Leaving the Sovietsky, where she had chosen the room most appropriate for her boss, and on her way to pick up the boy from the old woman, Galina stopped to buy some provisions. Between Dinamo, with its monumental football stadium, and Belorusskaya, along the Leningradsky Prospekt, were some new shops and some street vendors. Pulling her *avoska* out of her pocket she stopped in one of the new shops, which called itself a supermarket. There had been a delivery that day, so the check-out girl said, but still half the shelves were empty. The girl explained, dawdling by the till and yawning to prove her point, that they were far too busy to fill them.

Annoyed Galina left the shop. Further down was a shop that had been opened just to cater to this new breed of tourists who had been coming to Moscow for the last four years. She couldn't see why the tourists would need special food, since they could get that at home and presumably came here to experience Russian food, but she could see why there were two tiers of prices. Foreigner prices would have been impossible for Russians.

As a child Galina had shopped with her mother and sister in the 'Bureau of Passes' but these special shops were different, there most things were exchanged for coupons and certificate roubles and were cheap, here you paid heavily in cash and could even use dollars. Only the queues reminded her of the past. Just one man, a poet called Voznesensky, had dared to write about the queues in the 70s: "I am fourteenth for the eye-specialist, twenty-first for Glazunov, the artist, forty-fifth for an abortion (when my turn comes I'll be in shape)."

They'd laughed so much at that when they were young. Now many of her friends had had abortions and Galina had known where to go, but had refused. She had wanted the boy. Wanted to give him the love she had lost as a child. She was going to give him the best she could and for him she planned their future.

Galina wondered what shops were like in the Federal Republic of Germany. Probably full of sumptuous goods, expensive no doubt but then foreign workers had lots of money, all drove cars and lived well. They probably didn't mind paying high prices, certainly the German never complained, but she thought they would expect the shelves to be full.

After some years of living in Moscow Galina's father had been posted to the German Democratic Republic, and all the family went too. She'd been to school there and although she'd forgotten many things about their troubled life her German language had stayed strong, almost fluent. Her major memories were the police, who all wore black, and their dogs and the disruption they caused at her school. She wondered if her boss would let her have a company credit card.

Galina bought some salami for the boy's supper, and some cheese, a bag of white bread rolls and some cocoa as a treat for him, bunging it roughly into her *avoska*, the string bag which accompanied her everywhere just in case she found a bargain. She was going to be studying again tonight, doing some more translations, so she needed the boy to be happy and quiet.

Suddenly she noticed a small plastic helicopter sitting on a high shelf. She stared at it for a long time before she bought it; as a present for the boy. When she put it in her bag she laughed. One day, she cried out loud in English, I will fly a helicopter, maybe all the way to England. And she stretched out her arms and whirled around, making a few people step back and curse her. "Silly wench!"

Blood Diamonds

The Russian Embassy is on Holland Park Avenue, near the gates of Holland Walk. Ali walked down the leafy wide road from the tube wondering if the area had once been full of Dutch men, possibly Van Dyke and his friends. "Van Dyke! It sounds like a bus load of lesbians," her alter ego would have said.

The door to the embassy garden was closed but, as Ali stared at it wondering how on earth to get in and join Pete as instructed, the door swung open and a man came out. She slipped in before the door closed and turned right through a small door into the Visa Office, which reminded her of a post office in a barn. Heaps of people milled around the barn, occasionally breaking through the long queues that straggled back from the various windows with apologies and shrugs. Behind the counter, protected by glass and visors, sat apathetic bureaucrats collecting and stamping papers, throwing remarks in Russian to people out of sight and occasionally closing the window heedless of the shouts of those nearing the front of the line (hence the need for the visor). There was only one window without a queue.

At the back of the barn, on a table by himself, sat Pete with a pile of photocopies and a list. He was ignoring the piles and talking to someone on his mobile phone. He waved his free hand when she approached.

"Can you check everybody on the list has a photocopy here. Thanks."

Ali ticked them off, hers was the only one missing and she added it to the pile. When she'd finished Pete ended his call and picked up the pile.

"Come with me," he said, walking to the window without a queue.

In front of a morose looking man he deposited all the photocopies and Ali's passport, which the man looked at, took away to photocopy and returned.

"OK," he said, "I send them."

"Thanks Sasha," said Pete, "maybe see you in Moscow?"

"Maybe, Pete, maybe. But you know how it is, how it is."

Ali recognised the tone of a Peckham-maybe.

As Pete and Ali left through the garden she asked him. "How did you manage that? I thought the Russian embassy was supposed to be such a nightmare! I have friends who simply won't go there to get a visa."

Pete grinned. "Then they haven't got the right friends. We are guests of the state. Can I drop you anywhere? Or do you have a car?"

"No, thanks, since we've finished so early I think I'll go and visit a friend who lives up here. By the way, do you know how long Alice has lived in that house in Herefordshire?"

Pete shrugged. "No idea. Any reason why?"

"Not really. Only that guy Tom you made me ferry across to Welshpool said the house had been empty for years."

Pete spread his hands, dismissing the subject. "How was he? Enjoy the trip?"

"He talked a lot and wasn't very polite. He won't be my next best friend."

Pete nodded, his mind having moved on already. "Now, I'll come up to High Wycombe the day we leave to see you off, I'm leaving a little later as we're going in the JetRanger and it's quicker. I said I'd pick-up Alice and drop her at Wycombe. You two can fly down to Lydd, where you'll meet Daniel and his student. From there you'll all fly in convoy to Middle Zeeland in Holland and finally on to Osnabruck in Germany, where we'll meet up with you and the rest of the crowd."

"OK, I've got all the maps, right up to Moscow." Ali said, rather proud of herself. "I popped into the British Airways shop at Heathrow while I was over there with a student."

"Oh, good. I meant to remind you to get maps but I knew I could trust to your good sense. Incidentally the GPS in your machine isn't plumbed in, so it tends to give up after an hour or so and you'll need to charge it every night. The one in Daniel's machine is, so if necessary you can follow him. Or use those maps."

"Where are we going after Osnabruck?"

"Oh, the next day we'll just go on to Schoenfeld, old East Germany. We're staying there overnight because Daniel's got some client he needs to meet. Then the next day we'll fly to Posnan and on to Modlin..."

"Modlin...that's Warsaw right?" Ali was glad she'd studied the maps or Pete's explanation would have been a mystery tour.

"Yes, yes, north-north-east. We'll stay the night in Warsaw because Daniel has a client he needs to talk to."

"Another one! He's doing a lot of business on this trip."

Pete frowned. "He's a busy man. It isn't easy to just cut off and run."

"He isn't still working as a pilot, then?"

"Yes, yes but you know Daniel, a natural entrepreneur, he's always dabbling in something. I don't think I've ever met anyone as naturally clever. Did I tell you his theory about the number twelve? God's number?"

"Where after Modlin?"

"Well, that's where we meet our guides into Russia. From there on we'll be escorted by a Mil Russian helicopter, probably the Mi-2 I should think or perhaps the Mi-8. We go on with them to Brest, where we stay the night."

"Brest's in Byelorussia, right?"

"Yup, you'll have to change money there but don't change more than you need for that night, inflation is rampant. 180 percent or more. "

"OK. I heard."

"Next day we go on to Baranevitchi, which is an Air Force base, we'll refuel and maybe have a bit of a look around if they let us, and from there to Minsk and on to Vitebsk. Again we'll spend the night there."

"Uh hu."

"And the last day we'll go via Smolensk to Tushino, you'll probably remember that as the Moscow airport where the MiG Duck was first tested, it is right on the Moscow River. Champs airport. Most legs won't be more than two hours, so we should be fine for fuel even if we get a headwind."

"All right? See you next week then." Pete walked off towards his car, humming lightly, his cricket arms swinging.

It occurred to Ali that in spite of his occasional bluster Pete appeared to live on a very even keel, to neither get wildly excited or deeply unhappy. He lived his own life and others merely intruded, were included or excluded. Daniel's mercurial temperament must come from the other side of the family. What could his mother have been like? Since she'd met them Pete and Daniel had been a secure father son unit, tied in a bond of admiration, proud of each other's brilliance, unable to see any weaknesses, it was hard to know how a woman could have fitted into that concord.

Ali's friend lived in North Kensington in a tall thin house, with a roof garden that tumbled down over the eves in a turbulence of beauty and conflicting colours; causing leaks, brick warp and rows with her neighbours. Paula, a former policewoman, had given up ferreting out felons to become an artist and paid for it by dividing her house into self-contained units, which she rented out to the sort of people who needed a pied-à-terre in Kensington but were never there at the weekends. It suited Paula perfectly since she loved to wander around the house naked, particularly when doing the cleaning. Many a surprised soldier or baffled businessman had arrived inside the door to find a starkers Paula hovering behind the hoover. Tenants were now warned.

Ali had lived with Paula for a short while after her break-up with Jake, and, either because of that or because Paula was ten years older, their relationship had become one of mother and child. However, acute as women always are in their female relationships, Ali had noticed that Paula only had friends much younger, whom she could impress, or much older from whom she could learn, but none her own age with whom she could communicate.

Paula, clothed in a blue smock and so covered in dry clay that she looked like a desert explorer, opened the door to her friend, using her elbow on the latch. "Oh, it's you. Want to come in and have a coffee?"

"If you're not busy."

Paula let her in but looked suspiciously at her. "You want something, don't you? Information on something? These days you only come when you want something."

"I thought you were an artist not a psychic."

"Old," remarked Paula, although she laughed, "old joke."

They walked up the narrow stairs into Paula's part of the house. Here Paula lived and worked. On the large hippiesque sofa was a breadboard covered with mud-pies of wet clay, some of which had leaked onto the tasselled shawls leaving a chocolate smudge.

"Help yourself to coffee," said Paula, sitting down, heaving the breadboard onto her lap and delving her hands into the mixture. "I can't do it, I have to play here until the thing sets but you can talk to me while I work."

One of the joys of Paula, perhaps a remnant of her police days, was her ability to talk while concentrating on something completely different. Ali made some coffee and came and sat cross-legged on the floor opposite Paula, her coffee balanced on her right knee.

"Look! I'm going to Russia to escort a student to the World Helicopter Championships. Call it instinct but I have a feeling there's a hidden agenda, maybe I'm imagining it. I don't know. I thought you might be able to help."

"Chaotic!" Paula continued massaging her clay. "Break me in gently, won't you! Help how? You want me to come to Russia too? Why are you going? Whose idea was it? Who arranged the trip?"

"Pete and Daniel Otravia, a father and son. Pete rang me and suggested it, he said I would teach the girl on the way."

"Sounds sensible. You are a teacher." Paula kept her eyes on the clay.

"I know. But then he didn't tell me anything. You know, like that we were competing in a Championship or about the practice time and why we were going. It all just feels odd. I feel they need me there for something they aren't telling me about. I suppose I don't trust them really."

Paula avoided saying what she really thought: that Ali was damn lucky to be asked on such a trip and shouldn't be whinging about some omitted details and asked kindly. "Odd! You don't like them?"

"I like Pete, the son's a bit showy off, you know the type."

"I know you. I like show-offs, being one."

"Maybe."

"And the student you are escorting?"

"Alice Charleston."

"Is she! The stepdaughter of the Greek multimillionaire? That does make it more interesting!"

"Is she? Charleston doesn't sound very Greek to me! So he's a stepfather is he?" said Ali, thinking of Alice's mildly flirtatious attitude. "I thought they must be quite wealthy."

Paula snorted and kneaded her clay a little more fiercely. "Quite wealthy! You live in a very abstract world don't you Ali?"

"I don't watch TV, if that's what you mean."

"Or read the papers, or listen to the radio. It's surprising what you can pick up, you should try it sometime."

"I know! 'Through the world the journalists come and go talking of Michael and Angelo'!"

"Very clever!" But Paula laughed, unconsciously rubbing her nose, leaving a clay smudge. "Remember that French guy who used to sing 'you have all your death to sleep, use your life for living'?"

"No." Ali drank her coffee. Paula looked at her, smiling maternally.

"Anyway, according to the Tatler, her parents came to this country when Alice was about five or six. Her father was very sick and died soon afterwards and after a short interval her mother met and married Charleston, who 'name or not,' is a Greek shipping billionaire with South African connections. He adopted her as his heir."

"Hence the bodyguard. Where did they come from? Her parents that is."

"They say Germany."

"They?"

"The magazines. This lot are intensely private, have never given an interview, never even had any 'friends say'. Even when the daughter came out."

"Came out? Is she a lesbian?"

"What are you like! She was a debutante of course, you have heard of them? They were around before you stopped listening to the world turning!"

"Ha, ha. Does it still happen, then? Presentations to the Queen? Curtsying, candles and cake?"

"In a down-market form."

"So, where do you think this private family and their debutante daughter came from?"

Paula stopped working the clay for a moment, then began again, stroking it into lines, which she twisted into sugar cane columns. "Put it down to a police-woman's suspicious nose if you like but when I hear of someone arriving here thirteen or fourteen years ago, that's say 1980 or '81, with no known history, I get a tingle. I say 'Odd!' The magazines say both parents were only children who came from a small village in Germany and all her family are dead. That may be true but I'd say they escaped from the other side of the wall. I'd say for Germany read East Germany."

"Then why not admit it? The Wall's down now, has been for some five years. Why pretend?"

"Well they're not exactly, since they don't talk to the press. Clearly there can't be anything too exciting or the tabloid sniffers would have sussed it out by now."

"Have you got a copy of the Tatler story and I'll have a read?"

"You cow! Do I look like the sort of person who reads such junk! I just happened to pick it up in the dentist. But if I go there again I'll pick it up for you. I'll see if I can find anything on the Otravias too, I like to keep my contacts warm at the station. They miss me terribly."

"Thanks."

Ali let herself out through the flower-clustered door, wondering if she was being a bit hysterical. Just have a good holiday and enjoy yourself, she told herself. An odd engine failure and a bit of gossip from a diamond merchant don't add up to anything; other than what they are.

Sightholder Heaven

A couple of days later Ali was offered another job, this time by a business near the South Coast, who wanted her to transport a family to a restaurant near Bournemouth for lunch and return to pick them up in the evening. "You do have a JetRanger rating on your licence, don't you?" she was asked.

"Oh yes," Ali replied, wondering why every job she was offered seemed to cost her money, and planning to quickly revalidate it as it had lapsed.

The result was that Ali drove down to the CAA, to pay them £100 for a JetRanger rating on her licence, to earn a couple of hundred for the flight. Flying's an on-edge business profit wise, she mused, waiting for the CAA licencing department to finish processing her licence. In the 'Ladies' she saw that on a sign on the door saying: 'Please leave this toilet as you find it. There is a toilet brush available.' Some wag had written: 'How much?'

When she got home a copy of the Tatler was sitting on the doormat, and, although Paula had failed to add an explanatory letter, the writing on the envelope was hers so she had presumably appropriated it from the dentist. However, the story dished by the journalist was somewhat different from what Ali was expecting. Primarily it was about Mr Charleston, his phenomenal success and ownings (sic), with only a small aside about Alice.

Charleston, who was described by the Tatler as a slight wiry man in his mid sixties, had come from an impoverished but well-connected family. Born in South Africa to Greek parents, he was living in England when the Second World War started. His parents decided to stay in London and his father worked in the intelligence service. When he was thirteen both his parents were killed by a bomb on their terraced house. Charleston was put into care in Hackney while other relations were sought. However, he escaped, managing to stow-away on a ship going to Cape Town. There he was discovered and befriended by the Captain, who employed him until the war ended. A year later the Captain died and Charleston took over his boat. He quickly realised that war-torn Europe was deeply in need of supplies and used his relations in Africa and Greece to fill the void. Before long he was running fifty ships. He then turned to other markets.

Ali skipped through the millionaire's growing successes, how many companies he still held privately and how many were in the public sphere, and concentrated on the sidebar about his stepdaughter. There, apart from elegant pictures taken by a couple of society photographers, they could offer little more than Paula had already done, only adding that she had an elegant figure. The few stories about her deb years gave the impression that her fellow debutantes had not been thoroughly enamoured by her life and charm. The magazine, on the other hand, declared her charm was substantial, claiming she had bewitched their reporter: hmm, thought Ali, the girl who would not talk to any journalist. Only one fellow debutante, a girl whose family had taken Alice to Annabel's in Berkeley Square, had anything concrete to report. She said that Alice was polite and a good conversationalist. "Indeed," the girl said, "she got on so well with my father my stepmother was nervous. However," she continued, "Alice is the sort of person who will never have close friends. Too reserved," said the debutante psychologist. "Too cold."

Poor lonely Alice, thought Ali, already marked for an independent heart at nineteen. She put down the magazine, no wiser about Alice but aware her stepfather was a winner.

The next day she picked up the JetRanger from Lydd Airport and flew to the Bee Inn to pick up the passengers. They were a Russian family. (Why is it that as soon as you have a subject on your mind it pops up over and again?) The mother, the heaviest member of the party and the only one who spoke good English, sat in the front with Ali, while her husband entertained the two children in the back. She happily told Ali all about her shopping trips, how she had bought twenty pairs of shoes, in various sizes, twenty dresses, twenty suits and so forth, to sell back in Moscow. Surprised, Ali asked if there wasn't any duty on bringing in so much shopping. The woman laughed. "This is Russia," she said obscurely. However, when Ali told her she was herself flying out to Russia in a small helicopter the woman grew serious and told her to take care. "Many kidnappings in Russia," she said. "Many, often no purpose. Stupid men think all foreigners have money. I tell them no, but they don't believe me. Russian men stupid. More money they have, more stupid. Oligarchs!"

≈≈≈≈≈≈

Five Carat Blue

On the morning of the trip to Russia, a letter from Paula arrived in the eight o'clock post. Ali was surprised. Paula was one of British Telecom's best friends, never taking the top off her ballpoint when there was a handy loudspeaker, but she was too busy to worry about why and shoved the letter into her bag to read later. She threw her little suitcase (small enough to fit under the Robinson's seat) in the back of the Ford Fiesta and, opening the one stalwart door, jumped in and turned the key. There was the usual reassuring scraping sound, followed by nothing. The car coughed and re-coughed but refused to start.

"Damn, Damn, Damn!" Furiously she hit the dashboard but no amount of kicking and hitting made any difference. It coughed again, almost started and died away. A little group of helpful Peckhamites who had previously been working in the gutter-garage gathered around the car.

"Battery sounds ok," said one, who had just been balancing his own wheel-less car on bricks. "Although it soon won't if you keep pounding away, man. Battery – man, think battery!"

Helpful hands opened the bonnet and prodded and poked, but nothing happened.

"You need a garage, man."

This cry was taken up and the spectators stood talking about what a rip-off all the local garages were and nodding sagely, until Dindas came out of the house.

"You'd better get going if you's going to take the train. Man oh man, go. I'll do the car."

Grabbing her bag and giving Dindas the keys, Ali was about to run for the local train when one of the assembled crowd broke away to offer his services.

"£10 for London? It's a good deal."

"Done. Thanks."

Her driver, clearly seeing she was late, drove an accelerated, although rather circuitous, route to Marylebone, while remarking on the poor quality of London drivers.

"I agree," said Ali, "Peckham seems to have some of the worst drivers in the world."

"I'm telling you!" He slapped the steering wheel. "And if you tell 'em they're so ignorant they'll..." He stopped.

"Punch you?" supplied Ali.

"I'm telling you."

On the car radio an interviewer was asking people on the street what they would do if they found a wallet full of money. One woman said, "Well, I would-not give it to the police, they'd just keep the money themselves."

Ali's driver whooped with joy and slapped the steering wheel. "I'm telling you," he hollered.

The train to Wycombe had (naturally rather than fortuitously) been delayed and, thanks to Ali's habit of leaving early, she arrived at the airport only half an hour late. Alice and Pete were waiting for her by the Robinson.

"Where the Hell've you been?" shouted Pete, who was hopping about like a stork with DTs, keen to be off. "And where's your car?"

"Wouldn't start."

"Shit! What was wrong with it? Not fuel again?"

"Ha, ha," said Ali, forgetting about the Gazelle and imagining this was some woman-joke. "I don't know. It just wouldn't start."

"What a nuisance! Never mind, you're here now. I'll leave Alice to you."

And he galloped off to the JetRanger like a man in five-mile boots and was away in minutes.

"He's in a hurry," remarked Ali. "Sorry I was late."

"Yeah, he's always late for everything. He said he has to do someone's flight test before he leaves for Russia. It was always like that when he was teaching me. Nightmare! On one occasion..."

"Typical! You ready?"

"You bet. And I'm looking forward to this." Alice was sparkling again.

Ali turned the Robinson key, the engine started with a cough and a surge like a tussle between two strong men over a metal implement. Alice and Ali looked at each other. "Not again," said Ali, beginning to feel jinxed. At least this engine was running.

"Do you think it's OK?" Alice asked, fiddling with her ubiquitous beads. "It sounds rather rough. My father says engineers never do any work but live the high life at our expense!"

Ali said nothing, but she thought engineers were probably trying just as hard as Alice's father to make a living, and were less likely to be living the high life.

She tried the carb heat but it made no difference, so Ali leaned back the mixture and ran up the rpm, then she pushed the mixture back in and the engine ran sweeter. "It's OK, just a fouled plug but we'll keep an eye on it. Perhaps it's the effect of living in that storage hangar with all that dirt flying around. If necessary I'll take the spark plugs out and clean them."

"Can you do that?" asked Alice, impressed.

"Well, yes actually. I trained as an engineer, though not necessarily for helicopters, I know what to do. I always carry some spares. It's quite educational being in Peckham, a bit like living in a street car repair shop."

"Wicked." Alice said, clearly delegating all responsibility for the machine to Ali. "It's wicked being with you!"

Maybe, thought Ali, once again missing the confidence-inviting tone in the girl's voice, but not an inspiring start to a 2,000 mile trip.

The beginning is often the end... the end is where we start from.

Although the weather looked clear from the ground the visibility dropped once they lifted off and the pilots saw they were in for a hazy trip. They left High Wycombe low level down the eastern route, flying at 150 feet over a rough stony path behind white oblongs of glider trailers. The Robinson jumped a sturdy post-and-rails as beautifully as any horse and they continued flying low above the fields to the east, eager to avoid those circling gliders that were staying close to the airfield in the listless climb-destroying air.

"Wild," said Alice, as they cruised over the broad dismissive backs of sheep at 300 feet, the quadrupeds concentrating on the hard fight for sustenance amongst the short dry grass. "That's wicked, I didn't know you could leave an airfield like that. I thought it was all runways and circuits..."

"Yeah, quite a few airfields have great entry and exit routes. Shoreham is another good one with a low-level passage down the harbour, over the road-bridge, and across the tributary out to sea. When you fly in from the East you can see your shadow caressing the boat loading cranes and following you along the beach with its wooden tide breakers..."

"Wow. Can we go there when we get back from Russia? I'd like you to finish teaching me my licence if you will." She smiled winningly, and Ali realised Alice expected only one answer.

"Of course. I'd love to." Was Alice ever opposed?

At Bourn End, Heathrow let them cut across the zone and they skittered across the polo grounds of Windsor Great Park, galloped past Ascot race-course and teased the queues in the mesh of roads south-west of the Airport. They skirt-ed Brooklands, where back in the 1920s the infamous Tommy Sopwith had had his first flight and crashing the machine had uttered the immortal words: "Bring me another plane, this one is broken."

Exiting the zone at the long unused runway of Wisley, Ali told Alice it was built for a diamond company that never used it. It now had deceptive barriers along the runway to catch-out students practising forced-landings there. As they made quick turn over the mock Tudor roof of the Black Horse pub, where Ali used to land with her students, a rush of white-aproned ants ran out onto the nearby football pitch, waving up at them frantically like disturbed termites.

Low green shoots heralded late growth in the vineyards as they passed over the geodesic roof of Dorking's champagne grounds. At Reigate Hill Gatwick Air Traffic Control allowed them to enter their zone, but the airport was busy and the helicopter was held north of the airport (Alice looked down and saw they were circling over Union Jack tails and long white bodies in the British Airways Terminal) before finally crossing the runway a few hundred feet behind a jumbo.

"Wick-ed!" cried Alice. "This is so cool. You're going to be a great teacher for me."

Following the railway line south, the Roman aqueduct reminded Ali of a past that held no helicopters and the tongue-shaped blue reservoir at Ardingly offered boats instead. They left the zone at Balcombe, heading between the wooded hills of Crowborough and the by-passed town of Uckfield direct to Lydd.

Over the water-inundated meadows of the Rye basin the girls peered into the mist. Lydd is an airfield hard to see, but Ali knew the survival shortcuts and quickly spotted the railway track that led to the zero four threshold. There they turned left and passed low level over groups of golfers, splashes of coloured jer-seys moving amongst bunkers and dunes. They dropped down to 200 feet, and, avoiding the golf balls, descended onto the disused runway. The helicopter settled on a newly painted white H, between a privately owned red Jet Provost and Daniel's student's R22.

Daniel and Gary were already in the cafe. Walking over to join them the girls passed through the empty and now dilapidated terminal, with its smell of overwashed carpets and peeling paint. In the early years of aviation Lydd had been a major airport, with 'society' arriving here in Bentleys, Jaguars and Rollses to fly across the Channel for the weekend. On the walls the girls saw reminders of Lydd's heyday when Bristol Belfasts flew out to Le Touquet. Used as a car ferry, the big, lumbering plane was hardly able to rise above the beach with its cargo of elegant but heavy cars, and passengers enjoyed wave-scraping sights all the way to the French coast.

On a raised platform by the viewing-area window, surrounded by a golden rail, the boys were eating buns and filling out their flight plan and customs declarations, helped by an old man in a flying suit. As the girls approached he rose politely.

"Hello," he said, shaking Ali's hand, "we meet again, delightful to see you. I hope all the practising went well."

Ali didn't remember him, but she knew female helicopter instructors were rare enough to be remembered, while male pilots were numerous. He turned to Alice effusively, kissing her on both cheeks. "Alice! What a coincidence! What a small world. How nice."

"What a coincidence," echoed Alice, her voice as dry as untreated leather. "How are you, Uncle John?" She pushed rudely past him and sat down next to Daniel.

Now blustering nervously, a well-meaning man caught in unexpected female ire, John said, thank you, he was well, had just flown in from France and was on his way up to Worcestershire. He asked if she had anything that she'd like him to take home with him.

"Hardly," said Alice blightingly, "I only left home this morning."

He nodded with more bemused smiles, and kissed her again looking as though he could face the 'monstrous anger of the guns,' but not the 'monstrous regiment of women.' I only have a pilot's limited powers of expression, his eyes pleaded, while she looked away angrily. As soon as he could he departed, saying he must fly on home before dark.

When he had gone Alice turned furiously to Ali. "My father's checking on me again. He can't trust me for a minute. I'll bet there'll be another friend-of-the family when we get to Holland, and another at every stop."

She breathed heavily but when Gary, who had flown with Daniel through the cross-London heliroutes, started talking excitedly about flying over the Houses of Parliament her mood changed and she began laughing with him.

"Imagine," Gary said, "being able to do that. You'd never think this lot would let such a thing happen. They're so nervous of every criminal who kicks a football and yet they let you fly right over the seat of government..."

"Wicked," said Alice interrupting his laudations, "I've done that route a couple of times and it's just wild. I love it. Did you see Buck House and the tower? I reckon if you had an engine failure you could make it down without getting wet. Pete told me that he once had a problem there and landed in Battersea Park."

She took a pen from her bag and began filling in the forms Ali gave her, slapping down all the details in a large, excitable hand which filled all the space available. Ali, writing in her small neat script, full of inhibitions, wondered if Alice was telling the truth, making up stories or simply paranoid. Why should her father have her followed? He knew where she was.

Daniel passed his half-filled form to Gary to complete, and told them about John, the recently departed pilot. "You know he was court-martialled twice in the war! Once for landing on a beach hundreds of miles south of where he should have been, and the other time for leading his troops to the wrong bomb drop, which he did on purpose to save their lives. Wasn't that just too cool? Wasn't the war a wild place for pilots! Wild! I was born too late. Damn it! I would have been a fucking hero. No question. Probably court-martialled too but certainly a hero."

Customs completed, they walked across the desolate historic tarmac and climbed back into the helicopters. "Can you believe," said Ali, "that this used to be a thriving commercial airport in the eighties and one of the few places where you could do your instrument rating. People stayed down here for weeks at a time."

"Blimey," said Gary, "they'd need a suicide watch!"

The two helicopters lifted in formation from the Hs and flew across the runway, directly on track over the flat beach to the water. On their right were the 'dark, satanic mills' of Dungeness.

"Danger areas are active," warned the ATC.

They crossed the Channel due east to Cap Griz Nez. Alice had never flown over water before but was undaunted, not expecting the engine to stop.

"Why would it?" she had asked Gary, when he showed some anticipatory nerves. "It doesn't usually."

"But it would be a whole lot worse over water," remarked the northerner, anticipation exaggerating his accent. "Ought we to carry floats do you think?"

Alice had made a derisive face but checked the engine oil with especial care.

They flew out of hazy but still weather on the British side of the Channel, into bright sunshine at Cap Griz Nez and increasing winds, which ruffled the sea into little white horses.

"Look at the reflection on the waves," said Alice laughing, "it looks like someone's dropped hundreds of diamonds down there. Shall we go and pick them up?"

"No, I prefer 1,000 feet, gives me time to get to the shore."

"Spoilsport!"

Alice's eyes gleamed with her escalating excitement and Ali thought that for the briefest challenge Alice would go down and touch the water, only Ali was not so brave. She wondered if Alice knew the cliche about no old, bold pilots, but then reflected they had just met one back in the cafe; his exploits were legendary and any pilot who'd been flying long enough to get a licence knew of him, though few had actually met him. Strange he should be a close enough friend of Alice's stepfather for her to call him uncle.

They turned left and flew along the white sand of the French coast. Calais sat in the distance, once teeming with Bleriot's compatriots but now silent. More than a mile of deserted runway with only an empty apron and a bar that made toasted sandwiches. The ATC waved them through with minimal conversation. Ali told Alice that much instrument training was done there on the long, unused airfield, and that even student Concorde pilots came here empty to practice their landings.

"One of the few places in the world where you can watch Concorde doing circuits," she said laughing.

Along the Belgian shore they dropped down to 200 feet, watching their shadow caress the beach and frighten the bathers. Alice giggled. "Let's hover over the swimmers in the sea! They'll think there time has come and some avenging angel is overhead!"

Ali, feeling like a real old bore, motioned her back to 500 feet.

They passed Ostende without a break in speed or height, the Air Traffic Control merely saying there was no traffic and they were free to transit the zone. Alice watched the large airport passing under them and almost screamed in excitement. "Wow! How can you be so calm? This is so wicked!"

Ali shrugged. "I've done it before."

"What? Flown to Russia?"

"No, OK, but I have landed at Ostende. It has the cheapest fuel in Europe. And you can get a really great steak and chips with excellent, fresh mayonnaise."

"Chips and mayonnaise!" Alice echoed.

They left Belgium and entered Dutch airspace just after the Costa beacon. The air was so clear they could already glimpse the sensuous undulations of Vlissingen over the other side of the water. Here the Dutch had deceived Nazi ships and led them onto the sand, here the Dutch had defended their country against Austrian, Spanish and English invaders, not always successfully but always bravely. Middle Zealand was flat, reclaimed land.

"Why is New Zealand, called Zealand? Look at its Middle brother!" Ali said to Alice. "The baby's far more mountainous."

"Baby's got the hump?" cried Alice. "Elder brother's a flat!"

They laughed excitedly, Ali catching Alice's mood as the dykes and reclaimed areas passed under the helicopter's belly and they approached the airfield.

Daniel made the approach call, telling the air traffic control they were joining from the south and would cross the main runway and land by the control tower. As he spoke they crossed a major road, without much traffic and proceeded towards a waterway.

However, the ATC refused that method of entry and told them to join downwind and land on the runway. Laughing, Daniel called back that it was too late, he was already crossing and he could see the runway was clear.

There was some shouting across the airwaves from the ATC, of which Daniel naturally took no notice, sailing happily across the runway to plonk down in the parking area outside the cafe. Only Ali, feeling rather a goodie two-shoes, took control from Alice turned downwind and followed the pattern to land on the runway as instructed. She then taxied over to join Daniel, who was faking yawns and indicating she was a teacher's pet.

"You don't have to do what they say," he said, as she shut down the helicopter. "They are there for your convenience you know. There wouldn't be an ATC without aviation." And lighting up a cigarette he began blowing rings.

A group of concerned looking Dutchmen came down from the tower, eager to reprimand Daniel and to prevent him smoking near the helicopters. But he shrugged, and, pointing out to Alice that: "Johnny Foreigner always lost his cool" and "I always call them Kaarl," he walked away telling Gary to go smooth things out with "Kaarl and his pals".

"See you in the cafe, mate," said Daniel, handing Gary his passport. "Tell 'em to give us some fuel too. Both helis to the brim. I'll get you a tea unless they have pop."

Ali expected Alice to join Daniel in the cafe and leave sorting out the annoyed 'Kaarl' to her and Gary, but she didn't. Instead she walked over to Kaarl and smiling very seriously explained that Daniel was not quite right in the head and that he didn't always understand things. She then talked so seductively about the beauty of Zeeland and how much they had loved flying up the coast, about childhood memories of sailing all around the Schelde and how exciting it was to be there again, that before long the whole Air Traffic Control staff were chatting happily about sand dunes, land reclamation and waterways.

This problem over, they then discovered that the airfield didn't take credit cards and they hadn't enough guilders between them to pay for their fuel. Kaarl, only just appeased, was beginning to look pretty sick all over again when Ali discovered an Eurocheque in her back pocket. Although it was scrumpled and scuffed it was at least legal tender and Kaarl agreed to accept it, although Ali hoped desperately he wouldn't cash it before Pete had paid her.

By the time the three of them joined Daniel in the small cafe he was surrounded by a group of curious, and somewhat baffled, Dutch men, women and children to whom he was explaining the sex appeal of helicopter aerodynamics.

"Well," he said, "I think that went off pretty well. I wish," he added, as the Dutch enthusiasts went off to look at the helicopters, "I caused this much interest at home."

He blew a smoke ring towards Alice. "What are you eating Angel?"

"Bitte baals and herring, it's good. Want some?"

"Bitter balls? No thanks, my own are sweet enough. Want to try them, young girls?"

Alice giggled and Ali asked Daniel who else was joining them in Osnabruck.

"Well," said Daniel, swinging back in his white plastic chair, "there's Pa and Tim, you met him at Shawbury, in the JetRanger with Robert (Mister White Socks!) in the back. He'll be interchanging with Graham porky-voice and his wife in their R22 since his Squirrel's gone tech. You remember the Navy-boys, Paul and Rob, they'll be there in the Guzzle, with another one from the army and one from the Wruff. There's a couple I haven't met, Steve and Sandra, in a Hughes 300. And of course the lovely Kevin..."

"Oh, please!" Gary butted in, "Group Leader Kevin!"

Daniel grinned, continuing, "the organiser and general gopher. He used to be butler to some rich mini-bar-brain who upped and died and left him the lot. Loads, and loads of lolly. Now he's bought a school, started this group and of course he thinks he's Mr Magic and we're all his poodles. You can't imagine a more self-satisfied wally." Daniel made a sick face. "Then there's his navigator - oh boy, does he need one! Learning to fly he got lost and landed at a pub to ask the way. Can you imagine finding that sour-faced puss leering at you over your beer. Makes you sick. You know he even looks like a trout." Daniel pursed up his lips and put his chin in the air imitating a very anguished looking trout fighting the line. Alice clapped her hands in delight.

"Oh, yeah and there's a low-time guy called Mike (some used car salesman who did well) who's bringing his own mechanic, a Boer called Joe, they're a couple of jokers coming in an Enstrom. Phut, phut. Wonder if it'll get there!"

He bounced his arms in derisive jerks.

"I thought Enstroms were nice machines when I flew them," Ali demurred, "very tough, take any kind of knocks without problem. I enjoyed what you can let a student do with them."

"Oh kinky! I can do it longwise in an Enstrom? They're fine for teaching, but so slow and no range. I'll bet you a penny to a stud muffin they'll have to go down in a field somewhere while we get them fuel."

"Stud Muffin?" Alice asked, getting bored with Daniel's scathing character assessments, "is that like tongue piercing; painful to eat?"

"Great isn't it. I heard it on 'Pets win Prizes'! And the winner is Stud Muffin! He gets the biggest bone!"

Ali made a disparaging face but Alice laughed delightedly.

≈ ≈ ≈ ≈ ≈ ≈

Lattice Crystal

Galina sat at her desk, hardly able to contain her happiness. As well as the profit she had made from the discrepancy between her friend's driving payment and that of her German boss, the man had tipped her $100. And she knew from her friend that he had also tipped him. Everybody was happy.

The German had rung her from the Sovietsky Hotel. He was laughing, his voice really happy when he said that the hotel was excellent, just what he wanted. So Russian, he said, which had made Galina laugh too: she didn't know a single Russian who could have afforded it.

He went on to praise her work. He said her translations were excellent and that he had been complimented on the breadth of his language in both Russian and English. Galina was delighted, but also relieved. The dictionary she was working with was old. Her father had given it to her long ago, in the days when she still lived in his house, but apparently it seemed the English of yesteryear was still acceptable to the businessmen of today. That her Russian was good was less surprising, both her mother and her stepmother had been intelligent women and were well educated, and her father's position and her own intelligence had allowed her to qualify for the Phys-Mat School Number 2 in Moscow. Later the school had lost some of its advantages, but when she won her place it was still one of the best in the Soviet Union. Then, of course, her family had had their problems and her father had thought it better to put her in a less serious school. For a moment she felt emotional thinking what might have happened, what she might have been doing now, had it not been for other people's personal egos and selfishness, but suppressed it and pinched the dollars in her pocket.

Moving her hand in her pocket she suddenly noticed her ID card wasn't there. Cursing she remembered she'd taken it out to show the boy how you could use it to open doors, and left it behind on the table. She'd have to be careful going home. If the police stopped her it was an on the spot fine, and if they were feeling really mean they could take her down to the police station. Of course if she gave them the $100s they'd leave her alone but why should she. She thought for a moment then decided to ring her friend with the car. They never stopped him because of his still warm government connections.

Yes, thought Galina, that was a good idea. They could stop on the way home and she would buy her friend a present and the boy some new clothes, although he'd better not wear them to visit the old woman or she would get suspicious. She'd buy herself a new dress too, and some shoes, the ones she had were starting to pinch her feet, which rather annoyingly seemed to be still growing. And, she thought suddenly, she would buy herself some chocolate. She grinned quietly, tapping her fingers on the desk in the rythmn of Happiness is a Warm Gun.

≈≈≈≈≈≈

Schraubenflieger

Daniel's group were the last to arrive at Munster-Osnabruck, an airfield south-west of Osnabruck and north of Munster and serving both towns. Back in Blighty the afternoon weather had turned showery, but Pete, the only one not already on the Continent, had made it out by flying low, dodging clouds and following railway lines. "I had to climb to let a train pass," he joked, "but went down quickly in case there was anyone else sharing my cloud!"

He laughed uproariously when he heard Daniel's story of the stupid air traffic controller. He grinned at the group with tears in his eyes. "Lucky Daniel knows how to handle them. He's a bit of a slippery devil, my boy. Kaarl 'eh! Personally I call them all Caroline."

Parked on the grass was a troupe of British helicopters. Next to Pete's JetRanger was Paul and Rob's fish-painted Gazelle with another Gazelle on the other side, this time in army camouflage. Behind the Gazelle an R22 was being unloaded by a couple of paunchy, middle-aged men, one had the inmate style hair cut of a man in his twenties though he looked to be closer to his fifties. To guess from the troutish-shaped face the other man was Kevin, the former butler turned Group Leader.

Another R22, painted in a Smarties design, belonged to the chipmunk-like man from Shawbury, Graham, and his wife Deidre. Next to them was a red-faced man wearing a baseball cap unpacking an Enstrom. Finally, there was a Schweizer flown by a thin grey-haired squirrel, Steve, and his considerably younger blond wife, Sandra. Ali cynically thought she knew what drew them together.

She parked on the grass near the tarmac next to the blue and white Schweizer, where, while Alice danced off to dally with Daniel, she waited for the fuel man. No one wanted to see their passports since, British or not, they had come from Holland.

A lanky, grey-haired man walked over and smilingly gave her his hand.

"How do you do. I'm Jaap, from Holland. You are?"

"Ali Gee," she smiled.

"Ali Gee! Ali Gee! Oh ho that is funny! I have seen this man. But he doesn't look like you. Very funny! Maybe you are taller? Certainly much better looking, I think. Indeed not bad looking for an old girl."

Ali smiled bravely, and hoped it wouldn't go on long, but it did. "Ali Gee 'eh. Of course you are too young, and you were still a flash in your father's lighthouse when he decided to become the same as you. And anyway it isn't his real name, but that is funny. Very funny. You don't think of changing your name? Maybe you should get married, although now in Holland many girls keep their own name, but I expect you would like to change yours, 'eh."

"Possibly," said Ali dryly, searching the distance for the fuel men and seeing them still helicopters away, filling up the Enstrom. Desperately she asked: "Are you competing in the World Championships?"

Jaap shook a sorrowful head. "I should be. I should be, but the mieren-neukers told me I hadn't enough hours. Of course for years I had been flying but I cannot be bothered to log each little hour, each little flight. What is that for time wasting? Only per year what I need. Only a Brussels' B-cat thinks such things necessary. So the mieren-neukers, what you'd call 'ant fuckers', they say I could only go by what I logged, not by what I flew. So now I fly over but sit and clap while you all win the games."

"Otherwise of course we would have no chance," said Ali, heavily humorous.

"Are you making fun of me?" asked Jaap, pursing his mouth a little. "Now you mock my English? That is something we Dutch never do, we never make fun of the foreigner. This is because of our cosmopolitan experience since many years. And because we learn to pull together, because of our dykes and flooding."

The fuel lorry moved up to the Schweizer.

"Looks like I'll be next for fuel, are you still waiting?" asked Ali relieved.

"Yes," said Jaap, "you take the fuel while I hang around picking my nose. My machine cannot compete but it can still drink the expensive fuel. This is a rich man's country, the further west we go the higher the prices. Rip-off Germany!"

"Is it more expensive than Holland then?"

"Of course. We all want to get rich but in Holland we do so more slowly!"

The fueller moved to Ali's R22.

"Hello?" he said cheerfully. "Fuel for you? Which do you want AvTur or AvGas?"

"AvGas, please." Ali slipped off the cap and stood back, wondering why the fueller, who had already done five or six R22s needed to ask. Reluctantly Jaap left her to go and prepare his own machine.

After Ali had signed for the fuel and put back the cap she found a dark-haired giant towering beside her like a beardless bear.

"Hello, seen the fueller?" He had just the trace of an exotic accent.

"Yes, he's just gone towards the green R22."

"Good. He's got my fuel cap. I stupidly put it on his seat. What a plonker 'eh! I'm Joe Noyes." He put out a large hand, but when she placed hers in it shook it surprisingly gently; unlike some handshakers who punish the comrade Joe was aware of his size.

"Hi. Ali." She didn't say Ali Gee this time; one moment of Dutch humour was enough for a night and she guessed this was the Boer. Judging by his size it was lucky they were in the Enstrom, a Robinson wouldn't get off the ground with him on board.

"Yes, I know. Kevin told us you were escorting Alice Charleston, of course we all know who she is."

"Do you?" Ali asked crisply.

"Yes. Don't you?" Joe asked ingenuously. His large eyes open wide.

"Meaning what?" She felt her hackles rising like an angry dog. She remembered her liberal parents had warned her that all South Africans were harsh speaking racists who believed blacks had small brains and large dicks and women only reached second-class citizens if they were blond with big tits.

Joe smiled lazily at her. "Meaning nothing. I'd better go find the fueller but nice to meet you anyway."

He walked off, leaving Ali feeling as irritated as if he'd left a pebble in her shell. Engineers, thought Ali crossly, always treated pilots like a child on her first day at school, never believing a word they said.

Alice came bouncing back with Daniel in tow. "Hello, fuelling all done? Let's get our bags and find our rooms. Apparently we're all going into town for dinner, they've booked a table in a square somewhere in Osnabruck..."

"Poor old locals," teased Daniel, "what have they done to deserve us?"

She punched him lightly on the arm and grabbing her bag danced off to the hotel. Daniel ran after her and Ali followed more slowly behind. By the green Robinson both Jaap and Joe watched them thoughtfully.

A fleet of taxis sat outside the hotel, presumably warned that a group of rich helicopter pilots would be staying there for one night only. Daniel, who had showered and changed at speed, insisted that he and Gary and the girls go immediately to the restaurant, the others following when they were ready.

The table for dinner had already been set outside in the market square adjoining the restaurant. A long trestle table lined with a miscellany of roughly joined white table-cloths and sturdy German tankards. There were candles on pewter bases running down the middle, with little bowls to catch the wax. Because of the slant of the street the whole table sat at a jaunty angle, like a 1940s flat cap on a gigolo's head. Daniel pulled out a chair for Ali and Gary sat down next to her, heaving a tired sigh. Meanwhile, Daniel walked around the table so he and Alice could sit opposite them.

"We'll be the interesting end of the table," he said. "Let the old bores guff-on down there, swapping war stories from the circuit at Biggin Hill!"

Even as he spoke, Paul sat down on the other side of Alice. "Since I'm highly entertaining I'm sitting next to you, if Daniel gets dull we'll chuck him up the other end, with his friend Kevin." He winked at her, while Daniel made a conspiratorial face.

Gary drank his beer and told Ali about his life in Liverpool, how well he had done with his computer company and then about the German Cessna pilots he had met at the airfield on their way back from Russia.

"Although they were invited to visit the country," he said, "the poor old Krauts found themselves being asked for more and more Deutsche Marks wherever they went. Fuel became more expensive and landing fees increased as they entered the heart of the countryside. It seemed that they must pay to land, to park, to fuel and to leave. And sometimes on top of that there was a so-called 'chocks tax'. When I chatted to them the Krauts were incandescent, saying furiously they had gone there to shore up good relations and came back hating the greedy Russians. The less angry pilot told me, 'we are returning home because we are tired of subsidising a collapsing regime'."

On Ali's other side sat Steve. Steve had an accountancy firm and knew everything you would ever need to know about local politics or pricing. Their conversation moved stolidly from car tax to the poor condition of the housing market, and back via capital gains to income tax. Occasionally Steve would glance at Alice, as though hoping he could ask her to supply her tax bill. He didn't ask Ali any questions, either because he didn't think she earned enough to pay tax at all or because he wasn't interested. To her surprise half way through dinner he started to tell her, unasked, how he met Sandra.

"I was at a dinner party," he said, "given by one of my greatest friends, there were about twelve of us. Most our age." (What, thought Ali, do you think we are the same age? Oh dear!) "I noticed her, of course, being so young and blond, but she didn't say a word all evening, so I soon lost any interest on that score, even though I was sitting next to her. I'd been a widower for some time by then, you know, my friends were always setting me up with 'suitables', who never were. Anyway, in general conversation the table had discussed politics, travel, the economy and all the usuals, when somehow we got onto helicopters. I remember the conversation went something like this: 'That's when Mil started to lose money. It was defeated in a tender by that long thing by Kazan or was it Kaman...' Then suddenly this little blond voice pops up, 'the Black Shark!'

Of course we were all spell-bound, us old boys. 'What?' I asked, and she replied, blushing shyly, 'Kamov, the Ka-50 Black Shark, won the contract for the Russian army helicopters, for the first time since the 1960s.' The others all lost interest then but I was ...well to say bowled-over is to say Botham was a decent batsman, gobsmacked, and the rest. 'Are you a helicopter expert?' I asked, thinking it was almost too good to be true: a quiet woman, blond, young and an expert on my favourite subject. 'No,' she says, 'Russia. I'm doing a PhD in Russian Government Finance.' Well, who could not fall in love after that, 'eh?"

"Who indeed," murmured Ali, "who indeed."

Wit is the only wall between us and the dark.

She glanced over at the far end of the table where Joe was sitting with Jaap, talking Dutch. He looked up and smiled at her and she looked away, embarrassed and annoyed.

Jaap, turning to the table and now speaking in English, said he would tell a bilingual story. "Since we are all here picking our noses. So, no one will understand it except Joe. I will tell it anyway, OK."

Alice gave a poorly suppressed yawn and muttered, was it worth telling a story no one would understand? Which received a smile of incomprehension from Jaap. Having freely mixed beer and wine the boys encouraged him. "Go on Jaap, we'll guess, don't worry."

"OK, well your English Queen..."

"British," said Gary. "Don't forget the Welsh and actually she's more Scottish than English."

"And German, don't forget the Georges," added Daniel whimsically.

"Yes, so, your Queen Elizabeth, she is at an Agricultural Show in Delft. She is walking around the show meeting people, asking what they do, 'Ha-lo, sir,' said Jaap in what he considered an upper-class British accent, "and what do you do?" Dutch accent, "Mam, I grow flowers." English accent, "splendid, splendid, and you madam?" higher Dutch accent, "well, Marm, I have chickens." English accent, "splendid, splendid. And you sir?" Dutch accent, "I fuck horses." English accent, "pardon?" Dutch accent, "yes, that's right Mam, parden.' Good 'eh? You understand? Vakken is to breed and parden are horses."

Everyone laughed happily, except Alice who made a face and twiddled her wineglass, muttering the Queen would not say 'pardon', it was vulgar. Daniel pretended to smile but was watching both girls.

"OK," said Daniel, "since we are going to Russia I have a Russian one. It's knock-knock joke. "

There was some heckling from Rob and Paul about the chances of Daniel getting one knock up, let alone two, which Daniel ignored.

"I'll do both parts. No hang on Alice can do it. Alice say Tolstey as your second response, OK?"

"Tolstey?"

"Yes, it means fat."

"Oh, Daniel," asked Alice simperingly, "do you speak Russian?"

"A bit, I can get by in most languages. It only takes a bit of flair, I expect you'd get the knack given time," he smiled rhapsodically.

"Wicked."

Daniel began. "Knock knock."

Alice: "Who's there?"

Daniel: "Tolstoy."

Alice: "Tolstey?"

Daniel: "Nyet! Tolstoy."

Alice: "If you are not Tolstoy why do you want to come in?"

"Oh!" said Daniel disappointed. "You've heard it before?"

"Yeah. At school. We had White Russians there."

The drunken pilots laughed happily, and threw bread. Ali watched Daniel and Alice and wondered what it all meant.

The candle burning in the middle of the table, now the lights had faded, caused Alice to loom large in the shadows. Daniel watched her as she sparkled in the gloaming, thinking she was like a fire-fly darting restlessly around the table with her quick fire talk, her witty evasions and her daring conversation. And so rich. Ali was quite different. She sat silently sipping her bitter lemon, or playing with her fork like a depressed teenager, deep in thought, apparently oblivious to her surroundings. In a rare moment of insight Daniel wondered if she ever realised how aloof she seemed. How she appeared to despise them, her active but less intellectual colleagues.

Daniel thought it was odd that everyone lumped them together because they were girls; Alice and Ali will do that, this, the other, when in fact they were as far opposite as shining silver and dirty rock. Alice was sexy, easy and fun, while Ali was difficult and scratchy. Big too, like a cart-horse beside the nimble thorough-bred Alice. He wanted to like Ali but found her edginess foiling him at every teasing thrust. The only thing the girls had in common was the similarity of their names and that, as he knew better than anyone on the trip, was not a coincidence.

The candle spluttered and Daniel saw it was burning down on one side only. Absentmindedly he leant over and began crushing the higher side, the red seal breaking into a myriad of white rivulets of hot wax. As he looked up he noticed Ali was watching him.

"Crushing the rebellion?" she asked, with that slight tang she used when she spoke to him. "Won't the candle do as it should?"

"Ah these insurrections," he replied lightly, "I spot red candle communism at work!"

She laughed wryly. "Is that the way to start our flight to Russia?"

"Ah, but like the candle Russia is red no longer," he spoke lightly, wittily.

No, thought Ali, Russia is no longer red and South Africa is no longer cruel, where could her liberal parents find somewhere to despise. How confusing life must be.

Daniel, seeing Ali had dropped back into thought, called over to Alice. "Well my little sparkler, fancy a trip deeper into the town? Shall we go buy emeralds from some blue-eyed salesman?"

"I thought you call it 'going on shore'," Alice countered flashing her eyes, "or is that only when you're inside Whales?"

"In that case let us dip our toes in the sea, walking hand-in-hand along the shore while leaving our shoes on the sand," mumured Daniel, missing her joke.

"Oh, no," said Alice blithely, "Ali will hold our shoes."

"Now the great winds shorewards blow..." muttered Ali, knowing no one would recognise the quote. "Now the wild white horses... champ and toss in the spray."

When Ali was getting ready for bed she suddenly remembered Paula's letter and getting herself cozily under the duvet, drew it out, ready for a good read.

'Hi Ali,' Paula wrote, 'I'm just off to talk to a girl's school about pottery and I look like a PANDA! Not sure if it's the thought of talking to a group of nine year olds, STRESS! or potter's dust, but my hair's gone grey over-night. WORSE! I've got excema all around my mouth! Looks like I've missed with the lipstick. These youngsters are not only going to think their speaker is a two-toned weirdo, but one who is so DRUNK she doesn't know where her mouth is! What a DISASTER! It'll probably put them off pottery for life. Just as well! I don't need competition right now!

'As to your questions. First, Daniel Otravia not only worked for a detective agency, he part-owned it. However, in spite of many wealthy and well-connect-ed clients they went bust at the end of last year. Just shows you really don't make enough money in feley-ony to run a helicopter.

'Two: Alice Charleston. Her name before Charleston was von Twit Toenburg, which sounds German enough, but, though her place of birth seems shrouded in mystery, I did manage to discover the von Twit Toenburgs used to own property on both sides of the border. Knew my nose still smelt well! And her father had had a previous marriage with two children, who must be around twenty-five to thirty now. Not surprising since he was quite elderly when he died, but here's the interesting one; one of those children escaped to the West as well. But my informant, who is giving me juicy gossip at the rate of a dry onion, claims they don't know each other. Odd! I'll drip-feed you more as I have it.

One other thing may interest you. Alice put her name down for these Games over a year ago, but with a different pilot, a girl named Georgie. Then one day Georgie disappeared. No one seems to know where she went, although some suggested as she was an Ozzie she might just have gone home.

'Well I'm off to embarrass the teachers and shock the girls. I hope I won't get arrested, it might be an old colleague. Hope you win! Paula.'

Baguette Cut

When Alice and Ali got down to the dinning room for breakfast next morning Jaap was already ensconced at the long table eating an egg, which he splashed around like a dog in the river. He made a half effort to rise, bread crumbs spraying onto the floor like dust. Alice countered his movement with a polite hand motion and a muttered, "No need…"

"So," he spluttered, his mouth still eggy. "So, Alice, excellent are the fuck bullets, shall you take them this morning? They are soft boiled. Very good. Fuck bullets for your well-toasted soldiers."

Alice laughed. "Why do you call them fuck bullets?"

"Look at them! Clear fuck cartridges, Dutch slang."

Ali helped herself to fruit just as a group encompassing Kevin, Charles, Steve and Sandra arrived. She waited for Jaap to offer them fuck cartridges too, but Jaap by then had turned into Der Spiegel and didn't even notice their arrival.

After breakfast they were encouraged out to the front of the hotel with their suitcases, where Kevin had organised a bus to take them to the airfield. He did a head count and found three were missing.

"Who's not here?" he snapped. He hated lateness, it was very trying and he knew it would be Pete's doing. He hadn't wanted Pete to come and he particularly hadn't wanted him to bring those girls, but he'd been over-ruled by the committee, which was very unusual and even more annoying. He suspected it was because the young one was famous and rich. Very irritating. He didn't like that at all. Girls without husbands to control them always caused trouble sooner or later. So did Pete.

"So, who isn't here? Can you all look around you?"

Ali, who had already earned a withering comment from Kevin for being the last on the bus after she went back to the hotel room having forgotten the GPS, looked nervously around. The others knew from experience it would be Pete and Daniel, plus Gary, presumably because he was waiting for Daniel.

"Pete and Daniel aren't here," said Ali compliantly, "or Gary."

"Typical," spat Kevin, looking as though he'd just swallowed some acid. "Absolutely bloody typical. Will someone volunteer to go and get them before we miss the daylight?"

Since it was only nine thirty in the morning Ali assumed he was making a joke. But Daniel was right about his fishy looks, now accentuated by stress, his forehead appeared to recede and his pouting lips showed an excess of protruding teeth, and he did indeed look like something dead on a fishmonger's slab.

There was an explosion of door-slamming and the three miscreants staggered out of the hotel, Pete and Daniel drooping like aged peacocks after a night of imbibing but Gary looking as healthy as a bodybuilder. He was laughing, propping-up Daniel under one arm, holding both bags in the other. Alice giggled and jumped out of the bus to take a photograph. Ali wondered if Gary would still be laughing at the end of the trip.

"There you are!" snapped Kevin sourly. "Hurry up and get on the bus."

"Ah," Jaap remarked, "a man with butter on his head should not walk in the sun!"

There was some faffing around at the airfield while everyone got ready. Kevin, his already tense spring tightening further as Daniel discovered he'd left his passport in the hotel and Pete that he needed another coffee before flying, took off early with only Graham and Deidre in their R22 as companions.

"Must go and sort out the over-night parking," he said, lifting off and heading away to the east.

"More likely worried his GPS might run out like the speeding Irishman's fuel," returned Daniel, but Kevin had already changed frequency.

The others took off from Osnabruck about an hour later, heading towards the former East German border. The faster turbines swished on ahead, Pete apparently trying to outrun the Gazelles, while the slower Enstrom soon lagged behind, accompanied by the only minimally faster Steve and Sandra in the Schweizer. Alice and Ali flew in loose formation with Daniel and Gary.

West Germany at this time of year was busy harvesting and large red combines ran up and down massive golden prairies of healthy corn. Some fields had not yet been touched but spread out in swathes of yellow, odd lines running up to rounded ends which looked like partially erased messages drawn by children in sand. Other fields were further ahead in the cycle and there tractors were followed by clouds of brown dust permeated by white wings as Jonathan Livingston Seagull and his greedier companions danced behind the plough shears. Above them the sun shone in endless blue and there were no shadows to cool the halcyon heat.

Daniel called to the girls over the radio: "Look there are no crop circles here!"

"Perhaps Martians only visit the UK," Alice returned.

"Quite right too!" replied Daniel, "only place worth visiting."

They flew over neat farmhouses with gardens, tennis courts and swimming pools, accurately placed cow barns with clean pigs and delicious smelling yards full of cultivation paraphernalia. Bright blue rectangles of plastic covered silage, like child-coloured cubes of sugar, were piled in ordered heaps next to tractors and other machinery. Every now and then they came across well-tended forests, whose efficient management led to squares of different heights, where patches of growing conifers bordered on the fully developed trees. From above it looked like a dark-green quilt with differing amounts of duck-down stuffing. Everywhere the land felt prosperous and modern; even the weather was content.

The contrast as they moved on into East Germany was startlingly bleak, even now that the wall was down and DDR souls were flooding into the promised land. The soil seemed drier and more arid, the farms more haphazard and less cultivated and the machines rustier and smaller. The girls noticed to their surprise the hedges were much thicker than the ones back in the West, as though they alone had been able to bloom out of control. There seemed to be less agriculture and more forest. Whereas in West Germany there had been autobahns, here there were roads: winding, dusty roads. A sharp cross-draft began to undulate the aircraft.

As though in response to the depressing view below Daniel began to climb, to test the Robinson for altitude prowess. At one moment the girls completely lost sight of him as his reduced speed in the climb made him drop behind them.

"At this rate we'll lose him," said Alice nervously.

"It doesn't matter," said Ali. "I did a flight route, we're not going to rely on either his navigational skills or our own failing GPS. I prefer to do it the old-fashioned way and actually know where we are!"

A few moments later, though, Daniel was back, having used his extra height to dive to VNE and catch up with the girls. He overtook them and began to lead again, calling over the radio.

"The map of the world from 15 thou was A.O.K. you should have come with us," he said, adding patronisingly, "just remember VNE reduces at 3 knots per 1,000 feet over 7,000," and off he scampered again, waving and climbing.

"Alice," said Ali, finally steeling herself to ask the question that had been running through her mind since reading Paula's letter. "Did you have another pilot before me? For the Games I mean."

Alice looked surprised. "Yes, I told you. She was teaching me to fly. We thought we'd enter them together, it was her idea actually. But then about six months ago, just before Pete called you, her father got sick in Australia and she had to go home. I guess she decided to stay there. Lucky for you, isn't it!"

They flew on in silence. Below them were the toll booths of the former Berlin corridor, strange isolated apparatus which looked like the starting gates of flat racing: horses thundering through, escaping to the rich grasslands of the decadent west.

Ali glanced at the map, noticing the 'corridor' was still shown there. Partly to break the growing tension in the cockpit she said lightly to Alice, "my mind is a corridor, the minds about me are corridors."

Alice looked at her and suddenly smiled. The atmosphere in the cabin relaxed as though sunlight had just shot in. "Yours or someone else's?" she asked.

"T.E. Hulme. A War Poet from the trenches."

Even as Ali replied she was wondering with a deeper level of her mind how tension arises and clears like that, whether Alice had caused it and, if so, knowingly or unknowingly. Alice's voice broke through Ali's thoughts.

"Too early then, for me, if you mean First World War."

"I do," said Ali shocked. "Why? Is the Second World War yours?"

"Yes," the girl replied, "it was my dissertation subject at school."

"Oh," Ali was startled by Alice's erudition. How many Peckham girls knew there had been two wars, let alone thought of doing dissertations.

Fumbling a bit, she asked. "Was there a special topic... yours... I mean... The whole Second World War sounds a bit big...?"

"Yes," Alice replied gaily. "The effect on Germany of losing, compared with the effect of Russia of winning, that was my angle. I got a prize for it."

"Hello, girls," Daniel's voice came grittily over the radio. "Can you see us above you again? We're trying an experiment."

Ali looked out and above. Way above and ahead was a buzzing blue bottle, the boys' R22.

"How high are you?"

"Fourteen thousand feet. Come up this time and join me, but keep the rpm at the top of the green in case you have an engine failure. I want to time you!"

As the girls climbed up, Alice quite amused but Ali irritated by Daniel's desire for control, Daniel said he was changing frequency to talk to Berlin ATC. The girls swapped too and discovered he was making calls for both of them.

"So masterful!" said Ali ironically, and suggested they descended. "After all we didn't ask him to do a formation call. Let's lose him. Flipping bully!"

Alice laughed. "OK, I dive like a dancer, sing like a bee," she cried, doing the first and, worrying the helicopter towards VNE, made it do the second. Ali pointed out that Alice had gone over the red line and, chastened, the younger girl reduced her speed back to normal levels. They had already lost Daniel.

Air traffic control told them to fly around the south east side of Berlin and make their approach from the south to Schoenvelt. Ali answered saying they could no longer see the other helicopter and would make their own calls from now on. The ATC replied 'copy' and when Daniel tried to make a formation call a second time they gently reprimanded him for not listening out on the frequency.

"Ha!" said Ali, "that'll teach him. Not that he cares much about a telling off from Kaarl, or is it Caroline! He's probably had much worse than that in his life."

"Oh, yes?" asked Alice, her voice deepening with curiosity. "Tell me."

Ali paused. "Well, I only know one piece of gossip and not related to flying."

Alice said nothing but her eyes indicated curiosity.

"Well, Daniel used to be a detective." Alice stiffened but didn't speak and Ali continued blithely unaware. "Apparently he was employed by a woman to follow her husband, whom she thought was cheating on her. Fairly standard job from what I hear. Anyway, this guy was a bit of a lad and it seems his wife thought she was funding his lifestyle in London, while she was living quietly with the children in the country. So, as well as having Daniel follow him, his wife had cut his allowance, and hubby was a bit short of cash. Then he decided to pawn her jewels to get some cash. And, of course, the day arrives when the wife is coming up to London for some terribly smart dinner and is expecting to wear the jewels. Well, the husband hasn't got any money to get them out of hock. So, guess what happens?"

Alice shrugged, staring at the summer scene ahead.

"Well, Daniel was sitting in a cafe, watching his prey, when the bloke gets up and comes to his table. Sits down and says: 'You've got a pretty good job following me all the time, 'eh?' Of course Daniel starts to deny it but the chap continues louder, 'I guess my wife is paying for both our good times, 'eh?' Anyway the chap goes on to suggest that Daniel gives him the money to get his wife's jewels out of hock, put it down to expenses and then they can both go on having a ball. And he did!"

Alice swore. "No wonder the agency went bankrupt! Did the wife find out?"

"Guess so. He lost the job."

As they flew east they first saw the reflective flash of the Berlin lakes, followed by the grey outline of Berlin to their north. The richer architecture of West Berlin soon turned into the angles of Eastern high rises which, drab and uncoloured, filled the landscape like something out of a pre-talkies movie. To the south, though the land was greener and more cultivated than the areas around the former corridor it still held a haze of poverty, with small fields and hand-workers. "Summer surprised us," thought Ali, "coming over the Starnbergersee with a shower of rain... what branches grow out of this stony rubbish?"

Arriving due south of Schoenfeld they turned north, and seeing the airport in the distance made their way towards the long, grey strip. The ATC held them for a short while at the edge of the airfield, and they circled over a frighteningly chemical-blue coloured lake before being allowed to cross over the main runway behind the vast air-shaking expanse of a landing Antonov. Daniel sped up behind them overtaking as they arrived on the apron and doing a neat torque turn to land exactly on the pad.

Alice parked, as instructed, on the end of a long line of helicopters along the tarmac. "Helicopters to my left, helicopters to my right, helicopters all around me," misquoted Ali excitedly, while Alice shut down using her checklist.

Here the British and Dutch crowd were joined by two French Robinsons, one with a couple of young men on board and the other with a man and a girl. Having shut down, Alice left Ali to go and say hi to the new boys. "I'll just practise my

French," she murmured, leaving Ali to do the fuelling.

Daniel jumped out of his machine and spotting Alice immediately followed after her, instructing Gary to try and get fuel as quickly as possible. Gary ignored him and sat down on the grass next to the taxiway.

"Bossy boots," he yelled after his departing co-pilot, bringing out a bar of chocolate which he ate from the wrapper, smearing the melted grunge on the grass around him as though a dog had left a wet trail.

As Alice's voice teasing the French pilots wafted over the grass Ali found herself once again waiting for fuel. Here in Schoenfeld, however, with the extra helicopters queuing up for liquid energy, Ali thought she might remain forever on the sticky tarmac watching the approach of a pinkish purple sky in the still warm sun. Was it cynical of her to think of Elliot's Love Song of J. Alfred Prufrock? *When the evening is spread out against the sky, like a patient etherised upon a table.*

For piston fuel the oilmen had a small round truck, like a pot-bellied pig on wheels, with a hand pump. Having taken the GPS out of the helicopter to charge it, Ali leant against the helicopter and watched the fueller grasp the splintering wooden handle, working it back and forth like a slimmer in the gym. The other man, balanced on one of the two remaining rungs of the stepladder, held the nozzle against the tank's protruding mouth, curling the black rubber hose high above his head not to show his flamboyant agility but to prevent gravity working against the human pump below.

In the background Alice flirted. Her voice darted in and out around the boys like a firefly through the Frenchmen's mountains, while they leant towards her defying Daniel who tried to interpose his own body as a human shield.

Ali was so absorbed in the sight infront of her that she didn't notice there was someone approaching until Joe, the big Boer, leant on the Robinson beside her, causing the little machine to lurch on its skids.

"Oh, sorry," he said, straightening up, the Robinson echoing him with a skittish dance. He presented her with a dandelion, smiling on one side of his mouth. (Who says men can only do one thing at a time?) "For you! I'm sorry if we started on the wrong foot. I was always crass."

She looked at him, hesitating. Wondering. Nobody did things like this to her; she wasn't pretty: too tall and too well built. She looked at the long yellow petals of the flowering weed, then slowly took it from his hand. She held it delicately, uncertain whether to put it behind her ear, drop it or simply hold it.

"A dandelion? An apology that will be forgotten in the autumn?" She said, half-quoting again although she knew he least of all, a Boer engineer, would follow her train of thought.

Joe laughed. "Coldly, sadly descends the autumn evening. The field strewn with its dank yellow drifts of withered leaves, and the dandelions fade into dimness apace..."

"Very clever!" she spoke brusquely but was impressed. "You know Arnold. Or almost know him."

"I got some education in spite of being a boorish South African. Mostly, of course, I just swam and abused my parents' staff. Did you like my little flower, was it a sufficient atonement?"

"Thank you. But what did you mean? That she was rich?"

Joe looked over at the heiress and her party. "That she was well known. We'd even heard stories about her in the estranged south."

"You don't sound South African," she challenged him.

"You mean I don't have the grating metal accent of the erstwhile Dutch," he asked in a Boer accent.

"Yeah. I guess I do." Unwillingly she smiled.

"My parents were English. I learnt Afrikaans in school, later I went to Europe to work for EGL, they sent me to India for training and later still I found myself living in Britain."

"So you left? Escaped conscription?"

"No. I did my duty to my country. Some Afrikaners thought we were worse than the blacks, you know. More poisonous for being traitors. For wanting the end of apartheid."

"I didn't know," she said stiffly. "I just thought all the good guys left the country before they had to do conscription."

"Oh!" He said nettled. "Now who's crass, or is it called direct with girls? Girls are neither gauche nor sweaty. It was illegal to leave, you know. Many found themselves without a country that way, and the bold British didn't always welcome them in! Anyway, I stayed. Instead of running away I was trying to change the system from within. I also chose to be an engineer rather than a pilot for obvious reasons."

"Obvious to whom?"

He rubbed his nose, squashing it into his fleshy lips. For a moment he wondered if it was worth bothering to try and be friendly.

"Not you, obviously. I meant pilots kill, engineers only gave them the means to do it." He gave an odd half smile. "We had to work as police too. I found Angola better than the townships. The townships were really scary when I was there, there was a lot of black on black fighting..."

"As well as white on black." Ali spoke a little harshly, remembering all the things she had heard from her literature-informed mother.

He looked at her, consideringly. "Yes, that's true too, but it was the black on black that concerned us. Some families were so scared they slept in their cars, even with the baby, they were too frightened to go home. Too frightened to travel to the other side of the township. This is crime we are talking about, something that transcends colour! It might even be that there was less criminal activity then when we had a strong police force."

"Was it the necklacing time, hot petrol...?" She stopped, embarrassed, realising how ill informed she must sound to someone who'd lived through apartheid. "I read..."

He nodded. "There was that, and lynching, burning the house. There were lots of problems then and now, although now one of the biggest killer is Aids, and yet those in power won't accept it exists. My sister works there still, she told me that of the forty in her firm fifteen died in one month. And still the problem is ignored."

"But you of course," she snapped, "were better than the rest anyway, went on anti-apartheid marches and gave out pro-black leaflets..."

"No. I didn't," he returned with asperity, "and we employed blacks as servants, we thought we were giving them a living and didn't realise it was wrong. But I hadn't been to omniscient Europe then; didn't know wrong from right. I was just an ignorant colonial guy who thought it was enough to be kind and helpful, who went with the system. The same heart beats in every human breast!"

"Oh! I..." she was going to say more when Mike came up and joined them, followed by Paul and Rob, who was holding the Gazelle's fuel cap. "Sierra November fuelled?" Mike asked.

"No," said Joe, his voice calm once again. "I'm still waiting."

"I think the fueller's in love the time he takes," joked Paul.

"Who with? Ruby Palm?" asked Rob.

"What? The banker," added Paul. They exchanged glances.

Joe looked at Ali, but she was looking away at Alice and Daniel, once again estranged from reality.

Kevin had arranged for minibuses to take them to the hotel, chosen for its convenience for the East Berlin airfield. The British team scrambled into the first one, throwing their luggage into the open boot like children at their first camp. The air was quivering with bubbling excitement. It was the beginning of a trip that they had longed for, an adventure, a wonderful dream in progress. It had been dusty and dry, hot and thirsty on the airfield and they'd had to wait a long time for the fuel, but nobody objected. They were all so happy to be here, on their way to Moscow.

"Mega," said Alice.

"Nature with an equal mind," said Joe sitting down behind Ali, "sees all her sons at play; sees man control the wind, the wind sweep man away."

While the others talked effervescently about the flight, comparing what they had seen with how their machines had reacted, Ali turned to him contritely but not completely won over. "You really know your Arnold! Why?"

"It was taught, thought suitable in a Christian school. Why you?"

"Because..." said Ali, and was glad to be interrupted by Alice asking where she'd put her bag, but because was Jake, who was doing a PhD in English, while destroying his body with prescription drugs.

The hotel was small, an old white washed cottage that had been stretched and turned into a rather cute hotel. The hall was crammed with a vast wooden reception desk, curtains and lots of little breakfast tables, decorated and already laid.

As in any cottage when you opened a cupboard door the staircase tumbled into the room, immediately rushing off up to the next floor. The visitors were given the impression of far too many things and people crowded into far too small a space.

Alice and Ali had a small room in the eves with a double bed: a large white bed in a large white room, there were no chairs or tables (which were presumably all downstairs) but strangely there was a basket of flowers on the floor. However, the sheets were enterprisingly soft and the duvet was large and fluffy. While Ali looked for somewhere to charge the GPS, Alice jumped on the bed with the verve of a child on her first parent-free holiday.

"Pruuh. No springs! Do you think it's horsehair, he-air in the east."

Ali laughed and ran her hand over the mattress. "Could be, but it's softer than that... dog's hair?"

"Human," said Alice with macabre excitement, "former prisoners... probably Jews, there's a old prison camp not far from here... how long do you think they went on burning them?"

Berlin Oval

That evening Daniel had a meeting with a client and asked Alice to go with him. The others were going to a restaurant in West Berlin and most had already left the hotel when Daniel pounded on the girls' bedroom door, telling Alice he was leaving.

Ali opened the door. "She's in the shower, Daniel, and judging by past form you'll have at least half an hour to wait."

Daniel stamped his foot impatiently. "Damn! Women! I'm not waiting for her. Tell her to take a taxi and join me at this restaurant." He started writing the address on the back of one of his cards (professionally printed, Ali noted enviously). Then he stopped and, raising his head to smile at Ali, said in a much calmer, almost supplicating voice, "Do you mind waiting, Ali, to escort her into town? It's not far from where you are going. Only a block or two."

"And Daniel's already paid the chap in advance so it's free!" Alice added later when told of the change of plan. "Usually he seems to find a way to make me pay, so this will make a nice change."

Shrugging on her leather jacket, Ali laughed. Alice, now dressed in clothes that her co-pilot could hardly believe had travelled with them under the R22's seats, looked too fashionable and demure in gauze covered silk to be accompanied by a black-jacketed scoundrel like her, especially in Berlin, home of Cabaret, transvestites and naughty mornings.

"Shall we change places? Shock the client?" Ali only half-joked, part of her wishing she could be like Alice and have her life.

"Wicked!"

Alice enlivened the short ride into West Berlin by talking all the way. She said

Daniel had told her his client was a jeweller whose father had made a fortune during the Russian Revolution by stealing gold from the Orthodox cathedrals and churches. He also had mistresses in various countries, his business keeping him virtually always on the road. Alice had been shocked but Ali reckoned he had made it up just for that reason.

As the taxi arrived at the restaurant a short, middle aged man with an expanding stomach and retreating hair was walking up the street. He drew level as their car stopped in the gutter. Ali, following Alice out of the cab and turning to shut the door, heard a voice saying: "Heavens! It is my favourite pilot!"

The man advanced on her and, before she could protest, kissed her on both cheeks salutively, before taking Alice by the arm and leading her firmly away. Ali was left staring. Who was that man?

She turned towards the French restaurant, where she was meeting the others, still puzzling. Only when she was half way there did she pass a dress shop call the Kaiser's Servant and she suddenly thought Good Lord! Thomas Moore! Thomas Moore, least attractive client and apparently friend, or client anyway, of Daniel. Odd, as Paula would have said, odd!

That unlettered small-knowing soul coincidence.

The others were waiting for her in the French restaurant, where they had an edible dinner and were happily able to complain about the service before decamping to an Irish bar. Kevin, muttering: "French restaurant in a German city, what can you expect, the only amusing thing was the suggestion service was included," refused to tip the check-in man where he had left his umbrella.

Bored with the Irish bar, the group soon started to look for more genuine West Berlin entertainment. Charles found a transvestite bar nearby (special raunchy, all view) and had almost convinced the bouncer to let them in when he saw Ali. Immediately he was adamant, "We don't take girls," he said confusingly, "even in leather, this is a male-only bar".

Charles seemed keen to argue, to point out the missing logic but Ali shook her head, realising she just wanted to go home and think about things.

"That's fine," she said. "Really! I've seen all the transvestites I need to, I used to live in Brixton. I'll take a taxi home."

"I'll come with you," said Joe. "I could do with some sleep before Mike starts wanting me to think again tomorrow."

"All right," Ali agreed ungraciously.

The taxi-driver unwillingly consented to take them over to East Berlin, suspecting he wouldn't get a ride back. He didn't speak English but apparently all of the assembled party were determined to practice some schoolboy German and were keenly giving him instructions. He agreed to take them, expecting he'd get a pretty good tip from such a large group. When only two people got into the cab he was disgusted, but it was too late (and too difficult) to complain and he started off in the proposed direction. After a short while he realised he was lost.

"Could you tell me again where the hotel is?" he asked in German.

Ali stared at him blankly. She turned to Joe, "do you speak German?"

"Yes," he admitted unwillingly, "don't you?"

"Nope. I can manage Essen, but only because I've been there and I was hungry."

"Old joke," he said, but he gave a tantalising half-smile. "Hang on, I'll ask him what the problem is."

After a short conversation leaning forward over the seat back, which groaned at his weight, Joe reported back that the driver had no idea where the hotel was, and added he didn't either. "Over to you?"

"Not a clue."

"Ah! And another thing... how much money have you got in Deutsche Marks?"

"You'll love this... "

"None?"

"I'm not that stupid. I've got some, but only twenty, I didn't think it was that far away. We arrived so quickly. How about you?"

"Same or maybe a little more. I'd better tell him, but be warned we may have to walk."

"I know, tell him to go to Schoenberg, we might be able to find the way from there. Perhaps we could tell him about the money when we arrive at the hotel?"

"I don't think you understand bureaucracy. If we tell him now, and he likes us, he'll turn off the meter. But if we over-spend on the meter he'll have paper-work up to his ears to explain it. I'm telling him now."

The taxi driver realised it was not his lucky night. He agreed to drive to Schoenberg and to turn off the meter. So much for his fairy godmother. He'd got a couple of elves. Still, why not, he thought wittily, looking at his watch, it was elf hour!

As they blundered around in the darkness the cabby exhausted his silent store of jokes. It was now well past elf hour and stretching towards the witching one.

"It all looks different in the dark," said Ali, "I would have sworn I knew the way from the airport... it isn't far after all."

"Are ye too changed ye hills?" Joe added cheerfully, enjoying himself.

"Very helpful! But if you're really keen on Arnold here's one: "Cruel, but composed and bland, dumb, inscrutable and grand, so Tiberius might have sat, had Tiberius been a cat!""

"Look! The hotel."

"Fantastic!" Ali said. "One stark monotony of stone, long hotel acutely white..."

"It's not long. Rather cuddly."

"No, but I can't help that. I guess they didn't teach Arthur Symonds at the Christian school?"

"You guess wrong: 'Life is a dream in the night, a fear amongst fears, a naked runner lost in a storm of spears.' The Wood of Finvara. I always felt that was made for Africa."

"What a school you went to..."

"What a pilot you are. I never thought I would be swapping poetry with a pilot in a taxi in East Berlin."

"Oh, amazingly we are not as dumb as everyone imagines, some pilots have depths as well as heights."

"Just as some South Africans are not racist?"

She smiled. "Touché. I'm sorry. Perhaps there's a dandelion somewhere..."

"That will be 50 DM," said the taxi driver, glad to be able to get heard.

Joe found an extra 10 DM and they paid. The taxi driver left without a backward look, feeling he'd more than exceeded his Christian duty that night. Ali walked to the door.

"It's pretty dark inside. Do you think they left the door open?"

"Try it."

The door was locked. Ali twiddled ineffectively with the knob, hoping the noise might bring someone from within, but inside remained dark and uninviting.

"OK," said Joe, "we'll have to break in."

"Blimey, is that what they teach you in the South African army?"

"Yup. Watch."

Joe expanded his chest, extended his muscles, lifted a huge fist to the glass; then turned and walked around to the back of the hotel. Ali followed suspiciously. Somewhere ahead in the dark he gave a gleeful bark.

"Look here. A fire-escape. The good thing," said Joe happily, "about societies that live with regulations, is that you can be sure the regulations will counteract each other." He grinned, stopping, one foot on the first step of the fire escape. "I'll tell you a story. Have you time?"

Ali smiled and nodded.

"During the Communist years," said Joe, "I was travelling to Europe from China, through Moscow for a connecting train to East Germany. Only my train came in south of Moscow and the only connecting one went out of Moscow half an hour later from a station east of Moscow, just too far to reach in time. However, since I was in transit and not a tourist I could only have a transit visa, not a tourist visa. Transit visas did not allow you to stay in hotels but they did allow you to spend five days in Russia. I did not make my connection and had to sleep in the station. Which was forbidden. I and a few hundred also unconnected Russians slept, were woken by the police every few hours, waited until they left and then slept again." He grinned.

"Nothing changes. Now, here in the newly liberated German Democratic Republic, I imagine you must not leave the door unlocked after 10 o'clock but at the same time you must have an exit onto the fire escape: ergo... one window..."

Ali laughed and they bounded up the metal stairs. The paint-peeling window opened with an aged scrape and both of them slipped in easily. To their amusement they noticed the fire door was locked with a chain and padlock.

"Good night," she said, moving towards her room, then paused and added, "and thanks. I, er, might have been a bit stuck without you. I guess I thought all taxi drivers spoke English. And knew the hotels."

"Like England," said Joe, with a rueful half smile. "Good night, Ali, sleep well."

In their bedroom Ali found Alice, lying awake but not sparkling, very angry in fact. During the course of dinner Daniel had told her not to misbehave with the Frenchmen, as though it was any of his business, and she was incandescent.

"How dare he?" she asked turning her head angrily, the beads, which she wore night and day, whipping her pillow. "The git! Who does he think he is? What does he know about anything?"

"He's just trying to protect you Alice. You are still young..."

"Protect me! Why? He's not my mother! I could be married at my age, many girls are, my mother had... was. Bloody Hell."

"Incidentally," said Ali, not listening, "do you know that chap Thomas Moore?"

"Of course, he's an old friend of my stepfather's," said Alice deflected. "I told you HE'd be sending out family friends to meet us at every stop! Tom introduced Daniel to Janus. I've known him ever since my mother married Janus."

"Janus? The God of door-stops?"

"My stepfather."

"I thought he was Greek."

Alice snorted angrily. "You got that from magazines. I thought that you were better than that. Why do you read such rubbish?" She turned over in bed again and the beads went bang, bang against the mattress. She turned back and Ali saw there were tears in her eyes.

Oh girls, girls, silly little valuable things. Young, vulnerable girls.

"It is a Greek name as well as others... 'they' focused on that. Dirt grubbers! When they don't know something they guess or make it up. I hate them.

Janus is an International. He is South African. He is Greek. He is British. He's an aristocrat and a businessman, there are few enough of those, not that the press would recognise one anyway even if it hit them with a solid gold family crest. He's a winner, makes money with everything he touches, some is from shipping, some from his other companies.

He was born in the most international country in the world. Anyway, that does not matter. The point is Daniel would like anyone who was going to give him money... you should have heard him smarming tonight... I felt quite sick... grubber! He's nothing but a Russian General! The twit! I hate him."

After Alice had dropped into a restless sleep Ali stayed awake. Was Alice telling the truth? The world suddenly seemed full of South Africans, or International South Africans. While Alice's father was an unknown quantity and the diamond merchant was vile, Joe wasn't as bad as she'd believed, in fact he was sweet and funny in a raw, boyish sort of way.

But what did she know about men? She who met the beautiful, elegant Jake at university and fell immediately for his brilliance, his soft girl's face, his nimble brain and his academic wizardry.

Jake used to quote too, although she thought he was cleverer than Joe, binding his words into aphorisms. When Ali had talked about 'Peckham diamonds' it was Jake who pointed out that every week there was a diamond heist by the street cleaners. "A diamond crown that princes won't enjoy."

For Jake, Ali, whose bent was all science, had learnt to quote the desperate poets, Milton, Elliot, Pope, Larkin, Yates and Pound; the crying boys, Shelley, Byron, Tennyson and the War Poets. For herself she had read the lighter styles of Arnold, Belloc, Betjeman and Symonds.

She was proud of her ability to quote, even though she knew much of it came from a good memory. She had excelled in her love. He rewarded her with unexpected rages and inexplicable eruptions. Yet at other times he would be perfectly charming and gorgeous, making her laugh with witty, sardonic comments. Never was Ali able to tell in advance which of her remarks would lead to light laughter and love, which to a blazing, angry row. And somehow she came to believe it was her own fault.

As the furies increased Ali tried, and failed, to find a common denominator; to see where she had gone wrong. She saw no rationale in anger because she walked too fast or opened the door first. No logic in his hatred when she laughed too loudly at a joke. She failed to understand his envy when she did well, since that was why he had admired her in the first place.

The tension between them grew so great that anyone else would have 'taken the one road out of Corinth' but Ali clung on loyally, feeling that if only she could discover the problem he would regain that caring loving person he had formerly been. That, Jake's therapist told her, was the difference between men and women. When men don't like their woman they get a new one, when women don't like their man they try to change the one they've got.

The end came when she went to visit her mother and her close-knit family unit. There, alone amongst the bond of mother, stepfather and half-brother, Ali saw she was an outsider looking in. On her way home in the train she watched the passing fields and decided that what she wanted was to drift along for ever, watching the world but unattached to any of its facets; to sit forever looking out of a window on life. She even considered sterilisation, just so she could continue the relationship without any fear of compromising her offspring.

She arrived home to find Jake had tried to kill himself. An overdose of the very drugs he felt kept him sane.

After the drama and the police Ali went to visit Jake's therapist. She suggested that the kindest thing for both of them would be for Ali to leave, never to see Jake again.

Ali agreed, suddenly realising it was a relief. She moved in with Paula, and, needing an alternative therapy, put all her money and devotion into changing her private helicopter licence into a commercial one. Poetry and helicopters, that was her life now.

Work without Hope draws nectar in a sieve, and Hope without an object cannot live.

≈≈≈≈≈

Vulnerable to Chipping

Next to Galina's apartment lived a middle-aged woman with three daughters. When they were growing up all three girls had shared a room, while their mother slept in the kitchen. Now the first daughter had moved out, and although the second daughter was only fifteen she was already talking of moving in with her boyfriend, something her mother was totally opposed to.

"She's so young," said the mother, standing by Galina's sink and watching her scrub her her clothes against the washboard, "and so is the boy. Only eighteen. How soon before he tires of her and sends her back to me. If only she could be like her elder sister and catch the eye of an older man. Katrina Lizavetta is a clever girl, a beautiful girl and she has her own apartment, like you, although she has no child yet. Her man is a good man, he has worked hard all his life and he will never leave her. I'm so happy for her, so happy."

Galina smiled insincerely and continued washing the boy's nappy, putting it out on the balcony to dry along with her own under-clothes. She was glad they were worn, so the old woman would see how poor she was and tell the neighbours not to charge her for any favours, such as looking after the boy.

She knew this story well. Of course the woman used her tales of woe to come in to Galina's flat to spy on her, to nose around and see how well she was doing. But how could Galina turn away a woman whose daughter (as everyone knew) was kept by an older man, who sold her services to his friends so he could watch them having sex. The whole building pitied her, how ever much her proud mother kept up appearances.

"Very true, very true," murmured Galina, "and perhaps Rosanna would like to look after the boy on Saturday. I have to go into work for an extra day and I may be back late. Maybe she could take him to the park and give him something to eat. He loves spending time with her, so much, so much he thinks of her as a second mother."

Pink Pavé

The next day, before they flew on to Posnan, Kevin called the whole group together at the airfield.

"Normally," he began, with a quick glance at Pete and Daniel to emphasise they were lucky to be included in a group going beyond the norm, "General Aviation travelling through Poland has to stick to special Visual Flight Rules corridors. However, as Group Leader I am empowered to tell you we have had a special exemption to go outside the 'Victor Mike' corridors, thanks to our importance as a team travelling to Russia for the World Helicopter Championships, which is not easily allowed and took substantial extra influence to achieve. So I would ask you all to stick together and not violate their special regulations; bear in mind this is not yet a fully democratic country and we do not want to upset their political status. You will need to have your passport checked on arrival. OK. Does everybody understand everything? And are there any questions?"

There were no questions, rather a general silence with the inevitable British smiles, looks and raised eyebrows. The teams got ready and in due course lifted off in a raggle-taggle bunch. As they flew on to Posnan, Daniel, whose boredom threshold was quickly crossed, began telling jokes on the radio.

"What do you call a deer with one eye?"

"One i-dea," cried Alice across the airwaves.

"What do you call a blind deer?"

"No idea!" yelled Alice.

"Alors," said Giles, one of the Frenchmen. "Trop des Anglais. Nous changerons à une autre frequency!"

Meanwhile Kevin and Pete joined in. "What do you call a blind deer with no legs?" But Alice, even muttering "still no idea," got bored.

"Let's see the standard of French jokes," she said to Ali. "What frequency do you think they're using?"

"Probably the French Unicom frequency," Ali replied, flipping the dials.

"How do you know that?"

"I worked in France for a while. Flying a guy back and forth from Cannes to London, and around the local area in a JetRanger. It wasn't the cheapest way for him to fly but he loved helicopters."

"Wicked."

"Do you speak French?" Ali asked.

"Yes, I'm fluent in French and German."

"Of course," said Ali, remembering she was from German descent. Alice looked at her briefly but said nothing, listening to the radio. Sure enough the French were on the Unicom frequency, babbling away about food and other various things just as silly as British jokes.

"So the nationalities at play," quoted Ali. "Not one but all mankind's epitome: stiff in opinions, always in the wrong, everything by starts and nothing long."

They fiddled around from one channel to another, while flying over poor-looking fields tilled with old-fashioned equipment, sometimes even drawn by a horse or ox. In one field there were rows and rows of grey lumps, which turned out to be people picking things, bent double, only their arms moving jerkily from rut to bucket. As they moved slowly up the field with extended arms they looked like baby elephants nosing for biscuits in the grass.

"Potatoes," said Alice.

"Isn't it too early for potatoes?" asked Ali, but Alice merely shrugged and replied "maybe," not interested enough in Polish poverty to debate the subject.

"Why aren't you married, Ali?" asked Alice.

Ali gasped, embarrassed and as unwilling to discuss this subject as an unemployed man his job. She was about to reply defensively that there are a lot a single men but there is a reason why they are single, when Alice continued. "My mother was married at eighteen and I'm already a year older, do you think standards and life have changed substantially? Do you think we all have to wait until our late twenties and early thirties to find the right man for us?"

Ali made a noncommittal answer but, while Alice continued on her theme, wondered about Mrs Charleston, the frail elderly woman with her Dresden china hands, who married at eighteen and had her only child in her forties. What kind of shock must that have given her! A whole life prepared, destroyed or enlivened; impossible to guess.

Gradually the helicopters began to spread out, the English pilots flying ahead, the French lagging behind.

"Look," said Alice suddenly, "three o'clock! What is Jaap doing?"

Ali looked over Alice's right shoulder and sure enough there was Jaap descending steeply down into a field that looked like old pasture with a possible ridge and furrow effect. There were no livestock in the field that the girls could see but a long line of thick green trees bordered one side.

"Shall we keep an eye on him?" suggested Ali. "You know what a nutter he is. I bet you anything he's gone down for a pee."

Alice giggled. "Wicked. Let's go down too and spring out on him!"

"Urggh, no thanks. I'd rather keep a dry distance."

The girls giggled together and flew towards the distant field, where they could see Jaap. Having landed, leaving his machine running, he had got out and was standing next to the spinning blades, slightly turned towards the skid as though to shield himself from an invisible audience.

"You're right!" giggled Alice.

"What a nutter. I hope he doesn't walk into his own blades."

"Ooh, ouch. But at least I could flirt with him safely!"

"Alice! How could you!"

Ali flicked back onto the British frequency just in time to hear Daniel saying: "Has anyone seen Jaap?"

Alice grinned. "Don't tell him! Old fuss pot. It's none of his business. Jaap's OK."

They flew low past the field and Jaap, having done up his flies, waved happily, quite unaware he might have started an incident. He hopped back into the helicopter and Ali, realising he was on the French frequency, hastily changed stations.

"Hi, Jaap, you there?" she asked in English.

"Ooh la la en français seulement, s'il vous plait!" Came over in anguished French. "Off zee frequency English. You sink you own the world but not 'ere."

"Excuse moi," said Ali, aware her accent was rather Essex, "je voud-ray par-ler avec Jaap."

"Ah bien, mais seulement en français!"

"Ah oui, vray-ment."

After a little persuasion Jaap admitted that having found a suitable field for a pee he no longer had any idea where he was.

"Huh," said Alice, "a blind deer but definitely not still!"

"Whatsat? Is that you Alice dear?"

"En français!"

"Suivez moi, mon brave," said Ali, and then, once Jaap was up and following, remembered Daniel. She changed back to the British frequency. On it Daniel was having a tantrum.

"Where are Alice and Ali? Where is Jaap? What frequency are the French on? Don't any of you idiots know anything?"

"We're here," said Ali calmly. "Jaap's with us and we're on our way to Modlin. Where you?"

They arrived at Modlin, leaving the forest and farmland and coming into a flat alluvial basin centred on a wide river. The tide was out and the retreating water had left craggy lines in the mud flats like the gills of a kipper, a few boats bobbing on the thin sliver of water that trundled between the gills. Beyond the river an open, treeless approach over a green delta led to the airfield, which looked as neat and prosperous as a French vineyard. Ali relaxed, forgot the outstanding questions and gave herself up to serenity.

The girls parked on the edge of the grass and Steve and Sandra popped down beside them, but they hadn't even shut down when a furious Daniel was opening Alice's door. "What the Hell do you think you're doing? Running around all over Poland without saying a word. This isn't the UK you know. This is foreign territory. I told you to stay close to me."

He punched the air, anger distorting his handsome face. Ali, thinking this was way out of proportion to the offence (if such it was) wondered if he was in love with Alice. Her instincts told her he was wasting his time. While you can never really know someone, however much time you spend with them, you can sometimes intuitively know their destiny. Ali already knew Alice, with her money and her hidden class, would never marry the flamboyant and emotional pilot, not necessarily because of those things, but because they both wanted to be the centre of attention. 'For 25 years I've been flying next door to Alice.'

While Daniel was screaming at Alice, and Alice was screaming back, Ali completed the shutdown. She'd put on the rotor brake and was getting her things out from under the seat when Joe walked over. "Friends who set forth at our side falter, are lost in the storm!" He grinned. "We, we only, are left."

"Except it was only a storm in a pee cup!"

"Wauph. What would our schoolmaster have thought of that? Go wash your mouth out."

"Um, well in this case I would say tant pis."

Joe replied, "Tant Piss, she can't miss, coz she's got a bladder the size of a football."

"Eloquent, though not very poetic. Another one for the Christian school?"

"Certainly was. You know what we used for footballs don't you?"

Ali looked at him, not sure if he was joking. He half-smiled and walked away. She reached into the helicopter to pull out the GPS for charging, but it resisted. Refused to come away. Yesterday it had come out so easily.

"Alice," she asked, rather fearfully breaking into the festering row. "Did you do anything to the GPS? I can't get it out of the case."

Alice shrugged. "Take the case too. It unclips. You can charge it with the case on, I've done it before." She turned back to scream once more at Daniel.

Unable to shift the machine from the case Ali did as suggested, and once the machine was in their room, on and charging, she thought little more about it.

In Modlin more nationalities joined the British team, including a Swiss man and his son who were going to take part in the competition as independents. Alice remarked they could hardly expect to win as the son, who was only about thirteen, didn't look strong enough to hold the bucket through the whole slalom, let alone manage the navigation on alien Russian maps which missed out anything secret or likely to compromise security. Leaving Ali to do the fuel she went to welcome the new arrivals.

Here they didn't even have the old-fashioned fuel truck with a hand pump. All fuelling was done with buckets, jerrycans and a filter, which arrived heaped onto a low cart drawn by a very thin young man. As Ali glanced at her watch he smiled happily at her, sitting down on the edge of the cart to wait for his friend to arrive with the stepladder.

After a short while another man appeared carrying a green brown stepladder from which splinters stood out like huge thorns on a rose-stem. On one side was a trailing, broken string. Dumped near the Robinson, the ladder teetered on rickety feet until the men adjusted it, talking in Polish. Still talking, one man climbed carefully up the bowed steps, while the other one held the legs, his horny hands oblivious to the thorns. He handed up the filter and the first jerrycan. Then, leaving the ladder, placed another filter in the neck of a second jerrycan, pouring fuel from the bucket. Predictably the can fell over, falling off the cart and spreading a fat squid of liquid across the apron like gleaming honey. The pourer returned the bucket to the cart, picked up the jerrycan, leaning it against the wood of the cart. But when he put the filter in the neck this time it unbalanced and fell under the cart. He retrieved it and the other fueller turned to get down and help. Worried they would take all evening to do just one helicopter Ali tried to help.

"Couldn't you pour fuel from the bucket into the filter?" She asked.

The fuel man looked mystified, shrugging his shoulders.

"Shall I hold the jerrycan?" Ali asked.

The fueller looked puzzled, and then, when she leant down to hold the can, began to laugh. The first fueller said something to him and they both laughed, the second fueller kissing his hand to Ali. He then made some gestures first pointing to his wedding ring and then suggesting she hold the ladder for the first fueller, whom, he showed her by the same means, was unmarried. By this time, however, the first fueller, having emptied the jerrycan, was now down on the ground again. The two men conversed some more and the second man went off to fetch a third man to hold the jerrycan.

Ali found Sandra by her side. "So," she said, "you are using your Russian?"

Ali stared at her blankly. "My Russian?"

"I hear you are a Russophile."

Sandra did not often talk to anyone, preferring to listen to what others had to say and reserve judgement. However, when she did she started her sentences with "So!" as though they had previously been in conversation and to which she had now discovered the solution.

Ali blinked. "No! Not me! I did aeronautical engineering at university. If that's what you mean. I'm a flying instructor. At best I read a few Russian writers."

"Oh," said her interrogator, unable to hide the disappointment in her voice, "so you are not fluent in Russian?"

"Absolutely not," said Ali, feeling guilty as though she had been caught lying and longing to say she could learn, if Sandra gave her time. "You must be thinking of some other pilot. I'm terribly sorry. Try Mike, I know he was learning some words. I think Daniel says he speaks some..."

"Yes." Sandra sighed, let down. After a block of silence she grimaced and asked, "How old are you?"

Ali looked at the girl, wondering if this was a sequiter, or whether there even was such a thing. She wondered if that was another of those words only to be found in the negative. Sandra repeated the question a little louder.

"Thirty," Ali replied crisply, wishing all these helicopter owners would be less forthright but somehow unwilling to lie.

"Oh! You look younger. I'm twenty eight." She stared for a moment at the three fuellers, who were now putting the second jerrycan's contents into the Robinson, then looked back at Ali, as though expecting a response. Ali remained silent, nervously uncertain what was required, and eventually Sandra walked away.

Once the assembled company were all fuelled, ready for the following morning, they got their bags and clambered into the meretricious pre-Walesa bus provided to take them into Warsaw. Ali was about to sit next to Alice when Sandra, her husband following a little behind, brushed past Ali and sat down beside the younger girl. Ali sat behind them, followed by Steve and from there heard Sandra now quizzing Alice. "So, you are a Russian expert?"

Alice made a face. "Hardly!" she said derisively. "But your husband said you were. Is that what you mean?"

Even from behind Ali could hear Sandra's cold smile. "I work for the government, my speciality is Russia. But I believe you did a thesis on the effect on Russia of losing the Second World War."

Alice bristled. Worse than curious! Sandra's profile indicated that there was a whole lot more hidden behind the inquisition. Defensively Alice met the question with a question.

"How do you know?"

"I read it," said Sandra. "You made some good points but you idealised the Russian character. I thought you were looking for too many heroes and like anyone brought up in a free environment totally under-estimated the fear of Stalin and his henchmen in the era..."

"I won an all schools competition for it," snapped Alice, "anyway how did you get hold of it? It wasn't for public analysis."

"Then you shouldn't have had so many copies printed and bound."

"That was Janus, he was proud of my win." As soon as she spoke Alice regretted having given so much away.

Sandra's smile was that of a fat feline who has trapped the mouse. "Umm. In my opinion you sounded like a rich girl who has not lived enough in the real world to understand poverty and its ramifications. An only child – you are an only child aren't you - and the daughter of rich parents, who had never had to fight for anything. I thought that..."

"Excuse me," said Alice. The bus having arrived at their destination she jumped up and, flying over Sandra's knees, propelled herself along the aisle and down the stairs. When Ali caught up with her she said explosively, "Don't ever leave me alone with that woman again. EVER! EVER! EVER! She is mad!"

Alaskan Diamonds

Daniel was again spending the evening with a client, but this time he decided to leave Alice behind and took Gary, Paul and Rob instead. "I'm leaving my darling Alice in your charge," said Daniel to Ali, "I hope I can trust you!"

"Pigs," said the disgusted Alice, as she joined Ali and Joe in the Proletariat Bar, "I hope their hangovers vastly outweigh the enjoyment of getting them!"

The girls and Joe drank Czechoslovakian beer from Pilsen, watching international racing on cable television in the international hotel. After a while Joe, flicking peanuts into his mouth, suggested it was time to eat. "The choice is simple," he said. "We can eat here: international food in an international atmosphere, or risk wandering around Warsaw trying to find somewhere decent before they close everything. I'll bet curfew is around ten o'clock."

"How's the international cuisine?" asked Alice, glancing at the imported pinewood clock above the bar.

"Bit like Tiberius."

Alice looked puzzled but after a moment Ali followed him. "'Oh, composed and bland! Funny man."

Joe grinned, rather pleased. "So, what you reckon, re food that is?"

"Let's try outside," said Alice, while Ali, determined Joe shouldn't get the better of her with quotes, added: "No one will ever know what brilliant feast is waiting if they don't go further than the railhead."

"Funny Girl," he whispered, smiling at her, while she wondered peevishly if he still hadn't had the better lines.

Across the square from their hotel, in which foreigners were formerly obliged to stay, an elegiac building proclaimed the splendour of the communist philosophy. Built in the best tradition of Stalingrad architecture, the government workshop dominated the skyline with stark, straight angles and a large grey statue of

Lenin. In contrast the square was full of rickety tables where men in 1970s polyester shirts (repeated designs of grandfather clocks and ships at 45 degrees to the vertical) and women with neurotically moving hands, sold clothes of thin, shiny material, orange and blue plastic shoes and trinkets from Taiwan.

"What is a communist?" asked Joe, as they crossed the square towards the plastic shoes, "but one who hath yearnings, for equal division of unequal earnings."

"Was that Arnold?"

"No, Ebenezer Elliot. He was called 'Franklin reborn' but they actually overlapped by nine years. Even the most lax Buddhist wouldn't allow that."

On the far side of the square a low, brown bunker paraded a prominent MacDonald's sign. The queue to enter snaked back several blocks, and although Joe thought it might be a laugh to visit MacDonald's in Warsaw, Ali and Alice stoutly over-ruled him.

"I want something Polish. A sausage or something," said Alice.

"Poland isn't known for food 'as luscious as locusts'!"

Alice giggled, "I'll risk it for a brisket, so on the bus, Gus! Whata you know, Joe? God, I'd soon pick up this poetry thing, no problem!"

"There's probably more protein in the locusts," said Ali, but hearing her words lost in Joe's laughter with Alice she felt an odd heartburn and wished Alice had stayed with Daniel for the evening. Then felt guilty and confused.

They walked behind the statues and conflicting grandeur of the main square and soon found themselves in narrow streets with drab, partially empty shops and cafes with dirty blinds. The cafes had little tables with formica tops, squashed together so there was only just room for the people to sit at them, touching back to back, service being a one side only, bang-the-plate-on-the-table affair. They seemed to be full of people, but behind the grimy curtains in one cafe a group were just getting up. Alice opened the door and the three pilots stood back for the dour cafe-eaters to pass.

The waiter looked suspiciously at them as they entered, clearly wondering why they didn't stay in their expensive hotel instead of coming to slum-it in his kitchen. He asked them in haughty Polish what they wanted.

Joe and Alice tried speaking in German, but he waved them away and walked off. He returned after a while with a piece of paper, covered in plastic, with various words written on it in Polish. They guessed it must be the menu because a line of Zloty signs ran down one side.

On the table next to them two boys, in the same kind of shiny shirts as the shoe-sellers in the square, and two girls showing lots of cleavage in loosely knitted vests, were eating red soup with bread. One of the boys had a plate of meat in a sauce with lots of potatoes and cabbage. Ali pointed at the soup. The waiter shrugged and seemed to be moving away when Joe and Alice hastily started pointing too. Shrugging again he moved off to the small door, source of meat-based smells, to shout at someone.

"I expect there's only one thing on the menu anyway." Joe said, before explaining: "Years ago I travelled on the Trans-Siberian Express and even before we left Ulan Bator the kitchens were out of everything except Borsch and Goulash and long before we entered Moscow that too had gone."

Their soup arrived accompanied by bread and plates of meat, cabbage and potatoes and a piece of paper with an amount written on it in pencil. The price for the three soups, bread, meat, cabbage and potatoes was equivalent to three pounds. On the paper was a little plastic cushion of 'ketjup'.

"Wow," said Alice, "if only I knew the Polish for champagne I'd order it." Then thinking of Daniel she added tactlessly, "but I'd rather be here with you than drinking champagne with that Russian General!"

Bits of fat swam around in the soup, and the meat was lumps of gristle. Ali, picking at the bread and potato while the others tucked in, asked Alice, "You mentioned that last night. What is a Russian General?"

"Oh," said Alice, red eyebrows shooting up into red hair, "in Russia they often invite a General to parties to give them 'ton'; he arrives in full dress with medals and everyone thinks they've come to a real celebrity do, but in reality he's paid. It's a con."

"Oh," said Joe, "like Potemkin's houses?"

Both girls looked attentively at him.

"Prince Potemkin, Catherine the Great's co-ruler decided as a beautiful, humanitarian gesture to build modern houses for the proletariat, with all the mod cons of the time. But all he really built was the front facade, which he showed to her and others. Behind the fabulous frontispiece was nothing and certainly not the splendid modern housing for peasants that Catherine believed was there."

Ali played with her meat. "Sounds like Peckham Diamonds." She pushed her food aside. "It's lovely but I just don't feel hungry any more."

Alice gave her a contemptuous look. "We're spoilt," she said, "decadent! You should be able to eat anything. Sustenance!"

"Even if it makes you sick?" asked Joe neutrally. While Ali gave that peculiarly English withdrawal-smile.

"Poor people don't get sick," said Alice, with the complete assurance of youth. "At least," she amended, "not from perfectly acceptable food."

"Not even when the ship goes wop and the steward falls into the soup tureen," asked Joe, filling his mouth happily.

"What?" Asked Alice, wiping her soup plate with the bread. "What is that?"

"A quote."

"Another one," said Alice, her eyebrows now flopping back. "Did you get prizes for this at school or something? Yours?"

"Kipling's...the Just-So Stories. Weren't you brought up with them?'

"No, nor Tintin neither. I think you had to be English."

"Or South African," remarked Ali ironically.

"Same thing," Alice sneered. She took Ali's soup and started to eat that too, while Joe added, "why then you will know, if you haven't guessed, you're fifty north and forty west."

"Warsaw," said Ali, unable to repress a smile, "is fifty-two north and twenty-one east."

"So," asked Joe half smiling, "what then? Steward-less soup?"

Ali laughed but Alice screwed up her nose, scooping into her soup loudly. "Silly. All very silly."

Russian Brilliants

On Saturday, after work, Galina had to meet her father for their yearly reunion. Their differences were profound but he never forgot that she was his daughter and once a year he would give her dinner and some money. This evening he had asked her to meet him in the Red Pelican, an expensive restaurant with a rather sleazy reputation, where he was known as a regular.

Galina always made sure she was late for their appointment. It was anyway more powerful to be the second person to arrive and she liked to keep him waiting several hours, but more than usual Galina, who was aware the restaurant was a meeting ground for unrelated old men and young women, did not wish to be sitting alone waiting. Even if it was her father she was waiting for. Tonight, though, she had a special favour to ask from him, a favour that involved a second meeting and a long drive into the country, and so she was prepared to be more than usually flexible. Consequently, she arrived only half an hour after the appointed time. Her father had not yet arrived.

Galina ordered herself a coffee and sat down at their table to wait. The piano player in the next door room played the opening chords of the Odessa Quadrille. She noted the golden luxury of the place with a cynical eye. Did her father want to remind her of what she was missing? How much better her life could have been? She had always been her father's favourite, their mother preferred her sister. Then, when their mother died, life changed rapidly and when father remarried a couple of years ago and had another family, well, everything changed then. Shrugging, Galina drank her coffee and studied the menu. It was life, it was Russia.

She had been there less than half an hour when the waiter approached with a letter. "Miss Reskarova?"

"Yes."

"Your father sent this round by messenger, with his apologies and instructions that you should order whatever you like." He bowed and drew back after giving her the letter.

Galina opened the envelope. Inside was a wedge of roubles, she didn't count it but noted the bundle was thick before she dropped it into her bag, and a letter. The letter was brief.

"Galina, apologies. Something has occurred. I cannot come tonight, but I have enclosed the usual obligation. I have instructed the restaurant you are to order what you like on my account and I will see you again. Same date next year?"

Galina shrugged, this was life as she knew it. He did not change.

She called the boy over and said she would like to order food to take out and a car to carry it, all on her father's account. After some discussion, over the surcharge payable to the boy and that payable to the restaurant, she ordered all the most expensive things on the menu. Then, after more discussion about how many of the dishes on the menu the restaurant actually had, she re-ordered, making sure she still chose the most expensive. Once her second choice (cold borscht with caviar, fried oysters, foie gras, lamb steaks in a cognac sauce, grouse, cold chicken and pelmeni dumplings for the boy, bottles of Russian champagne and coca cola) arrived she set off for home, determined to share it not only with her boy but with the daughter of her neighbour. For once they would dine well, her father would pay and she would lie about the dinner's origin so convincingly no one would ever suspect whence it came.

Kimberlite Kite

Next morning Alice and Ali were in the lobby, checking out of the hotel, when Daniel staggered past the uniformed bus boys with their shinning brass trolleys and came to an uneasy halt leaning against an ornate, well polished pillar.

"Hangover?" asked Alice sweetly, turning away from her cheque book on the broad, wooden desk. "Good night out with the boys, was it? Lots of tasty Polish beer?"

"Never get 'em. Strong men have begged me to lie under the table with them, but I go on regardless."

Alice returned to her cheque book, raising a bored shoulder, as she did so two men stepped up to Daniel, talking to each other in Russian. When they saw Daniel and the girls they changed into English.

"Buses are here," Grzegorz said. "Outside."

Most of the crew were assembled in the hall and followed Daniel and the girls out to the mini-buses. Made by Mercedes, these were long ten-seaters and the hotel had provided two. As they were about to leave Ali noticed Joe was not on board.

"Joe and Mike aren't here," she mentioned as off-handedly as she could.

"Oh, that's OK," said Alice, "they took an earlier bus, they're already at Modlin."

Ali wondered how she knew. However, when Kevin did his usual head-count he made no comment about the missing two, so presumably she was right.

It was a sad drive to Modlin. Their bus faltered down small, dusty roads without much traffic and through worn-down villages, whose houses though small and poorly built appeared to be making a valiant attempt to show, with plastic garnish in the gardens, that despite the brick work showing through the paint they were well up to historic Polish standards.

"At night," said Grzegorz, leaning through the gap in the seats between Ali and Alice, "many of these houses become bars, some during the day too and shops.

Income. Sometimes extra, sometimes all." But when Alice tried to ask him about the local nobility in a pre-communist past he laughed in amazement, as though such a time had never existed.

The few cars that were on the road drove as though they owned it, passing fast and often continuing some miles on the wrong side of the road. Several times the helicopter pilots's coach overtook thick-set horses dragging carts so loaded with potatoes that they seemed on the verge of toppling over. Sometimes there was a small boy or straw-hatted old man seated on top of the capriciously capacious mound. Every now and then they came across a pile of potatoes which must have dropped off one of the carts.

"Is much poverty in Poland," said Grzegorz. "Now may be better. Maybe no. Many Western countries want to come here. Many Westerners want to buy land, but government say no, yes, maybe. Land must have Polish owner, at least part. You understand?"

"I understand," said Ali, wondering about the affects of nationalism. Would America have grown as it did if all owners of land, at least in part, had had to be original natives? Or Australia? Would it be better or worse? If Poland joined the European Union would that affect its land policy?

The sun...disastrous twilight sheds, on half the nations and with fear of change perplexes monarchs.

She wondered what Joe thought about it, but decided against asking him: South Africans were bound to have an odd slant on nationality.

When they got to Modlin Ali noticed the Enstrom was no longer sitting next to their R22 on the tarmac.

"Where's the Enstrom?" Ali asked, almost to herself.

"In the far hangar," said Alice. "They had a blocked manifold pressure cable and went ahead to find an engineer to help them get the right tools."

"How do you know?"

"I heard Grzegorz and Sergei talking about it," Alice shrugged slightly. "I'm going to do the check-out, so go and look for them if you want. It's over there," she waved a hand vaguely.

Ali gave Alice the GPS to return to its clip and walked over to the hangar. But the metal sliding walls were shut and when she tried to open the little inset metal door it was locked. As she pushed it, hoping it might just be stuck and suddenly swing open, one of the big metal panels slid back and Joe's head popped out of the slit on an extended neck like a disembodied tortoise.

He looked so funny she started to laugh. Joe smiled at her and started to say something when Mike's head appeared too, below his pilot, his red face shining with whiskery delight.

"Hello! Looking for us? We're done. A combination of Joe and the local guys sorted it out. Travel with your own engineer and you can't go wrong."

He and Joe disappeared and then a crunching noise signified they had begun heaving at the heavy metal doors, whose runners appeared to have long ago been crusted up with dirt and rust.

"Give us a hand babe, will you," said Mike winking and laughing heartily. "Polish doors take more than two! Not enough polish."

Ali added her weight to their pushing and the door jolted unwillingly towards the side with the terrible graunching sound of rusty iron on antique runners, occasionally leaping forward and then stopping dead like a startled horse.

Sergei, their Russian guide, had parked his Mil Mi-2 on the apron the night before and had stayed at the hotel, but as he had spent the evening with Grzergorz no one had realised Sergei was to be their Russian mentor for the following few days. Now he clapped his hands, "to make myself obvious to all" and beckoned to the groups. "I calling a tarmac conference, to explain everybody what happening in next few days."

Everyone, apart from Sandra, who was frenetically cleaning her husband's helicopter, lounged over to listen.

"For today trip," he said, "you keep loose formation, stay behind Mi-2 lead. If anyone look too far behind, they are to shout loud and I wait for him..."

Alice started to giggle, while Daniel frowned at her.

"Very important is to stay together..."

Ali, losing interest in the rules of their flight, looked at the Mil and thought it reminded her of a big, floppy dog, always willing to please. A sort of cross between a Labrador and a St Bernard. It was hard to believe this was the smallest helicopter they had in Russia and that this twin was their basic trainer. The contrast with the R22 could hardly have been greater. Russian size, American delicacy, she mused. Which will win the Games?

"Do not land without authority," the guide said, glancing at Jaap, who smiled blandly. "Have taken many delegations to Moscow. Is better on airfield. Is safer."

"Very suspicious Russians," said Jaap to Ali, as they moved away to get the helicopters ready. "Peculiar is their way of not telling things. I had a Russian girl-friend, we lived together for three years and she never told me she had a daughter. Then one day this eighteen-year-old girl walks up on the stoop. My girl's daughter. And her mother had never mentioned her, not once! Secretive. Secretive as a communist. Slimy as an eel in a bowl of snot."

≈≈≈≈≈≈

Arboreal Cut

From Modlin it was only a short hop to the border and on into Byelorussia. If Poland had been poor agricultural land interspersed with trees, Byelorussia was trees, trees and nothing but trees. They swarmed under the helicopters like an unending bed of broccoli, on and on into infinity. Ali couldn't help feeling even Dante on his way to Hell might have thought there were too many trees here.

In the middle of the journey of our life I came to myself within a dark wood, where the straight way was lost.

Ali thought that if she leant out and rubbed her hands along the trees, many of which were pine, they would prick her hand like projections from the stuff-filled cushions her grandmother had used for hat pins.

Every now and then there was an occasional tarmac avenue amongst the vegetation. Seldom were there any vehicles on the road, not even a horse-drawn cart, but occasionally one lone car would appear from the far distance, meandering slowly along like a leaf on a stagnant river. Ali wondered where they were going, those who could not see the wood, or anything else, for the trees. One of Jake's poets had said a man who loves his race plants trees: those Russian ancestors (or were they Lithuanian when these forests were planted) must have truly loved their fellows. Or not.

More prosaically, one of the Gazelles swooped down to try and race a Trabbie, which rambled innocently down the road completely unaware it was about to be pounced upon from above like the Assyrians on the fold. When he saw the diving Gazelle the driver stopped immediately, jumped out, and starting waving madly at the pilot like one of those French prison escapees. He appeared to be inviting the Gazelle to land. Suspicious, Paul pulled up and hovered over-head, uncertain whether he was in for problems. Before he could decide how genuine this gift of friendship might be a Skoda came the opposite way, the man hoped back into his Trabbie and drove off. The Gazelle returned to the group, to await another adventure, and Sergei in the Mil, now catching up with the Gazelle, testily warned the group to stay together.

After more and more miles of sylvan pastures they finally came on to Brest, which they approached in formation, dropping off one by one to land, Sergei having finally caught up with the turbines and the French having condescended to fly beside the ignorant British language-grabbers for a short while.

Brest's vastly long concrete runway yelled to the interlopers of the military might for which it had been built. Close to the Polish border and at one time actually in Poland, it seemed that ghosts of MiGs, Tupolevs and even Concordski roamed here.

"All part of the Stalin-Hitler pact," murmured Alice, but Ali just had to believe her, knowing more of Second World War poetry than history.

Here the fuellers and fuel arrived in an enormous camouflaged Mil Mi-17 helicopter, capable of carrying 60,000 lbs. The back of the Mil opened like an oyster, its shell-like doors exposing huge round drums of aviation fuel from which they, like their Modlin brothers, filled buckets and jerrycans via a rubber hose and a foot pump. Filled jerrycans rolled out on wheeled wooden trolleys, long metal cross bar handles imitating the Robinson T-bar cyclic. Two men dragged the carts over the uneven ground to each helicopter, fuel slopping out of the buckets but tightly screwed into the cans. When Ali, thinking aloud, wondered why they used buckets, which were clearly unsuitable for this job, Joe supplied the answer.

"They haven't got enough jerrycans. It's that or scoop the fuel up in your hands. But doesn't it make your heart glad to see the proletariat at work, not loafing around like they do 'in West'!"

"Oh," she said, "yes, ha ha."

She felt obscurely guilty for not having realised they might be short of cans, and irritated with Joe for pointing out something that was so obvious. He really was a very tiresome man. She comforted herself with the thought he was clearly classist as well as racist, even if he was surprisingly well read.

The stepladder performance of Modlin was repeated here but this time Ali did not offer to help, nor did Sandra come and watch but again began neurotically washing her husband's helicopter. Two men filled cans by the Mil, while two other men trudged around to the helicopters in the field.

"From star-like eyes," Joe said to Ali, his half-smiling eyes caressing her, "he doth seek fuel to maintain his fires'. Would that make it high octane, do you think?"

"Depends on whose eyes," she replied snappily, adding reluctantly, "but it would make it cheaper!"

Joe sighed. "Yes, were it not for, 'As old Time makes these decay, so his flames must waste away.'"

"Not much use for helicopter travel then," she replied, but unwillingly found her lips smiling. She bit them crossly.

Joe was about to say more but Mike called him back to the Enstrom where a pair of uniformed men were checking and stamping the passports. When they arrived at the R22 and found Ali was alone with two passports they started sniffing like dogs on a scent.

"You are Ali Gee?"

"Yes."

"This is your passport?"

"Yes."

"Are you Alice Charleston?"

"Of course not, I'm Ali Gee."

"Ah! Then where is Alice Charleston, who does not carry her Identify Card."

Ali stared at them amazed. "I don't know! Maybe she's over there with Daniel or one of the pilots."

"Who is this Daniel?"

"One of the pilots."

"Ah! You said Daniel or one of the pilots. Therefore he could not be one of the pilots."

"What! I meant..."

"I'm Alice Charleston," said Alice, coming up with Jaap on her arm.

The men looked at her passport picture critically. One said, "You must carry Identify Card, all times." The other asked, "Are you bringing anything in to Byelorussia?" He opened the nearest door and peered around the Robinson. They lifted the seats, prodded the GPS and even pulled a fuel drain out of the luggage space. "Any money? Or jewellery?" Having examined the drain they gave it back to Ali.

Alice laughingly offered her plastic beads. Disappointed the customs men moved away.

Jaap chuckled. "Nutters these Byelorussians. More dumb than a Belgian with an Irish mother."

Once the helicopters were fuelled the pilots were transported over to the hotel in cars, three or four at a time. Ali and Alice squeezed into the back of a Lada with Steve, while Sandra sat in front next to the driver.

"So," said Sandra leaning back over her seat, which tottered slightly at the change of weight, "you girls are entering the Ladies' contest?"

"We're going to win it," said Alice.

Sandra smiled, perfect teeth bared like a dog. "Good. I'll cheer for you."

They arrived at the best hotel in town, its ugly concrete blocks reminiscent of the Tower of Babel and belying the idea that communists were not attempting to reach for Heaven. Kevin was in the lobby, his gills extended with seething anxiety. As Steve and the others eased their way out of the old Russian Lada he dived down the steep concrete steps yelling excitedly. "Has anyone seen Pete or Daniel?"

"No," said Steve, shaking his head, "I think they were still at the airfield when we left. They may have been waiting for the fueller. Here comes Mike, ask him. He left the airfield after us, but we took a more scenic route." He smiled at his wife, who had asked for the detour as she wanted to see some important political statue that was hidden in a wooded glen.

Mike waddled over, his face as usual lit up with happy glee.

"What's up chaps? I say Kevin you look down. Anything the matter?"

"Kevin hasn't seen Pete and Daniel and he wondered if they'd got left behind," Steve explained.

"Owe you money do they?" Mike guffawed. "But don't worry. They haven't left. There was a problem starting one of the cars so Joe's driven back one of the 'Fridges' to get them."

Kevin's gills shuddered. "What? That's all we need! Some bloody Kaas Kop getting stopped in the middle of Byelorussia driving without a licence. Shit! What happened to all the drivers?"

"I think Joe offered," said Mike, his round face as smilingly happy as ever. "The driver wanted to go home. They don't get paid much you know. Joe's a good navigator, and he drove lorries in the South African Air Force, so one little Fridgette ain't going to give him much trouble!"

"I just wish everyone would be more sensible, that's all," said Kevin storming off like a fish tossed in high seas, "and let me, as Group Leader, know what was happening."

"Well!" said Mike, "who rattled his cage? Anyone for a beer?"

The teams had dinner at Brest in the restaurant, a school mess hall adjoining the hotel. A large room, it had no shades for the lights which stood out from the ceiling on long white flexes like an army of downward pointing thumbs, their austerity softened by a long pink fishing net draped in elegantly unequal swathes from points along the wall. Each table had eight chairs, some were broken but rather than spoil the symmetry of the room they had been left, collapsing and propped up against the table. Diners would come in, pull out a chair, sit on it and immediately fall over. At first this gave the teams much hilarity, until they grew so bored of this game that even the military boys began to warn the prospective chair puller.

Ali and Alice sat at a table with Daniel, Pete, Gary, Joe and Mike. The peeling formica was covered with a thin plastic tablecloth with a blue and white check pattern. Daniel put down his transparent plastic glass and began to tell jokes.

"What's the difference between Prince Charles, an ape's mother and a bald man?"

"Old one!" said Alice wrinkling her nose. "One's the heir apparent, one a hairy parent and one has no hair apparent."

"Well! I've not heard that before," said Mike laughing affably. "Very clever, very clever."

After a dinner of soup, indeterminate meat, cabbage and potatoes, Pete decided to teach them what he called a vodka drinking game.

"A very simple game," he explained, "but you'd be surprised how many people get it wrong."

He picked up a plate and smeared the edges with salt, then poured a deep trough of vodka into the middle.

"Now," he said, "you must drink all the vodka without wetting your lips."

He demonstrated, telling the audience in an indisputable manner, "See! My lips are still dry. Now Alice you try."

Alice began to sip.

"No, no, right down, no cheating if you please! You realise if you swig vodka it doesn't make you drunk, while if you sip it, it cripples you. That's what all the Russians do."

Alice, caught up in the excitement, downed the contents of the plate. Whereupon Pete filled it and passed it to Daniel, who did the same, while his father shook his head at his wet lips amidst much laughter. And then on to Ali who, already understanding the game, stuck her chin on the side of the plate and tipped the liquid onto the table.

"Dry lips," she said.

"Huh," said Pete, "you cheated, we'll come back to you."

Ali was relieved.

When it came to Joe he lifted the plate and cried, "Your health, Master Bunyan, but do not get drunk, or you may not distinguish your limbs from your trunk," letting the contents of the plate dribble down his shirt like sweat. Pete either didn't noticed or made no complaint and just kept filling and pouring.

Every time Alice or Daniel drank the plate Pete would say, "No, no, wet lips, start again!"

Alice grabbed a second plate and plastered a rather swervy salt line along the ridge. "Sh-OK Daniel, I shallenge you to a race."

Daniel picked up his plate. "Pah, tshoo to your one!" he slurred, grabbing the vodka bottle and downing two in succession.

"Shey, I didn't hay go," yelled Alice, jumping from her chair and onto the table, where she did a handstand that almost compromised the lurching table. "Copy that twice if you can."

Mike giggled and Gary yelled lustily. "Hey! Look! A natural redhead."

Daniel pushed his chair back muttering. "I've got to go and see a friend." He got up. Staggered back a few paces. Steadied himself and walked through the long red plastic curtains that covered the exit into the kitchen. For a moment the table froze, staring amazed at this swift disemboguement. Then, behind the curtain, clunk was followed by crash. Daniel's hand appeared underneath the gap; a delicate, almost girlish hand lying beneath the rough plastic skirt, disembodied like a picked flower. Alice flew off the table singing a Russian folksong, and nearly prostrating herself on the next table where Sandra, Steve and Kevin sat watching with evident disdain. Mike dropped his head in his vodka-washed plate. The other four looked stunned for a moment, then, while Joe saw to Mike and Gary to Alice, Ali and Pete got up to look behind the curtain.

Neither Pete nor Ali were drunk, although Pete had played his game as deeply as any, and between them they easily lifted Daniel's light body up and carried him across the restaurant and back into the hotel, to the elderly iron-door lift. Scrunching back the gate Pete put Daniel gently on the floor, propping him up where the lino seemed least worn. Gary, seeing there was no room for Alice, who was still on her feet but staggering on his supporting arm, said he would bring her up shortly.

Once on the fifteenth floor Pete and Ali lifted Daniel again and, with Pete holding his shoulders and Ali his feet, carried him to the room he shared with Gary. As his bottom sagged between them like an aged mattress he groaned and tried to lift it.

"Sshsh, Daniel, be quiet," said Ali, her voice as kindly as a well-paid nurse, "you're OK, keep still."

His eyes flickered but he didn't struggle any more.

Pete propped him up against the wall while Ali opened the door; there were no keys in this hotel. They laid Daniel gently down on the narrow hospital-type bed where he lay prone between the stark metal uprights. After a while he groaned again and clawing the thin sheet heaved himself into a sitting position. He got out of bed and staggering, weaving and bumping into the wall, slid along it to make his way to the adjoining bathroom, where he collapsed onto the raised platform that gave the loo a dominant position. Ali noticed his razor sitting on the edge of the bath, hunched like some blue and white superman on the edge of a life-saving leap. Next to her the boy threw up into the yellowing bowl, his hand gripping tightly to the plastic rim as though he might fall into the abyss. Unfortunately the water in the hotel was turned off at ten o'clock and now it was ten thirty.

Pete pulled ineffectually on the clanking chain, watching his son silently as the ball-cock bounced noisily in the empty chamber.

As idle as a painted ship, Upon a painted ocean. Water, water everywhere, Nor any drop to drink.

Ali felt deeply sorry for Daniel. He reminded her of Jake when he'd been on a binge, she remembered how lovely Jake had been when he was ill; gentle as a baby. Their relationship had momentarily become one of mother and child; certainly something his analyst must have thought appalling.

Leaving the heaving Daniel in his father's charge, Ali walked down the corridor until she found the floor attendant. She was asleep, her head planted on her arms, her scarf cutting out the cruel electric light. When finally aroused she pointed desultorily at a back room, where her supervisor was also asleep, and let her head drop back into position. Ali knocked on his door and, when he finally groggily opened it (shoes off, shirt open to the waist) she asked for the water to be turned back on.

He shrugged, partially closing his eyes. "No English."

"Water. I need water. Sick man."

Shrugging again. "Nyet. Nyet. Off."

When she insisted with eloquent speech, he simply shrugged for the third time, and firmly closed the door.

Stupefied for a moment, the resourceful Ali recalled seeing Steve and Sandra drinking bottled water at one of the fuelling stops. Hoping they were still awake and still liquid she knocked tentatively on their bedroom door. When Sandra opened it, half dressed, her face lighting-up with curiosity, Ali explained Daniel's problem and begged for the only remaining water in the hotel. Sandra laughed. "We have a little nurse here," she called to Steve, who emerged naked apart from the briefest g-string, "who needs water".

With great amusement Steve and Sandra gave her two bottles from their well-provisioned suitcase. "We'd heard about the tap water," they explained, making bilious faces.

"Oh," said Ali, who'd been drinking it without thinking. "Oh, yes." She wondered how the Byelorrussians managed without bottled water.

By the time she got back to Daniel's room news of his condition had reached the whole group and the teams were all trying to crowd into the room; happily watching Daniel be sick and adding helpful comments which would usually have been restricted to engine performance.

"Amazing," said Kevin, happy for the first time on the trip, "how much comes out of such a small body."

"Pretty good power to weight ratio, I'd say," added Charles humorously. While the military boys, pointing out he ran on low on fuel but was high on alcohol, joked about alternative fuel sources.

"Get rid of them," Daniel pleaded from his collapsed position, relieved she was back. "I can't stand them, the oafs!"

Ali wondered where Pete had gone. Then remembered the pallor of his face as he impotently pulled the chain: he had held himself together longer but now he too was in silent suppuration on his own small bed. She turned on the gawking crowd.

"OK, people," she said firmly, "that's enough. Daniel needs his space now, go and find another peep-show."

Shuffling them out, she firmly closed the door and pushed a chair against it.

"Thank you, thank you," said Daniel, drinking his water and being sick again. "You're an angel, marry me please."

As the bowl began to overflow the brim with bile and stained white paper Daniel stopped puking and Ali persuaded him to get onto all fours and drag himself back to bed. Having negotiated that mountain, he lay still and shut his eyes, opening them periodically to thank her again with tears.

"Kiss me," he said, "kiss me. No one will ever kiss me again, I'm so disgusting."

Kindly she bathed his head with a small amount of the bottled water on a handkerchief, soothing away the vomit-encrusted hair.

"Oh," he said with a shudder, "I'm revolting, disgusting. No one will ever love me. Would you marry me if we could rush off tomorrow and just do it? Let's do it."

Even while she murmured "tomorrow" appeasingly, she thought about it on a deeper level. Would she? Marry in haste, repent in leisure. Who had said that? But it might be nice to be married. To avoid all those difficult decisions one had to make as a single person. To abdicate ones authority for a while. Come on, pointed out her deeper mind, not with Daniel! There you wouldn't be leaving your decisions to him, you'd be taking over responsibility for his actions!

Instinctively Daniel realised he was losing her attention. "Lie down with me," he begged, holding her hand like a child, "kiss me."

And Ali did. He kissed her and she kissed him back, feeling the softness of his lips and the sensitivity of his mouth. She stroke his face; he was a very attractive man.

"You must be special," he murmured, his senses highly aware of the smell of vomit even in the cold furniture-free room. "I think you are special."

They kissed again and Ali felt confused. She told herself kissing him was no more sensual than kissing a dog. That there was no chemistry, no physical attraction. She supposed what happened was that the dislike she'd always felt for him, the contempt, had now changed into something maternal enough to allow her to nurse him, so this was just a sort of motherly relief.

"We'll get married tomorrow," said Daniel, drunkenly comfortable.

But Ali merely felt confused and when Gary put his head nervously around the door, pleading to be allowed to go to bed, she left without compunction and some relief.

"Sleep well boys," she said, giving Gary the remains of the water.

The girls' room was just opposite and when she opened the door Ali found Alice in tears. Sobbing with the heavy, body-shaking cries of a child. Ali put an arm around her shoulder. "It's OK. It's just the vodka. You'll feel better..."

"It isn't OK!" replied Alice furiously. "You don't understand. Nothing good ever happens to me. No body loves me. My father didn't care, even my mother didn't really love me..."

"She does, you should see the love in her eyes."

Alice looked up drunkenly. "Who? Oh yes, her. You don't and you can't understand."

She wrested herself away from Ali and began weeping dejectedly, big wet pillow-sopping tears. Ali felt powerless to help her. She never cried herself. She was a person who withdrew when the pain became hardest, empathising with herself from a distance, her quotes ensuring her survival; how then could she comfort another closely? She had no idea what would soothe and what would irritate. Gingerly she rubbed Alice's shoulders and rearranged the girl's beads, which had slipped sideways and were hanging down to the floor, noticing how heavy they were for plastic.

After a while Alice began to snore, granulated noises like a drill graunching through heavy concrete. Ali moved away to her own little narrow, single bed and began to read a poem by Philip Larkin:

For nations vague as weed, for nomads among stones, small-statured, cross-faced tribes and cobble-close families... life is slow dying.

≈ ≈ ≈ ≈ ≈

Great Diamond Race

Galina, Rosanna and the boy ate and ate until they couldn't fit anymore in, and even then there was still plenty to put away in the fridge for the next day. Rosanna asked no questions. Later, though, Galina knew the girl's mother would come snooping, but until then she could relax. She poured her friend some more champagne and gave the boy some coca-cola. Galina was so excited by the first party she had ever given that she even told Rosanna a joke from her childhood.

"The Interior Minister telephones Walter Ulbricht," she said. "He says: 'Thieves have broken into the Ministry this evening.' 'Have they stolen something? asks Ulbricht' 'Alas, yes," replies the Interior Minister, 'all the results of the next elections."

Galina roared with laughed and the boy echoed her, but smiling Rosanna looked a little puzzled even though she giggled obediently. Eventually she asked. "Who was Ulbricht?"

"President of the GDR for years and years, but of course you are too young, he died in the seventies and was replaced by Honecker," said Galina, remembering that most girls did not concentrate in school these days, and that her neighbour's daughters were particularly unintellectual.

"Oh," said Rosanna brightly and for a moment Galina wondered if she even knew who Honecker was, but apparently she did as she suddenly murmured. "Oh, yes, mother said you came from Germany."

Galina laughed inwardly. What a woman her neighbour was. She wondered what piece of information she had left lying around that had led to that conclusion. It was true that her father had been in Germany in the late seventies and into the eighties, but after the disaster and his wife's death the family had all been beetled quickly back to Moscow and had never been allowed to leave again. She had certainly not 'come from Germany' as in being German, but she wasn't going to give the nosy snooper any more information.

Instead she walked out onto the balcony, and after glancing at her fourteenth floor view of the opposing block of flats smiled and went back into the room. She asked Rosanna if she'd like another cake and turned on the television. Later, when the girl went back to her flat, she would finish her latest translation.

≈≈≈≈≈≈

Rough Diamond

Next morning Alice was too limp to fly and she sat lethargically in the helicopter, half asleep, leaning against the door all the way to Baranevitchi. When they landed she refused to leave the helicopter and revived only briefly when Daniel, who, having more practice, held his hangover better, tried to persuade a military pilot to swap a ride in the R22 for a ride in a Mig, calling loudly for Sergei to translate.

The pilot of the Mig refused, although he would have liked a flight in the Robinson, and listened curiously while Daniel explained how the T-bar worked. All the pilots, however, agreed to a group photograph, which Sandra took, the Europeans ranged alongside the Russians looking scruffy and social beside the mighty Russian military in poorly-cut matching suits with tatty metal medals. When the Russians wanted to swap their medals for something foreign, Steve, who must have thought of this before leaving England, suddenly produced boxes and boxes of cigarettes, pens, and button badges. Ali wondered if he would offer them some water. Remind them of the toxic nature of what they daily drank.

Sergei, standing beside Ali and like her watching the scene from a slight distance, murmured, "So we play. Russian and English. My children say I scenic."

Ali looked curiously at the pilot, in spite of regulation black boots which made his feet huge, he was attractive with solid Turkish looks and a moustache that would have graced a World War One aviator, but she doubted he meant that.

"Scenic?" she queried.

With a large gesture he indicated the group, the collapsed white and brown control tower, which must once have been smart and shining with new paint but now appeared to droop with lack of care, looking more like an abandoned pig shed than the home of modern warfare equipment, and the helicopters.

"Before we had some problems, things much better now but still problems remain. So I scenic. My children think all is best now."

Ali, thinking only of the building, remarked prosaically they needed a carpenter but Joe who had come up behind her quipped, "When the forts of folly fall, find thy body by the wall. Or was that more suitable for last night?"

She looked at him, detecting amusement in his face. How large and reliable he was in this world of Alice's volatility, Daniel's ebullience, Pete's games and scenic Russians. But Daniel was far better looking.

"Can you imagine it?" said the pilot. "When I tell my children I flew with woman pilots, they will really scenic then."

"Yar," said Joe, "in South Africa we only let them women sit in the back. That's when we let them out of the kitchen at all."

"Very funny," Ali sneered. "Every prospect pleases, and only man is vile!"

As they left for Minsk the British pilots' helicopters each flew past a Mig and a Scud missile, mounted on large plinths and apparently just on the point of leaping into action like the Concorde in Heathrow. Here the missiles dominated 'finals' in both directions. Were they there to prevent anyone who shouldn't landing by mistake? Or were they a bigger deterrent? A proof that the mighty

Soviet Union had not gone quite yet?

Baranevitchi was in an enclave, hidden in the midst of low green mountains. As soon as they left the airfield it disappeared, swallowed like something in a science fiction movie, and when they looked back they could see no sign of it. They were once again surrounded by trees, trees and more trees. Funny, Ali thought, she had never thought of Russia as the haven of trees it was. She equated Russia with snow, not leaves.

The field of bubbling green broccoli had become darker green with distinct humps, more like green-painted stucco. Ali wondered how long it would take a lone pilot flying here to be discovered if he had an engine failure. Weeks? Months? Years? Forever? Were there wrecks of old Mils still lying down there, hidden in the undergrowth? For that matter were there villages down there under the foliage, lone livers or even families, unaware that the regime of the Tsars had ended and there had been a couple of generations of communism, now also ended? Unaware they were now free. Free to do what, she thought, wondering if their lives had changed at all, or even a little.

Of course, she thought, looking at the somnolent Alice, were any of their group to have an engine failure they'd be picked up in a moment. Carried away in the accompanying Mil, lest they bred too many wicked ideas in the minds of the under-canopy men.

Alice snored quietly beside her, her head lolling against the doorframe, her belt tightening as she rolled with the movement of the helicopter. The narrowness of the cockpit kept her upright in a way her relaxed muscles were unable to do. Her beads had escaped the confines of her T-shirt and shuddered with her breathing and the vibration of the helicopter, so they seemed more alive than their owner.

As Minsk airfield approached Ali lowered the collective to reduce power and the helicopter nosed left, surprised that she should have been so clumsy she eased in more right pedal: nothing happened. She pushed harder on the right pedal. Again nothing happened. Instead her foot met resistance. Her heart leapt disproportionately and she kicked at the right pedal, her mind trying to convince her it was just imagination: nothing wrong, really.

The helicopter continued to yaw left. Ali pulled up on the collective and the nose obediently yawed right. Thank God! It wasn't an engine failure, but looked like a tail rotor problem. She pulled the collective up and down a couple of times. The tail wagged like a friendly dog. Shit! Tail rotor. Or, at best a pedal problem. At least she could still fly, only landing was going to be a problem.

Forcing herself to keep flying calmly, she looked around her. They were one of the last, most of the others had already landed or were currently on finals. Even Jaap, who as usual was at the back, and Sandra and Steve, who'd been taking pictures of his Robinson, had now moved ahead. At least then the way ahead would be clear. For some unknown reason she didn't want to call a 'Mayday'.

Her mind now thinking clearly she saw she had two choices: she could cut the power and go for a full blown autorotation on to the airfield or she could try for a run-on landing balanced on the narrow undercarriage. However, she was aware that if the helicopter's skids caught on something as she was landing fast the light machine could easily turn over. On the other hand if she got the autorotation wrong, there too she could end up in a heap of parts; smashed on the Byelorussian ground and going nowhere. And, more importantly in some ways, not entering the championships.

She decided to keep the power, do a 'run-on' and trust to the strength of Mr Robinson's skids and her own ability to hold it straight with cyclic, the only remaining directional control, throttle and lever. Subliminally she noted all the others were down now and the landing area was clear.

Her mouth dry but her mind focused, she made her approach. Slowed her speed as much as she dared and approached the landing point her nose yawing left, looking as though she was hoping, for some eccentric reason, to set-down sideways. She expected the swivel to move to the other side as she brought power in and to get more extreme when she encountered the friction on landing. She hoped to brace the swing with cyclic and, playing with collective and throttle power, keep it straight. She'd done it in practice with students enough times to be perfect. Only, the real thing was often somewhat different. More serious. No room for error. She had to hope her instincts were finely honed by years of practising with students.

Gently she made her approach, keeping the helicopter at a steady thirty-five knots, straight as she could. Closer and closer the ground came up towards her. Larger and larger seemed the blades of billowing grass. As gently as she could she set the front of the skids down. It skidded left, giving off a cloud of dry dust. She pulled in collective. It straightened. Then started to go right! Gently but firmly she reduced throttle and slightly lowered the lever. It straightened and shuddered, for a moment she felt it tipping and turning right and thought it might go over. She reduced the throttle more, and held left cyclic. It fell back. Gradually, slowed by the friction of those same billowing blades of grass, the helicopter came to a trembling halt. Ali gave a gust of relief. She put the collective all the way down. Mechanically she shut down the engine, realising she was trembling, and, once the rotor brake was on, collapsed her head onto her knees and part of the cyclic overhang. Her knees began to shake, her feet knocking against the pedals.

"Thank God!" she breathed. "Thanks, God!"

"Did something happen?" asked Alice, suddenly opening her eyes.

"No, nothing really," said Ali, sitting up and forcing a smile to her dry lips, "just a pedal got a bit stuck. It's OK now."

Alice looked sharply at her, but didn't say anything. If Ali hadn't been so obsessed by the landing she would have noticed an odd look passing across the girl's face.

Ali undid her straps, thinking silently within herself. To Alice she said, "I'm just going to check the pedals, make sure they are free. Do you want to go and find Daniel and tell him what happened?"

"Sure," replied Alice smoothly. "What did happen?"

"Nothing really. It's OK."

"OK," Alice averred, "so I'll just tell him a pedal got stuck but it's OK?"

"Please."

Alice walked off, still somewhat delicately, to find Daniel. Ali walked around the machine feeling her whole body twitching with malarial shivering. Ridiculous, she told herself, ridiculous. Keep calm. It's over now. She examined the tail rotor hoping no one had noticed anything odd. She walked back to the front of the helicopter and leant in to the Robinson's cockpit, pushing Alice's pedals, where the main obstruction seemed to be. She tried pulling up the carpet and getting under the mats.

"Can I help?" asked a soft South African voice behind her. "As one who's seen the odd tail rotor incident before I might be able to shed some light."

She lifted up her head and looked up, shading her eyes against the light, noticing the greenness of Joe's eyes. With post-incident clarity she noticed there were striations in his irises and that he had a strange, almost tight way of looking at her. She wondered foolishly if Arnold had anything for this moment.

"Thanks." She spoke harshly, trying to be blasé. "Did you see it happen then? I didn't think anyone had noticed." She found herself gesturing ineffectually.

He gave her a quizzical look and his voice softened further. "You did a good job! Impressive. You should be wanting everyone to see you!"

Ali shrugged, feeling closer to tears than she had done for years. Stupidly she wished he would put his arms around her, cuddle her. She turned into the machine, muttering. "I'm sure something must have got in behind the pedals but I can't see anything. I've checked the tail rotor and that seems OK. We're not missing any pens or anything."

Joe went around to the other door, flipped on his flashlight and leaning forward examined Ali's pedals. The light flickered up and down under the matting giving it eerie pink spots in the greyness. Finding nothing on that side he walked around the front and slipped in beside Ali, examining Alice's pedals. As his large body slid against hers Ali felt a tingling sensation shoot through her veins. Her heart lurched. His back muscles touched her arm and then her side, she felt paralysed. As unable to move as if she had taken hemlock. Her chest tightened. Her breath hurt. She suddenly wanted to press against him, to put her arms around his large body and hold him to her. To rub her cheek against his huge one. To take his strength and make it hers.

But often in the world's most crowded streets, but often, in the din of strife, there rises an unspeakable desire, after the knowledge of our buried life.

"Ah ha."

Joe's huge hand disappeared down the dainty void under the pedals and came up loaded. "Look at this!"

He opened his hand and in it was a bulldog clip. "This was attached down the line of the tail rotor cable. As you moved the pedals it was working its way closer and closer into the pedals, then, when it got up almost to the pedal, it stuck, restricting movement. You were lucky it didn't happen earlier." He almost made a comforting movement, but restrained himself remembering what a big bear he was. "I wonder? Does Alice usually fly?"

"Yes, only she didn't this time because she had such a hangover after last night. So I did all the flying."

"Umm."

"Umm? Are you thinking that if she'd been flying it would have moved up more quickly into the restricting area, but because I was flying her controls were moving less. Possibly if she had been flying the pedal would have stuck somewhere on route. Perhaps somewhere over those trees? Or worse, maybe the cable would have snapped. Or she might have thought it was an engine failure and panicked. Put it down. Smashed it. Or not." She heard the pressure ripping through her voice like a spring violently unwinding.

Joe turned, and in the restricted space his face almost touched hers. She could feel his breath on her mouth. His body shadowed her own but he apparently feared only for her humanity.

"It's only a theory," he breathed gently, "and it didn't happen."

"No, no, of course not," she snapped. Then, pulling herself away and back together, "how do you think a bulldog clip got down there? And when?"

He moved gently out of the machine, careful not to touch her. "Your guess is as good as mine," he said, looking down at the offending clip. "But it looks like the sort of thing you buy in the UK, these ex-Soviet countries are pretty short of these kind of luxuries."

"Do you think it was an accident?" she asked. "Left in there when the machine was last worked on at High Wycombe?"

"Don't you? Engineers can make mistakes." He half-smiled.

"Yes, yes, of course. I'd better go and find Alice, tell her it's OK."

She turned away abruptly and he watched her walk towards the lines of derelict Mils parked on the grass. Rows and rows of perfectly lined-up Mil Mi-2s and Mi-8s sat gleaming and rust-gathering in the sunshine. Their quartered windscreens looking like faces lost in a crowd. He watched her until she went out of sight, and even then he watched the space through which she had disappeared. Had she known what he was thinking, she would have been even more unhappy. He was thinking that this was a classic trick to cause a tail rotor problem, and that he certainly wouldn't be the only person on the trip to know it. Something so easy to explain away as an engineering mistake, something so easily lost in the ensuing crash. He was pretty certain someone had put that clip on in Brest. Was there, he wondered, some one who would gain by keeping the girls out of the Championships? Someone who, as Jaap would say, had butter on their head and was testing the strength of the sun?

Ali found Alice with Gary and Daniel, playing on the swings in the playground behind the Mils.

"Look at this," said Alice, as excited as a child, her hangover forgotten. "A playground for the party members, for the student pilots!" She swung higher and higher on the swings. Ali watched her, thinking she'd been much closer to death than a mere swing. Did she intuit it?

"There's a school here, we found it in the back. Classrooms and everything." Alice swung up again. "And have you seen that wheel for practising aerobatics!" She pointed at an enlarged hamster wheel, rusting, with broken straps but still standing as a memorial to Russian negative-g training.

"Did you find the problem?" asked Gary. "Alice said your pedals got stuck."

"Lucky it didn't happen in the air!" said Daniel, vying for height with Alice so the aged swing supports shivered and strained against their bolts. "Or you'd have to practice some of your teaching skills for real."

Ali frowned. "Yes. I found it."

"What was it? A pen that slipped."

"Yes," said Ali, wondering why she was lying, "yes. My pen had slipped off my pad. Stupid really. Could have been a disaster."

She wondered for a moment if Joe would say anything, then knew instinctively he wouldn't. Wouldn't because he knew it was not an accident. She felt cold, and even Alice looked up. Then she swung harder and laughed louder. "Wicked! Wicked!"

They fuelled up the helicopters in the usual hand-pump manner and Ali wished they were staying at Minsk. However, after Byelorussian tea and cakes brought out by friendly local girls who were only unwilling to feed Jaap, whom they mistook for a German, they got ready to move on to Vitebsk.

Daniel came up as the girls were getting into the helicopter.

"Watch what you do with your pens now girls," he joked winking at Ali. "Take care and don't give me another scare."

Waving his fingers, he went to join Gary, who had already started the Robinson.

Alice had recovered from her hangover now, but not enough to fly, and Ali was glad to continue on the controls, just in case a second bulldog clip had been placed as a back-up.

"Pity we're leaving so fast," Alice said. "There's a lot of history in Minsk, but I don't suppose Kevin cares too much about the past, does he? If anything," she added darkly, "I expect he'd rather forget it."

Ali nodded, but she wasn't in the mood for a history lesson. Inspite of the beautiful dappling sunshine, the elegant airfield, the lovely, listing light and the normality of the afternoon, she couldn't avoid the thought someone had tried to kill her. Or Alice. Or both of them. One the indispensable handmaiden of the other. And, of course, no one would want to kill her, so it had to be Alice. She looked briefly at the girl, who had shut her eyes. Why? Who would want to kill a nineteen year old, untried, untested girl. Why? Revenge for a deal done by her stepfather? Had she injured a fellow deb? Stolen her man? Or could there be something in the girl's past that was coming back to haunt them both?

Ali took off, her mind chewing over the possibilities endlessly like a piece of wheat stuck on the Russian's negative-G wheel. Either the bulldog clip could have been on the helicopter since the last bit of engineering was done, or someone could have put it on in Brest or even before. Who? And why? The truth was anyone could have done it, there was so much time spent faffing about, so much time when the helicopters were left unattended. And everybody knew enough about helicopters to do it, except perhaps Sandra, but even Deidre and Graham were both pilots, both would know about cables and tail rotors. Even Kevin, and he certainly wouldn't mind if they were out of it, still he probably wouldn't want any scandal, and he would definitely blame Pete. She tried to forget that three people had had the best opportunity to do it: Pete, Daniel and Joe. All three had been at the airfield when the rest of them were back at the hotel. But it could not have been any of them, could it? They were pals. Her pals.

Marquise Ridge

When the helicopters arrived at Vitebsk the fuelling Mil-17 was already there and its buckets and jerrycans were out, placed in rows on a small cart. The fuellers were already holding the T-bar, standing like horses in their straps, ready to charge into battle. The only thing missing had been the helicopters and now they too had arrived. The teams lined up on the grass, their tails pointing towards a large hedge. Joe and Mike parked the Enstrom next to the girls.

Dropping their luggage on the ground, Joe sat down on the grass by the helicopters while Mike went to see how long before the fuel cart rolled over their way. Alice flopped down exhausted beside Joe and with a groan fell asleep in the sunshine. Jaap walked over and looked down at her.

"Look at that a floppy doll," he said, "no stamina or as we'd say in Holland a 'flop drol', a 'flip turd' for the pan."

They were so used to Jaap no one bothered to ask him if a 'flip turd' meant what they thought it did.

Joe turned to Ali. "No more surprises?" He asked quietly, his green eyes holding a mesmerising tinge.

"No, everything was fine," she said, her stomach flipping, her heart lost in shades of green. Torn between wondering what he was thinking about, and wondering if green was a Russian colour, certainly not South African, that should be yellow.

"Good." He continued to look at her but didn't speak and she gradually became embarrassed and dragged her eyes away from his face. Bubbling in her chest was the desire to ask him what Pete and Daniel were doing when he returned to the airfield at Brest to pick them up. But, although her voice almost came to the surface, she knew to ask such a thing gave implications to the words that her mind could not credit. She felt the lonely depression that comes from confusion with the present and its consequent loss of control of the future. She wanted to curl up in a ball.

"Sikorsky," said Joe, smiling at her, "before he became involved with helicopter invention, used to design planes. One of these crashed because a mosquito flew into the engine and blocked the fuel intake. Can you imagine what he did as a result?"

"Designed a filter to protect the engine?" Ali suggested, drawn away from her brooding. "That's what I would have done."

"No, he started to design multi-engine planes because he felt there was an inherent danger of singles! That is the Russian mind. Bigger and better."

In spite of herself Ali laughed, and he laughed with her, a full happy sound full of genuine mirth, his gentle eyes watching her sleepily. He couldn't be a murderer, she thought with relief, a man who thought and laughed like that could not contemplate murder, could he. And she laughed again.

Pete and Daniel wandered over, plonking down on the grass beside Alice, apparently unaware she was asleep. Daniel still looked grey and a little dishevelled.

"We came here in '78," said Pete smiling, "for the third World Championships. Daniel was only a child but they let him hold my buckets."

"I was seventeen," Daniel pointed out. "That's the youngest age you can fly, and I won an award for the highest placed youngster."

"And it's been downhill ever since?" asked Ali.

Daniel stuck his tongue out at her. Roguishly.

"In those days," said Pete, "it was still a Communist country and it wasn't as easy to fly out as it is now. We didn't just have to have a guide, we had to have a navigator in each helicopter. The Germans didn't want that so they put their helicopters in a transport plane and had them brought over. And of course there was no South African team then."

"Or Americans I suppose?" asked Joe.

"Oh, yes they were here... battling away with the Russians, competitive that lot. Not like us, that's why we never win: we just like to have fun."

Alice muttered, "I thought that was girls," from her prone state, but Pete ignored her.

"Who won?" asked Ali.

"The Russians, they nearly always do. They practise a lot."

"I think," said Daniel, "there should be games which require skill only, which you can't practise for, then only the talented ones would win."

"Like you I suppose," muttered Alice sarcastically. "Oblomovist!"

"Impossible," said Pete, "impossible. I have a theory, which no one likes, that there should be no laws at all. No regulations and that everyone could behave just as they liked. Then you'd see about natural order, natural goodness emerging. The basic humanity of people would out."

"You think people are so nice they'd immediately start helping their neighbours, their brethren?" asked Joe. "Servare modum, finemque tenere, natu-ramque sequi."

"Did Arnold teach Latin?" asked Ali intrigued, while Pete ignored any interruption. Joe though turned a little her way and smiled.

"Yes, I believe so," Pete answered Joe. "I think regulations stifle people and turn them bad. True freedom, true democracy is no regulations at all."

"Are you going to tell us what it means?" Ali asked Joe.

"Believing in ourselves and following nature, more-or-less," said Joe, while Alice muttered from her prone position, "tell him he's a fucking show-off."

"People don't like it when they realise how deeply I'm going," Pete continued, "I mean no laws at all! None."

"Sound like chaos to me," said Joe. "What would you do when two people wanted to own the same piece of land."

"Ah! There you see! You can't even think in the right terms. There would be no ownership of land."

"Like in Communist Russia," pointed out Ali.

"And look what happened here," said Joe. "Communes were forced to give up their grain by Stalin because they wouldn't do it freely! They were certainly not the success Lenin envisaged. Why should anyone grow crops, work at all unless either they see benefit in it for themselves or you force them to, which means rules...?"

"The trouble is," continued Pete, disregarding their caveats, "that so many people with vision are nutters, not leaders, they go off half-cock like the Unibomber. Now he had good ideas but we couldn't follow him, so then we are destined to follow half-men, shallowtons with no vision. Better then to have no rules and no leaders."

"Why should anyone do anything?" asked Joe again.

"For the common good, which is their own good... but I agree it is a difficult concept to make popular."

"All this," said Ali, as the fuel men finally reached the Robinson, "from not allowing the Russians to practise their slalom!"

The local guides were waiting, in aged German buses parked at the edge of the tarmac, to take them to their special tourist hotel. After a short drive on winding roads, now beneath the green broccoli canopy, they arrived at a chunk of concrete which towered above them in angled, dirty masonry. A myriad of black-eyed windows gave it the appearance of an angry, dirty giant, glowering down on a minuscule unimportant populace. Ali thought even the council behind the building of Peckham's estates would have been ashamed of this: the best hotel in Vitebsk.

"This is new," said Pete. "Wasn't even built when we were here in '78. Must be luxury."

"That's sixteen years ago," Alice pointed out, but he didn't reply. "Sixteen years ago," she repeated to herself, staring at the building. She turned to Ali.

"Did you bring the GPS in for charging?"

"Shit! No, I forgot. Sorry, I had a lot on my mind!"

A flash of anger passed through Alice's eyes but she just raised her eyebrows. "Too bad," she said stiffly, walking away.

The hotel lobby had a large money-changing outfit, like a mad cowboy-western vision of a post-office. One side was filled with wooden bars stretching out of a concrete base and reaching to the ceiling, these had metal bars across them as a grill and a little upside-down U-shaped speaking hole, which bisected the counter. Behind this ugly barricade sat bored tellers with heaps and heaps of pretty well worthless Byelorussian notes, stacked in bundles of a million, and an abacus. To change money you had to queue, in a line designated by less permanent looking wooden bars, with your foreign currency and passport. You exchanged the foreign currency for a paper ticket, while verifying who you were with the passport. You then took your passport and the ticket through another queue to the moneychanger, where you gave in your ticket and got your money, again using your passport to verify your person.

"It's just like trying to buy a book at Foyles," Ali said to Alice, listening to the musical clack of the abacus. "And about the same amount of language difficulties."

Alice laughed, "that's not entirely true, they're a bit more friendly here!"

"Nyet!" snapped the teller to someone ahead of them who was trying to show two passports, changing money for a friend. Both girls laughed. "Well, maybe not. At least in Foyles you can buy a book for a friend."

Unlike in Brest, where they had been able to pay for dinner on the hotel bill, here the two had to be separate, paid in advance and in cash. All payments were made on the way into the dinning room and in exchange the pilots each received another little blue cloakroom ticket.

"Probably because having got a money-laundering place they want to use it," said Charles grinning widely. Being an accountant he found these things hilarious. "And, of course," he added chuckling, "they want to clean out your dollars."

Dinner was in a large echoing hall with a high, wooden-beamed ceiling. The chamber was attached to the hotel in such a way you had to walk through the money-changing area to get to it, much to Charles's delight. Perhaps to disguise the lofty height of the ceiling, the room had been draped with the national flags of all the teams. French, German, Russian, Byelorussia, American, South African, British and Swiss flags were all suspended above them forming a canopy. Underneath the flags were plastic flowers in baskets, wrapped around with fairy lights, some working, others just green filamented glass. Below that the bare wooden tables sat like a barren Alaskan shoreline under a distant sky.

"Where did they get those flowers and baskets?" Ali wondered.

"Made 'em, of course," said Alice. "What you think? They flew across to Alaska."

That there was nowhere else to go in the town was clear, since all the members of all the national teams were gathered in the dinning hall, mostly sitting on parochial tables chatting in a number of crossing languages. Ali noticed the new

South African national flag on the table next to theirs.

"Look, we've been joined by some newcomers," she said.

Alice nodded. "Oh, yes. Because it was too far for them to bring their own machines they came here about a fortnight ago. They've been learning to fly the Mils somewhere down south and now they too are on their way to Toshino. Rumour is the Russians haven't shown them how to start the engine, so they have to have an engineer with them all the time. No chance of them winning then." She smirked.

Ali looked surprised. "How do you know?" And then, seeing Joe also on the South African table, "did Joe tell you that?"

"Joe? Oh, yes," said Alice. "Water?" She poured the two pink plastic beakers full of tap water. "Do you think it's safe to drink it?"

"Which is worse? This or vodka?" snapped Ali, unhappy that Joe had been sharing secrets with Alice and not with her. She sat in sullen silence.

"Hello, girls, can I join you," asked Mike, standing at the edge of their table, his red face gleaming. "My pilot's gone native, so I'm on my tod. Personally I think he's after their team mascot, have you seen her? All blond hair and long legs."

The girls looked over reflexively, and then grinned. The mascot, sitting on the table wearing nothing but the flag, was a fluffy lion. Mike winked waggishly at them. "That Joe," he said, "you can see he's a ladies' man."

"How's your Russian?" Alice interrupted. "Someone told me you know a word or two?"

Delighted to be able to show off Mike began with: "ПπßO (PEE-vah), that's beer you know..."

"Are you sure? Sounds a bit Greek to me."

Mike looked a little put-out and poured her some beer, but any further practising was interrupted by the arrival of a thin girl with a tray covered with plates of sour-smelling meat, which she placed on the table, picking up their paper tickets in exchange.

"cIIacдo" chortled Mike happily, while the girl looked at him darkly and withdrew.

"Was that thank you?" asked Ali, while Alice inspected her plate. "The way she looked at you, you may have propositioned her."

Mike thought that very funny and chuckled happily, while looking around for his friends.

Once they had eaten there was nothing else to do, and the girls sat dawdling on the table, wondering what to do next.

"We could go and refold the maps," said Alice, fiddling with her beads, "or try and guess where they'll send us on the navigation leg."

"What do you think locals do in the evening?" Ali asked.

"Sleep probably," said Mike, beginning to doze in his seat.

"Or make babies," said Jaap, who had been at the South African table, and now came to join them. "Ah, eventually I return to you beautiful ladies. I like to practise my Dutch, one tends to forget it, given the chance. I have a friend in New Zealand, who emigrated after the war, now he cannot speak any more Dutch and has to talk to me in English. Odd, hoor. Now Ali Gee, from London, where the taxis creep by the bus-stops teasing the 'punters' as you call them, I have a tale to tell."

Both girls looked hopeful.

"You know," he said, "already the Mafia are strong here. There is a man who works for Coca-Cola and is posted to St Petersburg. He soon discovers the taxi drivers won't take him to the door of certain, foreigner-patronised, restaurants. This is on account of the Mafiosa tax. They drop him a little way away and the cost is half. Once they believe in equality, now they eat from the other wall. Capitalism or communism always we have tax!"

Alice frowned. "The Americans too have their Mafia," she said fretfully. "Why is everyone so anti-Russian. We haven't even got there!"

"We're not..." began Mike, jerked from sleep by such injustice.

"Ah, yes, Miss Alice," replied Jaap, raising his voice to drown out Mike, "but how many Irishmen emigrated to Russia?"

Alice paused and Ali, smilingly mystified, offered him some compromising beer.

"Yes, willingly. You like my story? I was told it by a man on the Afrikaners' table, I am showing off with other peacock's feathers. And what a peacock. You know his name is Slaghek, to us it is gate, hit-gate, but to you... a whore hé! Doesn't that make you laugh? Worse than being Ali Gee's namesake, hoor."

He laughed, Ali poured him half a glass of beer from a pitcher, while Alice, looking offended on behalf of her friend tried to speak again, but Jaap was unstoppable, raising his voice another decibel he said, "Ah, you are from Den Haag, meisje?! Such pouring."

"What do you mean?"

"Half glasses, we call that Hague measures. With half a glass I forget the story now, something to do with the stork. I'll tell you later when I remember it, do you mind if it is midnight, hé?"

"Yes," said Ali. "I do."

"Ah, well. Half glass, half hope, hé."

≈≈≈≈≈≈

Oblomovshina

Next morning the teams assembled for breakfast, hopefully looking around for someone to feed them. The dining room, as Jaap remarked, was as empty as a parish church on a weekday morning. No tables were laid and there was an absence of the usual breakfast smells. The South Africans, who were up and lively in spite of heavy beer drinking the night before, starting singing Sarie Marais in loud voices, emphasising the verse, 'breng me truk naar the aulde Transvaal'; presumably implying breakfast could always be found in the Transvaal.

Eventually a squat woman in grey dress, carrying a grey mop and grey metal squeezer bucket appeared. She ignored the group, put down the bucket with a clank and began dipping her mop in the grey water, sliding it lethargically across the equally grey linoleum. However, when the South Africans upped the volume she waved her fist at them, cursing in Russian.

"зáBTPaK," said Mike who had added a few more Russian words including what he thought was 'breakfast' to his vocabulary, thanks to the elegance of Irina the translator.

"Nyet!" said the old woman stodgily, waving her fist and pointing to the ceiling.

"Le petit déjeuner est sur le plafond?" demanded one of the Frenchmen, to general amusement.

The old woman shrugged, pointed at the ceiling again and kicked the bucket along, muttering to herself in Russian.

Eventually, one of the receptionists, alarmed by all the noise, came out of her office. Mike saw her first and pleased by the success of his Russian, rushed up to her crying "зáBTPaK, зáBTPaK!"

She shook a tired head. "No dining now," she said. "Make own breakfast in kitchen. Is kettle for purpose. Upstairs."

Collective examination showed the teams that on each floor there was a little kitchenette, with room for two people in it at one time. Ali nobly said she would make breakfast for her floor: Alice, Pete and Daniel, Steve and Sandra, Gary and Jaap. As she went to fill up the kettle Pete, who had squeezed into the kitchenette with the girls, put his hand on her arm.

"Right to the top now, Ali dear," he said, "don't be mean. Women always half fill a kettle, a very bad habit. They don't seem to know how to fill it to the brim."

Ali and Alice glanced at each other, raising eyebrows.

"Hague measures you think?" asked Alice.

"Clever!" Ali picked up the tea-pot, noting the lip had been crudely mended and there were brown spots down the spout and around the base like dribbles off an old man's willie. She put it under the tap, washing it before she filled it.

While Pete's attention was drawn away by Alice asking a precision-flying question, Daniel said quietly to Ali. "Mother was brought up in the Sudan and they had to save water, so father tends to generalise a little from her. Don't take it personally."

Glancing around, to make sure no one was looking, he kissed her neck.

Ali, obediently filling the kettle to the brim, again felt that strange bond between Pete and Daniel, that desire to protect each other from the outside world. Something so alien to her that they might as well have been from Mars. Would, she suddenly wondered, such closeness go even to the depth of murder. She was shocked by her momentary thought and forced herself to wonder instead would she have found such a bond had her real father not been killed in a train crash. Her eye fell on Sandra, standing alone as usual, and wondered what her parents thought of her marriage to a man so much her senior.

Seduced by the wooden bars of the Foyle's money changing area, Ali now had millions of Byelorussian dollars (about £20) lying around and didn't know what to do with them. With inflation running at 180% she knew they'd be worth nothing by the time they returned and she wanted to give them to their guide Irina as a tip but the girl was nowhere in sight.

On the airfield everybody was getting ready to go, then Ali saw Charles still waiting for his helicopter to be fuelled, she walked towards him.

"Hello Ali," he smiled, "Jaap has just told me that to get a haircut like mine I must have fallen off the stairs! What a character 'eh?" He laughed awkwardly, passing his hand over the offending inches.

"Have you seen Irina?" Ali asked. "I...er...I want to give her the remains of my money." Ali's face turned modestly puce at her own magnanimity.

"Good idea," he said, still palpating his pate, "we've all done the same. Apparently she gets more this way than in her proper job as a teacher, even plus her husband's job as a policeman. The economy is really shot here. I think you'll find her in the tower."

He smiled to himself, watching Ali walk away. In the back of his mind he knew he shouldn't let Kevin behave badly towards the girls. He knew Kevin was over-inclined to controlling behaviour and he flattered himself that he had more influence over him than most. But then did it really matter, in the long run; afterall people would be and do what ever and which ever they would, regardless of him and his better thoughts. The only really significant thing in life was money. Did inter-personal relations really make any difference at all, he wondered, watching the large red-headed girl dispose her tall body over the cracked concrete. He stroked his pate again and returned his mind to worrying about the quality of Byelorussian fuel.

As Ali strode towards the vast dilapidated tower, with its heavily chained entrances, she saw Irina come out of an open door and start walking her way. She waved and the girl stopped suddenly, the large bag she carried at her side bouncing against her hip in protest.

"Hello, Ali, you all ready to leave now?"

"I am. I just wanted to come and say goodbye and thank you and give you this."

Ali handed her a sheaf of notes, which Irina put spontaneously in her bag without looking at them.

"Thank you, you are very kind, you and your friend. I hope you will have a good trip through Russia."

"Thank you, but I'm not kind, I think I am you in another world, if you know what I mean. There are not so many differences in our lives."

Irina smiled politely, without speaking and Ali wondered if she had understood. "I wish I spoke Russian," she murmured, "I would love to be able..."

Irina inclined her head. "Your friend speaks Russian very well. I was surprised, it is unusual in Westerner to speak Russian, especially so good."

"Alice?"

"Yes, young Alice. She is good girl."

They were interrupted by Mike, who had also changed too much money and was keen to practise his five latest Russian words with Irina.

Ali turned and walked abruptly back to join Alice in the Robinson. As soon as she climbed in, before even doing her straps, she said accusingly. "Irina says you speak good Russian, I didn't know. You didn't tell me."

Alice looked at her blandly, as though wondering if it was her business.

"You didn't ask me! Yes, I learnt it at school. It was nice of her to say it is good, it is actually rather rusty. I didn't have many natives to practise it on."

She began her checks and started up the helicopter and Ali said no more. For some reason she felt as let down as a student pilot told of bad weather on the day of his qualifying test.

This time the take-off was more of a formation, as though the teams were now vying for the position of best discipline. However, it was not long before they were once again strung out over the forested countryside. The weather was sultry and oppressive, the cloud base not more than 1,800 feet, which forced all the pilots to fly at much the same level. Even the Gazelle boys were not in the mood for frivolous frolicking and only complained a couple of times about being kept down to the flying speed of the pistons.

≈ ≈ ≈ ≈ ≈

Fire Crystals

They landed at Smolensk, where their passports were stamped for entry while they had lunch. Ali noticed how dry it was now, how the dust seemed to sit in the air and coated everything with a fine, dry film as though they were living in the desert. Sitting on the airfield she saw dust devils in the baking heat whipping up the sand like ice cream cones. Unusually, Alice ate little and slipped away quickly, saying nothing to anyone. Ali found her in the helicopter, a map in her hand, programming the GPS.

"What's up? Afraid we won't find Toshino?"

"Ali!" She spoke abruptly. "I need your help. You will help me won't you?"

"What do you mean?"

Alice put her finger on a part of the map. "You see this dacha, here in the woods."

Ali looked at the map. There was a tiny village marked on the American satellite maps. If there was one dacha or many there it would be impossible to say, but Ali was prepared to believe Alice, whom she was discovering knew far more about Russia than she let on. "I see a village, what of it?"

"It's only about twenty miles off our path, actually a bit less guessing that the guide will want to avoid the area around Katya and will make a deviation to the right, that puts us ten or tops fifteen miles off course."

"Umm?" said Ali, not wanting to admit she had never heard the word 'Katya' before.

"Well I just want to fly over it, see it from the air. You don't mind, do you? We won't get lost, I've programmed it into the GPS." She smiled, seductively charming.

"That GPS isn't plugged in, remember. It can fail at any time. And I forgot to charge it last night."

"I know, but we haven't used it much so it should last two hours, that should be enough for us to find the dacha and return to our guide without anyone the wiser. Besides, Pete said you were one of the best navigators he knew! Instinctive he called you."

"Kind of him," said Ali, as dry as the dust-laden air, "but even I find it confusing above miles and miles of trees. I don't know, Alice! Why do you want to go there so much?"

Alice sighed sentimentally. "It was the home of one of my ancestors. I have Russian roots, did I mention it?"

"No."

"Oh, well I have, anyway, so my mother says. I imagine we were the whitest of Russians and escaped in the most dramatic manner, with lots of torment, probably taking the train to Vladivostok, coming up through Shanghai and battling through the rest of China, into Indonesia and walking and walking for days on end. But anyway, that is where the family came from, and I just must see it since I'm so close. I have this sort of longing to see my roots... a strangely filial pull... I'm sure you understand."

The sincerity on her face was harrowing and Ali was moved. She hadn't realised Alice was so romantic. And part of her did understand. She had, after all, once gone to visit the site where her father was killed, and another time to the place where she met Jake. Pure sentimentalism. Hard to know what pulled you out of the rational into the mode of visiting, but she too had travelled miles out of her way to pander to her emotional imagination.

"All right. But if the GPS goes down we go straight off back to the guide, OK?"

"You're a star! Thank you so much." Alice was laughing again.

They took off as a group, but Ali and Alice were soon hanging back behind the rest of the group. Usually Daniel would have noticed and have been up their tail-rotor, asking what they were up to, wondering where they were, but today he was absorbed in the nearness of their destination, and his chance of winning a gold medal in the individual competition, and left the girls alone.

As Alice had suspected the guide diverted around Katya, a controversial area for Russians where 22,000 Polish officers had been killed during the years of the Stalin Hitler pact, and at that point the girls deviated off course a little towards the village on the map and Alice's family dacha. The moving-map showed the course and Alice, partly following it, partly looking at the map, flew as straight as a hungry homing pigeon.

"There it is," she cried her voice high with excitement, "that's the village. Now wait. Our house is on the east road out of the village, about two miles."

Ali wondered how she could be so sure, but said nothing. Flying at 500 feet, they followed the small winding road, whose only traffic was one small boy and a dog. After two miles they saw a small round building, half hidden in the trees. Ali almost laughed. It was like a most magnificent summerhouse with Russia-citadel style, coming up from a round base, through an onion, into a peak with a bottle-opener on top.

"Is this what we are looking for? It is pretty but..." She stopped herself from saying it was hardly worth the stress of the trip, but that was what she thought.

"No," Alice replied, "that is the dower house or the summer house. Ours is further on, by the river."

About a mile away Ali saw a wide river with open banks and not far from it, set back in the trees, was an enormous, rambling pile of stones, which from this angle could either have been ruins or a house. As they got closer Ali had the impression of turrets poking out of the trees, and smooth round shapes in white, forced uneasily onto the edges of straight brick, interspersed with green branches. She was reminded of something she had read about Peter the Great's followers who, having returned to Russia after their trans-European trip, built their houses in a myriad of differing styles: this looked like they had put them all in one building. She wondered if the trees had grown since Alice's ancestors left it, or had been there to protected it from visitors at that time. Probably there was no one to visit, here in the bundus, miles from anywhere.

"Humm!" Ali mused, "you can hardly believe communist Russia could still have such places. How many families live here now do you think?"

Alice said nothing, concentrating on the house and her flying. She started to descend towards the flat bank of the river.

"Alice!" shrieked Ali, "what are you doing? We can't land! The guide will kill us."

"The guide won't know. It's just for a second. You stay in the helicopter, keep it running and if anything happens pull up and high-tail it: literally," she giggled, "out of here as fast as you can."

"What?! I can't..."

"It's nothing. I just must see it at ground level. I'm sorry. I can't help it. I can't resist it."

Ali groaned. The girl was mad. "This is Russia, Alice," she emphasised, "not Britain. They kill you for less. They cut off your head here for being a lousy sportsman, think what they'll do to two idiot English girls."

Alice laughed excitedly. "Don't you believe it! Communist countries have no power; ex-communist even less. Trust me, we'll be fine. Even if we have to buy our way out."

She landed gently on the mud near a long sandy path, and murmuring, "you have control," jumped out of the helicopter and ran up the path, disappearing into the woods. Ali saw glimpses of her Gloria Vanderbilt jeans flashing though the trees as she approached the house, and then she was gone, hidden behind a turret, which seemed to mock Ali like a wagging finger.

In the middle of the journey of our life I came to myself within a dark wood, where the straight way was lost.

"You shouldn't have let her go," said the turret. "How will you explain this to Pete, let alone her parents! You may have had trouble getting a job before but after this...wow...talk about not safe in taxis! Not safe in helicopters. Not a suitable guide for a young headstrong girl. Tut, tut," said the turret, and stared at the sky.

Ali stared at the gap of her absence. This was madness. How long should she wait? She couldn't fly off without her. How could she? How would she explain it to...Pete...to...to anyone. First I had a student, then I had none. She'd have to wait, but how long? Should she shutdown and go and look for her? The GPS might fail and, even if she could manage the navigation, the fuel wouldn't last for ever. She stared through the trees to the garden, realising with a shock the lawn had been recently mown. Even inside the helicopter Ali could smell the sweet scent of cut grass. That incredibly evocative smell, the reminder of British summer, croquet and pimms on the lawn. Ali struggled with a sudden sense of longing. If she, the girl from Peckham, felt like this, what must Alice feel? Then another, less romantic, thought; cut grass means someone cut it, someone lives here. Did they hear us land? And if they did what will they do? Catch Alice? Where was she? She checked the helicopter clock. Alice had been away seven minutes, it felt like seven years, but even seven minutes was a long time in failing GPS terms. Where was the girl? How long did she need to search for that ancestral feeling?

At that moment the GPS turned black. Ali stared at it. Struck it, hoping it was a momentary aberration. A loose connection. But it stayed black. That was it, then. It was all up to her. Stuck without navigation aids amidst the trees, in an alien land. They would never escape now. They'd be thrown into a Russian gaol. Tortured. God knows what. Her emotion welled up. And suddenly she laughed. How dramatic was this? What was she doing to herself? She put the friction on the collective and picked up the map. She knew vaguely where they were. She searched for the river amongst the heavy green of the chart. Found the small town. Then found the road out of it, and where it met the river. She was pretty certain she knew where the house was, at least certain enough to be able to fly to Toshino. Finding their guide and the group might be more problematic, but given their speed compared to that of the slower Enstrom and Schweizer the chances were they would all arrive at Toshino together. At least they would if Alice came back soon.

Where was she? The clock said fifteen minutes.

Just as Ali's worry-gauge had turned purple Alice came back from the far side of the opposite turret. She ran towards the helicopter, holding her beads in her hand and jumped in. Slamming the door so it bounced and she had to lean out and re-shut it properly.

"OK," she said, "you fly. We can go now." And burst into tears.

Ali, relieved they were both in one helicopter, lifted quickly, followed the river back to the summer house and once again above the trees set heading in the direction of Toshino the old-fashioned way: using the compass and map. Once they were on course she thought about Alice, still snivelling beside her.

"Alice? What's up?"

"Nothing," said Alice, "it was beautiful, lovely. I just feel so sad. I miss it so. And there was no one there."

"Did you think there would be? Do people still live there?"

"Yes, I think so. It looked inhabited. There was furniture inside and although the shutters were up the gardens were maintained and the woodwork painted. I expect someone loves the place."

Tears poured down her cheeks and she turned away and lent her forehead on the door. Ali flew on, amazed Alice was so sentimental about a place owned by her ancestors.

As though reading her thoughts Alice said defensively, facing the fragile, composite door. "You don't understand. I am Russian, we feel things more deeply than you... than... than Westerners."

"You're not German?"

Alice snorted. "My grandfather was German, but I am Russian." She spoke proudly and Ali thought for a moment she sounded Russian but didn't ask her any more questions. Was Alice now telling the truth, or was this another version? Did that mean her father and mother were Russian? Ali remembered her mother had looked English, aristocratic and most unlike anything she knew as Russian, but as this trip was constantly proving she was a provincial with little international insight.

They caught up with the group stragglers not far from Toshino. As they had expected Jaap was one of the hindmost. When he saw them he waved happily and vaguely.

"I wonder what he's been doing to be so far back," said Alice, who had stopped crying and was watching the approaching tails. "What do you think? Another pee? A bit of sightseeing? Or was he just hanging around picking his nose!"

She laughed and Ali felt relieved. Perhaps this was just the mercurial nature of a young, indulged girl.

They overtook Jaap and were soon onto the French, and then the Enstrom. Joe saw them and smiled through the perspex. Mike nodded his happy head. The girls were pleased with the speed of the Robinson.

"This is a good machine, Alice," Ali murmured. "You should buy it, I think it's the best Robinson I've ever flown, certainly one of the quickest."

Alice made a face and said nothing. Leaving Ali to remember that Joe said with helicopters like guns you never really knew them until you'd worked them. What was the R22? Not a Kalashnikov, more like a Bereta 92 in air gun form.

More and more trees. Spiky and individual members of one group. More rows of hairbrush bristles under her hand.

As they approached Toshino Ali saw it was inside Greater Moscow, deeper into the city than Northholt or Brooklands in London. You could see the city behind shimmering in the summer heat, the buildings giving an uneven outline. The field was flanked by rows of high-rises of differing heights, and as they approached the airfield Ali saw a large, diamond-shaped expanse of twinkling blue and white. At first this looked like a lake, then it revealed itself as a bulbous manifestation on the Moscow River. Behind the faux-lake were what looked like two great brick pillars attached to nothing but simply marking the entrance to the airfield. Diverging behind the pillars was a light green meadow protected on one side by a flea market, fenced off from the road. As the pilots approached their vision was filled by long square blocks of concrete with glass windows, lines of white and grey stripes. As they flew onto finals the stripes turned into lowering eyebrows over slit eyes and finally revealed themselves as tight balconies which almost met the sheltering overhang from above. These buildings, surrounding three sides of the airfield, might have seem fascinating on the architect's drawing board but here in the Moscow oasis they looked like rows of cheap false teeth, made only for the purpose of ruining a fairy princess's mouth. It was odd, Ali thought, that an airfield which was itself set in such a beautiful site, surrounded by a river with a large diamond shaped lake in the marshy trees on the fourth side, with an approach through the forest, should have been made so ugly by human endeavour.

They flew over the watery bulge. Glancing down she saw the Robinson belly swimming underwater amongst drifting white clouds, there was barely a ripple in the still water and Ali felt more excited than she had for a long time. She knew they wouldn't win the championship or even place, but wasn't it marvellous to be here. She, Ali nobody from nowhere! She glanced at Alice, but she was staring stright ahead, frowning, living in another, tougher world.

Towards the centre of the Toshino field the teams landed one after another in the shadowy sun.

Come in under the shadow of this red rock and I will show you... fear in a handful of dust.

Ali watched their grey image as it bumped alongside the taxying helicopter, reaching the taxiway and their parking space first then, as she did a turn on the spot, getting left behind and dropping back to sit like a black cat on the tail boom. The fuel lorry drove over immediately and Ali noticed that he had a mechanical pump.

"Wow!" She said, "did you see that Alice! Mechanism has come to Russia."

Alice laughed in an absorbed way and went off to ask Pete about numbers and, as she murmured, "things for the competition".

All around the airfield were defunct Mils and Kamovs, sitting unused and presumably rotting inside, rotors drooping towards the ground. Some wore thick white canvas covers, others stood naked in the evening sun. Ali wandered up to the nearest Kamov, wondering if she would ever get a chance to fly such an incredible looking beast. She stared up at its double rotors and thought it looked like some kind of fantasy Christmas tree design.

Joe slipped round from the other side of the Kamov. "Crazy aren't they," he said. "Appealing, like a strange ugly dog which pulls at your heart-strings."

Her own strings fluttered a little too, but she sublimated them with cold speech. She put her hand steadyingly on the canopy.

"Umm. I've always wondered what it would be like to fly something without a tail rotor, with two whirling rotors above. What do your feet do?"

"They still give yaw control, but in a different way, through the rudder, like a fixed wing." He motioned at the back of the helicopter, where huge panels dominated the aircraft. "Looks like a couple of trawler gubbins doesn't it. They're very stable, I'm told. I've never flown one either. Apparently they were made like this for the navy, so they didn't bump into things on deck with the tail rotor."

"Is that right? I didn't know. I just thought it was another design."

"Kamov out of Gogol's Overcoat you think?" Joe said, grinning.

For a moment she didn't understand him, then she saw his happy face. "Is that some rather stretched reference to something someone said about Dostoevsky?"

"Spot on! 'We have all come out of Gogol's Overcoat', the most frequent Dostoevsky quote and not even necessarily by him. Shall we steal one and fly out of the armpit?"

Laughing she tried the nearest door, it was locked. Disappointed she turned around, and found Joe had been standing so close behind her she was almost within the circle of his huge arms.

"Oh."

He smiled at her. A full smile. They stood silent for a moment, she could feel her blood rushing around her body and hear her heart pumping for Britain. Then he leant forward and gently took the lapels of her shirt in his hands straightening them like a mother preparing her child for school. Ali's stomach contorted.

A gentle knight was prickling on the plain.

"Miss Gee bicycled down to evening service, with her clothes buttoned up to her neck," Joe said his voice deep, pressing her collar lightly on her neck like a caress. "Oh heck! Like waves around a Cornish wreck!"

Ali grimaced. "I may not have lived with Ali Gee all my life but W.H. Auden I have. If you knew how often boys like to say 'Back-pedal brake babe', or 'Miss Gee knelt down in the side-aisle, she knelt down on the knees; lead me not into temptation, but make me a good girl please'."

He laughed. "I'm cut in half!" he said but his eyes looked like a Labrador dog awaiting a chocolate. Ali thought he was going to kiss her. She shut her eyes. Then they heard Alice's voice calling, exasperatedly.

"Ali, Ali! Oh, there you are. The bureaucrats are here wanting to stamp your passport, you were supposed to stay by the helicopter until they arrived!"

"Yes, sorry," said Ali shaking herself free, although Joe had anyway dropped back as soon as he heard Alice's voice. She followed Alice back to the helicopter. Behind her she heard Joe murmur: "She could feel his hot breath behind her, he was going to overtake, and the bicycle went slower and slower, because of that back-pedal brake."

Excentric Excelsior

While they were waiting for transport to their hotel two members of the South African team came up to introduce themselves to the girls.

"We saw you last night," said a large, blond South African, approaching Alice in a half-tentative, half-brash manner. "Jaap told us you were a lekker wife!"

"Oh, no!" The other smaller man broke in, "No! No! How cruel! A mooi meisje; a beautiful girl."

"What is a lekker wife?" asked Alice uncomfortably, not in the mood for this, "I thought 'lekker' meant tasty?"

"Who told you that?" asked Dennie, the big blond South African. "You know some Afrikaans?"

"Dutch, don't you mean?"

"Ach well, it's not the same, we are the modern face of language. But, I'll tell you, my friend Lauren here," he gestured towards the small dark man, "thinks you are 'meer mooi dan lekker' and he is the Italian Stallion, so you'd better watch out for him."

"Huh," said Alice, reviving with their scintillating humour, "to me he looks more like a macaroni pony and a Lilliput at that!"

"Lekker stuk indeed," said Lauren admiringly, while Dennie creased up with laughter.

Unimpressed, Alice decided to make use of the South Africans to fill her in about other teams. "Tell me, who are those tall blond women standing by a JetRanger?"

Dennie followed her perlustration. "Oh, those. They are the American ladies team, Catherine and Julie. Your boys Rob and Paul have nicknamed them the Whirly Bitches? British men are so unkind!"

"Oh yeah," said Paul, walking up with Rob, "but our women love it! We don't have to go catching the kaffir serving maid. How's your chilapalapa talk?"

Dennie offered him a playful fist, Ali looked towards the girls. Two blond women were standing by a Robinson, one a fiftyish blond Californian with that Barbie doll perfection (slim hips, full rose lips, button nose) that made her seem like a breakable twenty-five. The other looked slightly younger and shorter but similarly perfect.

"They obviously don't come from the Mid-West," said Paul, "at their size they'd have been eaten as part of the average breakfast."

"Bet you can't sleep with either of them," said Paul. "Bet you a bottle of pop, you don't even get past first base."

Rob measured the Americans up in a long glance. "Make it a case! I'll take on Barbie if you take on one of the Russian babes."

"Cora or Clarice?" breathed Paul in shock, while Rob almost crippled up with laughter. "That's not fair, I don't speak Russian. I say you take Cora and I'll have the Whirly Witch."

"Her name is Catherine," said Alice, her voice strident with irritation: unlike Ali, who found it amusing, she hated this kind of thing. "You are children," she added, "and stupid."

The boys moued at each other. "OK, Alice," said Paul, "you're right, witch was unfair, she's more like Irma."

Alice hadn't heard of Gormenghast and didn't know what they were talking about, but knew she didn't like it. She stormed off to talk to the German ladies team, Ali followed her more moderately.

The German pilot was a short, plump woman with cropped purple hair and several nose and ear piercings. When she laughed, which she did when Alice introduced herself revealing a mouth of perfect teeth, it came out with a whoosh like the firing-up of central heating. Her co-pilot and navigator, Dagma, was black. Alice, who had never seen a black, woman pilot before, was curious.

"How did you get to be a pilot? You're a novelty to me."

Dagma took it well. In American-accented English she explained that her parents had escaped from the war in Ethiopia to Germany when she was a baby. Her father had worked as a public relations officer in an engineering firm, and when she showed an interest in flying he encouraged her to become a helicopter pilot, seeing the PR value that would accrue. "He was right," she said indulgently, "Germany had seen nothing like it! I'm a bit of a sensation. A *Berühmtheit*. What you'd call a celebrity."

"Poor you," said Alice.

Ali smiled silently. Dagma was as tall as she was, but slimmer. Whereas Ali looked like a battering ram, capable of knocking down walls with a strong arm, and Alice like a still growing boy, Dagma looked like an elegant tree sprite, a wood nymph or a supermodel. She wondered if Dagma would be such a celebrity if 'the first black woman pilot in Germany' was five foot two and looked like an elf.

An elderly Lada, with one of the back doors tied with string, lumbered up and stopped near the foreign helicopters.

"Blimey," said Ali watching it slide to a halt on the dry frictionless grass, "it's like being back in Peckham. Except without the diamonds."

Alice looked at her curiously and then, when Ali explained, extremely amused.

The driver got out, said he could take four and asked who wanted to go first.

"I'll go," said Alice, adding warmly, "Ali? You coming?"

Ali shrugged. "I don't mind. I'm not in a hurry," she said, glancing around her, looking for Joe almost without realising it.

Alice shrugged too, rather resentfully, and got into the back. Pete sat in the front and the two South Africans, remarking that Alice had better be chaperoned, got in beside her. They were about to go when Daniel suddenly pushed Ali forward. "Get in, get in, you can't leave Alice alone. Move over fat boys, we've one more."

Ali squeezed in beside Alice and the old car ground into gear and set off slowly, heaving bouncily across the airfield ruts to the road.

"Cozy in here, isn't it!" said Lauren, "and I can't even cuddle Alice. Want to sit on my lap, beautiful?"

"No thanks," said Alice peevishly, and, leaning forward, asked Pete which hotel they were staying in. The driver skirted a broken down Lada, its bonnet open, steam pouring from the radiator. Pete watched the manoeuvre with interest while he replied. "Travulbodz, it was a communist party members hotel, meant to be the smartest thing around. We are guests of the government."

Alice sat back and dropped into a daydream, refusing to answer any of the South Africans's questions. Pete turned to the driver and began asking him questions in slow, clear and rather loud English. Ali, noticing the smell of petrol fumes, watched the way the driver shook the steering wheel back and forth between his hands as he darted in and out of the pulsing traffic, wondering if this steering wheel shimmy was necessary with Ladas.

The hotel was deep into central Moscow, outside the Garden Circle and the Boulevard Ring but inside the Moskovskaya Koltsevaya Avotomobilnaya Doroga. It was an unusual building, with four turrets, two at each entrance, decorated with tiny tiles (which Gary suggested might well come in stick-on sections). A circular arch led to a grey-brown courtyard with two untended tubs of flowers. Their driver stopped outside the arch and helped them open the boot. For a blinding moment Alice suddenly had a flash into the future. She saw herself passing the hotel and slowing down because of the heavy traffic, nostalgically looking back to this moment, before the driver of her Mercedes put on his flashing blue light and they sped to her meeting, sometimes driving along the pavement. She shuddered. "Ali, what do you think you will be doing in ten years time?"

Ali grimaced. "Probably running supplies to small Alaskan airfields, getting stuck in bad weather and sitting in cheap hotel rooms with cans of beer and CNN."

Alice frowned. She thought she had better employ Ali in the future, if that was her most ambitious vision.

The lobby of the hotel was gargantuan, with stained marble floors that were cold to the touch and well-padded chairs in the window recesses. Three girls and a man stood behind the polished wooden reception desk, happily free of clients. At the far side were a bank of lifts, above the doors were old-fashioned round lights in a cage showing the floor numbers. The lift doors had an iron mesh exterior, with a red-brown material cover inside that concertinaed up with the door or spread out to hide those inside the lift from any audience.

"Perfect," said Dennie, "for sex on the rise...Alice where are you?"

Alice sneered and took her own and Ali's passport to the marble desk to register, in exchange she was given two old-fashioned door keys. Meanwhile the South Africans tested out the *gezellig* chairs by dropping into them, watched blandly by the Russian staff.

Pete was on a lower floor than the girls, so he left the lift first and they chugged slowly up another two floors. The lobby they got out into was painted brown, with brown plastic leather chairs next to a brown, plastic leather sofa in a brown alcove opposite the lift. There was a brown desk at this end of the corridor where the concierge should have been sitting, but which was now as empty as an alcoholic's vodka bottle. There was one window, high in the alcove opposite the lift, which oozed an eerily muddy-coloured light to the in-flooding sunlight. Along the corridor were bare lights without shades. There was a pervasive smell of boiling tea, with an uncurrent of salami.

"Shit," said Alice, "do you really think this is the best they can do for their officials, or do you think we got the servants' quarters and Pete and Daniel are in the best accommodation?"

"Wait until we've seen the rooms," said Ali, absentmindedly pushing a dead fly off the sooty parapet, "but I'm not holding out much hope."

Their room was at the far end of the corridor. A brown door led them into a small lobby with doors to three rooms: one had a small sofa and desk, another two beds and, just before the bedroom, was a bathroom with an enamel bath on feet and a clear plastic shower curtain decorated with painted cherubs. Some of the wall tiles had fallen into the bath. Ali picked them up and put them back in place on the wall, where they held until she shut the door.

"Blimey!" said Alice. "Either the officials aren't fussy, or they aren't high up enough to complain. That this is the best hotel is as unbelievable as a go-faster stripe on British Rail trains. I'd like to see Pete's room."

Ali sat on the nearest bed, which was a hard, army-issue type with raised edges. And single. "I don't think anyone got up to much naughtiness in here," she said. "You'd be crippled."

Alice looked out of the window, her gaze passing over a parking lot towards several blocks of flats. "We've got a good view of Moscow though," she said, "and we're at the back, so it will be quieter."

"I think I'll go and ask the landing-lady for some glue to stick those tiles back on," said Ali, "and a bath plug, and some loo paper."

"*Babushka*." Alice spat. "She's a *babushka*! But don't hold your breath. I did bring some paper though. And we can shower."

Ali strode down the corridor to find the *babushka*, embarrassedly aware that her solid locomotion sounded like the tread of a man, and expecting she would get nothing but a "Nyet". The small brown room behind the brown desk was empty. However, a cup of tea and a steaming samovar suggested that the woman might be back shortly, so Ali plonked herself down on the brown sofa to wait.

In spite of a slightly sticky exterior of the faux-leather the sofa was temptingly comfortable. She moved her hands over the firm material, deciding it was probably as close to good quality as things had come in pre-democratic Russia. Hearing the groan of the arriving lift she stopped her probing hands and sat upright: rather embarrassing to be caught by the floor-woman, or indeed some lost party member, lolling around on the brown plastic sofa like a decadent Western teenager.

Joe walked out of the opening doors.

"Hello," he said, throwing himself down beside her, "shall I be a party member?"

"What?" He was a mind reader.

Joe leant back against the cushions and put his hands behind his head. He turned his chin and looked at Ali, smiling.

"That's what this is for. Prostitutes come and meet their members, as you might say, here on the sofa. The party faithful bribes the landing-lady to go and busy herself elsewhere and they have a bit of breeding, as Jaap would say!"

"More likely to say pulls out his fuck cartridge," Ali returned.

Joe laughed. "You're right! He wouldn't be so prissy."

"Strange chap, Jaap," said Ali seriously, "he seems totally anti-authority."

Joe shook his head. "No, I don't think so. Apart from anything else he is Dutch and they generally believe in swinging with the model society they think they have."

She thought about that for a moment before replying. "Maybe. But you don't think it's a sort of subliminal power play? I can control the group through eccentricity."

"No, I think in Jaap's case he is totally unaware he is doing anything strange, if anything he thinks he's highly conventional." Joe spoke seriously but abstractedly as though he really wanted to discuss a quite different subject. "Look," he said, rather brusquely, "who cares about Jaap! Shall we play Russians?"

He put his hand on her leg, his voice turning light on the word Russians.

"Ha, ha," said Ali her voice disploding, her stomach leaping and falling. This change of tone unnerved her. Before he'd seemed serious. She put away the implications unthought. Now he was joking about. Perhaps Jaap and Mike were right in saying he was a womaniser. She knew nothing about him. He probably had a wife and four kids, was just hoping for a bit on the side like the many married men she'd avenged Jake's memory with. She got up.

"Let's hope playing Russians means we win the championships. See you later."

Joe watched her go, his gentle features crinkled by confused wrinkles.

I have known them all already, known them all, have known the evenings, mornings, afternoons, I have measured out my life with coffee spoons.

Cubic Zirconia

After testing the propped-up bricks in the shower, Alice and Ali took the marble stairs to the main hall to collect their 'welcome pack' of Russian goodies. Alice got hers first, but discovered that her badge said 'GUEST' instead of 'NAVIGATOR' and went off to complain to Lyuba, their guide and translator.

Ali, delving into her pack, felt a warmth behind her shoulder. Joe, the contents of his bag crushed in one large hand, lent over her shoulder as only he was tall enough to do. She smiled, amazed how his presence, even when he wasn't full of joking quips, filled her with a kind of silent joy and conscious she had to force herself not to lean back against him and rely on his strength. She was even happier when he said: "When the One Great Scorer comes to write against your name - he marks - not that you won or lost - but how you played the game."

"That's lucky! Since we don't have a hope in Hell of winning. Is that Arnold again? Mind you his father was at Rugby, perhaps he pushed him into winning."

"I don't think so. But no, anyway, this is an American football writer called Grantland Rice who wrote a poem called Alumnus Football, a sort of early twentieth century Nick Hornby. He left a football trophy too. He was a sort of journalist poet, just like you are a pilot quoter, and I am merely one more man to fill the quota!"

Ali smiled, she knew that literature was full of women seduced by men who play with quotations, and yet she liked it, but perhaps she, like Chekov's Masha, was about to be deluded. She opened the neck of her bag and began looking through the gifts. There were a few little badges made of weak metal, the Russian equivalent of Peckham diamonds, which bent as she tried to pin it on. There were also flags and memorabilia of Moscow, and a programme which included a timetable of the following days' events.

Joe, reading his own, asked: "Have you noticed how early in the morning all the competitions start: 'all games are planned by old men, in council rooms apart'. Bet the old men will be still in bed."

"Do you think so?" she replied seriously. "It's hot here in the summer, I thought that was a sort of response to the heat-in-the-helicopter option and the number of teams to be got through. I must say I don't think it's a bad idea; hot helicopters can really drain you, although we used to take the doors off and then it's rather lovely but if we did that in the navigation Jaap, at least, would lose his flour-bags. I must say it is kind of the Russians to give us these gifties, but what will we do with them?"

Joe gave his half smile. "The terrible gift that brought them such suffering...?"

She shuddered. "I hope not!"

She remembered how the poem went on: 'Who doesn't desire his father's death?' and shivered. If someone had de-railed the tail-rotor on purpose, why hadn't they tried again? Don't think about it. Just enjoy your holiday. How can I not think about it? asked her mind. I cannot think about anything else.

"Are you OK," Joe asked, "you seemed to have gone away deep into thought."

She looked at him, wanting to ask: "Did you try and murder me? Tell me it wasn't you. Tell me, tell me something else, tell me something better."

Subjugating her perversely wilful mind she gushed brightly, "I was just think-ing we were way off Arnold now. Was Dostoevsky another school favourite?"

"No, that was when I was in the army."

She laughed. "I don't believe you! Couplets for conscripts? You'll be telling me next Dennie and Lauren also quote Russian literature."

"They might. We had an informal alliance with Russia under apartheid. They were one of the nations not to knock us out."

"Are you sure? I thought South Africa was terrified of communism and that Russia supported African countries like Ethiopia?"

For a moment Joe looked annoyed and Ali found herself adding placatingly, "Anyway, it sounds more like cricket. Does Pete remind you a bit of that chap in Crime and Punishment, with his theories?"

"Raskolnikov? Maybe, but I have a feeling Pete just likes to play. I don't think he believes his theories, just that he enjoys them. Although to a lesser extent I agree with him. Too much regulation does indeed 'dull the mind and deaden the wit', preventing people taking the initiative. Men, like animals, need rules they can believe in, but not regulations for their own sake which confuse them and make them afraid of authority."

"Ah," said Ali, "if the man who turnips cries, cry not when his father dies, 'tis a proof that he had rather, have a turnip than his father."

Joe laughed and his face softened.

Alice skipped over, happily displaying her new 'Navigator' badge and the three of them went to the Upstairs Bar. Ali, who was used to being alone, felt tired after the stress of visiting Alice's ancestors, and realised she would rather have gone to her room with a book, but Alice was young and interested, longing to know 'what was Moscow'. And Joe wanted a beer; badly.

The Upstairs Bar, a misleading name because it was in fact the only bar, was a small room with a lot of windows and a few small tables. On the door was a sign which read: 'Table Service Only', in English and Russian. At one end, near the door, was an elaborate wooden counter, behind which two harassed young men stood trying to work out how to give table service to the fifty or so importunate foreigners who had crowded in asking for attention, and were now some three rows deep around the bar, shouting and impeding what table service there was. For an hour the waiters resolutely broke through the cordon of thirsty drinkers, muttering "Nyet" and "No table", insisting on giving table service to those happy early birds seated on the five small, round tables. Then, suddenly, their resolve broke and the two young men fled back behind the bar and began serving the customers from there, while still indicating with their haughty manner this was something quite beneath their dignity.

As they waited in the jostling crowd for beer Joe remarked to Ali, "Often in the world's most crowded streets there rises an unspeakable desire: for a drink!"

Laughing she replied, "We certainly have the din of strife, I can hardly hear the Americans above the vain glorious!"

With the scrum of people there was a lot of pushing and shoving and Joe, who would rather have spent the night glued to Ali's side, found himself jostled away by Pete who was keen to continue their discussion on lawlessness. Steve and Mike took Ali's elbows and pulled her off to the window, curious to hear more about her celebrity partner, while one of the Frenchmen somewhat lacking in gallantry offered Alice a chance to arm-wrestle.

"You know," said Giles, "in France we love the dogs."

"Racing? Greyhounds you mean, or is there poodle racing in Paris?"

"Comment? Oh, my lovely Alice you joke. No, we believe a dog is an animal, the British no," he spread a flattened hand, "it is a friend and for the Americans? Well, if I suggest it is a lover you say I call the woman a bitch! But we return to Paris for this story. One day I was walking home after work and I see a woman with her dog and he is, as you would say, performing outside my house. My house! Then the woman she walks on, leaving the doings on the doorstep. I am outraged. As you English like to say, a man's home is his castle. So, I roll up Le Monde (sacrilege in itself, ne c'est pas) and I pick up the doings and follow the woman and her dog. Unfortunately she does not go straight home, so we amble along, down the river, past the supermarket, she stops for a cafe and then for a Pernod. But at last we arrive at her house. So, I wait until she has gone in. Then I ring the doorbell and she comes out. And I drop the dog's doings from Le Monde down on her doorstep! Ooh lala! What an excitement of excrement! She calls her husband to hit me. She yells for the gendarme. So much, for so little. I just turn and walk away. Ah bah!"

Alice laughed so loudly that various people turned from their beers to stare, and Giles was delighted. "Ah, c'est jolie ça, ma chere n'est pas?"

"Only with trust," said Pete, lighting his pipe and sucking hard, "can society exist without rules. Do you know which nation has the most positive response to trust."

Joe did not.

"Norway, the most trusting nation in the world, they believe in each other, and hardly a rule to be found, while the Russians cannot trust each other for five minutes and everywhere you turn you bump into a new regulation. What does that tell you about rules, 'eh." He took another drag on his pipe.

"That you need them for positive reaffirmation of society?" suggested Joe. "That the Norwegians are trusting because they have been involved in the rule-making process, while Russians have not and find many of the regulations contradictory and self-defeating."

Pete was delighted. "Ah, again you show you lack of understanding of law-less-ness. Lack of trust, like obsession with rules, leads to a suspicious poverty-trapped nation, and then the growth of pointless self-defeating bureaucracy."

Joe took a swig of his beer and gave up any idea of spending the evening with Ali; this was going to be an all-night discussion.

"Most dictatorships," he began, "have only one rule, the whim of the dictator, and an individual's trust is inversely proportional to the position they hold..."

Bored with the Frenchmen, who the girls found had a desire to fall into French whenever they could, Alice and Ali agreed go out to dinner in the Chinese restaurant on Daniel and Gary's floor of the hotel. Afterwards they went back to the boys's room for a drink and some flight planning. The boys had the same type of rooms as the girls, but each railway carriage room had one bed and the desk had been dispensed with.

"They obviously know men snore," said Gary.

As they lent over the maps Daniel sat close behind Ali and put his arms around her. "Oh, little Ali Gee," he sang, "what a babe you are, who knows the map, and scams the crap. What a girl you are."

Handsome countenance, light amusing persona, so much more attractive than Joe, the big and kind intelligent elephant, but why was Daniel flirting with her? She wondered what Joe was doing, whom he was with and why she wasn't with him. Out loud she asked why Mike and Joe weren't competing.

"Ah, our big lad," said Daniel lightly. "He certainly made it his business to be friendly with you, Ali darling, once he knew whom you were travelling with, did he not? The big friendly farmer."

He pinched her cheek while Gary pronounced, with the seriousness of evening booze, "I don't think he needs to compete, anymore than I do. There are other things in life than being number one all the time."

Alice giggled. "You mean large, successful computer companies?" she asked. Adding heavy-handedly, "I think computers are just so interesting."

"You know," said Daniel, looking crossly at Alice, "that Jaap has been allowed to enter the competition after all."

"No! How come?" asked Ali.

Alice grinned at Gary and twirled her beads so suggestively that Daniel reached over and slapped her hand.

"Apparently the Swiss man was told that his son was banned from the competition for being too young. However, they didn't want to disqualify him completely or, since they'd forgotten to mention it when he entered, they'd have to refund his money, so they let him take Jaap as his navigator. Presumably the

Russians realise there is no chance of competition from them. Which means overall the rules were fudged a bit, Jaap is a late entry and from a different nationality. What a cock up, 'eh? Funny if they won now."

"Unlikely though," said Ali.

"'Tis too," said Alice, "we're going to win."

Human Fence Posts

Early next morning they were picked up from the hotel by an aged Lada and escorted to Toshino through the steady flow of hooting traffic, weaving in and out of broken down trucks with steaming radiators. The competition was scheduled to begin as soon as the Opening Ceremony had been completed.

Passing through the prohibitive gates and onto the airfield they drove through a row of young men in uniform. Looking back the girls could see they were placed every fifty feet around the airfield.

"Look at that," Ali said, "human fence posts!"

Alice looked back too. "Cheaper than the real thing. They've got an employment problem in Russia now. What can they do with these young conscripts now there is no Afghanistan to fight in?"

Gary, who had volunteered to prepare the helicopter for the still snoozing Daniel, said ponderously: "The opposite of the UK. There we are downsizing. Replacing humans with the computer, here they bolster up their flailing and failing technology with manpower. This is a market we are only just touching."

"Besides," said Alice, "Gorby might try a comeback by kidnapping one of the helicopter teams."

What they didn't notice was a young girl with a baby, standing outside the Human Fence Posts. Her long red hair was tied back demurely, her baby balanced on her hip playing with a plastic helicopter, which he flew off the helipad of her shoulder. She had not been allowed to approach the airfield beyond the uniformed men, but she saw the car and watched its progress down the stoney path to the airfield with an almost ghostly smile on her face. Once it was past Galina turned away and trudged back towards the Metro station, wishing she too could ride in the plastic helicopter.

The opening ceremony was a splendid, if only partially rehearsed, affair. Divided into nations the teams processed around the peri-track of the airfield, holding banners and national mascots. Each group was led by a muscular man carrying the flag of his country fluttering from a wooden pole-support in a leather belt holder, while above them a Mil Mi-8 helicopter flew circuit after circuit, each national flag fluttering in its turn in the slipstream.

The Russians, wearing cheap, poorly-cut but identical suits, marched with complete uniformity, holding their banner proudly aloft. In contrast the various foreign teams, in much better quality clothing but with occasional bouts of individuality which ruined the overall picture, slouched along getting out of time and sometimes falling back into another country's group. Only the Americans equalled the Russians in national pride, heads back, chests out, happy to be from the Greatest Nation on the Earth, which reminded Ali that Pete had told her neither nation was above cheating; something to which she gave all the credence one would extend to a man who equated practising with cheating.

"You can't trust nations," Pete had said, "and you can't trust anyone, however much you like them, don't forget that, will you Ali? Only with lawlessness can you trust people to do the right thing because they know they are their own ultimate authority, that the buck really stops with them."

"Prisons must be citadels then," said Ali, but Pete just smiled, continuing to point out that nations, like rules, caused more crime than they prevented.

After the marching all the groups stopped in their nationally defined areas and formed little enclaves of parochialism, while flags were again paraded overhead by the Mil-8. One after another the national flags progressed across the sky above the airfield and their national anthems were played. Ali felt moved and proud to be part of the British team. Alice was completely overcome and tears poured down her cheeks. Paul, Rob, Sandra, Steve, Kevin, Mike, Graham, Deidre, Robert, Tim and Charles all stood to attention, their faces pulled with emotion. Even Daniel and Pete stood tall, while she noticed Joe had moved over to join the South Africans. Only Jaap wandered around like a lost dog looking for his companions. Again she wondered what it was about nationhood that gave a man or woman a real sense of belonging, of being someone special. But, at least here in this sporting helicopter meadow in Russia, that was clearly true.

Once the last flag had been dragged past by the Mil, the Russians gave each team a special saltless bread, plaited into an elegant braid and curled around into a circle. In the centre was a heap of salt into which torn-off bread-pieces were to be immersed to give full flavour. Alice was the first to plunge in, while the others dipped with more reluctance, and Pete and Daniel, both living skeletons, just pretended to nibble delicately.

Finally, a Hind flew over the airfield, giving a talented and complex display of Russian domination of the airspace.

"Look ye there," said Rob, "they can only make left turns. What ya think? One or two Robinsons to knock them out of the sky?"

"One Robinson with a female pilot," replied Paul, with a brief sideways glance at Alice. She sneered silently.

After the ceremony the teams went into the tent for the briefing. Each pilot was given a theoretical number, which they had to somehow convert into something practical that could be stuck onto the helicopter. Luckily the efficient Alice had brought some duct tape, since Pete and Daniel hadn't thought about it and Ali hadn't noticed anything in the rules, but then she had skipped through them quickly between attempting to fix her car and watching for the abundant-with-jobs telephone to ring. With quick fingers Alice created both numbers and planted them on the helicopters.

Rob and Paul sat behind Ali and Alice during the briefing, a long script slowly translated from Russian into both English and German. The microphone screeched and belched like a man with asthma and the translators gave up on it immediately. The Russian speaker, a thin man who was Chief Judge, sturdily ploughed on shouting through the electronic wheezing, until eventually he too knocked the offending instrument aside and began bellowing at the crowd. Great detail was gone into over timings, the size and position of the numbers to be stuck on the helicopter, ways of flying over the judges and what would happen if the teams got lost or there was any other emergency. There was also a timetable of when each team would have its GPS blanked out to avoid any cheating and where they would be stored. The Gazelles soon got bored and dropped into quiet conversation.

"You know Cora's going to have my babies?"

"Did she say so?"

"Near-as. She said 'gudmrning', in return to my greeting."

"I just don't think I could activate. Even Whirly Wizard is beginning to give me the droop."

"Ha, don't give me that. I saw you throwing things out of your pram in excitement!"

"So, she's all over me like a rash! I may have to take the champagne and be done."

"I'll need proof."

"I'll need Bollinger. A case."

Once the briefing was over the teams wandered away to their national tents. Each team had been given a small, white canvas, girl-guide affair, with wooden benches outside and a bench-and-table construction inside, for planning and discussions. Ali and Alice, who had worn matching skirts for the opening ceremony, were about to change when Alice realised she had forgotten her sneakers, and would have to enter the Timed Arrival in high heels unless she could find someone prepared to take her back to the hotel. Sandra came to her rescue.

"So, Alice," she said, regarding the girl's feet critically, "I think my shoes should fit you. I'm not as tall but my feet are big."

Alice slipped on Sandra's sneakers, which fitted her perfectly and was just thanking the girl when Charles's wife Nancy noticed the exchange. "Hey, Sandra," she cried happily, "with your jeans and stilettos you look just like one of the Russian tarts! All you need is an older man..."

Sandra smiled politely, even as Nancy blushed and stammered, realising her mistake but Alice turned away furiously muttering, "Cultural oaf!"

The first competition was the Timed Arrival and Skittle Drop. As each competitor lined up at the start ready for departure they were given a map, embossed with the route of a short navigation, which they had to complete in a certain time. The route ended back at the airfield, where the team had to do a one-minute descending square around a field, passing the penultimate finishing line on time, drop a skittle in a hole in a dog-house roof from a certain height and fly over the final line, where the timing stopped.

Pete and Daniel were the first of the British team to go. They started off on time and disappeared over the lake towards the first checkpoint. The next team, a Russian Mil flown by the South Africans, had taken off before Pete and Daniel came in sight for their last leg. Alice, who'd been timing them on her stopwatch, nodded her head.

"Good, supposing they haven't made any mistakes out there, they're dead on time. Although they forgot to put their landing light on as they arrived back at the airfield, which means they drop points."

The British team watched as Pete and Daniel crossed the first finishing line and began to do their descending turn; only they didn't descend. They did the one-minute turn, but then found themselves ahead of time, and so slowed down to a hover taxi for the last bit, and then suddenly descended to cross the penultimate line and make for the dog-house.

"They've blown it!" said Alice, turning off the stopwatch in disgust. "They will get penalty points for hovering and for not descending. They really are idiots. You know," she said to Ali, "Pete's done this competition every time since it began, he flies brilliantly and yet he still doesn't know the rules. It is quite amazing."

"Don't forget," Joe pointed out, "he doesn't believe in rules. It would be against all his principles to learn the ways of the enemy."

Ali laughed but Alice inverted her eyes in irritation.

The Robinson hovered up to the doghouse and Pete dropped the skittle right into the hole. They hovered on to the finish line and landed.

Rob and Paul looked at their watches. "OK lover boy," said Paul, "we'd better go, ten minutes to lift off."

"You wait until I'm drinking the Bollinger," said Rob, as they walked off towards the Gazelle. "You'll be crying then, dyke-rider!"

Ali laughed and Alice turned on her. "You shouldn't encourage them, they're shitty sexists! They should have their balls cut off."

"Come on! It's only a joke. They're just boys having a good time."

"Come on yourself," Alice snapped, "we'd better go and get our helicopter ready. You know what we're doing, don't you? Have you read the rules, yet?"

They were sitting in the Robinson when the Russian ladies team took off. Alice timed them and saw they did a perfect round. Even their drop into the doghouse was quick and fluid.

"Shit! They were perfect," said Alice, "but we're going to do at least as well. We can always beat them on something else."

Ali said nothing, wishing they'd had more practice and fearing that Alice was going to be deeply upset.

A few minutes before their start time Ali started up and took off, flying over to the waiting line. Two minutes before take-off she lifted again and went to the start, where Alice was given the map with the route printed on it. They planned the route, while waiting for the starting flag. As the time got closer Alice began a countdown. "OK, five, four, three, two, one, GO. Lift. GO."

Ali took off and started on the heading Alice directed, noticing as she did so the German ladies were just starting their descending square.

"Good, good," said Alice, "excellent. There is the first check point, fly overhead and turn. Good. Exactly on time. Fantastic we are doing well."

Ali was a good navigator, capable of making up for Alice's inexperience, the route was fairly easy and the Robinson was correctly judged for time, so they found all the points without any problem and turned exactly on time to make their approach to the airfield.

"Don't forget to put on the landing light one minute out," Alice reminded her.

"Yup, tell me at a minute."

"OK now."

"On."

"Good. OK off now and start the descending square. OK, three-quarters of a minute to go, half a minute, excellent we are half way round. Good. Good. Good. Over the line." The stopwatch clicked. "Excellent. Exactly on time."

Ali hovered up to the doghouse and stopped. Alice unravelled the rope with the skittle as they went.

"OK! Up, up, up. That's it. Right a bit, bit more, right and more... and OK."

She dropped the skittle. Then.

"Oh SHIT!"

Ali, now going towards the finish, asked, "What happened?"

"I missed," said Alice, and burst into tears.

Ali landed and a prematurely white-haired American judge took back their papers. She noticed Alice's tears and smiled sympathetically. Ali said nothing, flying back to their parking space while the distraught Alice stared out of the window. "Shit, shit, shit!" she said, "we were doing so well."

"Don't worry Alice," said Ali clumsily, "we will do better in the other phases, this was a good practice."

"Yes," said Alice through her tears, "but we won't win! Won't be in the Moscow papers." And tears dropped on to her lap.

Pete and Daniel came up to congratulate them on having had a good round, until the last moment. Daniel tried to put his arms around Alice to comfort her, but she brushed him away and walked off. He watched her looking peeved.

"She's very upset," said Ali diplomatically, "she really thought we might win."

"Well really," said Pete, "you should have practised more if you wanted to win so much. You can't expect me to do everything for you!"

Lyuba, the translator, came up to the Robinson. "Hello," she said, adding somewhat unnecessarily, "I'm the team translator. I wanted to meet you."

"Great," said Ali, "good to meet you too."

Lyuba was a slim girl with long dyed-hair, in a colour Ali, seeing it everywhere, was beginning to think of as Russian-red. She was dressed in the usual seventies synthetic clothing but had a lovely, friendly smile. Ali liked her immediately. She asked her if she flew and the girl explained that was how she got into translating. She had been at military college and learnt to fly Mils in the communist era, although she couldn't afford to now. Eventually the technical side of learning to fly helicopters had been too much for Lyuba and she had transferred into aviation translating. As this clearly left several questions hanging Ali tactfully avoided asking her anymore, instead she asked if Lyuba had met Alice yet.

"Oh, yes, your friend. I spoke to her last night, but we spoke in Russian. She is good for a foreigner. Almost fluent."

"So I was told in Byelorussia," said Ali. "I think she has Russian forebears."

"Oh, yes," said Lyuba, "for example, she told me to call her Galina Reskarova while she was here. She said it was her patronym like in Puskin and the other Russian writers. She seems to be well read in Russian literature."

"Really? She hasn't quoted any to me!" snapped Ali, irritated by the thought that Alice might have some other unadmitted skill. Lyuba blushed, uncertain how she had offended and, after hastily changing the subject and talking about more mundane things, left to see if anyone else needed her services.

Guiltily aware of her rudeness Ali strolled over to join Joe, who was standing near the show ground watching the doghouse disasters. Alice was not the only person to drop the skittle and Joe was having a very good time. He welcomed her with delighted amusement.

"Jaap and Hans, the Swiss man, have just started off. I can't wait until they get here, there's bound to be some kind of disaster. So far the Gazelles did a perfect round, but the German ladies got in a right old stew, and the fat girl almost landed on the roof. Finally, Dagma used the skittle to hit her with. It was a real scene. They were disqualified for going over time and when they landed I could see them sitting in the helicopter having a right old ding-dong!"

At that moment the Swiss-Dutch pair arrived going at fast speed. Ali checked her watch. "Are they late?"

"Looks like it, watch them in the square. Loads of people have forgotten to descend until the end, and one pair flew right over the doghouse without stopping and landed by the finish. They then tried to throw the skittle from there, nearly hitting the rotors. It was hilarious."

Jaap and his co-pilot, though, did manage do the descending square correctly and hovered over to the doghouse. However, Jaap had obviously not read the rule that said you had to drop the skittle from over thirty metres. They did a low-level hover, just over the hole and Jaap dropped the skittle, getting an excellent, speedy hole-in-one and being disqualified for low-level dropping.

"Hey ho," said Joe, disappointed, "I expected something far more eccentric from Jaap. We'll just have to wait for the rest of the competitions. How is Alice?"

"Miserable. I think she really thought we could win. Now we haven't a chance."

He looked at her sympathetically, and almost absentmindedly stroked her shoulder. "You could still come second, if all the other ladies get disqualified in one sector or other. Getting a disqualification in one area doesn't put you out of the competition you know. And you're still level pegging with the Germans. They were well disqualified." He chuckled again.

"How about the Americans?"

"Right up there with the Russians and the Gazelles. You don't think Blondie and Blondie are going to make mistakes do you!"

"Et tu Brute!"

"You're not suggesting I'm like the Guzelles I hope!"

"Well..."

"Besides," Joe said, "I'm in love with someone else."

"Oh," said Ali, not sure whether to laugh or cry.

Paul and Daniel walked towards them, Ali was glad to see Alice was with them and looking more cheerful. She was even flirting a little with the boys. In the distance they could see Rob clearly trying to chat up Catherine. After a while they saw him laugh a bit strangely and walk towards them.

"God," he said, as he drew up with them, "I got it right about them being bitches, especially her; Whirly Catherine!"

"Threw you over did she?" asked Paul.

"Over me like a rash!" said Rob, "God, I could hardly hold her off!"

"Looks like you owe me champagne, brother," chortled Paul.

"Hey, I haven't finished yet, this was just for openers."

"And, what happened? After she'd trampled on your opening lines and buried you in a heap of dust?!"

"I was only asking her if she'd like to have a drink in my room this evening and she said, 'I've already changed my three sons' nappies, want me to change yours too? You're about the same age!"

"What a bitch!" cried Paul curling up with laughter. "Hey baby, want to suckle my dummy!"

"Oh, she's just playing hard to get," said Rob. "She'll be all over me yet."

"Oh, yeah! I can already taste the champagne."

"Besides, I don't know why you're laughing, how's it coming on with Clora, or is it Clorinda?"

"Never you mind, I'm working slowly, my boy. Later I'll show you how an adult goes to work, baby!"

Kevin walked up, his face dark with anger. "There's been a incident," he said. "Daniel, in my position as Group Leader, I'll need to talk to you."

"What's up, Kevin," asked Rob immediately serious, "not an accident?"

"No, but someone has turned the American flag upside down and they are furious. Threatening to walk out of the competition altogether."

Paul and Rob looked at each other and sidled away, before falling into heaps of giggles in the tent. Kevin's lips tightened. "This is not an amusing affair. Daniel may I have your word you know nothing about it?"

Daniel, who was almost crying with mirth, said he wished he'd thought of it, while Pete turned furiously on Kevin demanding to know why he thought Daniel would be involved and Alice, who was shocked and not amused, said she thought it might be the Germans.

Kevin turned to her, "What makes you think so?"

"Ali and I saw them going into the American tent a few hours ago."

Kevin nodded curtly and went off to find out what was happening.

White Death

After the day's events the British team met in the Chinese Restaurant, on the fourth floor of the hotel, for an evening of funny-foreigner stories. These were mostly based on the hotel staff and Russian translators since, in spite of Paul's storming of Cora and Clorinda, they had little contact with the Russian pilots, who never came to the hotel or drank in the bar. When asked why, Lyuba merely said it was "so strange," failing to point out that the impoverished pilots could not have afforded one beer at the 'foreigner prices' of the Upstairs Bar, let alone a round, or indeed that they were actively discouraged from mixing with the strange pilots.

Daniel began with an inspired imitation of Lyuba. "Can you believe it, Danielle," he said, swinging his hair, "Rob stole the scent the French team gave me and sprayed Sergei's jacket. So strange! It's not as though he smells like a dog."

Rob and Paul creased up. "Hey! Lyuba, Kevin's room wasn't ready until he gave receptionist $10 then it was."

"Oh, Daniel, this is so strange!"

"Hey, Lyuba, you need to help the hotel with their translating. Have you read in the hotel information this news about a long non-stop hooter in the telephone station? I'd say give the devoshka a new brassiere!"

"I'm sorry, Daniel, I don't quite understand you. You say translation is wrong?"

"No. Lyuba, it's just so strange."

Rob had a story about the floor walker, a man apparently on rails, who traversed the lobby looking at no one and there for no obvious purpose, but who constantly strode up and down the hall.

"This was a hoot. Old Ivan the Terrible was on his route when Paul, totally smitten by the sight of Cora or Clorinda at the window, was passing backwards across the hall. Naturally our boy was oblivious to sight and sound with Cora on his mind so he walks backwards and then bang! Ivan who walks like a Russian driver, had hit him amidships. It never occurring to him that he might deviate his route for a man who didn't see him."

"So strange!" said Daniel, enjoying his acting. "Oh Rob, can you believe it?"

Even Ali, looking sheepishly at Alice and laughing slightly, told a story Lyuba had told her. "The French team, disgusted by the food, asked Lyuba to take them to the Special Shops in town. At first Lyuba denied such shops existed, then she compromised and suggested that there might be 'foreign shops, very expensive,' and finally agreed to take them there. However, even there the French had found it difficult to find food to their taste and eventually had been forced to buy caviar and smoked salmon at inflated prices."

"Can you imagine it," breathed Daniel, "so strange."

Gary told a story about how his plate was snatched every morning by the waiters. "There I was half-way through my herring, my fork half-way to my mouth and this half-wit comes up and tries to take my plate. I say I haven't finished and she backs off, but half a moment later and her colleague is back at my white matter! I bark a little, and he backs off. But give it another turn of the wheel and he is back, smiles all over his swede trying to grab the gaffer. I think I ought to give him one on the bonce. But I just say, 'Hey mate, leave it alone, I've hardly started'. And he looks at me like a lunatic in a juice bar and backs off, but not for long. Eventually the dildo-head claims that in Russia if you leave your knife and fork crossing each other it's signal to take away the plates! Yeah! Even if I'm still holding the buggers I suppose!"

"So strange!" purred Daniel.

Charles, who had been to pick up his wife Nancy at the airport, told an Aeroflot story. "When she arrived there were loads of people checking in with all their luggage wrapped in cling film! God knows why! Nancy didn't dare ask them, because you know how sensitive these Russians are! Ask them their name and they'll want to know why you ask. And she noticed a sign declaring: 'You must not import cliches'!" Charles chuckled, certain he was not your average accountant, adding that when he asked for salt this morning his waiter had told him salt was called, 'White Death' in Russia.

"So strange."

There was a silence and Daniel turned to Alice, a sly grin flashing off and on his face. "So. Alice the Slice, you must have the best story of all, keeping us waiting so long. What is it? Something about the sexy Sergei who is so scenic, or that elegant pilot Alexei, son of Tzars?"

Alice looked haughtily at him. "Christ, Daniel, you are such a child. Yes, I have a story, all right. It is about the English who say 'Spa-siba, Spa-siba' and complain at every possible moment, the spoilt brats who think it's life failing when the shower won't work, but won't actually get down to fix it but call in a 'little man who can'. Shit Daniel but you haven't suffered enough to get a wrinkle on your hands while people here have lived with death in their families, yet you think they should adapt to you and your constant 'sank yous'. The clever Russians can manage a 'sank you' and the whole Roman alphabet while you're still thinking it clever than you can translate pecknama into advertising or babushka into grandmother. You know Daniel they laugh at you, they call you Diplomat Daniel."

Daniel smiled. "That's not so bad, 'eh, diplomat."

"Yup," said Alice, "it's the name of their cheapest vodka."

Bort A Lada

The second day Ali, Alice, Daniel and Gary arrived at the airfield at 5 am, as the briefing was set for 5.15. They left the hotel in a gleaming, light-holding mist and journeyed through awakening streets before the traffic jams started. Under the street lights the dispersing fog formed peaks and, as they passed under a low stone bridge, a hovering bird caught the light in its wings, beating the hairy air into a spectrum of dew-drop-laden colours like a tiny pulsating rainbow.

The Lada dropped them at the airfield gates and the team drifted sleepily down the path to the airfield, where the early morning dew was just lifting off the damp grass, forming ethereal cushions of low level cumulus. Clouds hid the helicopter skids in puffs that reached halfway up their doors and wafted around the airfield in bubbles, so it looked as though they had stumbled on a film production of Helicopters in Heaven.

"Wow!" said Alice, "look at that, Paradise in Moscow. Daniel can you waltz? We should dance through the lifting dew, over the clouds to Olympus."

"And down the long and silent street, the dawn, with silver-sandaled feet, crept like a frightened girl," quoted Ali.

"Crapped more like!" chortled Daniel doing a handstand.

This was the day of the Precision Flying competition. Two chains were attached under each helicopter, one shorter than the other. One chain had to be dragged perpetually along the ground, while the other was prohibited from touching it, with subsequent penalties for violations. The helicopter flew over a square course, forward, backwards and sideways with spot turns at each corner, before landing as close as possible to the centre of a stretched bar-code.

"Hum," said Daniel, noticing the square as the mist lifted, leaving it now a patch of beige mud, "well-worn precision tracks! Those Ruskies have practised this thing to death! No wonder there is noplace in the competition for someone like me with inborn brilliance. Pets win prizes for practising!" He slouched off towards the British national tent.

The British team had heaped things around the sides of the tent and from one pile stuck Kevin's umbrella. This he carried everywhere, having heard Russian weather was as unpredictable as their bureaucracy. The South African tent next door was crowded with cases of beer, donated by fans, Dennie claimed, which piled against the sides of the tent protruding in angular lines through the canvas. Jaap and the Swiss man shared the British tent as their team was too small for their own tent. Jaap said the other teams were worried they might steal their secrets or their beer.

"Interesting is those national qualities," Jaap ruminated. "As French and German speakers we thought their tents would be as open to us as the elephant's turds but no, was closed even as mouse's sphincter."

"As! As closed as a mouse's sphincter," screamed Alice. "How long have you been speaking English, Jaap?"

Jaap turned to her surprised. "Oh! Now you see me as an enemy! I wonder why all the nations are not at war. We let in the foreigner, but we hate the way he behaves, embarrassed by his moral codes and infuriated how he garbles our language, ruining it for eternity." He shook his head, as though to loosen the butter.

"I have noticed an interesting national characteristic. Even while they mock us for our language, the British are the only nation in the world who like to be laughed at: they started with men in skirts and now they enjoy to lose competitions. Eddie the Eagle, your proud boast. We have Ruud Gullet and Marco van Basten and you have Eddie and drunken footballers."

None of the British replied but Joe, who divided his time between Beer Tent South Africa and Tent Britain, declared cheerfully, "Every human creature is a profound secret and mystery to every other."

"Except the British," said Ali, "who are clearly welcoming to all others, Mister South African, in spite of what you do to our grammar and our Empires. Back in your box."

He looked at her, his half smile tremulous with desire. "Some more than others I hope, Miss World."

"Come on Ali," said Alice taking the girl's arm possessively, "stop fooling about. We need to watch the games."

In the Precision Flying event the British girls surprised everyone by improving their position from near the bottom to half way towards the top. Alice being good at giving clear orders that begged submission and Ali at carrying them out to the letter, they sailed over the parched and well-dented ground at one height, the little Robinson gliding like a swan on a glassy lake.

"Keep your height exactly as it is," ordered Alice tersely, "and go backwards, quite slowly, we are up on time. OK now left turn, no height change. Good. Good. OK side to the right, but don't let the lower chain lapse, it's slipping down. Good. Excellent. OK turn again. Up a little, enough! OK forward faster now. We're getting behind time. Now go for the landing square. OK. Down. Back a bit, down, left a bit, down. Good. Not bad. Not perfect but not bad."

When they read their scores on the Marker Board, an easel set up beside the briefing tent (which was difficult to get at because the translators used the area as a base and all sat around it drinking bitter black coffee) they saw they had come level with the American girls and second to the Russians.

"Wow, Alice," said Ali, genuinely surprised and pleased, unused to winning, "look at that. We're equal in this with the Gazelle's girls!"

Alice frowned at the table remarking, "Maybe, but they're all ahead of us overall, except for the Germans. We must beat them at least. I hope the others haven't got too much of a head start. Perhaps they'll let themselves down in the navigation. We should be OK there."

The Gazelles had also again done well, better than the Americans of both genders and Ali and Alice, and as well as the Russian women, who were now leading overall. Pete and Daniel were only just behind the Russian women, having somehow kept the helicopter together for an excellent and precise round. Alice remarked it wasn't surprising since you didn't have to learn any rules for the precision flying.

"See," said Daniel cockily, "even without practice we're ahead of you."

"Yeah, but not if you divided it by the number of years you've been flying compared to the number we have," countered Alice swiftly.

In the Slalom, however, Pete and Daniel were disqualified. They had been too hungover to walk the course, got the gates mixed up and although they muddled through the red-spiked poles they confused the order. When they finally placed their bucket in the middle of the table without spilling a drop of water, they were eliminated.

"Honestly," muttered Daniel, "there shouldn't have to be an order of gates. It should be just the quickest way of getting through! After all we were within the time, did all the obstacles and had a dead-centre drop. But just coz we hadn't practised we were out. No wonder the pets win every prize."

The score board showed that the Whirly Women (as the British team had taken to calling them, much to Alice's disgust) and Cora and Clorinda were tied in the Slalom, with the Gazelles just behind and the American and Russian men tied with the Gazelles.

Ali and Alice did a solid slalom round, but lost much of the water from the bucket, which then swung under the helicopter like a pendulum so Alice had difficulty steadying it enough to pass through the long gawky poles the Russians had imported from the Ukraine. By the time they reached the end of the course she had got the bucket under control, only to lose it again as Ali climbed to the required height. She just managed to plonk it down on one side of the table. They also incurred penalty points for dawdling too slowly. Daniel smirked and pointed out that if he had known the rules as well as Alice he'd have won.

"Then why don't you learn them?" she snapped, before turning to talk to Jaap.

In the bar that evening Joe, Alice and Ali were talking to the South Africans behind the American girls when they saw Rob approaching Catherine in a cool, devil-may-care manner.

"Well, Ms America, you are quite a pilot. Still level pegging with the Russians, and ahead of quite a few of the men. I'd like to buy you a drink for that."

Catherine gave him a long up and down look, before moving her knee in his direction. "Oh, go play with your rattle, baby," she said. "We're talking adult here."

Joe gave a low whistle, "Wowhoo. She means to have him!"

"You think so?" asked Ali surprised. "Doesn't sound like the way I'd do a come-on."

He laughed, moving a little closer to her. "I'm sure. Look at that body language. She wants him on her terms. No wonder she wins all the time. She's quite a woman."

"Fancy chancing your arm yourself do you?" asked Dennie, walking over and attempting to balance his glass on Alice's head. "You lusty little lover boy! Go ahead Joe and pull out Rob. " He smiled lecherously at Ali.

"God!" said Alice, shaking off the glass angrily, "men are disgusting."

"I agree with you," said Lauren, "but luckily women are not, they are lovely."

"Oh, piss off. Bantam of the Opera!"

"Oh my darling!" cried Lauren. "Marry me, marry me now. I'll let you beat me on our wedding night."

"No way! Lekker Man."

Fighting his way back from the bar Jaap joined them with a beer.

"I'd buy you ladies one, but it isn't worth the fight. This is like Amsterdam on a futball night."

"Hey, Jaap," said Dennie, nudging him, "you been trying for the Whirly Bitch too, you've torn a hole in your pants."

"No, forsure," said Jaap, "it was the result of an outstanding screw on the table."

"Don't tell Rob," choked Dennie, as they all dissolved into tears of laughter and Jaap stared at them bemused.

As the evening wore on Sandra fought her way through the crowd to come up beside Ali, "So, I'm told you live in Peckham. What is that like?"

Ali rasied her eyebrows curiously. Here they were in the middle of Russia, streets full of new smells, sights and sounds and yet such was a person's fundamental love for her homeland that she was asking Ali about Peckham. Sandra the Russian expert. Perhaps Russia was old hat to her and Peckham new and exciting.

"Actually," said Ali, "in some ways it's similar to Moscow. Ugly, poorly built high-rises, surging crime rate, not too healthy for cars. Yet it is a place of contradictions. A warm Saturday night may be full of car races, boys jumping across bonnets and the splintering of 'Peckham Diamonds' on the pavement. Yet watching the fray will be my neighbour and his friends, who give me a beer and listen to music, while watching the 'fireworks' amongst the cosy Georgian enclaves and the harsh Stalingrad edges.

Peckham was once a country village and everything from the Gothic two-storey castle, where some eccentric householder has painted the walls like a rainbow to defy the graffiti artist, to the dog-poo park with the monument to the heroic dead reminds you of this sylvan lineage!"

Alice raised her eyebrows, "Oh yeah?"

"Certainly! My neighbour grinds her own spices and each morning I wake tantalised, imagining I'm in India. I fetch my paper from the local shop, where the Asian owner calls me 'Madamluv'. And there is the small boy kicking a coke can in the morning, balancing the boy selling drug in the evening."

"So," asked Sandra quickly, "is it the same boy? Same frustration? A whole generation? These things worry me. How can a happy future evolve from this early formation?"

Ali shrugged, refusing to be judgmental. "Peckham Rye on a Saturday teems with people just like Oxford Street, but the gospel preacher alternately sings through his microphone encouraging his laity in a body-joggling capriccio or rains curses on the godless. Sundays is a myriad of multi-coloured batiks; head-dresses of sharp, piled cotton cloth glowing against warm brown skin, as large ladies squeeze four or five into small cars going to church."

"Ah, yes but don't forget Peckham has the highest crime rate in the whole of the United Kingdom," said Sandra, "that is less romantic."

"Sure but there is more to Peckham than the newspapers's emphasis on street crime, drug drops and multi-cultural stabbing. Where there is multicultural death there is also multicultural life: you don't get much of that in Lower Bridlington on Sea. And then of course there are the street diamonds..."

"What?" asked Sandra, pulling nervously at her blond hair, while the others looked strangely at Ali.

"Diamond mines?" asked Dennie. "In London? Or is that just a description of the women: like Alice they sparkle, they reflect your glory and best of all they are worth a mint." Alice slapped him.

Obtuse Angles

Day three was the Navigation competition. It was scheduled to last all day. This, as they were told in the briefing tent, meant that those teams from the national squad who had already flown the course had to be separated from those yet to go, lest they told them something that would enable them to cheat.

"Don't you love 'em," Rob chuckled, "as though having had a briefing from us would help Pete and Daniel. They can't even read the rules, what good will it be me telling them where the judges are or the map reference for the bomb drop?"

"Ah," said Paul, "but it means we shall be alone with the lovely Whirly Witches. Locked up in a room with only videos and vodka, beer, peanuts, long legs and blond hair."

"In your dreams, pervert! You stick to Cora and Clorinda."

"I can hardly get them to leave me alone. They recognise grown-up power."

Ali and Alice were one of the last teams to go, only a few others, including Jaap and the Swiss man were scheduled to leave after them. To prevent the waiting teams from getting bored they were offered lunch at one end of the false teeth building, a Party school in less celebratory times. They picked their way through old-fashioned desks, with conjoined lift-up lids, to the canteen. The walls had been newly whitewashed. Lunch was chicken soup with bits of gristle floating amongst the oil slicks. Ali took one look at it and refused to eat, but Alice tucked in happily saying she liked Russian food, and she couldn't understand why Westerners were so fussy.

"It's all about survival," she said, yet again. Then, relenting, told Ali a story Lyuba had told her about forging her helicopter licence. "They used an egg," she said giggling. "When one pilot had had his licence stamped the others rolled a hard-boiled egg over the wet stamp and transferred it to their own licences. Of course that was enough, here in the land of bureaucracy. Have stamp can fly!" Then chastened she added, "but don't tell Daniel, he'll only use it to mock the Russians."

All the competitors were given a piece of writing in Russian to show to locals if they were forced to land, either because of bad weather or an engine problem. The script explained they were foreigners, spoke no Russian and would need help to be returned to Toshino. There was a number for the locals to call. Alice looked at the hand written note and chortled, pointing out mistakes to Lyuba. Jaap was also given one and was told he must not land unless it was really important. Landing away from the airfield would be a disqualification.

The Gazelles, the Whirly Women and the German girls had already finished when Ali and Alice watched Pete and Daniel pick up their maps and go off to examine them in an enclosed tent. They came out half an hour later, climbed into the helicopter and after a hurried start-up, taxied up to the departure line, where they were given their flour bags for dropping on the target. The French judge, holding an ancient analogue stopwatch, monitored the hand's progression to zero. Then a German judge brought down the starting flag with a sharp whoosh. Enclosed in the helicopter's own bubble, watching the exaggerated mime, the pilots sat like excited children viewing a silent movie. If they missed the departure time by more than a minute they would be disqualified, but Pete and Daniel lifted in a swift clean bound, disappearing over the trees like a bluebottle scenting meat.

Ali wondered where Joe was. She had been expecting him to watch her take off. Alice said he'd gone shopping in Moscow with Lyuba. "Shopping in Moscow?" Ali asked stupefied. "Why?"

"How would I know?" replied Alice fretfully, nervous now about her nascent navigating. "Perhaps he wants to buy one of those babushka dolls that heap up inside each other."

Ali bit her lower lip. If Joe was seriously in love, wouldn't he want to watch her flying, to empathise with her tribulations? It seemed not.

Rock meeting rock can know love better, than eyes that stare or lips that touch. All we know of love is bitter, and it is not much.

≈≈≈≈≈≈

Uncle Sam

Lyuba and Joe visited several shops before she dropped him at Belorusskaya metro station, saying she had "to make visits before return airfield". Joe waved, walking jauntily under the road, via the underpass to the station. There his eyes explored the railway station, visualising a past occasion when he had arrived from South Africa, full of hope and excitement. The Moscow he had visited then had been drab and grey, very different from the one he had been expecting, but his Russian had improved and his knowledge of life outside Africa soared.

Smiling his half smile he turned his back on his past and went into the metro station. He took the green line to Novokuznetskaya, there walking over to Tretyakovskaya and changing to the orange line, heading for Alekseevskaya, a route he had done many times in the past. Then the walls had been lined with propaganda and party slogans, now, though, capitalism was sprouting in the underground. Joe passed rows of magazines, but unlike the West where these were put out in bunches here they were sold singly on a thin frame like a traveller's clothes put out to dry. He towered over women sitting on the ground, or on a low stool, with one or two pairs of socks or large white knickers spread out on an old box. Corridors were clogged like coronary arteries by men and women selling shoes they had made from reeds, cake and biscuit vendors, touts with tickets and peddlers trading fruit and vegetables brought in from the country.

He also passed begging babushkas, and there he stopped and emptied his pockets of the remaining coins, even occasionally giving a ten-rouble note. He knew there was a sort of pension system for these old women but so little that it hardly covered a month's rent and, if the women had no families to support them, they were dependent on begging to keep alive. It saddened him to see it and he like Sergei earlier saw that not all change here had been for the better.

At Alexseevskaya more memories assaulted Joe as he left the metro station and walked down asphalt pavements: here he had had his first kiss, quivering with excitement and the likelihood of being seen. Across a mud path, he jogged up a set of concrete steps into a low block of flats. A large woman sitting by the door halted him with a question, and Joe replied in Russian that he was here to visit Olga Stevnkova on the third floor. Without a smile, but with some kind of acknowledgement she waved him through and he went on to a bank of vinyl covered lifts. Nothing had changed since he was last here. Even the missing linoleum on the lift floor had not been replaced. He pushed the tin bell, which disappeared behind the vinyl and had to be pulled back before the lift would move.

Eventually he arrived at the third floor and turned right out into the corridor. Nothing had altered, the same shards of broken glass, the same holes in the wall. In front of him was a padded door with a bell, which he rang. After a few minutes a woman in her forties opened the door, her face lighting up with pleasure when she saw who was standing there.

"Joe," she said in Russian, "welcome, welcome. When I heard there were helicopters at Toshino I wondered if you would be coming to see me. I am so pleased."

He kissed her on the lips. "Olga, my darling," he said, "I have missed you."

Deep Blue Hope

Finally, it was the girls' turn to get their maps in the small, stuffy tent. As they studied them, hardly able to breath in the close air, Ali noticed they were slightly different from the American satellite maps they had practised on. Several things, such as airfields or sets of buildings, seemed to be missing, and she spent a few moments concentrating before she realised these were not the same 1 in 1,000,000 or 1 in 500,000 they were used to using. Having realised that she thought they should probably be able to work with the charts, but she couldn't help wondering what would happen to Jaap when he tried to use them. She and Alice plotted their course.

They lifted from the start on time. Only a few seconds after the flag dropped Alice yelled: "Go!" and started her stopwatch. The first leg was uneventful with good ground features and predictable wind. They found the turning point and set out on the second leg. Here the helicopter was flying over banks of thick trees, the wind had increased and, with no natural or artificial markers to use as navigational points, the girls did not realise how much it was drifting them right. Only when Ali saw, with a sudden sharp shock, a small church, which should have been on her right appearing on her left did she accept that they were paralleling their course. Making a quick mental calculation she told Alice they would dogleg back on track. Consequently they arrived three minutes late at the second checkpoint. Alice clicked her stop watched irritably but didn't cry. She pointed out it was on the third leg they'd have to drop the bombs, so Ali had better speed up while looking out for the target, and then prepare to slow up and drop down, to give Alice a more precise aim.

On track, but now five minutes late, they saw the targets: painted crosses in an area cleverly disguised by the reedy grass of earthy tussocks. Alice saw them first having spotted the judge's Mil Mi-2 hiding in the nearby trees. "Must be around here somewhere," she chortled excitedly, forgetting all her earlier annoyance and not even wondering how they had parked the large whirling rotors without scything the overhanging branches.

"Hey, there they are, now slowly, slow down! Give me a chance."

She opened the door as Ali got close, trying to judge the wind and the time lapse of dropping from the moving helicopter. The first one went wide, but the second hit the forward part of the target, and learning from these she dropped later and the third flour bag hit the centre of the mark.

"Woppee! Wicked!" she cheered herself, and Ali, relieved that her charge was happy, laughed too.

"Well done, Alice, now all we've got to do is find the way home and remember to put on the landing light on finals."

They landed two minutes late but had found all the turning points and hit at least two of the targets. Alice seemed quietly pleased and even heard the news that the German ladies had landed exactly on time without wet eyes.

The last team to go was Jaap and the Swiss man. Ali and Alice joined Pete and Daniel, who were out of hibernation now the last team had set off, and watched them leave in the right direction. After they'd gone there was little for the teams to do except wait, and watch the organisers who were setting up a beer and vodka table for the celebrations when the last helicopter landed. The Gazelles were nowhere to be seen but Pete said they had last been spotted shinning up a pole in the sitting-out room, while impressing the Whirly Witches with their singing. Daniel, he pointed out, had already climbed much higher.

"Now the competition's over, prizes drawing nigh, will Jaap be back ere sunset falls, or much later than that," sung Joe to the tune of 'Now the Day is Over'.

Ali turned to him frostily. "Hello, there you are. I heard you'd gone shopping. What on earth could you buy here?"

Joe gave his half smile and dropped his hands briefly on her shoulders, removing them slowly like a gentle caress. "Would you believe different types of vodka! Lyuba showed me a shop where I could buy hundreds of types, from pepper to 100% proof. Now you see why Mike and I came by Enstrom. It may not be fast and we may run out of fuel at every possible moment, but by gum it is a good porter for life's necessities!"

In spite of her beating heart Ali smiled, finding herself checking his eyes for honesty.

One of the Russian judges came up to Pete waving his watch. "Friend is gone too long," he said confusingly. "More fifteen minutes."

"Ah," said Joe delightedly, "could that be Jaap do you think? Finally showing his worth."

Pete shook his head and listened while the judge explained there was a time limit on getting back and if they went over the judges might be forced to break radio silence, although that would disqualify him, so should they wait a little longer.

"I shouldn't worry," said Alice, secure in her knowledge of the rules. "If he's over the time expiration he's disqualified anyway, so you may as well call him."

The judge looked at Pete, who nodded, while Daniel said he would call if they liked. "He might prefer to hear my voice," said Daniel fallaciously.

"Jaap, Jaap," said Daniel, shouting into the microphone as though Jaap might be able to hear him through the molecules of the air, "where are you? More the point, do you know where you are?"

"Hello Jonger," said the Swiss man, relaying the message since Jaap was unable to transmit as his stick, and consequently his talk button, had been removed to make room for the flour bags. "Yes, forsure we are fine, but since we are the last to go and so wouldn't be holding anyone up and since we realised we couldn't win we've flown off towards Red Square, which we can already see, to do a Matheus Rust. We call you from the square."

"Get back here!" Daniel ordered arrogantly, and with some peevishness in his voice presumably thinking that if anyone was going to land in Red Square it should be him. "Don't you dare go wandering around like a lunatic. Already the Russians are threatening to send out a Hind to bring you in! Do you know where the airfield is? I repeat..."

"Yeah, yeah, yeah," said the irritated Jan, "all right, all right, we are on our way back. But I can tell you we think you are a load of spoilsports! Jaap says you are a group of putteren."

"What do you think that means?" asked Ali, but even Joe had no idea.

Across the lake and over the forest they could see the small R22 turning towards the airfield, clear regret in its bobbing flight home like a tired bumble-bee. Joe laughed and Daniel pulled down his pants to moon at the approaching helicopter.

"Jesus, Rob," said Paul smirking, "that arse makes my Cora look beautiful. I'd watch out if I were him, flashing that kind of thing around here with all those lusty American babes."

"Gits!" spat Alice, her face burning furiously, "why don't you grow up!"

The boys burst into uncontrollable fits of laughter.

In the evening the teams dined in the Great Hall of the hotel, a sort of preparation for the final ceremony in a couple of days.

"If this is the dress rehearsal," Ali said to Joe, picking at some dog meat, "let's hope they are practising to make the food at the real thing at least edible."

"The beer's good." He replied, taking a deep draught and looking at her softly.

After dinner the girls were in the hall with Daniel, Joe and Gary when two teenage Mongolian-looking girls in low-cut, bright green nylon tops came into the hotel. The night receptionist, a short man whose breast proudly proclaimed the hotel logo in purple thread, immediately jumped up, his hands already waving dismissal. However one of the girls pointed at Daniel, saying in broken English. "We come see him, Mr Daniel, he is come with us."

The receptionist halted uncertainly and glanced at Daniel waiting for his response. Daniel, excited by the idea of two girls arriving out of the blue to see him, and certain this must have something to do with his status as a helicopter pilot, laughed delightedly, gestured the receptionist away with an imperious hand and walked over to them.

"Hello girls! How did you know my name?"

"You are famous," said the fuller girl, touching her hair, "we like fame very much. Like you very much. You excellent pilot. We watched you perform."

Daniel gave an excited smiled. "You like me perform, 'eh! Hey guys, none of you have fans like this. Where shall we go, girls?"

"We go Night Club. We know very good place."

"We have limo," the slimmer girl said, putting her hand on his arm. "I am Alya."

Alice, who'd been watching the girls through tense eyelids, now cried, "Great! We'll go too, won't we Ali. I haven't been to a nightclub in Russia and I'd like to. OK girls let's go."

"Nyet," spat the chubby girl, "nyet. Have only space for two boys." She looked hopefully at Gary, obviously thinking Joe too big to fit in a space for one boy.

"Nonsense," soothed Daniel charmingly, "of course you must come Alice, come on." And he took her hand and brushing past their would-be hostesses they raced out of the door towards the shadow of the parked limo.

For a moment the Russians were nonplussed. Then they galloped into gear and pursued the couple out of the lobby, Ali and Gary following more slowly.

By the time they reached the limo a shouting match was in progress. Alice, already sitting in the car, insisting she was going, Daniel agreeing and the girls yelling, "Nyet! Nyet!"

Ali was fascinated by Alice's self-control; not once, in spite of her anger, did she slip into Russian, although she must have known to do so would have rid the place of the girls immediately. For some reason she wished to remain just a non-Russian-speaking tourist.

Gradually the girls began to give up. There were lots of hand gestures, some swearing (as usual recognisable even in a foreign language) and shrugging. Then, apparently dismissing the evening as a wasted job, they made signs to the tourists to get out of the limo. Regretfully Daniel and Alice climbed out of the long black car and the girls drove off.

Back in the foyer Ali saw Joe. He looked angry and when she approached him uttered tersely, "Why do you care what happens to Daniel?" before marching off huffily.

She watched him go, her stomach churning with conflicting emotions. She didn't understand him. What had she done?

"Take no notice," said Alice, coming up beside her, "he'll get over his jealousy and we probably saved Daniel's life."

"We did?"

"Sure. You read about it often in the papers, these whores coming up and enticing young foreigners into the dance halls, where they get them drunk, steal their money and sometimes even blackmail their families into giving more money. You want to watch us Russians. You know the date-rape drug started here."

"Oh. Did it." Ali felt lost. Small, provincial and lost.

"Funny, though," mused Alice, "that the girls knew Daniel's name. Odd, don't you think?"

"Perhaps they are helicopter buffs," Ali hazarded, but, seeing Alice's eyebrows again disappearing into the thatch above, asked, "OK, what do you think?"

"I think someone told them. Someone who doesn't have Daniel's best interests at heart."

Ali said nothing, but remembered Paula's letter. Could one of Daniel's former clients have followed him all the way to Russia to get revenge? Feeling a little more cheerful she thought she might send Paula a postcard.

On the fourth day there were no more games and, with only the Freestyle to go, which only Daniel had entered, the group were free to amuse themselves. Or rather, since their hosts were too hospitable to allow them a moment's boredom, there was an invitation to visit the Space Centre which directs the Mir satellite, Star City.

Early in the morning the teams, and the family members who had joined them by 747, piled into another long and decrepit pre-Bresnev bus (trying to avoid those seats which appeared to be unnecessarily keen on commemorating history) for the drive towards the suburbs. Alice got on the bus nervously, taking Ali's hand and whispering, "make sure that lunatic Sandra doesn't come near me."

Ali, who had already noticed Joe was not with them, saw Sandra was also missing. "She's not here," she said, keeping her voice and her thoughts neutral.

"Good. Then I only have the other half-wits to avoid."

The Moscow traffic was heavy, held up not only by the usual number of broken down cars which blocked the lanes with their steaming radiators, but also the helpful police interfence. While the bus sat in a long line of cars and buses, all keen to leave Moscow and all spreading dark fumes behind them like mobile chimney stacks, small children walked along the outside of the bus begging with plastic cups or open palms at each window. Cursing, the driver jumped out of his seat and, hopping down the steps, opened the door. He yelled something in Russian, shooing them away, and they moved on to the cars behind in the queue. Here, though, they were more successful, many windows opening and small coins being handed out.

"Gangs use children," said Charles, who had been talking to one of the translators. "People always want to give to children, but the kids don't get much of the money themselves."

"Are you sure?" asked Alice, her eyes gleaming. "I've heard about the street children in Vietnam, they seem to be very much begging for themselves."

"Maybe so," Charles spoke appeasingly but his eyes were curious, "but this is Russia, where the underworld is more organised than anywhere else in the world."

"More than China? More than Vietnam? I hardly think so!"

"I don't know." Charles gave up, bending his head to check his hair growth, his smile an interweave of obsequious and patronising.

Little sheds of corrugated iron sat in the gutter or on portions of pavement as though hundreds of road sweepers had set up camp, which judging by the floating rubbish they hadn't. Gary asked Lyuba what they were for.

"Garages," she explained, "our government has no garages so individuals make their own car protection. Once you had to go on list to get a car, now everybody is owner, why is so many and so much traffic."

Some of these little movable garages were just conjoined sheets of corrugation, while others retained the shape of the car within. Jointed at the middle, half a car swung open upwards to give De Lorean like access. Gary took photos of them and wondered if he could market them in Liverpool: a new invention from Russia. But did it have the ring of Taiwan?

The bus chugged on through suburbs of flats and high-rises and then through fifties-built drab villages on the outskirts of the town. Every now and then there was a neat little 'common house', as Lyuba called them, from the past. Crumbling slightly, there was still delicacy in the latticework around the wooden roof. Occasionally, attempts had been made to shore up porches and verandas with bits of driftwood and tin. Ali noticed the trees were dusty at this level, and wondered if she had had to land on the trees would there have been a large cloud of dust sweeping around and settling on her grave.

Finally the bus turned into some black wrought-iron gates, impressively decorated but so rusty at the hinges that a fat baby could have knocked them over with a careless waddle. As they drove down dilapidated tarmac to the dirty concrete building ahead there was grass growing between the paving stones and the outhouses stood empty, their wooden struts splintering into ragged strips and their bricks desquamating into chips, their neglected doors leant open, hanging on their hinges like a drunk clinging to his chair.

"Odd, isn't it," said Charles tentatively, his foot turning in a jagged crevasse as they jumped down into the cracked concrete car park, "that they can put a satellite into space but they can't fix the earth station!"

"Matter of priorities, I should say," said Alice testily, "reserving their money for the important things."

Charles heard the heat in her voice and glanced at her, again puzzled. Daniel remarked blithely, "Oh, Alice is a convert! She can't see anything wrong with anything in Russia. It is her form of Paradise!"

"At least I don't muck up things from sheer laziness," sneered Alice. "Or look down on others for practising. I suppose you think tennis players should not practise either!"

"What rubbish..." began Daniel, increasing his strides as Alice began walking away, glad she'd had the last word.

Ali and Charles climbed up the steps, past colossal round pillars into the heroic Soviet-style entrance hall with a marble floor. There was a musty smell in the air, and Ali wondered how it was possible for such a large chamber to remain airless. They waited a few moments, while Kevin discussed something with Sergei, and then the guide began the tour with an introduction to the many uses of the station: training, monitoring, living areas, research and development.

As the tour progressed they again and again saw signs of a lack of money: photographs along the walls (including Ms Sharman the British scientist) with brown edges curling in the stale, damp atmosphere; the lino in the corridors so full of holes you could see the maze of string-work beneath and the bicycles, leaning against the wall, so rusty their chains were brown and flaking. The teams saw where the astronauts changed, where they ate, and the centrifuge where they did their g-force tests, but the benches they used were disintegrating and the cutlery corroded. Everywhere there was a feeling of deadness, of lacking inhabitants. It reminded Ali of Alice's parent's hall with its aura of desertion. It felt as though all the scientists and astronauts had gone into space, leaving only the guides and tourists to fill the vacuum.

They visited the museum and saw pictures of the Cessna in which Yuri Gargarin had died and the tiny capsule in which the first astronauts had returned to earth. They heard stories about how long it took the astronauts to walk independently again after being cramped in such a small space, and saw broken parts of the earth-returned space modules. Bits of which, the docent told them happily, had been used by peasants as animal pens and roof enhancers, until they were retrieved by the scientists.

On the edge of the plant there was a large under-water swimming area in which astronauts did various experiments. Huge glass windows gave the scientists, and now the tourists, excellent views of how the subjects behaved in this weightless aura but, the guide told them, the pool had not been used since 1989, as the station could not afford the cost of the water.

"No sense of proportion, Ruskies," said Kevin, coming up beside Charles. "I wonder if any of this lot have had their wages paid."

Charles shook his head and said mildly, aware of Alice's angry back, "Possibly not."

"Certainly, I'd say. Remember the translator in Byelorussia! Damn cheeky to expect us to tip and give so much..."

"But it's so little to us," Ali broke in. Kevin looked at her with dead trout's eyes, for a moment she thought he wouldn't deign to answer, then he said. "You are missing the point. It's a point of principle. Wages should be the first thing paid, before you go seeking glory. I would have imagined you of anyone would understand that idea!"

Ali blushed and looked away.

"The Russians," said Kevin, staring at a particularly worn piece of lino, "spent forty five billion dollars between 1958 and 1973 on space travel, even the Americans only spent twenty five billion, and which is the richer country? Which had more need to support its population?"

"I'd say it was a matter of perspective," Alice broke in, turning round quickly, her mental guns blazing through her soul's aperture. "Which might not be something those from the West with their total petty-minded self absorption can understand!"

Kevin's fishy lips almost disappeared but before he could reply he was interrupted by the guide, who said they were now going into the control room where they would see the satellite on screen and there should be no unnecessary talking.

The control room was an enormous barn with rows and rows of television screens, behind which sat lines of working men and women. In spite of the size of the room and the height of the ceiling there was the hot, moist smell of people working at fever pitch. In front of them, partially filling one wall of the room, a monumental movie screen on which tiny objects moved. Before Ali could concentrate on what was happening Charles kindly began explaining.

"That's the main body of the satellite, look now! Can you see them docking? Notice the mechanical arms... there! Now, if you look in the distance, at the far side of the screen, you can see the moon..."

As they watched the docking was complete and everybody in the room gave a rather muted cheer. Muted perhaps because too much exaltation would be unseemly in the presence of foreigners, most of whose countries didn't even have a spacecraft, let alone all their expertise.

The guide then led them to the shop, where Ali bought lots more Peckham-metal ornaments, because she felt she ought to. Charles and his wife Nancy also bought heavily, while Kevin sniffed there would be no room for these things in the Robinson and he hoped Nancy was going to take them in her hand luggage on the jumbo. "Oh, yes," said Charles, his face almost splitting with mirth, "and she'll wrap them in cling-film along with her cliches!"

Corrugated Iron

By the evening both Ali and Alice had had enough of team talk and delightedly agreed to join Gary and Daniel in exploring Moscow and looking for somewhere delicious for dinner.

"I cannot bear to eat another one of their 'foreign menus'," said Daniel. "If I have to eat another Russian derivation on the theme of Chinese I will be sick."

Lyuba told them they needed tokens for the Metro and allowed them to buy some from her. It was roughly four pence each time you went into the Metro and there were no zones or differing prices like London, so it was comparatively easy. Alice and her guidebook suggested they took the Metro along to Mayakovskaya, walk down a beautiful street to Pushkinskaya and then get back into the Metro there, to get out near the Kremlin. The others agreed.

Alice was sparkling more than any recently liberated Peckham diamond as they went down into the metro, following the guide book's directions. The green-line was deep and its three-lane wooden escalators were lit by fat plastic candles sitting on the wide banisters. Alice had made Ali promise not to tell the others she spoke Russian, and told them she could read the Cyrillic signs from her knowledge of Greek.

"It's close enough and I guess the rest," the edge in her voice underneath the off-hand dared anyone to challenge her, but Gary didn't notice and Daniel was too preoccupied with the fun of running up the down escalator.

"Nyet! Nyet!" A babushka with a red arm band at the top of the moving stair-way yelled at him, coming out of grey kiosk to shout volumes of Russian they couldn't understand.

"Come on Daniel," said Gary, nervous under his bonhomie, "you know Commies can't stand any independence, you'll get us in the nick."

Daniel, halfway up the staircase turned and began to run back, sliding on the bannisters and jumping in leaps in case the babushka followed him.

The Metro was an amazing place, more like an underground museum than a conduit to work. An impressed Stalin had built it after he had travelled on the

London underground. Where, however, the Victorian model was narrow and ceilings low, here Stalin had built a monument to remind his workers of the glory of their nation. The entrance halls were grandiose like cathedrals, the ceilings throughout the Metro were high and ornate, some set with scrolls, others with Art Deco design and others with reminders of great writers of Russia's past: Chekhov, Pushkin and Mayakovsky. Little Venetian bridges allowed movement between the platforms. On some stations statues lined the track, set back in little alcoves like the classical rooms of the British Museum. And like a museum it was virtually empty.

Ali wished Joe had come with them, but Mike had asked him to entertain his daughter, who had flown out with her mother to spend a few days with them visiting Moscow. When she'd pressed him, he took her hand and said sadly, "I can't Ali, I'd love to but I really can't."

And, in spite of his loving eyes, she again wondered about his devotion.

"Come on," said Alice, taking her arm, "it's this way. I remember reading about the place."

"Where are we going?" Ali asked, trusting Alice's guidebook more than what the girl had learnt from her teachers at school. Teachers Alice described as incredibly well informed people, considering they had had to imagine a country rather than visit it. "What does the book suggest, Alice?"

Alice shook her head. "I'll find somewhere."

At Mayakovskaya they found an Art Deco station, with elegant pillared architecture planned by Stalin and modernised by numerous large locked corrugated iron boxes, which sat between the marble columns.

"Look Daniel," joked Gary, "they even have car garages in here, I wonder how the cars get in!"

They left the station into a square dominated by a statue of Mayakovsky and, using the dying sun, found south. Although it was getting dark they could see that they were walking along a wide boulevard of tall buildings, some of which had been built in decadent Tsarist times. These were now converted into flats, although many looked empty. Empty or full the passage of Moscow climate and neglect had allowed the facades to lose much of their original glow, plaster was missing in many places and the paint was so dirty all the houses seemed coloured grey.

Gary drew Daniel's attention to the wide-bore tin drainpipes running onto the pavement and thence to the road. "Hey, Dan, look at the size of these! Must rain like Hell in the winter. Bet the pavement floods."

"I could live here," said Daniel, uninterested in the drainage. "I bet you can buy one of these palaces for less than nothing and live here in style."

"Um," said Ali dryly practical, "you'd need plenty of servants to live in barns like these. Not only to cook but to do the fires in the morning. Just think how cold it would be in winter, especially here in Moscow where it drops to about minus twenty, and then you'd need a team to clean the place. You wouldn't get me living there without at least twenty maids, and fifty outdoor staff."

"God! Where's your sense of romance. Think of the history, the drama, the beauty. You'd come and live here with me, wouldn't you Alice?"

"Absolutely. We'd have diamonds and rubies..."

"Peckham diamonds and hospital rubies," said Ali, but the others had drawn away from her cynicism, sparkling like their imaginary gems.

"...and flowers in every room, with fountains..." Alice was crying.

"Waterfalls," said Daniel, "beautiful waterfalls pulsating from natural stone, surrounded by flowers and dropping through gold rings..."

"Leaks probably," said Ali, "Russian leaks must be at least twenty degrees below Welsh ones." But there was no one listening to find her funny, even Gary had drawn ahead with the optimists. Where was Joe? Had he been there, she thought, he would have said: "The great houses remain but...those who sang in the inns at evening have departed; they saw their hope in another country."

They went back into the Metro at Pushkinskaya and travelled virtually alone down to Borovitskaya, which Daniel (suddenly knowledgeable) claimed was the nearest station to Red Square. Coming out behind a spout of modern, communist architecture they found themselves at the State Library. The rather poor map in Alice's guidebook directed them to the Alexandrovsky Gardens, behind the walls of the Kremlin. From here they could see the Golden towers of the Kremlin cathedral and Yeltsin's office behind the tall wall with its strangely Italianate watchtowers. Huddled under the walls in a corner of darkness were a group of men gathered around a brazier shining like hot red beacon amongst the dark colours of their clothes in the shadows. There was something nineteenth century about the effect, and Ali found herself expecting a man in rags with a knife to jump out singing 'all day long I'd diddle diddle doo, if I were a wealthy man'. She could hardly repress her giggles.

"Ssh. Don't say anything," Daniel whispered in her ear. "Don't give yourself away as a foreigner. They look stronger than us. They'd kill us for a couple of dollars."

The four of them huddled together and walked on nervously past the Trinity Gate in silence. Russians in greatcoats regarded them malevolently but made no move towards them. (Later Lyuba explained this was the Eternal Flame and, far from being vagrants huddling for warmth, these were the guarding soldiers.)

They walked along the wall under a bridge and through a gate into the tip of Red Square, abeam the history museum. They debated whether to have a closer look at Lenin's tomb but instead went into the small, old streets of Kitay-Gorod, which Alice's guide-book told them meant Chinatown but had nothing to do with China.

"Bit cryptic your guide book, isn't it!" said Gary.

"Must be written by a Russian," added Daniel. "Doesn't it tell us a good place to eat? I'm starving."

"Too right!" Gary agreed. But Alice shuffled them down the Uiltsa Varvarka, a road in which monasteries and Orthodox churches reared out of the dark like gold-topped witches. It took them towards a square in what seemed like a residential area. As they walked down a narrowing pavement a young couple came out of a small gate and nearly fell over Gary, who had stopped to stare at an inscription in Cyrillic.

"*Pazhalsta*," they apologised together, "so sorry, my fault."

The boy let the gate swing, drawing their eyes to the dilapidated monastery behind.

"Not in very good nick, is it," remarked Daniel.

"No worries," said Gary cheerfully, "I was standing in the wrong place! I always had feet like Charlies!"

"Ah," said the boy, "you are English?"

"British!" corrected Gary, "Welsh on my mother's side."

The couple stared at the group, either astounded or trying to guess what Gary had actually said. Alice examined them for a moment, before asking them in English if they knew The Red Pelican Restaurant.

The girl glanced uncertainly at the boy and it was a while before either of them spoke. Then the boy said, "We know Red Pelican, but you cannot go there. Is not good place, very expensive."

"But I've heard very good things about it," said Alice. "It's in the guide book."

The girl laughed to show politeness. "Nyet. Not good place," she echoed. "We are Christians, have just come from prayer." She indicated the courtyard behind. "We show you better place."

Gary and Daniel, who were getting hungry and bored, agreed and Alice allowed herself to be led to the new place, but Ali was pretty certain she would find something incontrovertibly wrong with it. She was right. While Alice admired the decor in the first restaurant and, when that had been rejected for a terrible menu, the food in the second, while the furniture was splendid in a third, none of them were completely right. The Russians tried to insist on some places but Alice demurred and the boys did not even try to argue. Ali didn't want to, she was excited by the whole scene and wondered what Alice was up to. "Let us go then, you and I," she thought to herself, smiling, "through certain half-deserted streets, the muttering retreats of restless nights in one-night cheap hotels." If Joe was there she knew he would have added: "Oh do not ask, what is it? Let us go and make our visit."

Reluctantly the Christians agreed to show them the restaurant Alice wanted. They walked through a large, brightly lit square, full of young people and sharp posters and on into a smaller, darker side street. The Christians stopped in front of a large door with a couple of steps off the street. There was nothing here to make it obvious that this was a restaurant, but when Karl rang the bell an uniformed man appeared. When he opened the door a heavy curtain immediately fell behind him, obscuring any view of the inside from uninitiated eyes. He said something in Russian.

Karl replied, and although Alice's gaze followed their every word she didn't say anything but let Karl argue and bargain, finally getting them a decently priced dinner. There was a lot of head shaking, refusing and walking away by Karl but eventually some kind of compromise was reached and Karl turned to them.

"Price of 1600 rubles, which far too high, but he give us oysters for that, so perhaps is worth it."

Daniel, who like the others had been amazed at the cheapness of the deal, asked Karl and Karine if they would be their guests. The Russians agreed and the six of them followed the uniformed man into the subtly lit hall with its muted maroon drapery and swirling gold-decorated ceiling. There was a large mirror with a gold-painted frame at one end of the hall, draped in swathes of maroon velvet; a trompe d'oeil which, in spite of showing a second gleaming chandelier as ornately glass and gold as the first, deceived Ali. The Christians looked around with a mixture of awe and relish at the silks and satins, the velvet and the brocade. The fact that light had faded the colour and mites had torn away bits of the fabric not denting their delight.

The group followed their guide up a broad, gently sloping oak stairway, with heavy red carpet and gleaming stair-rods. Above were doors, covered in thick, dark green and gold, velvet curtains, surrounding a small landing. Ali was beginning to find the place creepy, and almost expected to see a suit of armour and a replica of Ivan the Terrible. The Christians, however, were bubbling with curiosity and excitement and pointing things out to each other, and whispering. Alice had become suspiciously silent. The boys too were quiet, Daniel peaking a look at himself in a gold rimmed mirror on the stairway and more enthused by the place than Gary, who was wondering what was wrong with a thick cut steak and chips in the first restaurant. It was impossible to see out of (or into) any of the windows, which had shutters as well as thick curtains.

The dinning room was devoid of people, but a few gleaming tables were already laid, shining with crested silver, in groups of four and eight. Another crystal chandelier dripped from a ceiling embossed with gold moulding. Escorted by a waiter in green and gold livery, they passed through this room into one with a piano player at the end and a smaller, darker room at one side, here they could just view the outlines of a discotheque table through the gloom. The waiter led them to a table of six next to an enormous mirror that filled the whole wall, while the piano player struck up the opening cords of Lily the Pink.

"No one else eating?" Daniel asked Karl surprised.

"Is expensive," said Karl, "not everyone comes here. Is special restaurant."

As they settled down and began leafing through the menus, completely lost in the Cyrillic twirls and curls, there was a furore of noise at the entrance to the first room. The noise burst into the dinning room metamorphosing as a group of six diners, three men, in their forties and fifties and three girls, in their teens or twenties. Noting their ages and dress Ali was mentally stacking them as tarts and toffs when she noticed something about Alice. She looked at the girl.

There was nothing specific, nothing Ali could definitely say had changed but she saw Alice was completely obsessed by the new group, tensely watching their every move the way a jilted lover watches his ex-fiancée. However, Alice did nothing unusual, merely waiting until the group was settled at the table opposite, and then, turning to Daniel, sparkling away once again. Peckham-hard diamond, am I seeing the actress and the diamonds, Ali wondered.

The first course arrived and the Christians tucked in rapaciously. Even though they had at first claimed they had already eaten, to the pilots it appeared they hadn't ever eaten before. The only disappointment was the non-arrival of the oysters, which were replaced by an extra course. Strangely neither Karl nor Karine seemed in the least bit surprised at their absence.

All evening, as one course succeeded another, as red wine bottles replaced white, as the breadbasket was replaced by biscuits and then by cakes, Ali was waiting for Alice to do something odd. Not by a blink or a gesture did she do so. Throughout dinner she continued telling stories, flirting lightly with the boys, pretending to try out a few words of recently learnt Russian. Giggling at everyones' jokes, listening to their tales, she was the perfect mature debutante, equal to every opportunity. Until, the last piece of cheese finally finished and even the Christians completely satiated, she suddenly jumped to her feet.

"We must toast our Russian friends," she cried, lifting her full glass towards the light and turning to Karl and Karine. "How do you say in Russian...cheers? I know! It is nastarovia. Nastarovia, my friends. Nastarovia!"

Their glasses rattled and chimed with international emotion. Alice smiled around the table; the perfect hostess. Ali, pulled by the pressure of Alice's eyes, rose too clinking her glass all around. Then the boys and the Russians too were rising. All standing, all raising their glasses, suffused with proud nationalism. Alice still crying, "Nastarovia. Nastarovia".

As her voice reached its peak one of the men on the opposite table looked over. He smiled and lifted his glass too.

"You have an excellent accent," he slurred in slanted English. "We Russian table would like to salute our foreign friends. Nastarovia. Nastarovia".

"Nastarovia. Nastarovia. My new Russian friends. Nastarovia. Nastarovia".

Ali followed the direction of Alice's gaze, noticing that while she toasted the leader of the group her underlying attention was focused on another man, sitting towards the end of the table. He had a hard face with a large nose and a prominent forehead. His chin receded into his neck and gave his mouth the appearance of pushing forward ahead of the other features. He was bald. Somewhere, Ali thought restlessly, she'd seen that look before.

All the Russians on the other table were now also rising. "Nastarovia. Nastarovia".

"Nastarovia. Nastarovia..."

Again the man on the other table complimented Alice on her Russian accent, but this time he did so in Russian, and Alice thanked him in Russian. All the Russians twitched with sudden suspicious interest. Ali watched them with a growing sense of disaster. She waited for chaos to arrive, for the ceiling to fall in, but then Alice giggled and said in English.

"I'm sorry I've exhausted my Russian," and they all relaxed again.

"Nastarovia, nastarovia." This time it was Daniel toasting.

Daniel was quite drunk, he waved his glass and kissed all the girls, but Ali thought that he too had noticed something strange in the scene. Something was happening but she wasn't quite sure what. Perhaps she would have a chance to ask him later, after all he had been a detective.

After much toasting the British table kissed all the Russians on the other table and, after paying their bill and saying farewell to their Christian friends at the underground, returned to the hotel.

"Come and have a last drink in our room girls," Daniel insisted, "Gary's got a bottle of whisky and I want to have someone less boring than him to talk to into the morning hours, after all I've got to do the Freestyle tomorrow."

"So you have," said Ali, wondering if she could get Daniel to explain that scene in the restaurant. "OK, but just one quick one, I'd hate anyone to say we knobbled you!"

"Oh, I'm better with a hangover, fly like a moon chick."

"I've had enough," said Alice, quieter than she'd ever been. "I'm for bed like Ruska Doronin. See you in the morning guys."

The boys didn't understand what she meant, and in their happy flying state hardly noticed she'd said something odd. Ali did but didn't understand it. She had a feeling Alice was quoting Solzhenitsyn's The First Circle, which she'd carried with her all trip, and in which Ruska Doronin was one of the characters, but could not imagine what she meant.

Ali and the boys had a whisky and talked about Daniel's routine for the Freestyle. She wished Gary would go to the loo so she could ask Daniel about the restaurant but he appeared leak-free. Suddenly she looked at her watch.

"Shit! It's half past two. Your Freestyle may not be until the afternoon but we have to get up early to go and have a go on the Kamov, remember Alice got me a flight. Shit! I'll never forgive myself if I muck that up."

She got up and went to leave. Gary waved a drunken hand and collapsed back on his bed, but Daniel took her hand and caressing it in both his own came with her to the door.

"I'm going with my future wife, Gary, don't wait up."

"What was going on in the restaurant?" Ali asked as they reached the door. "What happened there?"

"We had a good evening," said Daniel, putting his arms around her and kissing her on the lips. "It was fun, wasn't it, Ali. Shall we run off and get married now? Shall we?"

"Leave me alone, Daniel," she said, opening the door to leave. "Play your games with Alice."

"Darling! What is that baby to me? You are love, she is lust. Tell me you love me."

"Of course, I love you," said Ali kindly, kissing him on the lips. "But really, what was really going on? Really?"

He kissed her again, his face creased with the blank smile of the happily pissed.

"Good night, my little fruit bug," he said, "sleep well. We will party again a demain! My little love."

Ali staggered out of the door, half-drunk and half-regretful, straight into Joe who was walking past the door. She grabbed his arm.

"Oh," she said stupidly, "there you are."

"Indeed," he said, moving away from her falling embrace, initial surprise turning to distaste in his face. He looked at his watch demonstrably.

"So!" he said, in a voice Kevin would have given teeth to be able to emulate, "I supposed you've forgotten that Daniel has the Freestyle tomorrow. I hope he's not going to lose just over some one-night floosie."

"What...?" she began but Joe had already gone into his room slamming the door with cantankerous calm.

Shaking she went back to her room. Collapsing on her bed she noticed Alice was asleep clutching her beads like a baby's comfort blanket. Shaking as though she'd had another tail rotor failure, Ali moaned quietly to herself. What had she done? She had had too much to drink. She had been trying to get Daniel to explain what he knew about Alice. She thought she was being clever. That she could charm him into telling her the truth. What a fool she was. And now Joe hated her. Joe. Joe. *But I was young and foolish and now am full of tears.*

Male ego, she thought. Large but brittle, the male ego withstood the tread of an elephant and yet shattered with the smack of a feather. While a woman defeated remains friends, a defeated male never forgives, never forgets. Look at Kevin, she thought, power ball ego, constantly wishing to be in charge, but foiled again and again by Pete and Daniel; they would never get anywhere in the helicopter world while Kevin was the leader, they were not nearly deferential enough. Such is male competition. Hoping that Joe had not reached that point she fell into an exhausted and alcohol-generated sleep.

Inside his room Joe walked to the window and put his head against the cold glass. He looked out into the almost black Moscow night and cursed. Bloody women, they're all the same. Women, he thought bitterly, could never stay the course. Always went to the first man who asked. Who was it said: "Her cabined, ample spirit, it fluttered and failed for breath...Eternal passion! Eternal pain!" Well, he got it in one!

He might have forgotten the quote but he remembered his wife. An Indian girl. He had married her against her will, arguing that his family believed in it and it would give her a better life. She just wanted to be friends but he was insistent and she gave in, only partly to go against the apartheid system. It was so exciting. So brave. And yet their marriage failed. Was it just that he was a shocking husband? Or was it that their beliefs were too polarised. She wanted to be a good wife; he wanted her to stand up and fight. He wanted her to be the strutting heroine on the stage of life.

After three months they were no longer in love, were arguing, and after nine months they divorced. She left the country. His parents celebrated, he stayed and did military service, only partly to make amends to his parents. And now Ali.

Ali was different. They shared more. Had the same interests. A big girl with ideals. Would his life stand scrutiny by a woman with ideals, Joe wondered. Even one who wanted him to be OK. Would she understand the historic context of some of his actions? Would she? Could she? Someone had said the worst thing was a woman with ideals, but Joe was too tired to remember either the full quote or the source. Instead he envisaged the effect on Ali if he claimed: 'My crimes are attributable to history'. Best not to tell her anything and let her discover, if she could, the truth.

Perhaps, anyway, love was nothing more than self-kidding. Comfortable clothes for desire. Perhaps he was just a few years off forty and wanted a sexy redheaded helicopter pilot with an equal eye-level. And perhaps she was screwing Daniel. But perhaps not.

Screwing Daniel!? That was like eating worms; you'd do it if you had too but not if there was a choice. He couldn't really believe something like that was serious. Irritating, but could you seriously screw a man like Daniel? If she was the sort of babe who could screw Daniel she was nuts. He was out of there. But maybe she had just been having a drink with Daniel. She'd been kissing him! But perhaps it was just a kiss. Is a kiss ever just a kiss? What was she doing in his room at two o'clock at night?

Joe didn't sleep well that night.

Kevin Confidential

Kevin did not sleep well that night either. Not because he was unhappy or because of the flickering street light that shone into his room through the flimsy (and somewhat dirty: he certainly would not have allowed such a thing in the Countess's home) curtain, but rather because he was delighted with his progress against the forces of Russian bureaucracy. So hard had some of his battles been with those who were supposed to be helping him into Russia (visas, invitations for visas, clearance, the impossibility of staying anywhere other than the accepted hotels and flying by accepted routes) that he at first wondered if the aim of his so called advisors was actually to keep them out of Russia, to prevent any foreign teams arriving at the Championships. Were they just making certain of a Russian win? Later he felt the problem was really the shapeless organisation, which had no powers of decision, could not say "Nyet" to a single party request (although they constantly said it to him). And men who were so scared of the system they were unable to be even minutely flexible or take any responsibility. He came to realise that they did not see that what they were doing was often actually obstructive to their own cause, let alone his interests, but imagined they were being in someway helpful.

Kevin had heard Jaap calling the Russians secretive and even his bright friend Charles calling them duplicitous, but he dismissed such euphemisms; the Russians were liars. But unlike the baffled Jaap or the intellectual Charles he knew why: fear.

Had Kevin been a literary man he would have said to himself: 'Say Russian and I will show you fear in a handful of dust', but, although he had dusted the books in both the Countess's London apartment and her country seat, Kevin was no intellectual. Fear, as Kevin knew from his guts, formed the reason for most decisions even in free countries, let alone here amongst the Stalin-schooled and Dumas-directed population. Fear and longing for power over their own lives, which they sublimated into tiny, devious actions; pointless lies that could only hamper the unenlightened foreigner and yet seemed to give them some footling impression of control. He congratulated himself that he, seldom afraid and always knowing how to grasp power, had defeated their most sinuous schemes.

The most tiresome problem was when he was informed by the Russian Helicopter Club that there was no piston fuel available between Warsaw and Moscow and that they would, therefore, have to fly it in at a cost to the arriving pilots of $10,000 US. Kevin refused this extra cost and rang all his team to tell them they would be rerouting via Finland. Then, lo and behold, the Russians came back with a new price of $5,000 US, which dropped to $1,000 US until finally they agreed to meet the bill themselves. Kevin congratulated himself that few organisers would have had the will power to meet their bluff so consistently. But Kevin believed in the mantra if you say something simple, repeat it often enough and politely never take "Nyet" for an answer you will always get what you (and ultimately they too) want.

Few of his followers, naturally, had any idea of how hard he had battled to enable them to be here in such state. True his room was the best, but theirs were pleasant enough, all things considered, even that of the plebeian Ali Gee, who constantly complained about the food and her spoilt brat companion who cried over trivia or the self-centred Ortavias. Waste of space. Ungrateful amoebas.

Organising was his strength. He had organised the Countess until her death, even when she turned to the bottle and had to be organised through one clinic after another (she was inclined to turn rough and abuse the doctors, making her an unwelcome patient in spite of her limitless money). Later he had organised her funeral and the lawyer to keep her greedy stepchildren at bay. And now he organised those invertebrate, GPS-dependent, helicopter pilots, who longed to fly to Moscow and take part in the world games but lacked the strategic ability to do so. Indeed they fed each other with stories of how difficult it was to penetrate Russia, how many people had flown out to buy cheap planes and returned defeated by the Russian bureaucracy, which nullified an acceptable price; anecdotes which happily made his job all the more important to them.

Kevin smiled at the flickering light and, spreading his chest, thought about the book he was going to write: 'From Butler to Boss,' it was a certain best-seller.

Gogol's Armpit

The next day Ali and Alice took a taxi to the area of the drooping Kamovs. Only their Kamov was far from drooping, rather it was uncovered and champing at the bit. Alice, who was now suddenly happy to admit she spoke Russian, chatted away cheerfully to both the taxi driver and, when they arrived at the airfield, the pilot. Eventually, after a long conversation with much laughter and gesturing, she turned to Ali.

"He says do you want to start it? You can sit in the pilot's seat. Fly it all you like. He says treat it like your R22. You can do anything in a Kamov. He says, it is the easiest helicopter in the world to fly. Then when you've finished he'll take it back and really show you what it can really do. Sound OK to you?"

"Fantastic, but aren't you coming with us? In the back."

"No, I'm going to watch you for a while, take a few photos. Then I'll pop over and see Daniel doing his Freestyle. I'll meet you over there."

"All right," said Ali, too excited to wonder why Alice, who had previously wanted to fly the machine herself had suddenly lost interest. "OK, I'll see you later then."

Ali climbed into the machine on the left side and after some misunderstood instructions from the English speaking pilot managed to get the Klimov engine to start. The pilot was happy and gave her a thumbs-up, before motioning that she should lift off. Ali put her feet on the pedals in anticipation of torque spin and the pilot started to shake his head and smile. He indicated that she should give him control and put his feet flat on the floor, she did too. Immediately he pulled up on the collective, and the helicopter leapt into the hover. Happily he grinned at her. "Very easy. No torque!" He landed it again and gave it to her.

Ali was not so flamboyant and she kept her feet hovering near the pedals while she slowly lifted the collective, getting the feel of the machine. Once in the hover she gingerly pressed the left pedal, conscious she was moving a rudder not a tail rotor, trying to get her mind around this agglomeration of plane and helicopter. The agglomerate responded sensitively, yawing left. Gradually she got the feel of the machine. She twisted left and right. Growing braver did a little dance with the pedals and the collective. Left the hover and taxied up and down, took off and did a circuit, admiring the flats and trees of Moscow spread out below her. Even here, inside Moscow's outer ring, there were many trees amongst the houses, perhaps trying to keep the air free of the already fearsome car pollution.

As Ali got more daring the pilot grew happier and happier, often smiling and laughing, encouraging her with hand signals. Then he took the controls himself to show her what the machine could really do and they spun around, up and down like a helicopter version of Nureyev. Ali was amazed something that had felt so stable in her hands, was now dancing so manoeuvrably in his. She said what a versatile machine it was but, although he laughed and grinned and gave her many thumbs-up, she thought versatile might be a first for his English.

Having said many goodbyes and thank-yous to the very friendly pilot, who told her through a more fluent friend that it was a privilege to meet a flying woman (clearly forgetting their own team was led by two women,) shaken the hands of several laughing engineers, refused to drink vodka and kissed them all many times, Ali left them to walk over to the other side of the airfield where the Freestyle was taking place.

As she walked past the lines of abandoned helicopters she saw Joe sitting by the British tent, watching the Freestyle with Mike and his family. They were laughing lightly together and Mike was demonstrating some trick with a bottle and an egg. She walked towards the tent, hoping to explain the unexplainable. However, when Joe saw her he suddenly got up, said something brief to Mike and his family and veered extravagantly away towards the South African tent, going inside out of sight.

"Hello, young Ali," said Mike as she came level with the tent. "What have you done to my engineer? He looks like a man with a debt problem!" He laughed heartily, nudging his buxom wife to make sure she hadn't missed it. "A man with a debt problem!"

"I don't know." Ali muttered, more to herself than to him. "Men are strange things."

"Men! Men! It's you women that are weird. Never mind, let me introduce you to my wife and daughter and the three of you can all curse us to Hell, 'eh. Right, lovey 'eh, right 'eh?" He winked at his daughter. "You've got to laugh at things, young Ali. Nothing is worth dying for."

Ali sat despondently down on the warmth of the seat Joe had just vacated and wandered away into the field of her imagination, pretending to watch the Freestyle. However, Daniel's performance was something special and Ali was a soul pilot, so that kind of display could not but call her back to reality.

Daniel started with a deceptively simple turn around the tail, moving into a turn around the nose, tail high. The machine seemed to skip from skid to skid as he danced it around its nose, like Essex girls around a handbag. Then, without any apparent increase in power, he accelerated straight up, corkscrewing in the pull round and round like an ascending whirling dervish. Next he dived forward into a descent, but just before he seemed to be about to hit the ground pulled up into a torque turn to the left, followed by a pull-up to pedal turn right, all within feet of the earth which could so easily have swallowed him up.

As Ali watched she was impressed, not only by Daniel's dexterity but also by his showmanship, which was something beyond the mere movements. There was undoubtedly something special about Daniel's relationship with both the helicopter and the crowd, something shared with few pilots, many of whom could have made the movements but few of whom had that extra verve that turned the movements into a show. As she pondered this she noticed Kevin standing next to her chair.

"Pretty amazing, 'eh," she said.

Kevin turned and looked at her, it was a while before he spoke. Then he said, "I think he is dangerous, I would have marked him down for that if I were the judge."

Ali was nettled. "But, you're wrong. That's his ability; to make the actually safe look dangerous, that is what showmanship is all about."

Kevin continued to stare at her, contempt no longer veiled. "I would have marked him down," he said again, and walked away to stand by Charles.

Ali watched him leave, wondering what she or Daniel had ever done to cause such disdain in Kevin, then overcome with the creeping feeling that it was all to do with his lust for control and little to do with their failings. She imagined saying to Daniel: "You should be proud that Kevin feels the need to patronise you." She laughed loudly and Kevin, talking to Charles, turned and glared her way once again.

It wasn't until the Ladas arrived to take them back to the hotel that Ali realised she hadn't seen Alice watching the Freestyle. She asked Mike if he'd seen her and he, interrupted from an amusing chat with his daughter, replied absently that he thought she'd gone in one of the earlier cars.

Arriving back at the hotel everybody drifted upstairs to the bar for a drink, before going to change for dinner. Although it hadn't yet been confirmed, it seemed pretty likely that Daniel had won the Freestyle and the British team was busy celebrating their pilot's win. Ali, however, now saw that Alice was not here either. She took the lift up to their room but it was empty and showed no signs of anyone (let alone a cleaner) having been there since they'd left it that morning. Back in the bar she edged over to where Daniel, in the centre of a group that contained the Gazelles, the American girls and the French and German men, was being energetically toasted. She finally managed to get his attention for a short while, between 'nastarovias', 'skolls', 'cheers', 'santés' and 'a la tiene,' which danced around their heads.

"Daniel, have you seen Alice?"

Daniel disturbed from his celebration wasn't very interested, but, seeing her so distracted, frowned with concern. "No, I thought she was with you."

"Well she was, but then she decided to take pictures while I flew the Kamov, and when I got down, a bit late, it was just time to rush off to watch your show."

"How long is it since you saw her?" asked Daniel, looking pleased.

"Three, four hours I should think."

"Oh, my God! You're supposed to be looking after her."

"What do you mean?" asked Ali, "looking after her! She's over eighteen. What's going on, Daniel? There was something last night too, wasn't there? What is it?"

Daniel sighed the soul-wrenching sound of the misunderstood, raised his glass to a Frenchman who was applauding him, and took her arm. "Let's go outside, they won't leave me alone in here."

They left the bar, watched by Joe who had just entered, and sat down on a long sofa in the hall.

"I rather think she'd gone to try and find her father."

"What! He's dead."

Daniel sighed and looked around for Pete, but he was nowhere to be seen. "All right. I think I'd better tell you a few things."

Ali felt weak. She leant back against the reassuringly hard edge of the sofa. "What things?"

Daniel took a gulp of Russian champagne. "Well, you see... I used to have a detective agency... I wound it up for various reasons not relevant here."

"Umm," thought Ali, like lack of money because you spent it all on helicopters.

"Anyway, last year, while I still had the agency, Mrs Charleston, that is Alice's mother, who had heard of me through jobs I did for friends, rather successfully and actually rather more remuneratively than they had hoped, came to see me. She told me her daughter, Alice, was hot to go to Russia. She was learning to fly and had heard there was some flying championships going on and she was determined to compete. Now Alice didn't even have a licence, so anyone else would not have been that worried, but old Mrs C was frantic. She said Alice was terribly headstrong and would go whatever, so she had given her permission, and had even said she would help her organise it. She, you see, had heard that I was a rather important helicopter pilot as well as a detective and would be able to arrange all these things. Are you following so far?"

"Like a hungry Corgi," said Ali testily, wondering when they would leave the subject of Daniel and get on to Alice.

"I'm telling you these things as I found them out. Anyway, of course I said that was all no problem, but what was the fuss? I pointed out, you know, that Russia is no longer the Big Red Devil and we can go in and out like Sainsbury's. Well, almost anyway." He took another drag of champagne.

"She swore me to secrecy; she'd heard of course from many of my clients I was admirably trustworthy, and I think you can attest to that yourself, considering I haven't mentioned a word to you before about this. I, you know, only ever did clients through word of mouth, never needed to advertise. So, then she explained that Alice was actually Russian herself, not, as we all thought, German. And because of this, and Alice's huge current, and even huger potential, wealth, she was deeply worried about kidnapping. That's where you come in."

"I do?"

"Yes, well, just a rather clever extra, which I thought of when Pete mentioned you were out of a job. You see you are both the same height, both rusty heads and have names similar enough to confuse a Russian. It occurred to me that anyone thinking of kidnapping Ali might easily end up taking you instead. So I bribed Alice's normal teacher (who was small and dark and not likely to be confused with Alice) to return to Oz saying her father was sick, and you took her place. Clever 'eh."

"Gee, thanks a bundle. You didn't think of mentioning this to me so I could go and get Kung Fu courses or something first though?"

"No, well naturally we didn't want to alarm you, but you must admit it would give a potential kidnapper a bit of a scare, suddenly finding two instead of one Alice."

"Humm, just like the Wonderland, go on then. Her father?"

"Oh, yes, well that all came out in the wash. It turned out that Alice's mother wasn't actually her mother but her grandmother. Her father had been some party official who had forced Alice's mother, who was only a girl, to marry him. Apparently Alice's mothers family were from old stock, so naturally very frowned on in communist Russia, but they'd been keeping their heads down and surviving, and then this chap comes along and threatens to expose them if they don't let him marry their daughter. But then he turns out to be a bastard so Alice's mother and family decide to do a bunk, to escape out of Russia - don't look like that! She told me the story - but in the attempt Alice's mother was killed and her grandfather was wounded and although he got out he died shortly after they got to England. So, to protect her, Alice's grandmother pretended she was the mother, and then anyway she remarried so they all changed names. But she is still frantic the father may come after his daughter."

"And even more so if she is easily available in Russia," said Ali.

"Indeed. However it seems Alice, the headstrong girl, rather than waiting to see if he might kidnap her has gone to find him."

Enlightenment suddenly dawned on Ali! "Oh, shit! Last night."

"What?"

"Last night, that man on the table opposite... he looked like her! Alike enough to be a relation. Alike enough to be her father."

"Not the nastarovia man, he was blond and heavy, quite good looking for an older man, but that couldn't be her father, wrong build, wrong colour, forget it..."

"No. Also at the table, a quiet one. With the babe with the big boobs."

"Which one was that?" Daniel asked ironically.

She ignored him.

"Yeah, of course, I thought he looked like someone, but I wasn't thinking she might have a missing father, I thought he was dead. And older. Shit what shall we do?"

"Nothing, at the moment. I've got to change for the ceremony, and you'd better do so too. Don't think of going it alone! If she isn't back after the prize giving we'll go out together. OK."

"After!?"

"It will look suspicious if I'm not there to get my prize. Not to mention rude! And besides I expect Alice is fine. She is probably chatting away to her father, catching up on old times and just forgot the time."

"OK," said Ali, trying not to think his prize seemed more important to him than Alice's life. "But after the ceremony we go looking."

"Maybe, oh, and Ali."

"What?"

"Don't go saying anything to Joe."

"Why Joe," asked Ali bristling. Daniel must have seen some of their friendship and be jealous.

"Because," said Daniel slowly, "it was him who arranged for those nice Russian babes to try and take me to the night club. That was how they knew my name!"

And, having delivered what he knew would be a crushing blow, he walked away waving fingers like his father, although his still remained unstained.

The dinner was everything Ali had expected; borsch in which strangely stringy cheese danced amongst thick strips of beetroot, stroganov with meat that would have troubled a canine's canines, peas that melted on your tongue like marbles, and lemon pudding with acid drops. Practice had made perfectly foul. Ali was inclined to think she preferred her gristle soup. However, even the finest caviar would have tasted like ashes in her mouth, all she could think about was Joe and Alice. Where was Alice and could Daniel be telling the truth about Joe? If Alice was with her father would he be kind and return her, or would he keep her in exchange for money? Joe had indeed been away during the day, the day the Russian girls tried to kidnap Daniel. He claimed to have been shopping for vodka. Could he actually have been finding girls to kidnap Daniel? No! Not Joe. Why?

Besides, if Joe was responsible for 'Daniel's girls' (and here her heart started beating so loudly she thought it was trying to deafen her thoughts) then he must also have put the bulldog clip on the Robinson. He had had the opportunity. But that might have killed her and Alice. Surely not. Not Joe! Most of her mind refused to believe it. Joe cared for her, she was sure, she'd seen it in his eyes. He wasn't a killer. But he was a South African, had been in the military; under apartheid. So were many people, good people, nice people (there was conscription after all) it didn't make them all killers. But she still had a problem with her intractable inner mind, which refused to give him complete absolution.

At the Prize Presentation the Russians won everything. The Russian Ladies won the overall individual trophy, a first ever. Their triumph was followed by the Russian men and then the Byelorussians. The Russians also won the team challenge, the Americans coming second and, thanks to the Gazelle pilots's scores, the British team third, the South Africans grabbed fourth place, leaving the German and French to fight out fifth and sixth. The American Ladies were second in the Ladies' Competition and to Ali's surprise they came third, beating the Germans. Neither the French nor the South Africans had sent a ladies team. Daniel won the Freestyle. Jaap and Jan received a special prize for the team that gave most amusement during the tournament: the Potemkin prize.

Just as Ali was wondering if she would have to go up and collect their medal unaided, Alice slipped into the seat beside her.

"Thanks for keeping my seat!" she whispered. "I went for a walk and got lost. I only got back as you were going into dinner and by the time I had changed I was late. I've eaten though, I sat over the other side."

"What! Don't you dare... I want more than that!"

Alice's face turned the milky yellow of her drawing room chairs. "Oh! OK. We'll talk afterwards."

Both Daniel and Alice were extremely happy with their medals, Alice saying to Ali next competition they'd come back and win, but Ali didn't give a damn. She couldn't wait to get Alice somewhere quiet where she could hear the true story, and could hardly wait for the national anthems to be played out before she was dragging Alice off the stage to somewhere private. Even then it was impossible, with every member of each team wanting to stop and congratulate them. The French wanted to kiss them, especially Alice, at least three times each, and the Germans wanted to bow over their hands, the South Africans to hug them. Only Joe stood back watching, saying nothing but Ali, though upset by his cold distance, was too interested in getting Alice's secrets revealed to worry about him.

After hours of kissing Ali finally got Alice to an alcove behind the dining room where they could talk undisturbed.

"OK, Alice, spill. Don't hold back. I know that was your father in the restaurant last night. Did you try and find him? Is that why we had to trail all over Moscow looking for the Red Pelican?"

Alice suddenly looked very thin and young, and very vulnerable. There were tears in her eyes. "Yeah, OK. I did. I knew that was his favourite restaurant. Last night when we kissed them all goodbye I picked his pocket. I knew he'd have a business card, they are the latest thing in Russia, all the smart ones have them, so I got his Moscow address. I knew the country place already."

"Where we landed?" Ali, while pleased with herself for such deduction, felt her heart sinking. This was all bigger and more confused than she'd realised. Alice was not just a gentle sentimental girl but a general who had planned a full campaign.

"Yeah. But then, as you know, he wasn't there. So, today, when you were flying the Kamov I went and found his house. I waited for him to come home." She stopped and tears suddenly poured down her face. Ali said nothing, trepidation mixing with embarrassment.

Another Frenchman came out of the dining room wanting to give Alice a congratulatory kiss, and then an American.

"Look," said Alice, once they had got free of admirers, "let's go upstairs. We'll never be uninterrupted here."

Once in their room Alice, sighing, returned immediately to the subject of her father. "He didn't come home from the office until late, and he was drunk. I stopped the car at the gates by walking in front of it. At first he didn't recognise me, thought I was some floozy he'd done down. When I told him who I was he got angry. He didn't want to see me. He told me to go away! He told me he'd got another daughter. His new wife had had a daughter. Another daughter! Just like that, as though one daughter per person was enough! He said that my mother was a whore, that I might not even be his and he didn't need me, and if I didn't get out of his way he'd call the police..."

Alice was crying so heavily now, Ali put her arm around her shoulder. "He doesn't mean it. He was shocked. He'll come around..."

"Nobody loves me," said Alice, "nobody. I thought he'd be proud if we won..."

The tears came thick and fast like tropical rain and then like a monsoon shower dried up suddenly. "I hate him!" said Alice. "He killed my mother. If she hadn't been escaping from him she would not have died. Grandmother says she was always frail..."

Ali comforted the girl until she fell asleep. Then she stayed awake for hours pondering all these things like Mary in the Bible. Her inner mind, skeptically, told her she hadn't been told the whole story, but her imagination was not even half way to guessing what might have been left out. Sadly she saw she was a pilot who could quote, but not a psychologist up to intuiting anyone's motives or actions.

Alice and a father. Joe and Russian girls. Daniel and a detective agency. A potential kidnapper, who far from wanting to kidnap his daughter couldn't even be bothered to meet her. Why was Alice's grandmother so worried over something that was clearly a minimal threat? What about the tail-rotor failure?

Ali didn't fall asleep until well into the early hours of the morning.

Yehuda Diamonds

Because the competition was over, and they were spending the next day in Moscow, no one woke Ali in the morning and it was nearly ten o'clock before she opened her eyes. She looked at the clock and then, seeing Alice's empty bed, realised she was alone in the room.

Gradually, as her mind began to focus on the memory of the night before, she realised that although Alice's side of the room was a mess as usual, the clothes she had kept smart for wearing while in Moscow were gone. The wardrobe doors hanging loosely open revealed their empty hangers. On the door Alice had pinned a note.

Ali jumped out of bed and grabbed the note, tearing it in her haste to get it off the door.

"Don't worry about me," said the note, "I've gone shopping."

Ali sat down and laughed crossly. "Oh, Alice, Alice. Shopping! Shipping! Shopping? For what? How naive can you be? Do you really think I'm going to believe you've gone shopping?"

Feeling a little guilty but quite determined, Ali began searching through Alice's mess for anything that might give her a clue, either as to Alice's father's address, where she suspected the girl had really gone, or anything else that might help. The only thing she found was amongst the pages of Solzhentisyn. A handwritten letter in Russian, with small neat writing that was certainly not Alice's large flamboyant script, which she was using as a book-mark. Possibly this was a letter from her father.

Ali dressed quickly and went to find Lyuba, hoping to get her to translate the hieroglyphics. By chance Lyuba was still in the dining room, but when given the letter was rather unwilling to translate it.

"This is written to Alice," she said, shaking her Russian-red hair in deep dis-approval of reading personal correspondence.

"Yes, I know Lyuba, but you must translate it. Please."

"But it is a private letter, from her sister."

"Her what!"

"Oh, dear! I really think I should not..." She tried to force the letter back into Ali's hands.

"Believe me you should. Lyuba, Alice's very life may be in danger. I have got to know what is in that note. She mentioned yesterday she had a younger half-sister, her father had remarried, I had just forgotten. What does it say?"

Ali hadn't forgotten that Alice had mentioned a new daughter for her father, but since it had clearly been a surprise to her too this could not be a letter from such a person.

Lyuba stared at the letter for a moment. Then she said, clearly finding a Russian way of absolving her conscience while doing what Ali wanted, and what needed to be done. "All right. I won't exactly translate but I will tell you sort of thing the letter says, if is necessary."

"OK, go ahead."

Lyuba read for a few moments, then she looked up. "OK. This is from her sis-ter. Name is Galina, maybe why she asked me to call her Galina. She plans meet-ing with Alice, and she gives address."

"Yes, where?"

"It's in the country, in a dacha near Smolensk, a long way from here. This let-ter was written some time ago I think, before Alice left England."

"Shit! That's why we had to go to that place. Nothing to do with her father at all. But is there no other meeting place? I know. Where was the letter written from? What is that address?"

"It is in flat. Suburbs. Long way, in big house. Do you have map? I can show you where. I could take you later but first I have to do the translating for South Africans."

"No, no I'll find it, just show me on the map where it is and what is the near-est tube station."

"Tube?"

"Underground, Metro...banlieu...oh, what do you call it...?"

"Yes, Metro station. I understand." Lyuba spread out the map Ali gave her, but then shook her head. "This is tourist map. Only is centre. Galina is beyond Garden Circle and further."

"But I need to find her! OK, never mind. Tell me the address and which Metro station and what to ask for."

Lyuba looked at the address again and wrote it in English for Ali. "OK, can you say this address?"

After a few practices Ali reckoned she could be understood. "OK, which Metro station. You'd better write that in English too."

Lyuba, who knew the area although not the big house, asked: "Do you have

Metro map?"

Ali, feeling parochial and wondering why the hotel hadn't given her one, admitted she had not.

"OK, in Metro is map. You look for dark red line. End of line is Vykhino, you got that. I write it for you in English. Now we are on green line, so you must change. Easiest is to go to Tverskaya four stops on green line, then walk to Puskinskaya on dark red line then all the way to the end."

"OK," said Ali, "that sounds easy enough. Thanks, Lyuba."

"No problem," said Lyuba smiling, pleased with her own use of the vernacular.

Armed with Lyuba's instructions and without telling anyone else where she was going, because by she now she had began to suspect them all, even Daniel, Ali set out for Galina's flat. The air outside the window looked busy, as though it was raining, but in fact the sun was shining and the clouds whizzing by at such a rate they would not have had time to reach saturation point and throw out precipitation. She walked along accompanied by skidding papers, with bits of rubbish tearing past as though in a terrible hurry. Seeing the frantic movements of the wind made Ali anxious too and she hurried along faster than her normal pace.

Not until Ali had left Lyuba and was on her way to the underground station did she suddenly wonder how the nineteen-year-old Alice could have a sister who was old enough to own a flat. Even if her father had remarried immediately after her mother died, still all the children must be less than sixteen. And if Alice had had a full sister wouldn't her family have taken her too out of Russia, rather than leave her behind. Although it was possible you could only get one child out at a time. Ali vaguely remembered learning about Trotsky at school, his wife had only managed to bring out the son and then couldn't get back for the daughter and committed suicide. Could this be a similar situation? What a choice for the mother! Then, with a physical jerk similar to a sleep reflex, Ali remembered Paula's letter. Hadn't Paula said something about two half-siblings. A previous marriage. But was it the old man, who pretended to be Alice's father, but was really her grandfather, who had had two marriages? Or was it Alice's real father? And if so, did that mean that he had had three marriages? Ali strove to remember if Paula had given a sex to the half-siblings, but didn't think so. She said one had escaped to the west, but what about the other one? That could be the sister. Unless it was a boy.

Ali easily found her way to the Metro, but once in there discovered that the names of places were only written in Cyrillic. Why Lyuba, who must have known that, wrote the name in English was a mystery discovered too late. Still, she thought, looking at the Metro map, it couldn't be too hard. Lyuba had said, four stops to Tverskaya, then change to dark red line at Pushkinsaya. OK the line there was purple but that must be what she meant. Going to the end of the line should not be a problem.

She went down into the Metro, noticing what a deep station the green line was, and using the token Lyuba had given her. But once faced by a choice she

suddenly realised she didn't know which direction to go in. She asked a few people, who either said "Nyet" and moved away before she could begin, or looked
strangely at her and said, "Nyet" at the end. Guessing that she could only be right
or wrong she got onto the metro in one direction. Standing by the door, balancing on a hanging strap in case she had to jump out quickly.

She guessed wrong. After four stops the metro ended. Still, that was not so
bad, thought Ali, now she needed eight stops and she would be back where she
should be. So she got back on the train going the opposite direction and went
eight stops. Now, she thought, I only have to change to the other line and I can
go to the end of the tracks and get out, just to double check she counted; should
be nine stops to Vykhino. So Ali crossed one of the little Venetian bridges and
changed lines. However, there were three different hubs in this Station and Ali
got on at Chekhovskaya, not Pushkinskaya. After nine stops Ali did not come to
the end of the line, but instead to Chertanovskaya, halfway down the grey line.
Ali went one more stop then realised she had gone wrong. So she walked over the
platform thinking it must go back the opposite direction, but it didn't, it went to
the end of the line and she found herself at Bulvar Dmitriya Donskogo, which she
recognised because it was the only station with three words, however unreadable. So delighted was Ali to know where she was that she thought she could be
clever. She would take six stops to Sevastopol'skaya, change to the blue-green
line at Kakhovskaya, which would take her to Kashyrskaya, then three stops to
Paveletskaya, one stop to Taganskaya and from there to the end of the purple
line. A short cut.

Somehow after Kakhovskaya things went wrong.

Ali got off and on trains, saw red lines, which then were no longer red having
somehow merged to become green, brown and blue. She scrambled over bridges
and clambered up stairs to different levels, down and up and up and down: but
she never found the purple line. Corrugated iron boxes began repeating themselves amongst the beautiful stations. Mayakovskaya, which she recognised for
its Art Deco, turned up again when it should not, so she traversed the platform
and got back to Tverskaya. She strode off in one direction secure it could not be
Chekhovsksaya, so must be Pushkinskaya, but found herself back in Tverskaya.
Hot bodies pushed around her. Many had eaten garlic sausage. Most had
skipped the morning shower. Clothes reeked of frying. More and more of the
populace seemed to be travelling. It was very hot. Airless. People were moving in
the opposite direction. Shoving. Swearing. Red-armed band babushkas circled
her vision crying 'Nyet'. Grey kiosks seemed everywhere. She ran up and down
escalators full of darkened lights and broken candles. Long deep escalators.
Pushing people who seemed to want to stand both sides of the escalator. When
she asked for Vy-kino, she'd almost forgotten the name, she heard 'Nyet' 'Nyet'.
Nyet. Nyet.

Ali realised she was starting to panic. Where was she? She had absolutely no
idea and no one was going to help. There was a train in front of her, doors open.

She jumped on. Decided she would ride until the line ended and then see where she was. Ten stops and she came out at... at what. Holding her panic she saw she was on the grey line again. What a magnet that line was. She looked at her watch. It was two o'clock. She had been lost in the Metro for more than two hours. This was madness. Breathing deeply she calmed herself. It was much easier in the air. She decided to go back ten stops. Change back to Tverskaya and go home. Ask for a taxi to take her to Galina's address. Why hadn't she thought of it before?

She found Tverskaya. Got back on the green line and went five stops. It didn't look right. She now knew what Aeroport looked like and this was not it, for all the name started ABTO3...

Ali panicked. She must be in the right place. It was just a different side of the station that had confused her. Desperately she looked around for signs amongst the confusing Cyrillic and suddenly saw something she recognised. Bblixoπ B ropoπ. That was the right way. She followed the signs. Now there was even a red line Het Bblixoπ, which she went to follow, but the babushka with a red armband waved her away. So she took the blue door Bblixoπ B ropoπ, and found herself out on the street. Now suddenly she remembered why it looked familiar; it read Exit.

She was back in the streets with their unreadable names and their way of turning through 180 degrees so you were going in the opposite direction from the way you started. *Streets that follow like a tedious argument of insidious intent*

Quotes flashed through her vision, accompanied by boy soldiers armed with machine guns who stared at her insecurity. She wished she'd got a compass. She hurried through the streets so warm it seemed a Persian cat was rubbing against her, trying to smother her. She hoped she looked purposeful, she didn't want to be stopped and questioned by the armed boys. She noticed Russian men passing her with wet patches between their shoulder blades, and realised her own body was damp, she felt the trickle of water in her knees and dripping down her calves. The hand that still gripped tightly to Lyuba's piece of paper felt clammy.

Scenting the sweaty smell of one of these hot men passing her she held up her address to ask the way, forgetting, as usual, that not everyone speaks English. The man skipped to one side and vocally brushed her away with a distinctive, 'Nyet'.

"Friendly bugger," she muttered. Breathing deeply the pungent smell reminded her of horses in a hundred-degree temperatures. Pushing on. Getting even more lost. It was so much easier in the air where you could see the bigger picture, down here in the claustrophobic pit of the streets it was impossible to judge the true direction.

In the middle of the journey of our life I came to myself within a dark wood, where the straight way was lost.

Ali noticed the manholes covers in the street were decorated with what looked like a turbine engine design. She asked the way again. Another drenched shirt. Another 'Nyet'. Then someone suddenly hailed her.

"Hello," he said, "England?"

"Yes, thank you," she shuddered with relief. "Do you speak English?"

He smiled broadly. "England?" he repeated.

Realising she had probably used up all his English she pointed to the name on her paper.

"Here. I'm trying to get here," she said loudly. "Can you help?"

He nodded. With amazement she realised she must have got off at the right stop afterall. She was cleverer than she realised.

"I am really near there?" she shouted hopefully .

He smiled again and beckoned her to follow him. She hesitated a moment, noticing he did have rather small eyes, and his clothes were quite torn. But then remembered they were all suffering in the hot Russian summer and berated herself for being so parochial. He was just being helpful. Kind. Like the taxi driver in East Germany.

She followed the man into a small side road, then into another road. He stopped again, helping her through the teeming traffic where pedestrian life is low scale. She tasted as well as smelt the pollution of the leaded fuel; they were no longer used to that in England. Cars shugged and steamed, stopped and crawled. People jostled. He helped her, gently took her arm. Showed her another road. Then the way into a courtyard. Ali stopped for a moment uncertain, but he was gesturing, pointing at the address. She followed him. The courtyard moved into a little lane between buildings with another courtyard beyond, with a tree surrounded by weeds. A *babushka* was walking ahead, stooping to one side with the load of her heavy bag, her narrow back hunched in a way that made Ali feel secure. She followed the man into another courtyard. After all if it was a big house it must have a courtyard. He took her through a rusty iron door and motioned her ahead, into the flag-stone-paved corridor which was dark with broken electricity.

She noticed to her surprise he was moving up behind her. Then, just as instinct began screaming 'Run', he clamped something across her nose. She felt softness like cotton wool and the digits of his hand strangely outlined as though he was wearing mittens. She struggled. But it was too late. Her head began to spin and, still fighting against his hand, Ali lost consciousness.

≈≈≈≈≈≈

Alice in Wonderland

Alice walked down to the Metro station and took the green line to Teatralnaya, where she walked underground to Okhotny Ryad on the red line and taking one stop to Lubyanka changed to the purple line. Her sister had told her she lived at the end of the line, in a flat in a big house. Alice imagined she was going out to the countryside, beyond the circles of Moscow's roads and somewhere where an old palace had been converted into flats, much as in the film Doctor Zhivago, which Alice had watched more than twenty times.

Now it was daytime the Metro was busy. Full. Alice pushed past fat women and smelly men, rows of magazines for sale and clothing like socks and knickers sitting on upturned boxes, but she stopped for the *babushka*'s with their hands out, giving them fifty rubles a time, delighted to see their faces glow with thanks. When veterans from the Afghanistan war got into the carriage and told their tales, some being pushed on in wheel chairs, Alice increased the amount to a hundred rubles each, and some veterans even doffed their hats to her like the peasants her great-grandfather would have employed. He, Alice believed, was a good, noble man, who treated all his employees well.

As they got further out of Moscow the number of people in the carriage decreased and veterans and babushkas no longer begged. There were only a couple of women in crochet jumpers, which showed ugly bras beneath and some elderly men in black trousers with pale jackets that had never seen water. She noticed the stuffing was coming through the seats in many places and that the carriage still used screws and nails instead of rivets to keep the spars in place, but strangely there was little graffiti and most of the windows remained unscratched.

Finally they arrived at the end of the line and Alice climbed out on the station. These stations were not as appealing as those in the centre of town, but Alice, her thoughts full of Galina, didn't notice that Stalin had not given the same consideration to the peasants out of town as to those in it. She swept on up the wooden escalator, noticing, in spite of her emotions, that this one was a very short compared to the depth she had had to travel to get onto the green line, and that many of the fat plastic candles had stopped giving light.

Once on the street Alice had a shock; all around her were tall blocks of flats. However, she thought, no reason to suppose these should not have grown here around the big house, just as they did downtown. She got out the map of little lanes Galina had given her to follow. When Alice had originally seen these she had imagined she would be walking through fields, now she saw she would be walking through man-made paths, but nothing wrong with that. Alice went into a little shop, thinking she would buy Galina some champagne and caviar to celebrate. There was no such thing available in the shop, which appeared to be halfway through restocking. Eventually she bought something fizzy in a can, which a woman fetched from behind a plasterboard wall, and some dried fish. She also bought mosquito cream, for some reason stored behind the checkout desk. Armed with gifts, she began her navigation along Galina's map.

Galina had drawn a big road in wavy ink, which Alice crossed to enter a little lane. Following this Alice found herself walking on a mud path between two wrought iron fences, built to about knee height. Behind the fences some idealist draughtsman had no doubt intended that a garden or lawn should grow, but no one had thought to provide the gardener, so a mixture of tangled weeds, fag ends and dog-poo graced the area. Alice walked on. Soon she found herself walking beside the lower part of tall blocks of flats, the upper part partially obscured from view by the trees, which grew behind the fences, and the sheer height of the blocks. The lower two levels of flats had barred windows. Originally the bars were in the starburst style, but some had rusted and been replaced by stair-rods and long lines of wrought iron, destroying the symmetry. On the balconies of the third floor Alice saw washing lines strung out, women were drying rags, under-wear full of holes and even string and bandages. Alice wondered why. There were also collections of useful objects: tyres, sheets of plastic, empty bottles and lengths of vinyl and formica all crammed into the small space.

On the opposite side of the path were the ubiquitous corrugated iron car garages they had seen on the street, some of these were car shaped and many were rusty and had holes. She peeped inside to see Ladas and the occasional eld-erly Fiat or Skoda. One or two were open as men worked on their cars, renovat-ing and restoring. "Great place," murmured Alice thinking of Ali, "for home garaging." Just like Peckham! thought Alice, who had never been there.

She walked slowly, occasionally deviating off her route but managing to find her way back again. A few mothers with babies toddled around, and men and women strode with dogs, sometimes dogs wandered alone, which, when they were of the fierce guard-dog type, worried her a little.

Even as Alice made progress down the streets to her sister's flat her heart flut-tered with uncertainty. Her grandmother had been so certain that meeting her father, and his excess of offspring, would be a mistake that she had made her promise not to try, but Alice had had her fingers crossed behind her back when she promised. She had been determined to meet her sister, had wanted to know what her own generation, her own kith and kin, were like after a life under com-munism. If you couldn't trust your own sister whom could you trust?

For her grandmother, she thought, she had done a lot. For her she'd been a deb, an atrocious occupation, something she had hated so much even the mem-ory made her feel sick. English men seemed only interested in class and money, which should have made her a success but instead made her hate them. Alice had thought she would meet the aristocratic gentlemen of 1950s films, instead she'd met brash bankers and 'Rent a Gren' army officers. The other girls all wanted to be famous and paraded around half-naked at Henley, Ascot and Goodwood so the press would notice them. Alice only wanted to be left alone and invisible to the press. She hadn't found a single friend amongst them and she compared the British boys with their braying talk and faces like chickens (large noses and weak chins gave them the appearance of being about to run forward and start pecking) to the strong virile Russians of her memories. Russians like her father.

It was true her father had let her go, but her grandmother lived forever with the fear he would kidnap her granddaughter and take her back to Russia. He must have loved her terribly to still be a threat to her grandmother after fourteen years. Yesterday's brief seconds with her father she dismissed. He was an oddity, unsure of himself and this world. He was older too, and the Russian world in which he had placed all his faith had changed so much in the last five years, no wonder he had become insecure. Did he blame himself for her mother's death? Perhaps. That would certainly make him diffident with her mother's offspring. But it was not as though she was the first wife. Her father, who seemed to specialise in daughters, had had two by his first marriage, two by his second; both wives had died. And now by his current wife he had three girls and a boy. This wife at least had stayed with the living.

All those sisters spread across the globe, but she only wanted to see Galina, her twin. Why had her mother taken her and left Galina behind? Reality made her doubt that Galina knew the answer, but perversity made her need to ask.

As she neared her sister's flat her heart failed a little and she paused. She knew little of her relations, but the chances were she was the luckiest, had done the best of all of them, and Galina's request to meet her could indeed be, as her grandmother had suggested, a trap. She also knew that her bodyguards Daniel, and by default Ali, had all been shaken off and she stood alone.

Alice stopped where Galina had marked the spot with 'X stand here'. She had been instructed to look up at the fourteenth floor and wait. Why, she thought now, looking up at the big house, which was just another block of flats, the idea of a fourteenth floor had not alerted her to the possibility of flats she didn't know. Trusting where perhaps she should not, hoping against possibilities.

After what felt like hours to Alice, standing brushed by the glares of angry Russian residents, a girl walked onto the fourteenth floor balcony and looked. Even from this distance Alice could feel a shock go through her, and then she disappeared. Alice waited, and waited, and waited. After about fifteen minutes a girl came out of the flats and walked towards her. Alice felt her stomach contract into painful leaps. There she was, looking as though she had awoken the morning after a heavy drinking session and gone to the mirror to find herself dressed in appalling, cheap clothes with heavy unattractive make-up on her face; to find herself prematurely aged at nineteen with a small child in her arms.

"Welcome, Alice!" said her sister, then in English, "you look so young."

"You speak English?" asked Alice, almost unable to believe it after all she had heard about Russian education at her progressive school.

"Ah, Alice, I learn it for you."

Alice felt her heart melt and tears start to her eyes, she jumped forward and caught her sister in her arms. "Oh, my darling," she said in Russian, "why do we meet now after fourteen years?"

Jolted by her emotion the child began to cry, and in his wail Alice heard her own heart, tears streamed down her face. Galina, after a brief return of Alice's embrace, stood back, said, "Fu!" to quell the child, and looking around her motioned Alice to follow her into the flats.

They went up three little steps and into a small hall, filled by a large square box that disappeared into the roof and two tiled columns. They passed a *dezhurnaya* with dyed hair, a grey shirt and a red armband, who watched them suspiciously but said nothing. She didn't smile. Alice wondered if this dark red dye was especially fashionable in Russia.

"Is that the concierge?" asked Alice in light English, when they were out of hearing. "I'm surprised she doesn't put off potential flat hunters!"

Galina looked back at her sister. "I'm sorry, Alice. I did not understand you. Can you repeat?"

"That woman in the...the box," asked Alice in Russian, "who is she?"

"Ah, Alice, that is guard, is normal in Moscow. Much bad people. She is very severe, even stops my friends visiting if she does not recognise them. Is good."

They entered a corridor with a selection of six formica-coated lifts. Galina pushed a small grey bell, which disappeared under the surrounding tin and had to be pulled back by her son's small fingers. When a side lift arrived Galina snorted and shrugged. "That one does not have button for fourteen, we wait."

"Why not?"

Galina shrugged, "I don't know."

When the middle lift arrived and the two vinyl doors swung open Alice saw half the lino on the carpet had been torn off and the back of the lift was covered in scratches. "Doesn't anyone maintain these lifts?" she asked.

Galina shrugged, and pushed another metal button, which again had to be pulled back into place. The numbers had been written next to each button by hand, when Alice asked why Galina shrugged, "I don't know."

The lobby on the fourteenth floor was exactly the same as that on the ground floor except there were no bulbs in the electric cords, which dangled from the ceiling like branches in winter. The only light came from a small shaft of daylight, which crept through the broken glass of a door from some stone stairs. The windows were broken and the fallen glass lay untouched on the concrete. This time Alice did not ask, but Galina said, "Boys!" with an angry shrug.

Galina pulled a flashlight from her pocket and led the way to a plastic-padded metal door, which she unlocked, hooking the boy onto her hip with practised ease. Beyond was a slim entrance hall shared with another room and full of shelves and bicycles. There was a little window at one end and Alice went to look at the view below. Galina called her back immediately. "Alice, come here!"

Shocked Alice returned, wondering. Galina unlocked a second padded door and Alice saw a narrow hallway, created by sheet-rock.

"Shoes, Alice," said her sister, "off!"

Alice took off her leather shoes and put on the green plastic sandals her sister offered. She paddled over the lino into the first of the two rooms, trying to ignore the way her sister lifted her Guccis to examine the leather. The first thing that struck her was Galina's love of kitsch and plastic. She smiled internally, realising she was storing all these things in her mind for Janus, how they would laugh when she got home. His taste was like hers, for the beautiful and delicate, not for these seventies' monstrosities like shelled mirrors, an expanse of flying ducks and vinyl cupboards. On a 1960s' convertible sofa of some ugly corduroy-like material lay a copy of Tintin-in-the-Ukraine: a surprise for Hergé.

Inquisitively Alice walked into the bathroom and saw that neither the basin nor the bath had taps, instead there was a complicated shower arrangement protruding from a couple of rusty pipes. The shower had an arm that swung down and across for use in the basin and up to convert into a showerhead. Turning back across squishy blue matting, she brushed through the long plastic-shell tendrils that separated the kitchen from the main room.

"I'm sorry I could not come to dacha," said Galina, putting the boy down on the corduroy sofa and following her sister into the kitchen. "I thought maybe father could drive me there, but then he must work. Did you go there?"

Alice nodded, unable to say anything, sensing prevarication. She walked through the kitchen, which was also the boy's bedroom, out onto the narrow vinyl and pine balcony and saw another block of flats in front of her and another to the left. They looked as though they had been made of containers, piled into towers of twenty-five floors and cemented together with concrete. Already the concrete was corroding, although Galina said proudly these flats were only three years old, and the sealant dripped down the sides of the corrugations like tears. Some humorous builder had added a small balcony, open to the prevailing wind and partly painted purple, to each container. Alice stared, no longer mocking, realising sharply that if her grandmother had not insisted they leave when she saw the opportunity in GDR, then she too would be living like this. Probably Janus would not laugh either. Certainly her grandmother would not. This was not kitsch choice, it was availability. The shock of such a thought held her rigid. Her ideals overturning like a shed in a storm. Alice turned towards Galina, who had followed her out onto the balcony, and pulled off her necklace, placing it around Galina's neck.

"It's for you," she said, "a present from me and from the past."

Galina lifted up the big flat plastic beads and weighed them thoughtfully in her hands. For the first time she smiled. "Was mother's?"

"Yes," said Alice surprised that Galina recognised it so quickly. "Do you remember it? Grandmother gave it to me."

"I had ear-rings," said her sister, "and bracelet. Sold now."

With expert fingers Galina peeled back the plastic, to reveal a diamond. "You wore this whole time? You took risk," she said thoughtfully, "big risk. Worth much money."

Alice shrugged. "No-body realised what they were. Ali even held them in her hands without thinking they were too heavy for plastic. Even Daniel! You know what they say, hide something in the open and no one will see it."

Galina shook her head. "In West maybe. This is Russia, Alice. Everybody sees everything." She slipped the plastic back on the exposed diamond, put the string around her neck and slipped it under her clothes. "We hope Russians have European eyesight."

Nothing Lasts Like the Temporary

Joe, who had had the foresight to bring a plug, wallowed in the bath oblivious to the rust-coloured water. His tiles had also fallen off, but he had fixed them with glue, just as he had improved the angle of Mike's showerhead with masking tape. Now he stared at the black centres of the white taps, which pointed in different directions like some women's nipples and thought about Ali.

He knew Alice would make her move today, and he was prepared. As soon as they arrived in Moscow he had visited an old friend from his 'exchange' period. Many people thought South Africa had been shunned by the entire world, without realising how underhand much diplomacy really is, especially in the self-protective and secretive Russian world.

Olga was older than him and already a single mother with three children. They had struck up a beneficial relationship which, although no longer of the type to upset his future wife, was still useful. He winced as he soaped his large body, thinking about women. Women, especially Russian women, were sensitive beasts, hard for a man to comprehend. Especially a man like him, who wanted the best for everybody but apparently didn't always understand the underlying trends of a woman's mind. Olga had often shouted at him. He wondered if Ali would do the same. Perhaps she showed her anger in other ways. Women, in his experience, had plenty of ways of punishing their loved ones.

Joe got out of the bath, shards of water cascading off his body and thought about drainage. When he had first come to Moscow almost twenty years ago they had had wide hollow tin pipes which ran from tin roof gutters onto the pavement, and joining the leaks from above, causing floods when it rained. He remembered walking through shoe-deep rivers and having to jump the surging cascades that gushed out of every courtyard and side road. He remembered how the asphalt pavements sloped down to the gutter and the road turned up so the water was trapped there, flooding the corrugated iron car garages, how the asphalt scarred with the strength of the water. Nothing had changed, only now most of the car garages had moved into the courtyards and the increased number of cars on the street were deluged in water up to mid-axle. Improving their drainage was only one way Russia could improve, given time. However, as Joe knew, there was a valuable Russian expression, *nothing lasts like the temporary*, which pervaded official life like sealant on a Lada.

As he dried himself the telephone began to ring. He walked into the bedroom, glancing at the clock. He knew it was Olga.

Peckham Plastic

Ali woke up in an empty room. For a moment she couldn't think where she was or what was happening. She wasn't in bed but on a wooden floor; she could feel the hardness on her shoulder blades and in her hipbones. Opening her eyes she saw above her a high, ornately decorated ceiling, with peeling paint and purplish mould in the plaster. Ali's eyes followed the scrolls and claws to grotesque faces at the corners, being reminded strangely soothingly of party cakes.

She turned her head, and splinters in the wood scratched her cheeks. She was in a large room with no furniture. On one side her eyes followed the skirting boards, and slowly registered that they too were in poor condition; the paint had come off in great strips and the wooden panelling looked as though some had been gouged out and taken away for firewood. She turned her head the other way and saw a house of chaos. Bits of paper, odd shapes of plastic and some huge hunk of leather. As her eyes focused on the rubbish she slowly realised this craziness was hers: her wallet and her library cards, supermarket cards, kidney donor card, people's addresses scribbled on bits of paper, all spread around her like large squares of confetti. For a moment she couldn't fathom what all these things were doing here, then it dawned on her with some relief that she had been robbed. Memory returning she recalled the man and the map. She tried to visualise his face, and failed. She remembered he had a mean-looking mouth.

She reached out to the piles beside her, trying to sit up as she did so. Her head spun and she felt sick. She lay down again. Whatever the robber had used it wasnot good for you. Still, in a strange way she was almost glad to realise she had been robbed, there was something so natural about being mugged, much more so than whatever was happening with Alice.

"Oh God, Alice," she groaned, again trying to get up. However, as soon as she lifted her head from the ground a feeling of nausea came over her, her head spun and she collapsed back again. After a few moments the sickness cleared and again she tried to get up. Rather more slowly. Each time she did a little better, actually managing to sit up for a while before the dizziness returned. Gradually she began keeping her head up longer and longer, before she collapsed again, until finally she made a push to get onto her feet. Breathing deeply, hoping that oxygen would help, she got to her feet and leant against the wall. She felt dizzy, her heart pumped exaggeratedly and greyness whizzed past her eyes as though she was in a centrifuge, but she stayed upright. Overtaken by weakness she felt as though she'd just spent a week in hospital, she looked at her watch wondering how long she had been unconscious, before realising her attacker had taken that too.

In the middle of the journey of our life I came to myself within a dark wood, where the straight way was lost.

Ali stood leaning against the wall for what seemed to her like hours but was probably really seconds, hoping her balance wasn't permanently impaired. Then not far away she heard the scrape of an opening door. Her stomach gave a tremendous leap of fear, what her mother would euphemistically have called butterflies.

Her attacker must be coming back. She could hardly believe it. What would he be returning for? Not money. He must have taken it all. She could see her credit cards had gone. What then? Her? Kidnap? She almost laughed. No one would pay a ransom for her. Even her mother would probably just shake her head and say she was always a wilful, difficult child and what a shame it was. She wondered if Alice's family would pay a ransom, after all it should by rights have been Alice who was kidnapped. And then her heart fell, remembering that that was why she was here: as a stooge, a patsy; a body double. No one was on side, certainly not the Otravias. Not Joe? Not Joe? She felt a heavy weight pressing down on her chest and breathed deeply.

Bracing herself she decided she would have to use the last of her strength to fight and hope to be killed in the fight, rather than languish slowly under some kidnapper, who would rape her and then chop off her ears and fingers at will.

As the steps neared the partly open door she felt a thump of recognition. Her inner mind already knew whose feet were pounding towards her, but her outer mind only accepted that they belonged to one of the helicopter party. Then as the door swung open revealing Joe, some long-barrelled, grey-green gun in his hand, she gasped. She didn't jump forward to defend herself, in fact she didn't move at all but leant against the wall too amazed to be other than deadly calm. Wondering what this meant.

≈≈≈≈≈≈

Moissanite Mouse

Alice and her sister talked for hours, catching up on so much. The only thing Galina could not explain to Alice was why they had been separated. Why, when her mother was escaping with one twin, she didn't take the other.

"Maybe," said Galina, "mother thought if she left one child, father would not chase her for the other."

Alice smiled at her, looked into her eyes hoping for another answer and said, "Maybe".

"Do you ever see our stepsisters?" Alice asked, but Galina shook her head. "They left. Went West. Only I am still here, and the boy."

Alice wanted to take her sister shopping, to buy clothes for her and the boy, but Galina refused. "No. Is nothing here to buy. You send me presents from West, Alice. I will organise safe place for clothes. These clothes," she made a face, "not good." She fingered Alice's shirt. "That is good. You send me many."

Late in the afternoon they returned to the hotel, Alice keen to introduce her twin sister and her nephew to Ali, and hoping everything could now be explained.

The girls went up to Alice's room, Galina exclaiming in delight at the hotel and later at Alice's medal.

"Special hotel," she said, "very good. You are championship winner Alice."

"No," said Alice sadly, "only third out of four women's teams."

Ali, however, was not in the hotel and when they walked up to the virtually empty bar the only people in there, Mike and Charles, had not seen her.

"Oh, well," said Alice, "perhaps she went shopping."

Privately she thought Joe would probably know where Ali was, so she sought him out, finally finding him in the hotel lobby where he had just returned from another vodka shopping expedition.

"Have you seen Ali?" Alice asked. "This is my sister Galina, and I wanted them to meet."

Joe took Galina's small hand in his large one. "Hello," he said in Russian. "How are you?"

Galina tilted her head thoughtfully, replying in Russian that she was well, but Alice looked at him in angry amazement.

"You speak Russian?"

"Only a little. South Africa didn't have many friends in the past, Russia was one of them."

Alice didn't pursue the subject, having more worrying concerns. "Have you seen Ali? No one seems to know where she is."

Joe didn't have a chance to speak before Lyuba approached them, also speaking in Russian she said. "Ah, Alice. I am glad you are here. Yes, I saw her this morning. She was worried about you and wanted me to translate letter for her. I told her address of your sister's flat and she left to go there."

Alice gawked. "What? I don't understand. Why didn't she wait for me here? And why isn't she back? Even if she got lost she must have arrived before we left the place. We were there for several hours."

"Maybe, Alice," said Lyuba, "she got lost. Decided not to go any further."

"Maybe," said Galina, "she is kidnapped. There are lots of bad men around who would like to take white slave and money. Foreigners always have money otherwise they not here."

Lyuba gave the girl a cold look and remarked Daniel might know where Ali had gone. Alice looked at Joe, but he said nothing and she wasn't sure whether he understood enough Russian to follow their conversation. She told Galina to wait with Joe and let him practise a few words of Russian and went to find Daniel.

Daniel was in his room, partially asleep and partially talking to Gary, who was up and dressed. Both boys were suffering from heavy hangovers.

"Have you seen Ali? Either of you?"

Daniel looked shifty and asked Gary if he would go out and try and find some Alka Seltzer. "There must be some Russian version if not, try anything. I'll even drink milk."

Gary grinned and, winking a sleazy goodbye to Alice, staggered out to see what he could find.

"So, what's going on? Where is Ali?" Alice asked crossly, annoyed he had been drunk. He was paid to look after her, not to sozzle his time away on her expenses. "Why weren't you keeping an eye on her? Where is she?"

"I don't know," Damiel replied petulantly, "have you asked Joe? There's something pretty odd about him, if you ask me."

"Joe! Don't be daft. He's in love with her. He wouldn't hurt her." Then suddenly she noticed Daniel was trying to change the subject. "What have you been up to, Daniel? What is going on?"

"Love indeed," said Daniel and seemed to want to debate the subject but when Alice repeated her question he gave up. "Nothing really. I mean nothing important. All right, I did mention something to Ali about your grandmother's fear of a kidnap threat, but we both know that is nothing but your dear old relation worrying the Hell out of an unnecessary situ."

"Oh, yeah! And I suppose you told her you thought it was rather clever to choose her because she looked like me!"

Daniel's face almost split with amusement. "Oh, my darling, did you work that one out yourself? You are a doll! I suppose I might have mentioned that if the worst came to the worst she was to be used as a decoy. But, you know, there was never any real danger, we all know that. Still, maybe I was too clever for my own good. I know how emotional all you girls are, and she is rather keen on me." He smiled at Alice. "I daresay she got mad and went off to make us worried," he added blithely.

"Maybe," said Alice, "maybe, but that sounds like more like you than Ali, doesn't it! Going off half cock and half-wittedly. I don't think so." She stormed out slamming the door and hoping it made Daniel's hangover much worse.

Even before Daniel had told her Ali was a decoy Alice had worked out why a pilot of similar height, with a similar name was chosen to accompany her, but she didn't really think there was anything to fear; now though Ali had disappeared and she was responsible.

When Alice returned to Joe and Galina they were sitting on the sofa in the lobby and getting on extremely well. Galina said Joe spoke very good Russian and he returned the compliment saying she spoke excellent English. When Galina went to freshen up, however, Joe looked worried and told Alice not to say anything to anyone else about Ali being missing.

"If anyone asks you where she is tonight just say she was tired and has gone to bed early."

"Tonight?" screeched Alice. "By tonight all sorts of dreadful things might have happened to her!"

"And what would you prefer? That we get the police looking for her?"

When Galina returned she agreed with Joe, who was still trying to convince the now irresolute Alice. "All police in Russia bad," she said, "once police involved, goodbye Ali."

Even though Alice's instincts told her that at least one of them was being duplicitous, she allowed herself to be persuaded. Particularly when Joe said that if Ali had not turned up by tomorrow morning he would go to the Embassy, and deal with Kevin and his inevitable tantrum.

Alice for felt afraid for the British girl but suddenly realised for the first time in her life there was nothing she could do. Alone in Russia with her sister, she had no way of overcoming the problem, the only people she knew were on her side were the Otravias and her sister, and yet she decide to allow freedom to Joe.

"All right," she said crisply. "I'm going to trust you, but if anything happens to Ali you will feel the might of my stepfather."

Joe looked seriously at her and said nothing for a long while, finally he spoke in a voice so devoid of any kind of humour that she was even momentarily afraid. "Alice, do you really think I would let Ali be hurt?"

Alice knew she had gone too far, that Joe was not the type of man she had flirted with as a deb, nor even the lovely usable elder she found in her stepfather. It suddenly crossed her mind that Joe might be one of those rare incredibly strong individuals who could not be bought, and she wondered if Ali knew it too. She said only, "Sorry."

≈≈≈≈≈≈

Star of Africa

As Ali leant back against the wall, wondering, Joe stepped into the room, tensely checking.

"Are you OK?" he asked gruffly.

Hearing his voice Ali felt the relief of a weary commuter discovering he has won the lottery; Joe must be on her side. "I'm a bit dizzy," she said. "I was mugged and I think the guy gave me some kind of drug, do they still use chloroform?"

Joe nodded. "Here in Russia." He stepped forward, then noticed she was leaning against the wall. "Can you stand? Unsupported?" Too late he realised his voice sounded harsh.

I would that my tongue could utter, the thoughts that arise in me.

"I'm not sure. If you were a kidnapper I was going to make a last ditch to fight you... but then it was you..." Her voice trailed away.

Joe made a strange noise. "Ooh." He stepped forward, inarticulate noises bubbling in his throat and put his huge bear's arms out and smothered her in them, kissing her on the lips before dropping back.

Love is most nearly itself when the here and now cease to matter.

"Look, I want to get you out of here. This was not part of the plan, but now it's happened we've got to get you somewhere safe. Let me get your things."

Stooping he gathered up all Ali's cards and note, stuffing them in the wallet, while she imagined him picking up her sword and shield. She started to laugh, thinking: "Heroes are created by demand, sometimes of the scantiest materials.'

"Looks like he got your passport...that's a bummer, that means officialdom... even with the helicopters I don't think we'll get away with it."

"What? My passport's at the hotel."

"It is? You weren't carrying it then?"

"No. Should I?"

He smiled, thinking that while Mike eschewed the rules Ali (like the majority of the population) was simply too lazy or uninterested to learn them. "Well, it is obligatory. The police can stop you and fine you if you don't have an identity card."

"I've got my library card."

Joe stifled a snort, imagining a policeman faced with Ali's library card. "OK. I'm going to take you to a safe place, you can cancel your credit cards there. I'll explain everything later, but now... can you walk or shall I carry you? I've got a car outside."

"But Alice?" Ali asked. "Is she OK?"

Joe put his arm around her shoulders and kissed her again, his forgotten gun wearing a ridge in her shoulder. "Yes, my darling." He stopped and then muttered inarticulately that Alice was fine.

Ali almost laughed. This seemed so far away from her normal life. Then the dizziness returned and she stumbled. "If you give me your arm," she said, feeling like an invalid, "I can walk."

He slipped his arm down so it was around her back and almost lifted her in spite of her size. "OK? Will this work."

She looked at him and grinned, her spirits soaring. "Yes, it's OK. I'm wonderfully OK."

He began laughing too, supporting her to the car. As they came out of the front door Ali saw they were still in the courtyard where the man had attacked her. Perhaps this was his stomping ground, his work place.

Driving to a 'big house' near the Botanical Gardens Joe murmured, "I am not Prince Hamlet, nor was meant to be; Am an attendant lord, one that will do to swell a progress, start a scene or two..."

Recognising the Love Song of J. Alfred Prufrock, Ali put her hand on his arm replying, "Indeed there will be time, To wonder, 'Do I care?' and Do I dare."

Unwisely Joe turned his head away from the frantic Moscow traffic and they smiled at each other seeing 'so much and so much', before the blare of horns returned him to competing with the concentration of cars.

Joe drove into a courtyard and parked at the back of another big house. They climbed up a fire escape to enter the house, Ali didn't ask why. The flat was on the third floor and had four rooms; the bedroom, where Ali could sleep off the effects of her drug; the living room where the owner of the flat and her daughters would sleep tonight, and the kitchen and bathroom. There was very little furniture.

A woman opened the door to them and Joe introduced her as Olga and then talked to her in Russian. She disappeared into the kitchen saying smilingly, "Lunch."

"It's all right, it won't be gristle soup," Joe said. "Olga is a great cook and you'll feel better when you have something to eat. You should have had breakfast, then the drug wouldn't have had such a bad effect."

Raising her eyebrows she replied rather tartly. "No doubt I would have done, had I known I was to be knocked senseless by a thief. Anyway, how do you know I didn't?"

"I heard you talking to Lyuba," he said ruefully, embarrassed. "I knew you were going to be a hero as soon as Alice disappeared yesterday, so I've had Olga and her daughters watching you ever since."

"Not closely enough to stop me getting mugged."

"No, I'm sorry. But she wouldn't have let him really hurt you. Only then she had to slip off and contact me, and I had to get the car. Actually it's Olga's, but she shares it with a friend who has a garage."

"I suppose you learnt Russian when you were in the South African army too, did you?" Ali said caustically.

"I did. I don't think you realise how greatly South Africa feared being attacked. I was in an elite force..."

"You mean you were a spy?!"

"I can promise you I never did anything you would really hate. I didn't cook anybody alive or anything like that, but I was in intelligence. But we can talk all that through in the future. For now I guess you would like to know what is going on with Alice and what I am doing here?"

"I would. Amongst other things."

Joe fiddled a moment with his big hands, before resting them on his knees. He leant forward.

"After I left South Africa I got a job with EGL, the European Gemological Laboratory. Although I started as an engineer, I soon became very involved with the diamonds, probably because of my military South African background. I'm not an expert but thanks to EGL I know a fair bit about them. For that reason, and because I knew his secretary, Mr Charleston, Alice' stepfather, sought me out and employed me to keep an eye on Alice."

"You too. This is like some mobile army: TAs – Traipsing after Alice!"

"You mean Daniel, I guess. Yes, I'll tell you more about him in a minute."

"Like why you had those girls try and seduce him?"

Joe ruffled her hair and slipped his head down into his shoulders, which in such a big man looked like a boulder falling into a crevasse. "Umm. OK. That too. But the most important thing is that Alice is carrying with her a string of diamonds worth roughly half a million dollars or more."

Ali stared at him. Her mouth went dry. "What? You are joking. No. Half a million dollars? In the helicopter! Where? My God! Why?"

"Quite so. That was what her stepfather wanted to know too. The diamonds were her mother's, family heirlooms that somehow they kept in spite of all the deprivations. Don't ask me how, maybe Mrs Charleston would know. Anyway, Alice is wearing them, disguised with a plastic cover to make them look like an ordinary girl's necklace."

"Jesus Christ her beads! Those are worth half a million dollars? Those things she swings around and sleeps on! Does she know how much they are worth? Or isn't that... I don't think I understand this at all... is that much money nothing to her, to them? I suppose it could be... but even so... and then you... why did he let her take them?"

"Well for one thing they are hers. They were kept in a vault in London, but just before you met Alice Mr Charleston was contacted by his bankers to say she had taken the diamonds out of the vault. As she is under-age, and he still pays the ferryman, he still has the last say. But he wanted to know what she was going to do with them, so he didn't say anything to her but employed me to keep an eye on her and see what she does and where she goes."

"Risky. He might lose them, her and you too, I would have thought. There's more than one person who would kill for half a million dollars."

Joe grinned, as though that was all part of the game. "Happen you're right," he said, "however, as you will have noticed rich men think they can buy safety and security, so he doesn't expect me to fail!"

"Oh, Joe!" Ali said nervously, putting her hand on his arm.

He immediately moved closer, put his large arms around her and kissed her. "My darling!" Then remembered he was in the middle of his story and leaving one arm around her continued. "One day Ali will inherit an empire with an income greater than some governments. Her stepfather sees she has the brains and the courage but he worries she is too volatile..."

"She's only nineteen."

"He was running his first company at sixteen so that doesn't weigh for much with him. He wants her to get experience of life. He wants her to fall into trouble and get herself out."

"Even at the risk of her own life."

Joe shrugged. "He may think that her life will be worthless if she cannot control her empire, but don't forget he did employ me."

Ali felt depressed. She didn't understand this coldness, she preferred kindness to sacrifice. "So why did she bring the diamonds? Wanting to bribe Yeltsin?"

Joe laughed. "Nice idea, but in fact Alice had a twin sister."

"What! She never mentioned it, but I suppose she wouldn't. Wow! This gets more and more complicated."

Ali felt rather tearful, but restrained herself. Twin sisters. Diamonds. Dead mothers, supplanted by grandmothers. Why? Why? Why, and why not confide in her, or why should she really. Again she felt like the student deprived of his cross-country test, was Alice always going to engender those feelings? At least, pointed out her deeper mind, she would be the one sending Alice off on her real cross-country.

Joe was more pragmatic. "Maybe. Anyway Mr Charleston thinks that Alice is probably taking the diamonds to her sister. You know now how emotional she is, he reckons that she thinks her sister got the short end of the straw and wants to give her something special. He told me that if he prevented her going out and giving her sister the diamonds this way, she would find some other way of doing it."

"But he still wants them back, right."

"Right."

"And, assuming she has now given the diamonds to her sister, you've got to steal them back. Right?"

"Only if she won't take a fair price for them."

"Oh." Ali thought about this for a while, wondering what it could be like to be so rich you could make this kind of little gesture to your stepdaughter's far distant family, then wondering what this meant for Joe. "Be careful. Diamonds like drugs make ruthless criminals."

Joe raised his eyebrows, smiled slightly but said nothing. Ali's head swam. She needed other questions answered but all she felt like doing was sleeping. Clenching her muscles for a moment she continued.

"Now you need to explain the other things: the tail rotor failure, the Gazelle running out of fuel and Daniel's dancing partners."

"The Gazelle running out of fuel I'm still working on, maybe Daniel can explain it but I wasn't there and I suspect it may have been a military problem."

"A military problem?"

"I'm guessing, but my experience is that often engineers don't record things like faulty gauges, or they'll have to fix them. As long as everybody knows about it, no one worries. But it could be two unrecorded problems came together, a faulty gauge and a new-boy who thought he had filled the Gazelle to the top without checking. The end result being insufficient fuel in the tank. Just supposition, but I know of no reason anyone would want to kill Paul and Rob, except perhaps Catherine if he doesn't share the champagne!"

Ali laughed. "So the tail rotor?"

"That is the problem. I thought it was Daniel. But maybe that was jealousy on my part..." then, seeing Ali frown, he added, "I'm only human, you know. I have a feeling someone else knows about the diamonds and wants them. I thought it was Daniel, he was always cuddling you girls and would have had ample opportunity to suss out the weight of those beads. Plus, having been a detective he is naturally suspicious, and because he is heavily in debt, and of course his father made everyone drunk the night before..."

"Including him!"

"Classic cover! But later I came to believe I was wrong. However, that was why I had those girls test him out. I thought if he was suspicious of them then there was a good chance he knew there was something more than an unlikely kidnapping involved but of course he wasn't in the least suspicious, in fact completely up for it. In fact, it was Alice who was suspicious."

"Sounds a bit like the ducking stool for witches: only the innocent drown."

"They wouldn't have harmed him. Our lady Olga here helped me find them, they are some relations of hers. You know Daniel doesn't for a moment really think Alice will be kidnapped. He thinks this is money for old rope. A risk-free job. And if, as I now think, he doesn't know about the diamonds, he will be even less worried."

"So why do you think Alice is still at risk?"

"Because someone knows about the diamonds."

"How do you know?"

"Because it was Galina who contacted Alice, not the other way around, and Galina died in infancy. That was why her mother didn't take her with her."

"Jesus Christ!" said Ali, jumping up to her feet, and immediately collapsing back swaying blackly. "Then Alice is in danger. What are you doing chatting here with me?"

"Don't worry. As long as you are out of the way Alice will be safe."

"Why?"

"Because who ever wants the diamonds thinks you have them. Thinks you were brought as a cover for Alice."

"I don't understand. And wait, hold on, since grandmother must have known Galina was dead why didn't Alice?"

Joe moued. "I'm not sure, but it is possible she didn't think Alice knew she was part of a twinage so never mentioned the twin having died."

"Now I really don't understand!"

"Trust me," he said, and kissing her again got up to leave, just as Olga emerged from the kitchen with some rather (incredibly) delicious smelling lunch for Ali. "I'll see you tomorrow," he said, "Olga will show you how to get back to the hotel, between you you can make up a story about how you spent the time. I don't want to know it, I need to sound as surprised as the others."

Ali smiled up at him. "I don't know sweetheart, I think you are a pretty credible liar."

"Not," he said kissing her almost too gently for a big man, "about the important things."

Ali Alrosa

That evening the whole team had dinner in the hotel. They were suddenly tired. The adventure had been magnificent, and even though they had not won the championships, as Grantland Rice knew so well, an Englishman does not enter to win, only to play the game. Daniel's win, of a small but special medal and as an independent, was just what they needed to feel victorious and yet remain good sports. But it was over now, and they were exhausted and ready to go home.

Sandra and Steve came over to join Alice and Galina on their table. Sandra now admitted she too could speak a little Russian, and was suddenly keen to practise her language skills. Although she had not mentioned she spoke Russian before, especially a Russian that both sisters quickly recognised as fluent, Alice professed to be unsurprised. "How," she pointed out, "could you be an expert in Russian government finance if you did not speak Russian?"

"So, where's your friend Ali?" asked Sandra, "I haven't seen her all day."

"No, she's tired. She's having a rest until we go off tomorrow."

Sandra nodded and turned to Galina. "So, what sort of life have you had here in the East?"

Galina bridled, unwilling to talk about her life, and tried to change the emphasis of the conversation, asking Sandra about her life in London. Sandra dismissed her reserve, talked only briefly about her husband and then returned to the subject of Galina's life, pushing and probing. "So, how did you survive with no mother, estranged from your father and with so little money," she asked, smiling harshly. "You must have had to do things you would rather have avoided."

"Why would you care?" asked Galina, appearing to Alice to be disproportionately angry. "What do you Western woman with rich husband care about us? Your life so pleasant now. Able to work only where you wish and to study."

Alice shivered at this side of both girls she had not imagined and studied them more deeply.

"You know," said Galina, calming down slightly, "should I ever become rich I would give money to others too. I would not keep privilege. It would not be just information I share but love and finance."

Sandra smiled palely. Perhaps she thought this an attack on her marriage to a much older man. She said, "I love my husband."

"Of course, Sandra," replied Galina. "Of course. Of course."

Alice, though, thought that the remark was rather sweet of Galina, assuming it referred to the fact that she had just become very rich, thanks to Alice's diamonds. Something, naturally, Sandra would not know about.

In the end, as much to keep the peace as anything else Alice told them about her life in the UK. Perhaps if Alice had been less used to speaking and behaving just as she liked, and more used to thinking about things she was saying, she would have thought it impolitic to tell her sister about being a debutante. But, however sorry Alice felt for her sister's years of deprivations, only for a fleeting moment did she think that Galina might envy her, might feel that their mother had let her down. So she happily broke into tales of horse shows, of her many ponies, of learning to fly and of being a most reluctant debutante.

"On one occasion at a dinner party," she said, "I was bored of talking about my neighbour's job in banking so I remarked that I was a transvestite hooker, to which my neighbour replied, 'oh, like aunty!' I thought there was some potential there but he turned away and talked to his neighbour ever after."

"So, a comedian?" asked Sandra. "Or was he serious?"

"English men sound very amusing," said Galina. "I would like them."

Alice shrugged. "Do you think so? I hated them and spent a large part of my deb season sitting under the table to avoid the 'chicken heads' or setting fire to the decorations, so I was soon returned to the country in disgrace."

Galina and Sandra both looked shocked and Sandra said severely that freedom was wasted on many people.

Only later when Galina told Sandra a few details about her life. When she talked about being a slave in her father's house once he had a new family. About discovering she was pregnant, and walking for thirty miles to get church-aid, having been thrown out by her father. About how lucky she was to get her flat (which she had bargained for in the 'house exchange' behind the Rzhevsky Bathhouse, and in exchange for which she had given German lessons, to cram the seller's stupid son into college) did Alice finally grasp how very different Galina's life was from her own.

Alice congratulated herself on having brought the necklace as a present for her sister, and on how much wealth that would bring her. And soon, she thought, they would be together again. Perhaps it would be best if Galina moved to England first, and then they planned going back to Russia, but they needed to make arrangements to buy back the family properties. For a moment even Alice considered it might be difficult but then she remembered that her stepfather would help; he had always been marvellous when it came to financial things.

After dinner Pete and Daniel joined them. Pete was very interested in Galina, telling her about his flying exploits during national service, which had included a long spell in West Germany and some time in Malaysia, most of which, given the speed at which he talked and his accent, Galina couldn't understand. She thought Daniel was charming.

"Women," said Pete, "who talk a lot are much friendlier than silent ones. Which is interesting given that it is not the same with men. Men speak to expose themselves. Women to communicate. It really is a quite different process."

None of the girls replied.

Russians Manqué

The next morning, when they all gathered in the hall ready to leave, Kevin discovered Ali was nowhere to be found. As Group Leader he naturally wished to return as a complete unit to England, but Ali had gone.

"Alice, Alice," cried Kevin, his teeth becoming more pronounced as his voice grew more acidic, "where is your friend? If she spent last night dallying somewhere with... with... well I suppose it would be a man... and cannot be bothered to get back in time I suggest we leave her behind. I assume you have the keys of your helicopter?"

Alice, her throat constricted by fury, said nothing, which Kevin took as assent.

Mike broke in cheerily to remind Kevin they still had her passport behind the desk, but Kevin, looking coldly at his friend continued. "I suppose, although it will be inconvenient, that Alice can fly with Charles and I'll have to fly home alone. I must say I find the whole thing pretty tiresome."

"Impossible," said Charles, "I'm not an instructor. Anyway we can't just leave the girl here in Russia. She might be in trouble."

"Then," said Kevin, annoyed at this disobedience from one of his most trusted minions, "we must call the police. Really Alice, I think you might have mentioned she was missing before."

"She's not missing," said Alice, finally finding her voice, "she's here... look!"

They all looked and there, entering the main door to the hotel, was Ali, her face drawn and her hair dishevelled.

"Ali, my darling," said Alice jumping up and embracing her, "what happened, where have you been? This is my sister Galina, I wanted her to meet you but she was about to go home."

Galina had in fact just arrived. Alice had wanted her to spend the night at the hotel, but she refused saying: "Gods would not allow it, they watch every one."

"The gods? The Heavens?"

"Guard, you saw her. Guard sit outside my apartment and watch who goes in and out. Is worse for me because so many of family have gone to West."

Ali laughed. In fact in spite of her rough appearance she seemed very happy, almost joyous. Alice and Galina were mystified.

"I'm fine, Alice. But a strange thing happened to me. I came to try and find you. Got lost, almost inevitably I suppose, and tried asking the way. Lots of 'Nyet'," she laughed. The girls laughed too, Galina saying, "Russians very rude on street. Walk into you and never say sorry."

"Then one man seemed to be helping me, with signs he said that he would show me the way. He took me down an alleyway and then boomp! The next thing I knew I was waking up in a deserted room with a headache and my things spread everywhere, except my money and credit cards, which had gone. I didn't have a clue where I was."

She paused for a moment and Alice said worriedly. "Have you been unconscious all night?"

"No, probably not that long at all, but he took my watch so I didn't know how..."

"You'd better cancel your cards," interrupted Kevin, somewhat crustily but feeling he should do his duty as Group Leader even for the tiresome girl. "It doesn't take long before the thieves have cleaned out your accounts and," he added, remembering this was only the pauper Ali he was talking to, "even if you haven't got any money they can run up a good old debt for you on those credit cards."

"Thanks. I've already done it," said Ali quietly.

"That was quick! Leave a phone for you did he, the burglar?"

"No. That was the family who took me in."

"What's that?"Alice jumped-in. "Some Russian family took you in over night?"

"Yes. The drug the mugger gave me made me very dizzy and when I tried to walk outside I collapsed. An old woman helped me to a seat and then invited me to stay in her house until I felt better. I stayed all night and came back this morning."

Galina looked stupefied but said nothing.

"You couldn't, I suppose," said Kevin tartly, "have used her phone for calling us, so we weren't worried. Or didn't that occur to you! I've been sick with stress, pacing all night wondering if..."

"Leave her alone Kevin," said Joe, who'd been listening on the sidelines. "She's been knocked around, scared half out of her life and all you are worried about is getting back to England on time. Welcome back Ali, I'm glad you are all right."

"Thanks." She looked at him and Alice noticed something almost conspiratorial in her glance, she opened her mouth to speak then suddenly closed it again. It suddenly sprung on her that Ali had stayed away for a reason, and that Joe was involved. This needed private curiosity, not public speaking.

"Well," said Kevin testily but trying to keep his voice in the polite cadence he used in his butlering days. "Now you are back, are you well enough to travel? Can we now return to that ordered land we came from, where girls don't go disappearing for days at a time and don't even bother to call."

And he stomped away angrily, to gather up the others and pay the hotel bill, while Joe murmured, "O strong soul, by what shore tarriest thou now?"

"So, where were you last night?" asked Alice. "With this old woman?"

"Yes. As soon as she put me to bed I went out like a light and didn't wake up until she shook me this morning. She must have given me her bed because there was only the one room."

"Wicked," said Alice sanctimoniously, while Galina added, "very kind woman. Very Russian."

Lamprey Lamproite

As they walked out to the taxi to return home it began to pour with rain. Rain that spurted up from the road causing little cones of water that looked like tiny crowns on the tarmac. Each car that zoomed past caused a vortex behind like that of a Jumbo in the distant sky, but more tiresome for being here under each squelchy foot. Kevin swore, remarking that if Ali hadn't disappeared they would have left before all this bad weather.

"The weather's doing water-sports," said Jaap.

"You mean Olympic winds and javelin rain against the window?" asked Daniel.

"No, the cats are pissing on the dogs: passionately."

Alice, Galina (who was accompanying them to Tushino) and Ali squeezed into the back of the Lada, while Joe went in front.

Galina laughed. "It's rain," she cried, "raining, raining in my heart." Turning to her sister still laughing she said, "do you still sing Beatles songs in West? And Rolling Stones, or is it all new punk?"

Even Ali noticed a mismatch. Alice, tears starting up, kissed her sister.

Once at the airfield the usual preparations began with fuelling and paperwork and it was another three hours before the whole team was ready to leave. However, finally the last bureaucratic ink dot was dry and their passports were handed back by the glum-faced officials. Alice hugged Galina goodbye, promising to arrange an invitation for her and her son to visit them in Britain. "I will send you an invitation," she whispered, "and we will be together again, I promise."

Both girls began to cry and it took quite a lot of tact from Ali to get one into the helicopter while the other stayed behind.

Preoccupied with her worries about Galina, Alice spoke little on the first leg of the journey and Ali too was silent. Thinking about various promises she had given Joe, what he had told her about Alice's sister and what she had forgotten to ask him about the other, the step, siblings. She meant to ask him when they landed at Smolensk but what with the pressure of fuelling again and Kevin in a hurry to get off and pulsating around like Napoleon in a snow-storm it went out of her mind.

So it was not until the girls had taken off from Smolensk that Ali noticed Alice was no longer wearing her beads. Her heart thumped against her ribs. "Where are your beads, Alice, don't say you've lost them?" She tried to keep her voice cool.

Alice smiled primly, "I gave them to Galina, she has more need of them than me."

Ali played her part well, asking reluctantly. "They weren't just plastic?"

"No, diamonds, and don't worry," Alice added with a giggle, "she'll know how to use them!"

Ali said nothing, watching the steady shiver of the air speed indicator. In the last month she'd been a stooge for a kidnap, been mugged by a common Russian thief, fallen in love with some highly dubious ex-South African intelligence man, nearly been killed in an accident and had innocently participated in a smuggling half a million dollars worth of diamonds. But discovering Alice had given away the diamonds to a con-woman filled her heart with dismay. However, she had promised Joe not to tell Alice anything until they reached the West.

"Did Daniel know you were smuggling?" asked Ali, hardly able to believe the control freak would have allowed such a thing.

"No! That's the funny thing. I dangled them under his nose, and he saw nothing, even in Poland. What a great private dick he must have been!"

"Probably why he went bankrupt."

"Yeah. Joe knew though. Janus employed him, to watch me. Margaret told me."

"Margaret?" asked Ali amazed, another new angle.

"My father's secretary."

"Ah," said Ali, whom could you trust these days? There was so much interplay here she was beginning to believe in Russian conspiracy theories.

"Alice did you really give Galina the diamonds?"

"I put the string around her neck."

Ali sighed. She knew she ought to wait, that Joe was right, that if she told Alice that Galina was not her sister the invincible girl would be bound to want to turn round and head back to Moscow to go and get them back, that she ought to wait. Worse, she also knew Alice would start crying and Ali hated that.

"Alice," said Ali, watching the other helicopters ahead, "are you sure Galina is your sister?"

Alice grew suddenly very still. A mouse watching the killing kestrel circling above; the kestrel itself completely intent on what was happening in the catchment area. "What do you mean?" Ali noticed absently the 'do you' got stressed.

"Well," said Ali carefully, "you said that she was your identical twin sister, but she doesn't look as like you as I'd expect, even given a different life-style. For a start she is older, at least five years."

"How do you know? She's lived a hard life. Poverty ages."

"She's a con-woman," said Ali, hopelessly unable to work up to the subject in the small helicopter, flying over endless trees, flying away from Moscow. "Your twin is dead."

"I know," said Alice and there was a noise in the right hand seat of the helicopter like a bubbling geyser. Ali realised Alice was crying again. "I know."

"I'm sorry, Alice. But I can't bear to think of you giving your diamonds away to a con-woman, shall we go back and get them?"

Alice continued to gurgle but now the noise changed to laughter interspersed with sobs. "Oh, Ali, Ali, you are wonderful... what shall we do? Land on one of the car garages. Storm in to her flat, grab the jewels, run back to the helicopter and fly away!"

Ali looked at her crestfallen. "You don't believe me!"

Alice stopped laughing. "I believe you. In fact although my father didn't say much to me he did say... 'I wish you'd died instead of your twin, she was always the better one of you'. And I believed him too." Tears began to fall again. "But," said Alice, more stoutly now, "if I hadn't gone on and given her the jewels we'd never have got out of Russia alive. Now we will."

"Rather expensive invitation visa, wasn't it," said Ali dryly. "Half a million dollars!"

"Is that what Joe told you?" Alice asked contemptuously. "They're worth more than that."

Ali said nothing. There was a growing tension in the cockpit and she wished she had waited until they reached the West. Clearly Alice couldn't give a damn. Why had she bothered? Half, maybe three quarters, of a million dollars was nothing to her, a toy to be given away to a rapacious cheat.

"Why do you care, anyway?" Alice spat. "It's not your money."

Ali felt hurt. How unkind that was. She'd been prepared to risk her life to help Alice get her diamonds back and suddenly she was stabbed for her thought. Didn't some poet talk about the brutality of superwealth.

Alice, though, apparently realised she'd gone too far. After a long pause she said in a rather constrained voice, "I'm sorry Ali, I shouldn't have said that. This trip has been difficult for me. Until I met her I thought, or rather I hoped, that Galina was alive. But then, when I saw her, I knew, I saw, I recognised, I just saw she wasn't my twin. She said that she had a vivid picture of mother wearing these and that she had had the ear-rings and the brooch. Well! There weren't any ear-rings or brooches. And, in fact, she never saw the diamonds at all, neither of us did. Nor did mother. But, you know, I kept my cool. I dealt with it like a... a... Trojan... as my mother... my grandmother would say... I coped... I pretended." There was another pause and Alice said, more to herself than Ali, "my mother would have been proud of me."

Ali stared at the trees, in her mind a quote from a twelfth-century writer: *you will find something more in woods than in books. Trees and stones will teach you that you can never learn from masters.*

"I'm sorry," said Alice again, and now her voice was soft, teasingly alluring as though she had realised that she was going to lose everything she had gained if she didn't bring Ali back on side. "I didn't mean to hurt you. But I thought it would serve my stepfather right if he had to worry a little. I mean, for Heaven's sake, two detectives, just for little old me."

Ali pondered for a while, then she said speculatively neutral. "Galina, if she isn't your twin, who is she? You recognised her."

"My half-sister. My father had been married before. There were two of them, she was seven years older and her sister nine years older than me, but her sister had also got out to the West, before we jumped the coop... long before, before I was born, and I never met her. None-the-less it must be through her that she heard of me, knew the possibilities. So, she'll probably get a good price for them anyway, and you can't blame her for trying. She's had a hard life you know. You should have seen her apartment."

"You gave them to her, knowing who she was?"

Alice shrugged. "Why not! I would have given them to the real Galina, so my stepfather wouldn't have had them anyway."

"Whose diamonds were these? Your mother's? In Russia?"

Alice laughed. "I suppose my mother's by default. By inheritance... something we had never heard of in Russia in the eighties. If she'd had them in Russia she'd have sold them long before. My mother hated suffering. Could not stand pain, her own or anyone elses. That's why she married my father, a party official, a man who could make things happen, even though she was a white Russian, an aristocrat from old line and he was from peasant stock."

Alice reached for the comfort of her beads, only to drop her hand listlessly when she remembered they were not there. The helicopter trudged on over the green broccoli of woods, but neither girl noticed the trees.

"No, they were family jewels, but they'd been sitting in the vault in England for years, since before the revolution. It's a family theory that one of our ancestors was Tsar Alexander II's mistress. She was from a British family (you may have noticed my grandmother is half English) and a rival to Princess Catherine Yourievska also known as Katharina Dologorukova. Alexander gave Princess Catherine Yourievska the diamonds as a present. She immediately sent them to England to be reset and they remained there because the Tsarina thought they'd been stolen and caused an outcry and they were too hot to bring back. However, our ancestor knew about the diamonds and had her own servant follow Princess Catherine's servant and steal them from him. Our family have had them ever since. Or so the story goes. "

"So you thought they were stolen jewels returning home and it didn't matter how really?"

"Something like that!" said Alice facetiously, and then she laughed, and laughed and laughed.

Ali stared amazed as the girl beside her gave up the controls and, hardly able to contain herself, laughed on. Happy tears poured down her cheeks and her chortles rocked the small helicopter, while Ali flew on staring bemusedly at the changing landscape.

Eventually Alice pulled herself together. She put out her hand and touched Ali's arm, gently like a child asking for forgiveness. "I'm sorry Ali, I wasn't going to tell you the truth, but I will. I wanted to give my step father the news myself, but..." She snorted and putting her hand into her trouser pocket drew out a packet of sweets. She placed them on Ali's lap.

"Here. Look for yourself."

She took over the cyclic and Ali looked at the packet on her lap. The cover said 'Humbugs'. Ali stared down at the package, feeling it crinkle and sag like a large packet of boiled sweets. She bounced it up and down, automatically weighing it, astonishment filling her face. "Diamonds?"

"Open it."

Ali pulled apart the easy-seal lips and saw inside a string of clear sparklers.

"You didn't give them to her... but you said... I don't understand."

Alice smiled. "I said I put the necklace around her neck, only I'd replaced the diamonds with moissanite copies. That was why Tom Moore came out to Poland, to give me the replicas he was making. He's good and they are better than paste. It's almost impossible to tell the difference: some people prefer moissanite." She paused. "Moissanite is a new thing, at least new in artificial form... only created in the eighties, it's made from silicon carbide exposed to extremes of temperature and pressure. Tom discovered a factory that makes it in North Carolina and he's been faking diamonds ever since. That's how he makes money. He does both but he makes more money from copies than from his legitimate diamond selling. The real diamond business is pretty cut-throat these days and Tom lost his position as a sightholder after a row with De Beers." She grinned.

"That dinner was a laugh. Tom pretended he wanted to meet Daniel about a job he needed doing, but really he was passing the replicas, I guess you'd call them Peckham Diamonds, to me! Daniel didn't notice a thing. Guzzling away on 'The Widow' I'd paid for, not a suspicion crossed his mind! Isn't he just the detective of a criminal's dreams."

Ali was so inured to the zigzag of these revelations that she hardly even felt surprise in discovering another twist.

"Why? Why have them made? Were you suspicious of Galina even before you left England?"

Alice drew her mouth into a long line, thinking before she spoke. "I was not sure. There was something in the way Galina wrote her letters, some of the memories she claimed to have had, or worse the ones she said she had forgotten... there were little clues. Little suspicions. I wanted to believe her though."

"Why didn't you ask your mother, I mean your grandmother?"

"I tried. I tried to angle the questions around to asking her, but she's very protective, very suspicious. All I said was I might try and ring my father while I was in Moscow and she went mad with nerves, made me promise not to. She was certain that my father would try and kidnap me, pretty ironic when he couldn't even be bothered to see me."

Ali made a sympathetic noise.

"So I had Tom Moore make up a copy. It wasn't ready in time, and I left wearing the real diamonds, and when he gave me the Peckham Diamonds I put them inside the plastic beads in the place of the real ones."

"Why didn't you give them to Tom Moore to take home?"

"Good Lord! I couldn't trust him. You've seen father's friends: everywhere! He'd be right round to Janus to tell him the tale. No," she said naughtily casual, "I just left them in the helicopter, I popped them in the GPS case."

"You left them in the helicopter! You left three quarters of a million dollars sitting in the helicopter on an airfield in the middle of Vitebsk... Brest... Moscow."

"Very good security on airfields," said Alice sanctimoniously, "besides, if you remember you always took the GPS out and brought it with us. Except that one time in Vitebsk when you forgot it."

Ali went pale, remembering that this was true.

The Marquise Essen

As they went from stop to stop they were shedding competitors and friends as each flew off to their respective homes. Every time they landed at another airport they were a smaller group of pilots. At every stop Joe was at the helicopter's side before the rotors had even stopped, checking they were OK, just being there. Ali would have laughed and Alice would have teased her, but now life had become so serious that at each stop Ali looked for him, was so pleased to see his stolidity there that she felt no inclination to laugh at all. Nor did Alice, who apparently seemed to empathise with his devotion. Ali had never known a friendship like it, but Joe couldn't bring himself to play games or not be there. Daniel didn't bother to check on the girls, but stayed with his father and Gary. He looked tired.

After a while, in spite of all the distractions, Ali noticed that Steve was not flying with Sandra but with Nancy, Charles's wife.

"Where's Sandra?"

Joe looked over at the projected helicopter, as though it might suddenly produce the girl, then said, "She gave up her place to Nancy, she's going up to St Petersburg with Mike's wife and daughter and she'll come home with them."

"More Russian experiences for her?"

"Indeed."

Some instinct struck her and she asked, "Is Mike somehow South African?"

Joe blew her a kiss as he walked away. "His mother was, from Cape Town, a lovely lady, my mother's closest friend."

Leaving Vitebsk, where they had spent the night, Ali told Joe Alice knew the truth about Galina.

"It doesn't matter now," he said, kissing her unnecessarily. "I rather thought you might tell her before we reached safety."

"Why?"

"You're a romantic and a risk-taker. Bound to do it, aren't you. I bet you even offered to fly back with her, to help her get the diamonds back!"

Ali snorted. "True. And she refused."

"Of course. She's not going to support your idea, is she? She'd have to initiate it herself."

Ali's brow crinkled up. "My darling, when we get back to England you and I are going to have to have a serious talk about what psychology you learnt in that funny African colonial service."

"OK, as long as we do it after we are married not before." He walked away blowing kisses, shocking Kevin whose face blotched like a mackerel.

As they flew from Essen to Eindoven the weather got worse and worse, the low cloud hung in and out of the tree-covered mountains. Kevin and Charles turned back, as did Steve and Nancy and Graham and Deidre, much to Daniel's derision. Pete surprisingly defended Kevin.

"He had a bad fall," Pete said, sounding as though Kevin was a prize jockey, "went into wires and has never flown as freely since. It is important to know your limits, not everyone can fly like Daniel."

Mike laughed. "I'd have turned back myself if it wasn't for Joe, he has a little bit of magic in him when it comes to flying."

Joe gave his rueful smile. "And I know how to use the artificial horizon and bad weather instruments," he murmured.

Pete gave him a long look, before turning to Ali. "You remember what I said about rules and nationalism?"

"Yes."

"Don't forget it. Never trust anyone who believes in nationalism above freedom and never follow the rules, they should not exist. It may save your life."

"I thought you used to be in the military," said Mike, confused but amiable as ever.

"I did," said Pete, "which means I know where I'm coming from. Do you realise," he continued, oblivious to his co-pilots who were clamouring to leave, "there are now more British military stationed abroad than ever before in our history. What does that tell you about our lack of trust and need to decrease the number of rules. You think about it. We have more laws now than we ever did and an increasing need to defend them. Terrible, quite terrible."

As he walked away, finally noticing his anguished passengers, Ali asked Joe, "Do you he's right? More than the colonial period?"

"I doubt it, but I don't think he minds if it is true or not, he only needs it to illustrate his theories."

Brilliant Blighty

The following day they landed at the barren airport of Lydd, where they were to separate, Joe and Mike going on to Sussex, Ali and Alice to fly up to Worcestershire. Most of the others had now left them, including the Gazelles and Pete. Only Daniel remained faithfully doing his job until the last moment. However, even he too was to leave them at Lydd.

Deciding not to stay for lunch but crack on up to Leeds Daniel and Gary came to say goodbye. They both seemed tired and even Daniel was not indulging in any histrionics, although his medal hung around his neck in case any passing refueller should be unaware of whom he was serving.

Gary had tried to get Daniel's win into the British National newspapers but was told that there was no room for this kind of news, as some middle-ranking footballer was giving up smoking and that, naturally, had priority.

"We're off now," said Daniel, leaning against the Robinson and putting his arms around Alice. He lifted the 'God-head' and offered her the metal to kiss. "But I'll be over to visit you in a couple of days. Your mother has invited me to stay."

"Good morning to my gold and next my god, open the shrine that I may see my saint," murmured Joe.

Alice smiled politely, disentangling herself from Daniel's arms. "I look forward to it," she said, making silent plans to have Ali fly her down to Shoreham that week. "See you then." He kissed her and Ali too, almost absentmindedly.

"You I will see again soon, probably in London I hope. I'll call you. Thanks for your help."

Ali nodded. Wondering how much Mrs Charleston was paying, and if it had ever occurred to him to offer her a cut. "Goodbye Daniel."

After refuelling the helicopters and having some lunch Joe came to say good-bye to Ali, who was already in the helicopter waiting for Alice to pay. She sat with her legs outside dangling over the left skid.

"Goodbye darling," he said, kissing her demurely on the cheek but with such passion it could have been on the lips. "I'll ring you as soon as I'm home. I miss you already. You do know that?"

She laughed at the platitude but knew it was genuine. "Goodbye, sweetheart. You know I'm staying with Alice tonight. Not going home until tomorrow."

He nodded. "Umm. Darling, can you do something for me? Can you give this to Alice's father?"

He placed something heavy wrapped in white paper in her hand, it sagged like individually wrapped bull's eyes. She weighed it in her hands. "Not more diamonds?!" she asked incredulously. Ruffling the treasures in her hand she weighed the options. "You bought back the fakes?"

"Clever! Too clever. Do you mind? If it causes difficulties I'll take it up later myself but this way is quicker."

"He who pays the ferry-man..." she said. "Don't worry, this helicopter is becoming more and more like an aerial Group Four van. How did you know that they were fakes? Did you blow on them? Watch for steam on the silicon?"

He shook his head. "It doesn't work with moissanite, only with cubic zirconia."

"Then...?"

"Two things, one is that moissanite is strongly doubly refractive, anyone who has worked with real diamonds can detect the 'facet doubling' by eye, the other is age. Simply put, I knew the age of the original diamonds and saw that these were not old."

"Love wine when it is old, women when they are young and diamonds when they are bright?" asked Ali mockingly.

"Poetry treats a serious subject with simplicity or with severity," he returned, "But only take them if you want to."

They looked at each other thoughtfully; testing and checking, arriving at conclusions with regard to each other that lovers do a million times and in every sphere of life; each time believing in their own ability to assess another's character and sincerity and so often wrong. Then Ali leant forward and kissed him on the lips. "A little test?" she asked. "A little trial for the Sphinx? Remember my darling that, 'women are falser than vows made in wine'."

He kissed her back, not just with passion but with understanding. Alas, she thought, life with Joe was clearly going to be fun and interesting. She hoped her tolerance could take it.

"I'll take it. How would you like me to give it to him? As a gift or as a reminder that the bill is due to be paid?"

Joe laughed. "As always you see through me. But don't do it if it is a worry."

"Oh man, how insubstantial thou art," she said. "You know I'm going to. And probably I'll end up ringing you, my love, while you are off testing an engine or something. So? How did you get them? Explain!"

"Mr Charleston gave me money to buy Galina off, if the diamonds were not real."

"And if they were?"

"Mr Charleston is not an unkind man, he didn't want Alice's sisters impoverished but he didn't want to lose the diamonds either."

Ali digested this for a moment and decided to put the harsher implications out of her mind. "Wait. Did you say sisters?"

"Sandra."

"No! I don't believe you! But Alice... did she... does she know?"

"I think she both knows and knew."

"Alice gave the diamonds... the fakes... freely, knowing?"

"Yes, to Galina. But Galina only knew about her stepsister through Sandra, who, thanks to her work with the Russian government, was able to contact her sister in Moscow. Together they concocted the plan to get the jewels, by fraud, by kissing. By turning love on the needy, emotional teenager. And, you won't like this either, it was Sandra who put the bulldog clip on the tail rotor cable."

Ali stared at him. Love, perverted or otherwise, family and corrupted she could easily conceive, but murderous intent?

"No! No! Not Sandra! That's too much. Besides when would she have had the opportunity? She was with us in Brest, went in the car with us..." And then Ali answered herself, "but not at Modlin. There she was the only one who didn't come to the briefing. Then she had the opportunity. Her helicopter was next to ours. It just took longer than she realised for the clip to take effect." Ali fiddled with Tom Moore's (high quality) fakes. "She was the one person I just knew it could not be... although of course it is so often the last person you suspect."

"You see! I knew you knew, clever clogs."

"Don't sweet talk me! But Sandra wanted to kill her sister and me? Why? And especially before she got the diamonds."

"I don't think she meant to kill either of you. She's an intellectual... she'll have looked at the statistics and seen tail rotor, or rather pedal failure, seldom leads to death but often to damage of the helicopter. In fact I'm pretty certain that when she heard you were an instructor she trusted you to get her sister out of trouble. I think she knew you would be OK. What she wanted was to damage the R22. She believed Alice when she said she was going to win the championships. Sandra just couldn't bear that. She was bitter! Enraged! Alice the indulged was to be the lucky winner too! She couldn't bear to think that Alice, who had always had everything, was now going to win a helicopter championships, and in Russia too. Their birthplace. "

"But we never had a chance. And Sandra was so bright. Why didn't she see through a young girl's boasting? Especially a young girl with no parents and brought up by grandparents."

"Jealousy blinds, my darling. We know that too, don't we? Odie et amo mea Lesbia."

On the way home from Lydd Alice was quiet for a while, letting Ali do the flying. Eventually she said, "did Joe give you something for my father?"

Ali looked at her cautiously. "Yes."

"You weren't going to tell me?"

"Did you want me to?"

"O Diamond! Diamond!" quoted Alice melancholically, "thou little knowest the mischief done!"

Ali just restrained herself from pointing out that Diamond was a dog and let it go, afterall this was the first time she had heard Alice quote at all; perhaps it was contagious. Her heart sang and she felt like laughing. She had never been so happy in her life.

Alice didn't say anything for a few more miles of the helicopter's journey, staring ahead at the passing countryside. Eventually she blurted out, "I'm a romantic. I like what you have with Joe, but I want to know, how much was...Galina... paid off..." The tears came down strongly; monsoon rain at its height.

"Oh," said Ali, her sympathy and love upset, "it's not like that."

"It is," Alice replied. "If you do something when you are poor that you wouldn't do if you were rich, then you've been bought!"

Ali snorted. "So speaks the rich girl! If you follow that through to a logical conclusion half the population of the world wouldn't work at all."

"They don't!" Alice snapped back childishly.

The helicopter responded with a turbulent leap and Ali gave it her concentration. Alice stopped crying and said nothing for a long time. She knew that what she wanted was unreasonable. The love of the rich woman who could say no to money, and yet she felt Galina and her stepfather had colluded to sell her short. She could not quite reconcile family love with this secret deal to return the diamonds to her stepfather: even if only the fakes. It was one thing to sell them in Russia and be done with them, quite another to take money from the same source she did.

"You don't understand," she said eventually in a sad quiet voice that quavered with disillusionment.

"I do," said Ali, stung, "I definitely do."

"Except," said Alice, "except I took my diamonds out to Russia for my sister. Then she turned out to be an impostor and I gave her something good, but not the real thing; just as she is not real herself. But my stepfather couldn't trust me to do the right thing. He kept me watched. Checked. My grandmother hired a detective for love, he hired one for financial reasons. He wants me to learn to be responsible and yet he bought her off."

This time Alice did not cry. She leant her head against the door, biting her lips. "Where is the logic in that?" she murmured again. "Or the love."

"So speaks someone who thinks love comes in financial denial," said Ali, sadly. "Believe me, no one let you down. What you did was crazy. Smuggling diamonds to Russia. You could have got us all killed. But in fact we all benefited in a way... and the only one who suffered was your stepfather. He paid twice; and that's only financially."

"No," said Alice quietly. "He didn't suffer. He never suffers. Never will. He is beyond that. You don't know him. He is strong beyond our understanding. You know what I wish? I wish I only had Peckham Diamonds."

Ali thought of love and of diamonds. She thought of Joe and Jake and after more miles, whereupon the house came in sight, she said, "No you are wrong. Sometimes, when the sun shines on them and they glint and sparkle, Peckham diamonds seem like the real thing, better indeed for being free, but the genuine article is always best. Even if you only have it for a short while."

Alice looked at her, strangely transposing love without an obvious connection, the way women do. "What will happen to Sandra now?"

"I think that is for you and your stepfather to decide. In other places in the world jealousy isn't the sin it is here... at least..."

"I understand," said Alice. "You know, Ali, I meant it when I told Galina I wanted her to come and stay, and the boy too. She isn't the real Galina but she is still my sister. Sandra too. We'll work it out the Russian way." She paused and then added. "Will you still teach me to fly? In spite of all you know. I'm much more..." and then she giggled, a bit of the old Alice resurfacing. "Well, I'm a bit more reliable now, and I promise I will listen to you and not... and well, I'll try not to show off... or cry!"

Ali laughed. Even if Alice hadn't changed Ali did want to teach her. Perhaps she even thought she could inject some common sense into her wild, vulnerable craziness.

"Do you know," she told Alice, "that a poet called Louise Bogan said, 'women have no wildness in them, they are provident instead, content in the tight hot cell of their hearts, to eat dusty bread'."

"Shit!" said Alice. "Thank God the world has changed."

Ali put the helicopter into a descent and began letting down to the park. Ahead of them in the gathering dusk she could see the bodyguard and her dog standing by the French windows and the curtains curling in the wind. Behind them stood the grandparents their hands waving politely but, even from a distance, their relief shining out like a yellow beacon.

Miles away in Peckham her phone stopped ringing. The answering machine came on, its reflective beacon cruising around the room. Joe didn't know about the flickering light, but he told the machine: "I happen to be in Peckham tomorrow. I wonder if I could come over and talk about diamonds.

HELICOPTER
LIFE
Magazine

Britain's only Helicopter Lifestyle Magazine!

www.helicopterlife.com